18·4·24
04.

Polly's War

Sunday Times bestselling author Freda Lightfoot was born in Lancashire. She always dreamed of becoming a writer but this was considered a rather exotic ambition. She has been a teacher, bookseller in the Lake District, then a smallholder and began her writing career by publishing over forty short stories and articles before finding her vocation as a novelist. She has since written over forty-eight novels, mostly sagas and historical fiction. She now spends warm winters living in Spain, and the rainy summers in Britain.

Also by Freda Lightfoot

For All Our Tomorrows
Polly's Pride
Polly's War

Lakeland Sagas

Lakeland Lily
The Bobbin Girls
Kitty Little
Gracie's Sin
Daisy's Secret

A Champion Street Market Saga

Putting on the Style
Fools Fall in Love
That'll be the Day
Candy Kisses
Who's Sorry Now
Lonely Teardrops

The Poor House Lane Sagas

The Girl From Poor House Lane
The Child from Nowhere
The Woman from Heartbreak House

The Poor House Lane Sagas

Luckpenny Land
Storm Clouds Over Broombank
Wishing Water
Larkrigg Fell

Freda LIGHTFOOT
Polly's War

10 CANELO

First published in the United Kingdom in 2015 by Harlequin MIRA, an imprint of
Harlequin (UK) Limited

This edition published in the United Kingdom in 2024 by

Canelo
Unit 9, 5th Floor
Cargo Works, 1–2 Hatfields
London SE1 9PG
United Kingdom

Print ISBN 978 1 80436 556 4
Ebook ISBN 978 1 80436 557 1

Cover design by Rose Cooper

Cover images © Arcangel, Shutterstock

Look for more great books at www.canelo.co

Printed and bound in Great Britain by Clays Ltd, Elcograf S.p.A.

1

Chapter One

1945

Polly Pride stared at her boss open mouthed. 'Laying me off? I'm thinking that's a mean-minded, low-spirited thing to be doing to a body, particularly since you know I'm the family bread winner just now.'

'Your Charlie no better then?' Jack Lawson had the grace to look uncomfortable, as well he might faced with the blistering power of Irish temper which now confronted him.

Standing with her fists screwed into her still slim waist, Polly Pride was an awesome sight even in a crossover pinny. She was still a handsome woman, her dark shining hair with its glimmer of red catching the light as she shook her head at him, greeny-grey eyes flashing dangerously. The fact that she was still known as Polly Pride for all she'd been wed to Charlie Stockton, her second husband, for near a decade spoke volumes. 'Indeed you know full well he's been off work these three weeks past. So how are we to manage without a wage coming in, will ye tell me that?'

Lawson's solemn face did not soften the slightest degree. 'Same as everyone else, Poll. By doing the best you can. Anyroad, your Benny'll be home from the front soon, and your Lucy's chap. That's why we have to let all you women go, to make way for our boys.' He raised his voice a little, glancing about him as if appealing to their compassion but more than one woman in the workshop shook a clenched fist and told him where he could stick the cards he was giving them all.

'Put 'em where the sun don't shine,' yelled one, not known for her finesse.

'Aye, and then take a long jump off th'end of Irwell Street Bridge.'

Many of the women no longer had husbands, brothers or fathers who could come home, and those men who had survived in one piece weren't necessarily coming home to them. Jack Lawson turned away, almost at a run, so eager was he to evade their accusations and sharp wit. The workers in this warehouse close by Potato Wharf weren't the only ones to get the chop, not by a long chalk. The building had served as a store for many things during the long war: cotton, timber, packing cases, even food. Now it was returning to its original purpose – a print works. There'd be no employment then for women like these.

The waters of the canal basin looked as black as ever, thick with oil and cluttered with rubbish, seeming to echo the women's dour mood as Polly and her friends made their way home at the end of their morning shift. For all they'd dreamed of this day for years, happily planned the celebrations for weeks, yet there was precious little laughter as they walked up Medlock Street and past Liverpool Road Goods Station, the taste of coal dust in their mouths and the booming and shunting of trains loud in their ears so they had to raise their voices to shout to each other.

It'd been the most exciting summer anyone could remember. They'd already enjoyed VE Day with jubilant street parties as well as the usual May Day Parades with Shire horses bedecked in ribbons and rosettes and the coronations of the various district May Queens. Now, with the surrender of Japan, hostilities really were at an end and red, white and blue bunting flapped joyously in the breeze, criss-crossing every street the women passed through, from bedroom windows more accustomed to blackout curtains during the long days of war. A Union Jack painted on a back yard wall, the hammer and sickle flying side by side with the stars and stripes; bright, brave flags heralding a day the likes of which had never before been seen, not even in Manchester where they knew how to have a good laugh. They'd soldiered on and 'made do' for nigh on six years, and they were only too ready for a good knees-up.

Bright eyed children in threadbare jerseys with holes in the sleeves. Boys in sleeveless pullovers and trousers they would 'grow into' hung on elastic braces, sparking their clogs on the setts as they kicked a ball about; girls skipping in skimpy cotton frocks, dirty bare feet thrust into scuffed sandals, not a hair ribbon among them to hold back shining bobbed hair recently washed and trimmed for the occasion but their singsong voices rang out with youthful joy and a certainty in the future, one their mothers were now beginning to fear.

'Ta ra,' the women called as one by one they peeled off and went home to make dinner for their children, trying not to worry about what the next week, the next day might bring.

By the time the remaining stragglers turned the corner into Pansy Street, a long string of a street which jostled with many another around the canal basin, they'd almost convinced themselves that they were doing a public service by allowing themselves to be sacked. Even so there was much bitter talk about how eager the bosses had been to take them on at the start of hostilities when men were scarce on the ground.

'It's all right for you,' Maisie Wright said, as she and Polly broke their linked arms for a moment to dodge a young lad wheeling a barrow load of coal to one of the barges moored on the canal. 'You can start up your precious carpet business again. It's the likes of me who are up the swanee. What am I supposed to do? I'm too old to go on the streets. I'd have to pay them to take me on,' she joked.

'Nay lass, you do yourself a disservice,' Maggie Stubbs told her. 'It's experience what counts every time,' and chuckling at her own drollness, was already yelling to her brood to 'get t'kettle on' even as she strode in through her own open front door.

Perhaps, Polly thought, ready as always to look on the bright side, Maisie was right. Could this be an omen? Someone up above giving her a kick up the backside and telling her to do something different with her life. ''Tis mebbe true,' she agreed. 'I could take over the carrier's warehouse and fill it with carpets, so I could.'

'Aye, that'd be grand,' Maisie agreed, happy to go along with the fantasy. 'You could have the swanky manager's office and I'd be foreman and have the pleasure of giving po-faced Jack Lawson the boot.' Both women enjoyed a good laugh at the prospect, but the chuckles soon faded as they neared their own doorsteps.

'Well, me darlin', the war might be over, but we still have a fight on our hands,' Polly said, 'if only to earn a decent living. But then we're expert at looking after ourselves, so we are.'

Even so as she gently closed her own front door behind her, some of the shine and laughter slipped from her face and a flicker of pain and worry seeped through.

In no time at all it seemed, the women were back on their doorsteps doing a bit of 'camping', revelling in the undercurrent of buzzing excitement, arms folded over their pinnies, as excited as the children at the prospect of the street party that afternoon to celebrate VJ Day. Others sat on their window sills, the sash windows pulled down to their knees to hold them secure while they vigorously polished already gleaming glass. Today was a day when spit and polish was important, for a husband, son or father could at any minute walk in.

At the far end of Pansy Street, a young woman knelt scrubbing a doorstep, her neat figure moving with the rhythm of her effort, nose pert and mouth tight with concentration. A lock of soft brown hair fell across her brow and Lucy Shackleton pushed it away with a tired hand then sat back on her heels to survey the length of the street.

'Have you not finished yon steps yet? You want to shape yourself. I haven't got all day.'

Lucy didn't even need to glance up to picture the pale oval face and blackcurrant eyes watching her through the window. It was a favourite occupation of Minnie Hopkins, owner of this fine double doorstep which, as she was so often at pains to remind her, should be clean enough to eat your dinner off, if you'd a mind.

Lucy tried to imagine the woman pulling up her rocking chair, which she rarely left, to eat her pie and pickles off the whitened steps. It almost made her laugh out loud but Lucy smothered the eruption of giggles with the flat of her hand just in time.

'Rightio, Mrs Hopkins. I've nearly done, then I'll get you a nice cuppa,' she called, as cheerfully as she could, then slid the donkey-stone with a final flourish along the edges of each step, to add an artistic touch.

'You said that an hour back.'

Lucy did not respond, merely surveyed the two steps she'd just spent the best part of an hour cleaning. She'd scrubbed them with a solution of washing soda so strong her hands were red raw, then whitened them with a donkey-stone got from the rag-and-bone man. They must be the cleanest steps in all of Pansy Street and that was saying something. But then nobody in this part of Castlefield would be seen dead with a dirty doorstep, despite all the muck dropped onto them from the movement of coal from barge to warehouse and back again, not to mention factory chimneys belching smoke in this city.

Manchester's chief claim to fame was that although its rows of back-to-back houses might be black, its cotton was the whitest and finest in the north, if not the world, its men the most inventive and skilful, and its women the hardest working and most good humoured. Give or take one or two notable exceptions, Lucy thought as she rubbed at an itch and deposited a smear of dirt on one round pink cheek.

'I suppose you're pushing to get off to that party. I'll have no slacking here, nor any work skimped.'

Biting her lip Lucy managed to hold her silence, which was ever the best armour against Minnie Hopkins's razor sharp tongue. She happily began wringing out her cloth and swilling the dirty water down the gutter. Today she didn't care about an old woman who picked a fight for no good reason. Today aprons and shawls had been abandoned in favour of summer frocks and flower-decked hats in honour of the occasion. Eager hands spread margarine and potted meat on thick slices of bread, set out cakes, decanted jellies and wobbly pink blancmanges with a recklessness that defied the self-sacrifice it had taken to save sufficient coupons to purchase such treats. There was laughter in the air, a voice singing 'Take me back to dear old Blighty', and Lucy could almost smell the very real scent of freedom along with the tar bubbles and sunshine.

Today she refused to fret about the fact she was bone weary yet had to do every job twice over in this house, though she'd no complaints from the other houses in which she worked as a cleaner in order to earn an honest living to feed her two children. What did it matter if here, at number 179, she was considered to be the lowest of the low, hardly fit to polish the mahogany dresser that took up the whole of one wall in the front parlour. She'd cheerfully dusted the many ornaments, the glass lamps with their crystal droplets around the rim, the gloomy pictures, mainly of highland cattle or young girls in smock dresses without complaint for today was a special day. Today was the end of the war.

Lucy lifted her gaze to examine the clear blue sky, cherishing the warmth of sun on her face and the blissful surge of happiness that swelled in her heart for she knew that soon, very soon, her Tom would be home.

She'd worried about him quite a lot lately, what with there being no word for a while – a long while actually. But that'd happened before, she told herself. She'd hear nothing for months then got a bunch of letters all at once. War seemed to be funny that way. Oh, but she would welcome him home, just see if she didn't.

The women were covering the food with cloths now, keeping a weather eye out for marauders and enjoying a brew of tea and a chin-wag before facing the onslaught of the afternoon's festivities. Down at the corner shop, Lucy could see Gladys Benson leaning over her counter to have a natter with her friend Lily Gantry. No doubt swapping tales about the failings and misdemeanours of their respective husbands, both of whom had already returned from the war to less than a jubilant welcome from their wives.

In her mind's eye she could see Tom striding up the street, kit-bag resting on his broad shoulder, a wide grin on his handsome face, fair hair shining. He'd swing Sarah Jane up into his arms and give her a big smacking kiss. Young Sean would be next. Then he'd look teasingly into Lucy's eyes, give her a big wink and she'd know that her man was home at last and that he still wanted her. Later, when the children were tucked up in bed, perhaps hugging presents from a father they'd hardly ever set eyes on before, Lucy would slip into bed with this handsome stranger who was her own husband and they'd start to get to know each other all over again.

If she was honest Lucy was a bit nervous about this part of her fantasy. Would he still fancy her? Would she still fancy him? She wasn't the giddy young girl she'd been when he went away. She'd become a responsible mother to her two children, though Polly would mind them sometimes so she could enjoy a bit of fun, like going to a dance or the Gaumont with her pals, shouting 'Put a Penny in' at the projectionist whenever the film broke down which was a frequent occurrence.

She'd held down several different jobs during the long war, had money in her purse, run her own life exactly as she pleased. Lucy knew that she'd changed. Perhaps Tom had too. He'd once seemed so strong, so forceful, sweeping her off her feet and arranging for them to be married in a hurry at the local registry office, for all Tom had known that Lucy had longed for a white wedding in the Catholic Church. They'd been hard up and far too young, had two children far too quickly, each following one of Tom's leaves home. Only this time he would be home for good. Filled suddenly with a mixture of apprehension and longing, she didn't at first hear the slam of the door behind her.

'What the hangment are you up to, dilly-dallying in the gutter? I don't pay you for day dreaming.' Startled by the sound of the sharp voice so close to her ear, Lucy dropped the bucket, which rolled noisily away.

Minnie Hopkins stood arms akimbo, brows beetled, small mouth sucked into empty gums. Her false teeth, kept largely for best, would be reposing in a glass on the bamboo table by her high brass bedstead. She'd slip them in later, when she deigned to put in an appearance at the street party, for all she'd stick chiefly to the jellies. In honour of the occasion she was wearing her best brown chenille frock with a marquisette clasp at the vee of the collar. Above this was tucked a lace front, that hid the scrawny neck as high as the chin. She looked like a miniature Victorian schoolmistress, holding a broom handle in lieu of a cane. Minnie Hopkins was famous for her battles with her yard brush. It was said that she'd chased away every likely suitor with it, which was why at well into her sixties, she was still unwed.

You don't pay me at all, your nephew does, you bad tempered old goat, Lucy longed to say as she gave chase to the bucket which seemed set on rolling all the way to the bottom of Pansy Street. Moments later, marching down the narrow lobby into the back kitchen, she deposited brushes, bucket and cleaning materials under the sink wondering, not for the first time, how the old bat's nephew could tolerate her as well as he did. He must be hard up, to manage to stop on with an aunt as mad as this one. Or else he had a patience born either of long practice or budding sainthood.

'I've done now. How about that cuppa?'

'I don't pay thee for idling over pots of tea neither.'

'I thought it was you what wanted one.' Cut her own nose off to spite her face, Lucy thought. Aloud she said, 'I've plenty other jobs waiting for me when I get done here, so if you don't want anything more, I'm off.'

'Meaning yer doing me a favour by finding time to come at all, is that it?'

'It's always good to be appreciated,' Lucy drily remarked, smiling politely and not quite meeting the sour gaze in case the old woman should interpret the merry glint in her hazel eyes as insolence and sack her on the spot. This had been threatened so often, that there were moments when Lucy almost wished she'd carry out the threat.

Coming twice a week to clean this big draughty house with its seven high-ceilinged bedrooms and heavy Victorian furniture was no joy, and with more criticism than thanks at the end of it. But then Lucy would think of Sarah Jane and Sean, the rent and gas and other bills that had to be paid, war or no war and, as now, she'd bite her lip, placate and calm the quick-tempered old woman, and go home at least with a sense of pride that she was doing her bit without complaint.

She'd made more money when she was working in munitions with Sal her sister-in-law, but that had meant leaving the children on their own too much. With cleaning, she could always take them with her if they were a bit off colour. And though it was hard work, she'd done all right, got a bit put by for a rainy day. Even so, she'd be glad enough for Tom to come home and take over this bread winning lark, so that she could tell Minnie Hopkins to stick her job and settle down to enjoying her children. What a treat that would be.

'So where did you find money to pay for a party, eh?' Minnie pulled out the bucket and cleaning materials that Lucy had just stowed away, and put them all back again in a different order. 'Or have you a fancy man wi' deep pockets tucked away some place?'

'Oh, you badmouthed old…' Lucy stopped, seeing the glint of satisfaction in the old woman's eyes. There was nothing Minnie Hopkins liked better than to stir up trouble but unlike many, Lucy had remained faithful to her husband throughout the duration so she refused to defend herself to this nasty minded old woman. 'We've all put in coupons. Which is more than you have, you mean old bat,' she finished under her breath.

'Go on, what am I?'

'Nothing.' Drat the woman for only being deaf when it suited her. Lucy yanked the curtain across the sink, nearly breaking the wire that held it. Her colour was high, though not nearly so high as her temper as she strode away, spine rigid.

Minnie Hopkins, not one to be outdone, or miss the opportunity to have the last word, galloped after her for several paces along the passage. 'Don't you give me any lip, madam. You're that sharp, you should take care not to cut yerself in the knife drawer. You can collect your cards for that bit of insolence, so don't bother coming in tomorrow. There'll be no job to come to.'

'Well that suits me fine,' Lucy staunchly replied, flinging her apron aside and slamming the vestibule door so hard the glass panel rattled. Once outside, all the fury drained out of her, leaving her weak and shaking with emotion. She had to go and sit on the kerbside for a minute and put her head in her hands while she wished, not for the first time, that her temper wasn't quite so hot, inherited from her Irish mother, Polly Pride, no doubt. Oh lord, she'd done it now. What would her mam say?

'By heck, a chap has to watch where he puts his feet on his own front doorstep these days. It's that clean I could eat me dinner off it.'

Lucy turned to greet the newcomer with a ready smile. She liked Michael Hopkins. He was a big, well-set-up sort of chap with a friendly open face, and a thatch of reddish-brown hair that hinted at a streak of Irish blood somewhere in his veins, descended no doubt, as her own family was, from one of the immigrant Irish who had come to work in Manchester during the last century. Not that he sounded Irish. He was as Lancashire as hot pot, and never short of a jokey remark.

'Your aunt's got a bit of brawn for your dinner,' Lucy told him. 'And you'd best take care you eat it all up.'

He pulled a wry face. 'Happen she thinks I need it,' and with the last traces of her ill temper gone, Lucy laughed, tidying her bangs and wondering if she had any lipstick left on, for she hated to be caught looking anything less than her best.

'If that's the way of it, she must be blind as well as...'

'Deaf? Daft? Or just plain cussed?' He stood with his hands in his pockets, smiling down at her. 'You and she been having another barny?'

'I've been given me marching orders.' Lucy screwed up her small face and rolled her eyes in a wicked parody of her employer.

'Again?'

'I reckon she means it this time. Says I've to collect me cards.'

'I don't think we've any cards to give you, have we?' Lucy gave a rueful sigh. 'It's me own fault. I was a bit rude to her. I've not to come tomorrow, she says.'

'By heck, that's serious. What'll I do without you, Lucy? Who else could I get to come every day and face my aunt's constant carping, yet still do her every bidding with the kind of tongue-biting patience you display.'

'I didn't bite me tongue hard enough today.'

He grinned. 'Let rip did you?'

'She started it,' Lucy protested, and then flushed with guilt at this childish remark.

Michael came to sit beside her on the kerb, resting his elbows on his knees. Lucy cast a sideways glance at the strong biceps beneath the rolled up shirt sleeves, the flush of freckles and sheen of golden hair on his fore arms. 'She doesn't mean half what she says,' he explained. 'It's only her way of blowing off steam. I reckon she just enjoys the drama of a good row. Livens a dull day.'

Lucy gave a disbelieving snort. 'She's a nasty minded old... sorry but she's got me all a-fluster. Accused me of having a fancy man. As if I would. What does she take me for? Tom could be home any day now. It's ages since I've heard anything, but they say everyone'll be home in a month or two.'

'Ah,' Michael attempted to look sympathetic but his heart squeezed with an odd sort of pain as he watched the way joy and sadness chased across her lovely face, flecks of gold sparkled in the hazel eyes one minute and clouded with uncertainty the next. Brown curls danced as if with a life of their own against the flushed curve of her cheek and he longed to reach out and run his fingers through them, to kiss the rosy mouth, savour the softness of her against him. He knew for a fact that Tom Shackleton had rarely penned a line to his wife for the entire duration. Such a man did not, in Michael's opinion, deserve to possess a lovely creature like Lucy if he couldn't be bothered to treat her with more consideration. Pulling himself back under iron control, he glared solemnly at the setts in the road. 'It won't be easy for him, Lucy, picking up the threads of civilian life again after so long away. He'll feel a bit at odds for a while. I know I did.'

Michael had been invalided out of the RAF in 1942, following a crash landing in a Lancaster bomber in which all the crew, bar him, were killed. He'd broken both legs which had left him with a limp, and suffered burns to his arms and chest, injuries which had taken a long time to heal. The guilt of finding himself alive while his mates were dead, never would. Consequently it was a subject he preferred to avoid since it had, at times, caused problems. Some folk could be less than kind when they saw a man walking around in civvies during wartime.

'We'll be fine and dandy,' Lucy said, 'given time, which we'll have in plenty now this dratted war is over. Once Tom gets home I won't need to go on me hands and knees scrubbing other folk's mucky doorsteps.'

Michael managed a weak smile, trying to imagine an existence that didn't contain the presence of this laughing, precious girl.

'You'll come to the party this afternoon?' she asked.

'Happen.' His eyes on hers were thoughtful.

'But you must. Everyone will be there, the whole street. There's pies and sandwiches, jellies and all sorts of goodies. Even Mabel Radcliffe has contributed a whole ounce of butter and a plate of home-made sad-cake. What d'you think of that?'

'Miracles will never cease. She's not known for her generosity isn't our Mabel.' His blue eyes were twinkling now, no longer solemn.

'Starts sharp at three.' And so filled was she with the coming joys of a new life with her husband, that Lucy impulsively kissed him full on the lips, then wagged a finger teasingly in his face. 'No arguing. Mam will have your guts for garters if you don't show up.'

'That settles it then,' he agreed, needing to clear his throat before he could get the words out properly. 'Your mam isn't one to cross. I'll be there.'

Lucy drew in a deeply happy sigh and, giggling like the young girl she still was at heart, skipped off down the street, joining in a game of hopscotch on the way as if she truly were a child revelling in the joys of life, before reaching her own front door quite out of breath.

Watching her go, Michael thought Tom Shackleton was a very lucky man.

Chapter Two

Polly Pride was waiting for her daughter at the front door and, snatching her arm, marched her straight into the kitchen, exasperation tight in her voice. 'So it's home you are at last, you little heathen. Will ye never learn to guard that devil tongue of yours? Whatever possessed you to risk losing such a fine job? Sure and you'll be the death of me, so you will.' The Irish in her always came out strong when Polly was agitated.

'How did you know?' Lucy gazed in mortification at her mother who stood, lips pursed, arms folded, disapproval oozing from every pore. She was a fine figure of a woman still, despite being very nearly fifty, which seemed tremendously old to twenty-eight-year-old Lucy. There wasn't much she missed in Pansy Street but this was fast, even by her mother's standards.

'Didn't Maisie Wright tell me while we were standing in the Co-op queue, waiting to collect our divvy. She witnessed the whole pandemonium.' Polly considered owning up to her temper being due to the fact that she'd suffered the same fate, but pride prevented her.

'She said some awful things about me cheating on Tom.' Lucy's eyes filled with a sudden gush of tears, whereupon Polly's soft heart instantly melted and she wrapped her arms about her daughter.

'Aw, m'cushla, I'm sure she didn't mean it. I know cleaning is not what ye should be doing, a fine intelligent young woman such as yerself. And aren't I in the same boat so who am I to throw the first stone?' It all came out then about Polly's employers laying off the women to make room for the returning service men. 'I

14

dare say it's fair enough and we mustn't fret. Now the war is over we'll get the business up and running again so we will. Once our Benny is home.' Lucy felt a quick surge of irritation. Why was it always Benny who did the right thing and not her? 'Our Benny might have his own ideas about that, Mam. Mebbe he won't want to go back to cleaning and cutting carpets. Mebbe there won't be enough work for him. The business has been closed for years. It'd be like starting all over again.'

'Don't talk soft. Aren't folk just itching to buy carpets to smarten their drab homes? And won't everything be grand for us then? I shall go looking for premises first thing in the morning, something small and cheap till we get up and running. The last thing we need is to be jobless.' Her face clouded as she half glanced back over her shoulder down the lobby to the living room where she knew Charlie sat, reading the paper, as he'd no doubt been doing all day through no fault of his own. She dropped her voice to a whisper. 'We need money coming in, me darlin'.'

Lucy's cheeks fired hot and red with evidence of her guilt.

'I didn't lose my job on purpose but that Minnie Hopkins has the muckiest mind in all of Manchester. She just got me paddy up, that's all.'

Polly snatched up a sharp knife and started hacking a fruit cake to pieces. Strictly speaking it wasn't a fruit cake at all, since it consisted chiefly of dried egg and chopped prunes but she liked to think of it as such. She wagged the knife recklessly in her daughter's face. 'Seems to me you fly too easily into a paddy, so you do. You need to clip a peg on that sharp tongue of yours, madam.'

'And where might I have got that from, d'you reckon?'

For a while neither woman spoke as each relapsed into self-righteous silence, busying themselves preparing sandwiches for the party. Polly set two slices of bread and cheese together with a couple of pickles onto a small plate and handed them to Lucy. 'Take that out to your Gran.'

'Why me?'

'Why not you?'

Lucy carried the plate, together with a large mug of tea out to Big Flo who spent most days in the Anderson shelter that still occupied much of the back yard, waiting for the bomb that she daily expected would carry her off. She was back in the kitchen in seconds.

'You should have stayed and made sure she ate it,' Polly said.

'Oh Mam. You mollycoddle her. What am I supposed to do? Ram it down her throat,' and snatching up a plate of potted meat sandwiches, stormed out of the house, slamming the door behind her.

Polly found her legs were trembling so much she had to sit down. Why did she always find herself criticising Lucy, making it seem that she didn't love her at all, when she loved the bones of her. But then why did Lucy fly off the handle at the least thing? Daughters were surely difficult creatures, far more emotional and pigheaded than a son. Independent to a fault, so she was. But Polly did so wish they got on better, as well as she did with Benny for instance.

Putting her hands to her face she found them wet with tears, squeezing out between her fingers and dripping onto her clean pinny, though she really didn't have the time. For all her brave words over starting up her business again, inside she felt a cold curl of terror. If only they knew what was wrong with Charlie. If only he was well and his usual cheery self, then it wouldn't matter that she'd been sacked, and Lucy wouldn't have to go cap in hand to get her job back.

'*Polly?*' That was Charlie now, calling from the parlour.

He always told her not to interfere, to let her children live their own life without advice or counsel from her. Wise advice in itself, if she could only bring herself to follow it. But then he was only their stepfather so how could he possibly know how a mother felt? Polly guiltily conceded that wasn't quite fair on Charlie, for hadn't he always supported her and been a fine father to her children, treating them as if they were indeed his own. It was simply that he'd not been quite himself lately, growing soft, or mard as he called it, in his old age, constantly complaining of aching bones made worse by his long days working on the freezing docks, so perhaps that was why he was less sympathetic. The pains had got so bad recently he could hardly walk and now had been laid off till he got over whatever it was. Aw, she was that worried about him.

And now to add to her concerns, she and Lucy had both got the push.

'I'll not be a minute, love. I'll just see to these sandwiches then I'll fetch you a cuppa.' She stood up, dabbing her eyes on her pinny, knowing that the minute she'd done the washing up and got this food ready for the party, she still had to clean through. Saturdays were her only chance and she was never one for giving a lick and a promise as many women in this street were. Polly Pride liked her house to shine, from top to toe. She allowed no room for a speck of dust, nor self-pity either.

Soon as they got the business going again, they'd all feel more secure, she told herself sternly as she set out spam sandwiches on a plate. Life would get back to normal at last and Charlie could have a nice warm job indoors instead of working on the wharfs, which he hated. Polly was quite sure that's what had made him ill in the first place. Or he'd caught some nasty bug from that filthy river.

When she was quite composed again, she picked up the plate of sandwiches and followed her daughter outside, biting back a further admonishment as Lucy shunted and banged plates about on the long trestle tables. Borrowed from the local Sunday schools and covered with well-darned sheets in varying degrees of whiteness, these straddled the cobbles down the centre of the street. Pop-eyed children hovered close, small tongues licking rosy lips as they waited for the magic hour when the celebrations and, best of all, the eating, could commence, her own grandchildren among them.

Polly's hands stilled in their jiggling of plates and folding of napkins, greeny-grey eyes growing soft as she watched them, eager to help for once. Young Sean, three years old, the image of his dad with his straight fair hair, and Sarah Jane, all dark and sulky, a budding Veronica Lake, tugging at her skirt.

'When can I put me party frock on?'

'As late as possible then you don't spoil it.'

'I'm hungry.'

'Have a banana sandwich then.'

Sarah Jane pulled a face. 'It's not banana. It's boiled parsnip with banana essence in it. I saw you make it.'

'Aw, who's a little clever-clogs then? Is it hungry you are or not?'

'No.'

'Please yourself.' Polly set the plate close by her granddaughter's elbow, knowing she would take one the minute her back was turned.

Larders had been ruthlessly raided for this day. Not since before the war had there been such a spread and none of the children could remember anything but war. When it was over, hearts would still ache for loved ones not yet come home and some, like Doris Mitchell from next door, would never see her son safe home again.

Oh, but what was she complaining of? Sure and wasn't she the lucky one? She had all her children and grandchildren safe and well. Charlie might be overworked and a bit below par but he'd mend so he would, and at least he'd been too old to fight. Benny would be home soon, along with Lucy's Tom and they'd all be happy as Larry.

And then it came to her, why her daughter was so scratchy today. 'Are you afraid that Tom'll no longer feel the same about you, after all this time away?'

A moment's silence and then Lucy nodded, eyes brimming with tears.

'Aw, me little one, won't he love every hair on your head, just as we all do,' but as she made to hold her close again, Lucy turned stiffly away, as if rejecting her mother's comfort.

Polly clenched her hands, trying not to mind for she knew there were many such concerns this afternoon, despite the sunshine and joy of the day. When would their men return? Would they be different, or damaged in some way? Would there be work for them to do? And how would each family cope with the changes? Some women were reluctant to give up their own jobs, while others dreaded the return of an almost forgotten husband. And there were those simply concerned over whether their menfolk would bring their own ration book. For an hour or two at least they could all enjoy the celebrations and forget about the aftermath of war and the new worries that peace might bring. Bellies would be filled, and some pleasure could be found in an otherwise grey life.

Conceding at last to the warm weather, Polly unbuttoned her cardigan, the wool of which had long since lost its stretch, this being the third garment it had supplied in six years. She'd go and take it off in a minute, have a good wash and put on her Sunday best. 'Is nobody going to make some tea? I feel like I'm chewing sawdust.'

Lucy laughed, her ill temper melting beneath her mother's good humour and the sunshine of this special day. 'I'll make it.' She hurried indoors and grabbed the kettle, filling it from the single cold tap over the sink.

She really ought to go upstairs and start getting washed and changed herself but her mind was still on how next week's bills would be paid. It would mean eating into her savings but then how was she to know that her mam would be laid off too, on the very same day. Life was cruel. It would be difficult enough for Tom when he came home, and she'd made it no easier by losing one of her best paying customers. Two children to feed and her wages more than halved. Mam was right. She should guard her tongue better.

For a long time Lucy hovered by the stove, waiting for the kettle to boil, her mind turning over the problems, worrying about her children, about Tom and how it would be for them after a married life spent mainly apart. She even found herself anxiously going over Polly's business plans. All wishful thinking, in Lucy's opinion. Once, Polly Pride Carpets had been busy and prosperous, had made them enough money to escape the mean streets of Ancoats and move them up in the world to a smart new house in Cheetham, but since the outbreak of war nobody had wanted carpets, even if such an item could be found, and the family had been forced to move again, to a more modest house in Castlefield for all it was better than many in Pansy Street, where Charlie could get work on the wharfs and the womenfolk too.

They'd got by well enough but starting up the business again would need capital as well as will power, and more hard work than perhaps her mother realised. Polly no longer had the youth or the energy she'd once enjoyed in abundance. Not that Lucy would mind having a go herself, given the chance.

As for Benny, his mother's pride and joy, perhaps he was no longer the biddable boy Polly fondly remembered. He'd always been streetwise, good at living by his wits as they all had once, yet also ambitious and filled with unrealistic dreams. Lucy wondered what these would be now, after six years of war.

Her troubled thoughts were interrupted by the sound of running feet, then Sean was beside her, face scarlet with excitement. 'There's someone outside. I'm only allowed to say it's a soldier, Mam, and he's asking for you.'

Lucy froze, then made a dash for the door, knocking a plate of fairy cakes to the floor as she ran, hardly noticing as she trampled over these fatless sponge treats. The soldier striding down the street towards her had light brown hair cut close to his bullet shaped head and eyes a familiar greeny-grey. Broad, almost stockily built with powerful shoulders and a ramrod back he did not carry a kit bag. The children gathered about him were carrying it for him. But he did swing Sarah Jane high on his shoulder and caught a giggling Sean as the little boy leapt into his arms.

Joy warred with disappointment as her pounding heart slowed to normal, this being her brother Benny, miraculously material- ised out of her thoughts and, pleased as she was to see him, he was not her lovely husband. Then Lucy became aware of an eery silence.

Somewhere a blackbird trilled its piercingly sweet note, not even the sound of a tram or shunting train marring the suddenly silent street. Nothing but the squeak of the telegraph boy's bike.

Not a soul spoke as he rode slowly towards the group of women hovering about the tables. Hearts stopped, mouths went ash-dry, skipping ropes dropped to the ground as even the children were attuned to the implications of such a visit.

He paused by one old man but only to ask a question, then the bike squeaked on as the boy struggled to pedal over the setts, carefully avoiding getting his wheels caught in the tramlines. Why didn't he get off the damn thing and walk!

Seconds later the waiting was over, the orange envelope was in her hands and Lucy knew, even before she opened it that Tom wouldn't be coming home next week, or even next month. He wouldn't be coming home at all.

–

Locked in a state of disbelief, Lucy felt too numb to grieve, though a part of her was only too keenly aware that her world had fallen apart and nothing would ever be the same again. She hadn't set eyes on Tom since before Sean was born when he was sent out to Italy and God-knows-where since, yet she should surely feel something other than this terrible sensation of resentment. To lose a husband at the end of the war seemed especially unfair somehow, as if war could ever be fair. She ached now to tell him all the things she'd never got the chance to say, to ask forgiveness for the quarrels they'd had, few as they were. She wished they'd made more of their marriage, that she'd been a perfect wife for him, since it was all the time they were to have.

Missing, presumed killed in action. Cold, unfeeling words that would live with her for the rest of her life. How could anyone *presume* such a thing? Yet she knew that to continue to hope year after year was a kind of death in itself. She'd seen it happen to

21

neighbours, to Doris next-door for one. Mrs Shaw at the end house for another. Even after they'd sent back what was left of her eldest boy, she still left his razor out on the shelf, just in case.

Lucy could never do that. It wouldn't be fair on Sarah Jane or Sean. She'd taken the children upstairs to her room and explained it all, as carefully as she could. They'd looked at her dry-eyed and uncomprehending. Then, as if seeing their bewilderment brought it finally home to her, it had been Lucy who wept, which in turn started Sean off, and Sarah Jane who had comforted them all.

After that Polly brewed tea, pot after pot, as if the hot steaming brew could put everything right. Sarah Jane put on her pink party frock, Lucy her best blue costume in an attempt to celebrate Benny home on leave, though her heart was no longer in it. And as if things weren't bad enough, a row broke out as soon as Charlie emerged from the front parlour to find this young stranger lounging in his favourite chair by the kitchen fire.

'I suppose you think you're the only one who's suffered during this dratted war?' Charlie demanded, prodding a surprised Benny in the chest with one finger. 'Well let me tell you there's many a family round here can say different. Mary Lee for one. She went out to the Co-op for a bag of rations and came back to find her house and half of Hardman Street had been blasted off the face of the earth. There were many such.'

'It's good to see you too, Charlie,' Benny drily commented. 'How are you?'

'He's not been too well and that's the truth.' Polly flapped around the pair of them trying to keep the peace. 'Hush, Charlie. Don't lay into him the minute he gets home. Glad we are to have our boy safe with us at last, are we not? Now sit down and drink your tea and I'll fetch you a bite of summat to eat.' She tried not to meet her son's puzzled gaze for Charlie had once been the gentlest of stepfathers. Whatever was ailing him was doing his temper no good at all.

People came and went all afternoon. Gran refused to emerge from the Anderson shelter as usual, and the whole day took on a deep sense of unreality. They at least remembered to thank Aunt Ida for her contribution of a tin of spam and Uncle Nobby for enough lettuce and tomatoes from his allotment to turn them all into rabbits. But nobody felt like eating, for all the sacrifices that had been made to provide such a spread.

Every now and then Polly would squeeze Lucy's hand or whisper that *presumed* only meant the authorities hadn't the first idea where he was. Some sort of bureaucratic mix-up and he was even now on his way home. Lucy tried to find comfort in these words and failed.

The only time any of them truly managed to lift their spirits was for the sake of the children. Later that evening, Sean, bewildered by the strangeness of what should have been an extra special day, marched into the kitchen and made a grab for his uncle's leg. 'Have you not fetched me a present, Uncle Benny?'

Benny, enjoying a glass of stout and a quiet read of the paper while his mother and Lucy washed up and tidied the table around him, gazed mystified about the room. 'Did you hear summat, our Lucy? I reckon we've got a squeaking mouse in the house.'

'I hope not,' Polly said, with equal seriousness.

'Well if we have, don't expect me to oil it,' Benny warned, making them all laugh and lightening the tension a little. Sean squealed with delight as his uncle swung him upside down before setting him back on his feet and suggesting he dig deep in his rucksack. 'Fancy me forgetting. Fetch Sarah Jane. Go on, you. Have a look in there. You might both find something of interest.'

Sarah Jane came running, half glancing at her mother as if wanting reassurance that it was all right to take pleasure in a gift on this sad occasion. Lucy smiled and nodded at her to dig deep.

'Happen you're too old for toys now?' Benny idly commented, helping the children to search. Then he held out a rag doll for Sarah Jane, and a small brown and grey dog for Sean.

Two pairs of shining eyes met his. 'Oh no, Uncle Benny. I haven't had much in the way of toys, there being a war on,' Sarah Jane gravely explained.

'Me neither,' Sean agreed, reaching for the dog. 'Can he sit on my pillow?'

'I reckon he'd like that,' Benny agreed.

There was a box of mints for his gran, cigarettes for Charlie, a scarf for his mother, and silk stockings for his sister. 'No questions asked,' warned Benny, tapping the side of his nose with one nicotine-stained finger, which for some reason took some of the pleasure out of the gift for Lucy, though not for the world would she say as much.

–

The excitement and trauma of the day meant it took a while to get the children to sleep, and their new playmates naturally must be suitably tucked up. But then as she lay listening to the even rhythm of their breathing in the bed beside her own, Lucy finally succumbed and sobbed out her grief, stuffing the pillow into her mouth so that she wouldn't wake them. The hours of darkness seemed to protect her from prying eyes and gave her at last some release from the build-up of constrained emotion, if not from her heartache. She slept for a few short hours after that, out of sheer exhaustion but the first shafts of a grey dawn found practical matters once more occupying her mind.

Her dreams of being able to spend more time with Sarah Jane and Sean were bitter dust in her mouth. She was particularly sorry about Sean. The boy was growing a bit wild and although Lucy did what she could, he was sorely in need of a father. Life had always been hard and she didn't need telling that it would become even harder without a husband to provide for their future. She might still get her allowance from the army, little as that was, but the long hours and backbreaking drudgery would continue indefinitely. Even when she'd finished work there was still all the washing, ironing and endless make-do-and-mend to do at home, not to mention the daily worry of finding something to eat.

And what about fun, she asked herself with a bitter twist of self-pity. She was still a young woman, with all her life before her. When did she get to enjoy that? Never, by the looks of it, for all the longed for peace had finally arrived, which brought on a fresh spurt of tears.

Losing one of her best clients had made things worse. She worked five mornings a week for Minnie Hopkins. In the afternoons she cleaned for Mrs Shaw, the Beckworths and the Taylors, while on Fridays she went right through the house behind the corner shop for the Benson sisters. Now, in one gesture of stupid defiance, she'd lost nearly half her week's wages.

There was no help for it but to do as her mam suggested, swallow her pride and go and apologise to Minnie Hopkins. Temper or no temper, she needed that job or they'd all starve.

—

'So, you've had second thoughts, eh? You've remembered them as don't work, don't eat.' Minnie Hopkins stood on her clean doorstep, arms folded, queen of her own domain and treated Lucy to her most blistering glare.

Lucy drew in a calming breath, gritted her teeth and forced her lips into a smile. It made her face feel all stiff and uncomfortable. 'I thought you'd might be having second thoughts yourself. After all, somebody has to clean this place for you. It's a big house.'

'Aye, and there's plenty would be glad of the chance to work here.'

Silence fell while Lucy wondered how much more humiliation she could bear. Should she reveal the truth of her situation and appeal to the woman's sympathy, or tell her she could keep her blasted job? She did neither.

Minnie was considering whether she could get Lucy back on reduced wages. The lass worked hard for all she was a bit lippy. For two pins she'd let her go, but Michael had a soft spot for her, which was why he paid her too much. Yet Minnie knew she'd be hard put to find someone else willing to take on the job of cleaning this great house. Stuck at the end of Pansy Street, a cut above the rest, it had been the bane of her life ever since the pair of them had been left rattling around in it. A real white elephant it was with its seven bedrooms and three reception rooms for all it had a fine Edwardian front to it, complete with stone pillars and one doorstep more than everyone else.

With her chin up, back straight, Lucy kept her mind on her two children, the gas bill that had landed on the mat that very morning, and the sight of her mother's face when she'd opened it. As if Polly didn't have enough on her plate, what with losing her own job, worrying over Charlie who was frequently in a sour mood these days, and sharing Lucy's grief. Not to mention Benny lording it over them all the minute he came downstairs, prattling on about how he was going to make his fortune on Civvy Street the minute his number came up and he was home for good.

'Aw, indeed you are so, and isn't that all settled,' Polly had agreed, placing a substantial breakfast the like of which Lucy hadn't seen in a long while before him. 'We'll be getting the business going again and you, m'cushla, can be my right hand man.'

Benny had laughed as he dipped a thick chunk of bread into his egg while Lucy's mouth watered to watch the precious yellow yolk run. 'Nay, Mam. I haven't made my mind up yet. I'll be looking for something a bit more substantial than second hand carpets. A job that'll make proper money.' Just as if he could take his pick.

'Don't talk soft, what else would ye be doing?' Polly had laughed at his dismissal of this precious dream but Lucy could see the hurt in the way her face stiffened up. 'Carpets made us plenty of money before the war, did they not? Brought us out of Ancoats and saved the lot of us from near starvation at one time.'

'That's all in the past,' Benny told her.

'So, they can make us money again in the future. I mean to buy machines to offer a service of cleaning and steaming. Now won't that be grand?'

'Sounds like too much hard graft to me, Mam. I've had enough of hard labour and square bashing. I'm looking for a job which brings in good money for less sweat and toil, if you know what I mean,' and grinning, he'd sliced the egg in two and put half of it into his mouth. Lucy had walked out at that point, unable to bear witness to the casual use of such good food.

She was fond enough of her brother, but he didn't seem to appreciate how hard it had been for *them* during the long war, what sacrifices they'd had to make. Money had been so tight at one time, she remembered scrabbling in the muck and wet of the gutter when she'd dropped a precious loaf of bread, washing it under the tap and baking it crisp again in the oven. And Lucy had no recollection of the last time she'd tasted a fried egg, since she gave her meagre ration to her children, which brought her troubled thoughts right back to where they'd started. Sean was already through the soles of that pair of shoes she'd got from Lily Gantry's rag shop less than two month back, and Sarah Jane showed an indecent amount of knickers in all her little frocks. Oh yes, for all she'd a bit put by and, for now at least, she'd continue to get something from the army. But she badly needed to keep this job.

She smiled steadfastly at her hated employer. 'I could make your dinners as well, if you like,' she recklessly offered. 'Michael's always asking me.'

Minnie Hopkins popped a pear drop into her mouth and sucked on it while she thought about this proposition. 'For t'same rate? We can't afford to pay any more.' The beady jet eyes seemed to pierce right into Lucy's soul and she could do nothing but comply.

'Yes, all right, for the same rate.'

'Right. You can get back to work this minute. I'm not feeling too champion this mornin'. Get me a cuppa, good and strong, then you can start scrubbing down the back yard.'

'My favourite job,' said Lucy drily, reaching for her sacking apron.

'What did thee say?'

'I said, just the job.'

'A thank you would be more appropriate.'

The old woman's hearing was too sharp for her own good at times, Lucy thought, offering her thanks as humbly as she was able. She brewed Minnie Hopkins a strong pot of tea, even offered a slice of the 'fruit' cake left over from the street party as a peace offering. As she headed for the backyard, bucket in hand, Minnie called after her.

'Only cook for two mind. You can make your own dinner when thee gets home.'

Lucy gritted her teeth. She'd be half starved by then after all this extra work, by which time Benny would no doubt have eaten them out of house and home.

–

Lucy baked a pie, consisting chiefly of vegetables but with a bit of pork added to make it tasty. The new regime meant she had to work harder and faster than ever in order to be home in time to pick up her children at the end of the morning, but Michael was delighted. He had long since grown tired of his aunt's paltry attempts at cooking. He made no mention of the fact that Lucy had only recently being sacked. Nor did he ask why she'd suddenly agreed to do the very thing she'd always resisted.

Once she'd served up, Lucy quickly untied her apron and, reaching for her coat and basket, headed for the door.

'I'll be in tomorrow then, as usual.'

'Right you are,' Michael said, pushing back his chair and insisting on showing her out, despite some caustic comment from his aunt about the girl being able to find her own way. 'I didn't like to say anything in front of Aunt Minnie, not after all that kerfuffle the other day, but I'm sorry about Tom.'

'Thank you.' She didn't know what else to say, and kept her face turned away as she fussed with coat buttons, bag and scarf, not wanting him to see the quick rush of tears.

'If there's anything I can do…'

'What can anyone do? He's dead, for God's sake.' Lucy realised she'd spoken more sharply than she intended, and instantly apologised. 'Sorry. I'm fine, really I am.'

'Are you?'

'I will be. I have to be. Anyroad, how can you grieve for somebody you haven't seen in three years, hardly even heard from?'

'You can if you still love them.'

She'd been all right until he said that, and until he gently touched her arm. Then before she could stop herself, Lucy turned her face into his broad shoulder and began to weep, overwhelmed by emotion and his ready sympathy.

Michael's arms slid quietly about her, strong and firm, holding her tight as he murmured soothing words of comfort against her hair, his mouth so close to her ear she could sense the soft vibration of him whispering her name into it. It made her shiver with a new, strange emotion. The clean, soapy scent of him, and the hardness of a strong male body pressed so hard against her own created a tension between them, one that even Lucy, despite her distress, recognised as dangerous.

They broke apart, the storm of sobbing over almost as quickly as it had begun and Lucy dabbed at her eyes with the flat of her hand, flushed with embarrassment.

Michael felt hot with shame at the fierceness of his need, his arms still seeming to be imprinted with the feel of her as he stood awkwardly on the mat, intent upon the downcast tilt of her head. The roughness of his jacket had rubbed a red patch on her cheek and he watched, dry-mouthed, as a tear trailed over it, managing by a superhuman effort not to put out a finger to catch it. He did offer her a handkerchief, one of his old airforce blue ones but spanking clean. 'It does you good to open the floodgates once in a while, for all you've soaked me through.'

Managing to smile through her tears, Lucy took the handkerchief from him and blew her nose then shyly met his gentle gaze. 'I'm all right now, thanks.'

'Well, you know where I am if you're not.'

'Yes.' She hesitated another fraction of a second, then turned on her heel and fled, her heart pounding in time with her feet on the stone paving slabs as she ran home. What in heaven's name had she done now?

Chapter Three

Belinda Clarke had been pleased and excited to get her callup papers back in 1940. She'd volunteered for the ATS, for special radio training, and later for service overseas, anything that sounded remotely exciting to bring some colour into her plain, drab life.

She'd certainly succeeded. She'd enjoyed her time in London, but best of all the years in Malta and Cairo where, in spite of the war, there'd at least been sun and a social life, if warding off the good-time johnnies was a bit of a trial at times.

It hadn't all been fun, of course. There were times when she'd been thoroughly browned off, and at others scared witless. But she'd survived, which was more than could be said for many so, by rights, she should be grateful to be coming home. She'd spent the last eighteen months of the war in South Wales of all places, and had left the demobilisation centre at Aldershot in the second week of September with perilously little cash, thanks to the prevailing live-for-today attitude, plus a few clothing coupons and a travel warrant. What she lacked in material possessions, she more than made up for with optimism and energy at the prospect of a new beginning.

But then she'd forgotten how plain and drab life in Cherry Crescent could be.

She dropped her bag and pressed the polished brass bell. Somewhere from the depths of the house came the familiar jangling sound. Belinda smoothed a hand over the grain of the polished wood. Blistered and cracked, it looked in dire need of a fresh coat of varnish, if such a luxury could be found. Someone had tried to clean off the strips of protective brown sticky paper from the red and green panes of glass in the leaded bay windows, and not made a very good job of it. If this were the depot, she'd have the perpetrator brought back and made to finish the job properly. Belinda smiled and again rang the bell. Where was everyone? Finally she tried the door, found it unlocked, and walked into the cool hall.

A solid, semi-detached house, sufficiently unlike its neighbours to lend it some class, it looked smaller than she remembered. Shabbier. But then she hadn't been home for how long? Oh goodness, she couldn't remember. Too long, perhaps.

There was the old grandfather clock that seemed to fill the narrow hall, ticking dully, and still ten minutes slow. The same dull brown panelling and green paint, her father's ancient barometer which he tapped every day on his way to the office, and the cumbersome Victorian hatstand with the wonky hooks. She'd forgotten how very ugly that was.

She flung her hat neatly on to it, watching it spin and settle on a hook, and grinned.

'Is that you, darling?'

Belinda went to the foot of the stairs to smile up at her mother. The sight of her, looking as serene and beautiful as ever in a lavender cotton housecoat that flowed over the curves of her girlishly slender figure, made Belinda feel instantly jaded and unwashed.

Her own demob suit was a dull brown, creased and dusty after hours spent squashed on an overcrowded train. Her tie-up brogues were more sensible than fashionable, for all they were highly polished. In her bag, apart from one decent silk dress from her days out east, there were a couple of outdated summer frocks among the serviceable underwear, two tin plates and an old army blanket she'd felt duty-bound to bring home as a memento.

Belinda Clarke herself, however, was very far from being either dull or plain. At twenty-six, she was fit and slender, athletic and yet feminine. The cheek bones high, the mouth wide and prone to easy laughter, and if the hair was cut mercilessly short yet it glowed honey gold, and the blue eyes sparkled with a ready mischief. Her whole bearing exuded confidence, as befitted someone who had attained the rank of corporal.

Her mother was scolding her for not having rung from the station.

'I took a bus.'

'Darling, with that bag? You surely haven't carried it yourself?'

Belinda let out a peal of laughter. 'Mother, I've been carrying my own bags for five years. Are we to continue this staircase conversation indefinitely, or will you come down and give your only daughter a hug?'

'Darling, of course.' Joanna Clarke half glanced back over her shoulder, as if reluctant to leave whatever she'd been doing, then floated down the stairs on light slippered feet, offering a scented cheek to be kissed. 'We'll have a glass of sherry in the conservatory. Just you and me.'

'I'd rather have a bath. I'm filthy.'

'No no, not now. In any case, you look marvellous, and you've hours and hours to make yourself beautiful before this evening. I want to have you all to myself for a while.' Belinda was instantly on the alert. 'This evening. Why, what's happening this evening?'

Joanna giggled, the girlish tones sounding oddly false. 'Everything's going to be splendid now you're home again. We've invited the Fentons round for a little welcome-home party. You remember Frank Fenton. You and he had quite a thing going once.'

Belinda groaned.

'No pouting, darling. Your father is quite set on it. You must at least make the effort to be nice to dear Frank, even if you have no wish to pick up where you left off.'

'Which I certainly haven't.'

'You know that Ron has gone into the business, don't you?' Joanna said, filling the sherry glasses to the brim as she very sweetly changed the subject.

33

Belinda laughed. 'Little brother working? Whatever next.'

'Oh, he's grown quite ambitious. It will be just like old times, all together again. Exactly the way it used to be.' Heart sinking, Belinda followed her mother into the overheated conservatory, lush with vegetation and sickly sweet, wondering how she was going to get it across to her overprotective parents that it could never be as it used to be. The naive, obedient daughter who had fled their fireside seeking adventure five years ago had not returned, and never would.

The dinner party was not a success. They all sat stiffly around the oversized mahogany table in the gloomy dining-room. Hubert drank too much wine and dominated the conversation with talk of Council matters and his hopes of being elevated to a position of even higher office next year, laying one finger against his broad nose as if to indicate it was all rather hush-hush. Brother Ron, seated opposite, wore his usual sour expression and seemed intent on not speaking to anyone while he devoured everything in sight.

Belinda upset her mother by refusing to wear the frothy pink number bought specially for the purpose, choosing instead a sensible green suit that had seen better days. The skirt draped softly over her slender figure but nobody could call it elegant. She brushed her hair until it shone, added the faintest touch of lipstick, but could see that neither of her parents were impressed with the result. She was soon to learn the reason.

The Fentons were well known to Belinda, owning a large chemical dye works on Liverpool Road. They were quiet, unprepossessing people, despite an air of self-satisfaction which seemed to proclaim they need make no further effort since they had already made their place in the world. Their greatest asset was their son Frank. He had followed them into the business, working hard to do his bit despite being excused military service, as they were at constant pains to point out.

Belinda had dreaded seeing Frank again, remembering too well his spotty face and eager bonhomie, so was greatly relieved when he didn't put in an appearance, hoping she could now relax and enjoy the meal. Her mother was evidently deeply offended, clearly believing that an invitation to her table far outweighed any other possible emergency which might have claimed his attention.

'He mustn't feel shy with us,' she said, and suggested Ron go round and persuade him to change his mind.

'He isn't in,' George Fenton insisted, as irritated as the Clarkes by his son's defection. 'Haven't the foggiest where he is.'

'Trying to avoid us, eh?' joked Hubert, though with little sign of good humour.

Always apt to talk too much when she was nervous or distressed, Joanna launched into a length discourse on how pleased she was that hostilities had ended, whether the authorities would be able to rebuild the terrible destruction in the city, and how dreary it had been for her to be evacuated out for the duration with Aunt Cora in Scotland. 'But Hubert was most insistent that I be safe.'

The very idea of anyone, even a German, daring to bomb Cherry Crescent, seemed a sacrilege beyond belief. Belinda managed, against all odds, not to say so, deciding that at least the enforced evacuation would have given her father some respite. Perhaps that was his reasoning behind the idea. The thought brought a smile, and very nearly a fresh spurt of laughter, so that she had to dash off into the kitchen on the pretext of checking on the apricot pudding, to get herself back under control. She stood at the back door, sneaking a quick drag of a cigarette. This proved to be a mistake for when she returned, still coughing slightly, it brought attention firmly back to herself.

'Don't you agree Scotland was a good idea, darling?'

Belinda resolved to hold her ground. 'If it suited you Mother. Unfortunately we couldn't all escape to Aunt Cora's. Some of us had to fight the war.' She regretted the remark instantly as being unnecessarily unkind for Joanna looked wounded and batted her long eyelashes in obvious distress.

'I did my bit, darling. I spent a great deal of time knitting dull scarves and countless balaclavas. For the poor sailors, don't you know.'

'I'm sure the poor sailors were most grateful,' Belinda said, sucking in her cheeks and wondering if she dare dash out again.

The soft mouth trembled. 'Cora got involved with the VAD but I truly couldn't. The sights she saw… Quite dreadful. I would have been ill, I swear I would.' Joanna pressed a lace handkerchief to her pretty nose, which had never smelled anything more unpleasant than cheap cologne, when she couldn't find any of her favourite Evening in Paris perfume. She looked about the table with brimming eyes, seeking understanding and ready sympathy, which she instantly received.

'Don't upset your mother,' came her father's voice from the head of the table.

'I didn't. I never meant…' Belinda bit her lip, hating to find herself in the wrong, on her very first night home.

Then George Fenton, obviously wishing to assist by changing the subject, enquired as to her future plans, now that the war was well and truly over. Before Belinda could think of a suitable reply, her father's voice boomed out yet again.

'There's no need for any daughter of mine to work,' pronounced Hubert Clarke, as if he were at a council meeting. 'Ron works with me in the business, of course. Belinda will help her mother at home and get involved in some appropriate charity, to give her an interest.' There were blotches of red on his plump face, the implications of his words plain to everyone. She would stay at home until the right young man came along. Hubert drank the last of his soup with a loud slurping noise, then smiled beneficially upon Belinda. 'You won't find me niggardly when it comes to giving you a good send-off.'

'Sent off where?' Belinda asked, in her coolest tones. 'Haven't I only this very day arrived back? Besides, perhaps I won't want to stay at home. I haven't yet decided what I might wish to do.'

'What is there to do but find yourself a good husband, and a bit smartish like. You aren't getting any younger.' Hubert, as he proudly and constantly reminded his family and friends, came from Bolton so prided himself on never mincing his words. 'Father knows best, eh?'

Belinda, used to holding her own against whole squadrons of joking men, had been responsible for the welfare of girls in her care and was no longer the shy, convent-educated girl who had gone away to war, merely smiled.

'Really, Father. That all sounds rather Victorian. I'm not a child any longer, you know, and I do think I'm capable of choosing my own job. I doubt radio operators are much in demand in Manchester these days, but I hope to find something a bit more interesting than helping Mummy at dinner parties or serving at charity coffee mornings.'

Councillor Hubert Clarke turned a dull shade of purple. He was not accustomed to having his word flouted by anyone, least of all a daughter at his own dining table. He would have said as much there and then, had it not been for the Fenton woman taking an obvious satisfaction in his discomfort. Even so, he wouldn't have his guests think him weak, or be bested in his own house. Hubert considered himself a man of some importance in his credit trading business, ably assisted by his son who ensured that customers kept up their regular weekly payments of a shilling in the pound for goods purchased. He'd never stood any nonsense in that department, war or no war. If they didn't pay, he sued, or pursued them until they regretted their lack of thrift. He hadn't become a self-made man of means without learning a trick or two. He was a man to be reckoned with in the city, with many useful contacts which served him well. He reminded himself of this fact now.

Joanna had placed a small chicken before him which he began, with great theatricality, to carve. 'We all appreciate how you volunteered to do your bit, Belinda, as we have too in our different ways, even your poor mother.' He wagged the carving knife at her. 'But it was your own choice to join the military and run wild. A feverish whim, no doubt, that got a bit out of hand. We're only thankful that the war is over at last, and my little girl is home again, safe and sound.' He beamed round at everyone before sinking the knife into the plump chicken.

'Feverish whim?'

'This is the reality now, lass. You can forget all that daft ATS nonsense and smarten your ideas up. You'll never catch a chap in that mannish suit, with your hair chopped off. Your mother will take you shopping tomorrow and sort you out, won't you, love? I've got some spare coupons I'll willingly donate for the purpose. I'd consider it a charity.'

If it hadn't been for the sheen of embarrassment on George Fenton's upper lip, not to mention Muriel Fenton's stifled snigger, Belinda might very well have imagined she'd misheard.

'I know you were never one for the glamour stakes,' Hubert relentlessly continued, 'but we can't have folks thinking my lass a dowd, now can we?' He passed her a plate of chicken. 'Eat up, and put some flesh on those bones. Chaps round here like a bit of flesh to get hold of on a woman.'

Belinda felt the sweep of anger run up her spine and freeze it rigid. 'How *dare* you! I'm perfectly capable of buying my own clothes. And I wouldn't *dream* of putting on weight simply to please a man. Besides, I'm extremely fit and intend to stay that way. There are other things in life besides marriage.'

'Nay, lass. Hold your horses. Don't take on so,' he mildly chided her.

Ron stopped masticating his chicken long enough to comment, 'Dad's only concerned for your future – that you shouldn't let the side down like.'

'Side? What *side*?'

'We can't have you rusting on the shelf.' Hubert Clarke had never been one to know when to shut up and draw a line under a point. He always had to score it deep. 'All I'm saying is that you've had your bit of fun. Now it's time to settle down and be the good daughter we deserve. Marry well and provide us with grandchildren. Don't you reckon we deserve that, George? Muriel?' He appealed to the Fentons, busily stuffing their scarlet faces with chicken.

For Belinda it was all too much. She was on her feet, pushing back her chair and actually gaping at him. 'Fun? *Fun, you say?* Oh yes. I've had loads of fun these last five years. It's been one long laugh from start to finish. What can be more amusing than picking up pieces of bodies and trying to match which bit belongs to whom. Or watching a friend's leg turn to green slime and then seeing her hobble about on crutches when they relieve her of it. Now that really was hilarious.'

It was unforgivable of course to relate such horror stories in front of her gentle mother, and at a dinner party.

Vaguely aware of Muriel Fenton rushing to the bathroom, Belinda watched in fascinated horror as her mother very elegantly slid off her chair into a dead faint on the carpet, her napkin still clutched tight in her hand, as if even in an unconscious state, she must not be found neglectful of her table manners. If it hadn't been so desperately sad, it might have been exceedingly funny.

As it was, Belinda simply folded her own napkin, dropped it on the table, and walked from the room. She'd start looking for a job first thing in the morning, come what may, and a place of her own to go with it.

Chapter Four

Polly stood in line for broken biscuits with a patience born of long practice. Far from disappearing with the end of the war, queues seemed to stretch longer than ever and black marketeering was as rife as ever, causing a lot of bother in certain quarters though it was no skin off her nose she supposed, if the government lost out a bit. There were times when Polly wondered if they really had won the war or whether it was all a big con.

'Are you queuing for owt good?' a passer-by enquired.

'We don't know till we get there,' said one wit.

Not that Polly minded queuing. Here at Campfield market it gave her time to look around and chat with friends. Polly had always loved markets, had stood one herself in her younger days. Just watching Billy the Potman juggle with his dinner plates and beat down his own prices never failed to make her laugh. What a showman! He should be on twice nightly at the Queens. When she'd queued at the butchers and got a nice long red skinned polony for tea, she'd take a little saunter down Tonman Street. She might find a cheap frock for Sarah Jane.

'There you are. Don't eat 'em all at once,' Madge Sullivan cheekily remarked as she deftly spun the bag to produce an ear at each corner and handed it over to Polly. Her wide girth seemed to fill the space behind the stacked stall, leaving her skinny husband hardly room to breathe let alone reach biscuit tins.

'Fat chance with my lot.'

'Got home safe, Poll, 'ave they?'

Polly explained about Tom being missing, and Madge tried to assure her that there was still hope. Other women in the long queue chipped in with tales of various friends and neighbours whose loved ones had come home, against all odds, and she nodded in agreement, without actually believing it possible. For all she'd been an incomer from Cheetham Hill, the folk of Deansgate Village had accepted her as one of their own, Madge Sullivan included. She loved the intricate network of canals and railways arches, the locks and bridges, and the wide sweep of the Bridgewater viaduct striding across it all.

'Millie Bradshaw's husband had been missing for four years when he turned up, nice as ninepence and just as brash.' Madge leaned closer over the biscuit tins, causing them to wobble perilously and a few stray biscuits to fall on the stone setts where they were gobbled up by an opportunist dog. 'And how's your lad, Polly. I hear he's home safe and sound, at least?'

'Hey, missus, we'll be here till next Preston Guild if you don't get a move on,' said one chap, clearly growing impatient with this feminine chit-chat. 'I'd like to get served today, if it's all t'same to you.'

'Why don't you save your breath to cool your porridge. You're lucky if you've an house to go to. There's plenty who haven't.'

Polly, anxious now to get away before the rest of the queue lost its good will and turned nasty, said, 'Benny'll be bright as a new pin and raring to go, once he's had a good rest, so he will.'

'Yer a lucky woman.'

'And isn't that the truth?' She hurried away, making no mention of her worries over Charlie. Nor did she refer to the rebellious stand her son had taken the minute he'd arrived home for good, threatening not to come into the business with her at all. Not that Polly gave much credence to such daft declarations of independence for all it'd shaken her a bit at first. Like a slap in the face it was, but then mebbe she'd rushed him, hadn't put it quite right, nor properly outlined her plans. Why, she hadn't even mentioned her dreams to go into selling new carpets. Full of grandiose schemes he may be but in his mother's opinion he could do no better than stick with the family business. Wouldn't he come round fast enough once he'd had time to settle? For this reason alone she preferred to keep these family concerns private.

She sauntered down Tonman Street, enjoying a bit of rare time to herself. At a second-hand stall she found a frock for Sarah Jane – blue gingham. She'd look a picture in it. To avoid any squabbles between her precious grandchildren, Polly bought a gaudy glass bobber for Sean's marble collection, then treated herself to a mug of hot Vimto, which went down a treat. After that, she turned off by St Matthew's Church and made her way along Liverpool Road where she'd heard of a warehouse to let. If she could get at least a part of it at a rent she could afford they'd be up and running in no time.

Charlie could work indoors again and be his own boss, which he preferred, and Benny would soon see the sense of coming in with her. Pity Big Flo was no longer the woman she'd once been, or she'd have given him an earful for rejecting such a fine offer. Wouldn't she just. But the loss of her own three sons, one after the other over the years had finally turned the old woman's mind. Didn't even know what day of the week it was half the time, poor old soul. Pride Carpets was still remembered though, a name to be reckoned with.

The warehouse had already been taken the landlord informed her, but softened her disappointment by mentioning another he'd heard going vacant, over towards Knotts Mill. Polly decided to take a look while she had the time. After all, Big Flo was being well taken care of. She'd left Benny in charge, giving Lily Gantry who usually sat with the old woman while Polly was working, a morning off.

The future, Polly steadfastly decided, was bright.

–

Benny didn't quite share his mother's belief that family responsibilities were good for him. Fond as he was of his grandmother, Big Flo was an old woman. She'd had her life and he was young and eager to be out and about to savour his freedom. What sort of a homecoming was this, to sit in the back yard with a seventy-nine year old who was only tuppence to the shilling.

He'd been shocked when he first saw her. Once a big woman, with arms on her like an all-in wrestler, she now seemed shrunken and wizened. When Benny took her the meal his mother had left keeping warm between two plates over a pan of boiling water he found her, as usual, staring into space in the shadowy depths of the Anderson Shelter, a strangely blank expression upon her face. The place had that sweet-sour smell of decay, of mustiness and the old tippler closet against which it leaned. It made him want to puke. On a table beside the old woman's chair lay a large book covered in newspaper clippings.

'He was my son tha knows,' Big Flo reminded him, with a hint of her old sternness.

'Aye, course he was.' He stared at the face of his own father, Matthew Pride, who'd been killed in the riots back in the thirties, protesting over the Means Test. Ancient history so far as Benny was concerned. He remembered grieving for him though as a young boy, and hating having to live with his uncle Josh, who'd taken over their lives completely. In the end, so far as he could remember, Josh too had turned a bit queer in the head, but Benny had no wish to live his life gazing backwards over his shoulder. Look to the future, that was the way.

'Did you know my lad then?' The wrinkled face broke into a childish grin, false teeth clicking with pleasure, as if this were a new discovery. Benny stifled the desire to say how would he not know his own father, but instead set the tray quietly before her.

'See, Mam's made you some nice lentil broth. Eat up,' he urged in jollying tones. 'Put some flesh on them old bones, eh? You should come inside, Gran, where it's warm.' The damp was getting to him already. Why didn't his mother pull the shelter down.

'Who are you to tell me what to do?' Big Flo's voice boomed out, as forceful as ever. 'Thee's nobbut a lad. Fourteen next week, Joshua Pride, so don't get high-handed wi' me. Yer not too big fer me to clock you one.'

Oh lord, Benny thought. Now she thinks I'm my own uncle. 'All right, don't get upset. Eat your dinner before it goes cold.'

Big Flo showed no sign of touching the food and after a long silence in which Benny struggled to think what to say that wouldn't make matters worse, he came suddenly to a decision. 'How about a walk? That'll put some colour in your cheeks. Fresh air, that's what you need.' He couldn't bear to stay another minute stuck in this Anderson Shelter. He'd go as daft as her.

He went upstairs and brought the old woman's coat and hat, changed her felt slippers for a pair of sturdy shoes, tucked a scarf about her neck. 'Exercise is good for you, Gran. Do us both good, eh? How about a tram ride? You like going on the tram, eh?' He'd go down to the city council offices, ask about jobs, or shop premises to rent, then he could do a bit of buying and selling on his own account. He had his demob money burning a hole in his pocket. There must be something good he could do with his future besides steaming and cleaning old carpets. Some way he could be independent.

Big Flo was remarkably easy to steer, if a bit wobbly, rather like an old car that kept stalling. Only once did she enquire where they were going and Benny told her the truth, that he was seeking employment. Unfortunately this set her off on the tale of the hungry thirties again and all the way in the tram she scolded him about his false pride over Polly working when he wasn't.

'I'm Benny, not Matthew,' he tried, but she wasn't listening so he gave up, humouring her as best he could.

He parked her on a bench, just outside the rating office, instructing her sternly to sit tight while he went inside. 'I'll be back in a jiffy,' he told her as he disappeared through the door.

He only needed a small shop, just to get him started. In truth that would be all he could afford, though once he'd a bit more saved up, he'd go for something bigger. What he was going to sell in the shop he wasn't too clear. Clothing maybe. Or better still, furniture. Whatever he could get his hands on. There'd be a good future in retailing once the utility rules were lifted. One shop, two shops, who knows where it might lead?

He marched smartly along the dimly lit corridor, boots ringing on the tiled floor. There were several men already waiting at the office to which he was directed, and a young woman tucked behind a newspaper. Benny ignored them all, stood at the small square window and pressed the bell. He could see the head of a man bent over a book into which he was writing in crabbed lettering. The clerk did not even glance up at the sound of the bell.

Benny pressed it again.

A woman in a tweed skirt and grey cardigan glanced briefly in his direction before returning to clacking the keys of an ancient typewriter. Benny wasn't used to being kept waiting, particularly by civvies. He drummed his fingers on the window ledge but neither paid him the slightest attention. A curl of anger started deep in his belly. He'd risked his life for idiots like this, pen pushers who'd hardly taken their backsides off their easy chairs.

With one sharp knuckle he rapped on the window again. 'Scuse me,' he said in stentorian tones. No response, save from the woman who, without pause in her typing, half glanced at the clerk, then quickly away again. Benny decided that either the man was stone deaf or pig ignorant. 'I haven't all day to stand here.'

From behind him came a stifled snort of laughter. He rounded upon the perpetrator, and stopped dead.

Bright blue eyes danced with merriment above the open newspaper, in the kind of classical face that might be plain or beautiful, perhaps depending on her mood, or on those who looked upon it. She was certainly arresting. A fresh, almost schoolgirl grin with a straight nose and a neat chin. The kind of face you could get to enjoy looking at. One that showed good breeding and class. The kind of girl Benny Pride didn't usually get anywhere near.

'I've been here two hours,' she said, twisting her mouth into a moue of disbelief. Relaxed again, it became once more a wide, laughing mouth, one he experienced a strong desire to taste. 'And it's not the first time. I've been here more times than I care to recall. It's always the same. He deals with you eventually. In his own good time. You just have to be patient.'

Benny was slowly gathering his wits. 'Two hours my foot. Nobody makes a monkey out of me.'

The girl giggled and ran her fingers through ridiculously short, honey gold hair. Benny preferred long curls that fell enticingly over a girl's face, and redheads rather than blondes, more the Rita Hayworth type but it suited her all the same, no doubt about that.

'I shouldn't think anyone would try,' she said and Benny puffed out his chest, aware he'd developed a good physique while in the army, and that this girl seemed to appreciate the fact.

He rapped on the window again, harder this time, meaning to impress. 'Hey up. I'd like a word, if you don't mind.' He'd no intention of being ignored while those bewitching cornflower blue eyes were fixed upon him.

The clerk lifted his head and adjusted his spectacles to briefly consider Benny. 'Wait in line. You'll be attended to in due course.'

In one fluid movement, Benny pushed up the small window, stuck his hand through the gap and grasping the man by the only bit of collar he could reach, hauled him to his feet. 'Stand up when you speak to me,' he bawled, in a voice the men in his platoon would have recognised. 'Straighten that tie, jump to it, and *get your bleedin' hair cut.*'

The clerk's jaw hung with shock as his dazed eyes took in the size of Benny, yet found himself quite unable to free himself from the clenched fist that held him in an iron grip. 'I b-b-beg your pardon?'

'No bloody pen-pusher tells me to wait in line. Is that understood? I've done all the waiting I'm doing. Six years of it. Now the sodding war is over and I haven't helped win it to wait about for fools like you to walk all over me.'

'Bravo,' cheered the girl softly from behind him, followed by a smattering of applause from the rest of his audience.

Benny's hand tightened on the collar, pulling the alarmed face closer to the window. His voice now was low, but uncompromising. 'You'll deal with this young lady first. *She* has been waiting fer *two hours.* You'll call her ma'am, and you'll be polite. Then

46

you'll deal with me.' Benny ignored the fact that there was a queue of men waiting before him. That was their problem. 'And you'll call me *Sir*. Have you got all of that? Is that simple enough for your small clerk's brain to understand?'

The clerk wagged his head, not without difficulty.

'Good. Get on with it then.'

'Right away.'

'Sir.'

'Right away, sir.'

And to do the man justice, he did. In a surprisingly short time he had dealt with the girl behind the newspaper and produced a list of empty shops, albeit a short one, for Benny to investigate.

Out on the pavement, Belinda thanked Benny for his help, though she had been less successful in her search for accommodation. The list the clerk had given her was for rooms only, and the rent would soon eat away at her savings. 'Not that I've found a job yet,' she complained. 'Five years hard labour for my beloved country and what do I get at the end of it?'

'Two hours in a rating office and the satisfaction of seeing authority crawl,' Benny replied, making her laugh again, a ripe gurgling sound that he instantly warmed to.

'I did enjoy that, I must say.'

She was perfectly delightful. As well as being stunningly attractive, her voice was soft and well-modulated, surely indicating that she came from a better part of the city than himself. Happen up near Heaton Park, or them new houses off Cheetham Hill he decided. He wanted to know everything about her. Most of all if he could see her again. 'What were you then? A wren?'

She shook her head. 'ATS. Corporal.'

Benny saluted, giving her a cheeky grin and a wink. 'Sergeant. Border Regiment. We must have quite a lot in common then.' He was struggling to soften his Lancashire accent. It wouldn't do to put her off.

Clear blue eyes regarded him with undisguised interest. 'Maybe we do.'

A stillness fell upon them and both seemed momentarily lost for words, but as she half turned to go Benny felt a desperate urge for her not to walk out of his life as easily as she had walked into it. 'How about a cuppa? Or a bite of dinner. I'm fair starving.' He could have kicked himself. A girl like this would call it lunch, not dinner. He felt suddenly unsure of himself, the cockiness that he'd displayed in the rating office now rapidly evaporating. He even wished he wasn't still in uniform, instead wearing a smart suit, maybe a double-breasted pinstripe, to show her he meant business.

Belinda was remembering how breakfast at Cherry Crescent had been even more fraught than usual that morning, so much so that she'd left without eating a thing. But then tension since the notorious dinner party while she searched for work and alternative accommodation had mounted daily. Her father objected to everything she did, even to the clothes she chose to wear. Trousers, in his opinion, were unfeminine and gave the wrong impression, whatever that might be. He was furious that she'd declined to go shopping with her mother, or agreed to have her hair curled. Even the fact that she refused to go to bed when her parents did, only served to spark off a row every supper time. If, as a result, Belinda barely stayed in the house long enough to sleep, let alone eat, was it any wonder?

She grinned up at Benny. 'Me too. Haven't eaten a thing all day. I wouldn't mind a bit of dinner myself.'

-

In no time at all the pair of them were laughing together over home-made pie and chips in a small cafe off Deansgate, swapping jokes and war stories, funny ones only permitted. Belinda recalled diving into the toilets on Victoria Station, attracted by the faint blue light over the door when a doodlebug had been about to drop.

'Trouble was, it was the gents. Fortunately it wasn't in use at the time,' and they both fell about laughing. People turned and smiled, entranced by the lovely girl who sounded so happy with her young man.

Then they moved on to dreams and ambitions, what they might do now that hostilities were over. She told him of the difficulties she was encountering at home, how her father was attempting to organise her life, her mother wanting to turn her into something she wasn't. 'And my brother Ron is no help at all. If Pops says jump, he jumps.'

'Nobody makes me jump if I don't want to,' Benny bragged. Eager to impress he told her how he meant to have his own business. 'I'd start out modest to begin with, just to test the market,' he explained, as if finance were not a serious consideration. He became so carried away by the intentness of her cornflower blue gaze that when she enquired what he might sell in his shop and from where he would find his supplies, he found himself claiming skills he didn't possess. 'I've always been good at making things. This utility stuff won't last. Folk will want summat better, so if I can't find the right stuff, I'll make it meself.'

It was all pure fantasy, born of hopes and dreams and the need to impress a beautiful woman. Belinda took it all in with flattering attention.

'I'm me own man,' he declared, rather grandly and somewhat inaccurately.

In view of how well they got on, it seemed natural for Benny to ask to see her again. He'd always been a bit shy around girls, the way they giggled behind their hands, and were only keen on spending his hard earned brass. But this one seemed different, this one wasn't daft and silly like the rest. She wasn't some tart on the make. She showed style, had class and probably had smart young officers queuing up to take her out. What if he had embroidered his ambitions a bit, and let his dreams run wild? Wasn't that the only way to get noticed by a smart lass like Belinda Clarke? He certainly wasn't going to admit he'd only been offered a job of cleaning mucky old carpets. When she agreed to see him again, he couldn't believe his luck.

'When? Tomorrow?'

Her eyes were dancing up at him and Benny felt the blood race through his veins. Yet again he was filled with worry. Was she laughing at him, or did those wonderful peepers naturally behave in that lively fashion, out of sheer happiness. Benny did hope so. He felt dazed, dazzled by the perfect loveliness of her face in exciting and startling contrast to the mischievous rebel he glimpsed beneath.

He walked her to Piccadilly bus station, watched her climb aboard the red and white corporation bus, still bemused by his good fortune. Only as it pulled away did he smack the palm of his hand to his forehead and start to run after it, shouting to her as she clung to the rail on the platform that he didn't know her address, or even her last name. And they'd arranged no time for their next meeting. 'Meet me in Heaton Park by the band stand,' he shouted above the roar of the engine. It was the only decent place he could think of, on the spur of the moment.

She was still laughing as the bus swung round the corner, and when he finally stopped to draw breath, Benny became acutely aware he was standing like a great cart horse in the middle of Portland Street, running the grave risk of being ploughed down by a passing tram whose driver clanged its bell furiously at him.

And he hadn't the first idea whether she'd heard him or not.

He turned smartly on his heel and started to walk home. So captivated was he by her, so bemused by his own good fortune at meeting this lovely girl, and so concerned over whether she'd turn up for their date that he quite forgot parking an old woman on an old bench more than an hour before. It wasn't until he marched through his own front door and saw his sister set the frying pan on the stove and start tossing in slices of black pudding, that he remembered. He stopped dead and swore softly under his breath.

'What's wrong? You've gone white as a sheet.'

'I'm in dead lumber, Lucy.' Thank heaven his mam wasn't home yet. He turned and raced straight out of the house again, Lucy's voice echoing after him, yelling to ask if he'd taken leave of his senses. He'd just have to hope Big Flo was still sitting tight on that bench.

His hopes, sadly, were in vain. The bench was empty. The half demented old woman had vanished.

Chapter Five

Polly was furious. Having found the untouched midday meal in the Anderson Shelter with not a sign of Big Flo, she was half demented with worry by the time Benny returned alone from the city centre. Couldn't he do a simple task like minding one old woman? Didn't she have enough to worry over without being able to trust her own son? And much more on similar lines, punctuating her words with frequent slaps about his shoulders and upper body which bounced off Benny as if they were made by a fly. She was for calling the police without delay, or for dragging the canal basin at the very least. Minnie Hopkins, who came galloping down the street at the first whiff of trouble, advised caution.

'Give her till tea time. Her stomach'll fetch her home by then.' Even so, the entire street turned out to search for the old lady.

All afternoon they hunted high and low, trailing the length of Deansgate, through St Anne's Square, along Cross Street, Market Street, even checking all the surface air raid shelters around Piccadilly Gardens in case she'd taken a fancy to one. Then back to Deansgate village and Castlefield where they searched beneath every railway arch, trawled around every likely wharf and tramped over practically every dingy stalk of grass down by the canal basin without seeing hide nor hair of her.

It was Lucy who found her, quite close to home, sitting in an air raid shelter of course, on a stretch of wasteland. It was growing dark by this time and nobody could begin to guess how she'd got there or when. Big Flo had her gas mask on, which she always carried in her portmanteau sized handbag, and her only response when Lucy gently scolded her for wandering off and not waiting for Benny, was to tell her that Jerry was sending buzz bombs now.

'Like a bleedin' homing pigeon,' said Lily Gantry, in her usual colourful language.

'At least she's nearing the end of the war,' Lucy said with a wry smile, once they had the old woman safely asleep in her own bed, a warm meal inside her and a hot water bottle at her feet. 'She might reach VJ Day soon, you never know.' Mother and daughter laughed, though not unkindly for it wasn't really a laughing matter.

'I wouldn't bank on it,' Polly mourned. 'She's hardly with us these days, is she?' Feeling a pang of guilt for leaving her mother-in-law to Benny's mindless care. 'Jesus, Mary and Joseph, she doesn't ask for much, does she? All she wants is an Anderson shelter, fitted out with a bed and a gas mask and she's happy as a bug in a rug. It's my fault, it is so. I shouldn't've left her.'

'You're not to blame,' Charlie insisted. 'Benny should've had more sense than to take her into town. Mind like a feather pillow, that boy has.'

Polly quickly changed the subject, eager to tell Charlie all about the warehouse she'd found, close to Knott Mill Iron Works and having easy access to Castle Quay. 'I've agreed to take the ground floor, which has plenty of space for the big machines I have in mind. We can just about afford the rent, so long as we all pull together and get the business going pretty smartish.' Polly thought of the savings she'd kept hoarded away in the bank for just such a day as this when the war came to an end. They weren't made of brass, as Big Flo would say, but they could manage if they all worked hard.

'What if I can't pull my weight? What if these dratted aches and pains of mine won't go, even when I'm working inside?'

Polly couldn't bear to think about such a prospect. She'd have him back up St. John Street to see that doctor like a shot. Useless though he'd been the last time, claiming it was nothing more than age creeping up on him, as if Charlie were in his eighties instead of only just over fifty. 'Then you can sit in a comfy chair in a swanky office and do the paperwork, and won't that be a relief? You know how I hate doing it.'

Charlie was only too aware that paperwork was something Polly never shunned. She'd sat up night after night making her plans: endlessly going over the estimates for machinery, drawing up lists and costings, yet she always made it sound as if she couldn't manage without him, as if she were weak and helpless, when all the time she was the strongest woman he knew. But then he wouldn't have her any other way. Charlie looked at her and loved the way her eyes shone with confidence and optimism for this new venture. He loved the way her head tilted and the impish grin that puckered her lips, the way she brushed back her hair with one languorous gesture. As always it made him want to kiss them, and he wasted no time in doing so.

'I'm the luckiest man alive and not a day over twenty-five, in my head at least,' he whispered, leading her upstairs to their private domain.

'And isn't it about time you realised that?'

–

When Benny arrived home the following afternoon, he felt greatly in need of sympathy after failing yet again to find a job or shop premises. Worse, he was suffering from deep disappointment over the fact that he'd waited two long cold hours in the park for Belinda, who hadn't turned up. She can't have heard him after all, over the roar of the bus engine and, since he didn't know where she lived, or even what her last name was, this put Benny in a self-pitying frame of mind. Yet no one seemed in the least interested in his troubles. He could almost feel the family shunning him.

Sean had apparently howled all the way home from the nursery because it was closing the following week. Lucy was almost as distraught, worrying over how she could possibly earn a living if she had no one to care for her son. It was all apparently due to the fact that since husbands had come home from the war, wives could now go back to being mothers instead of factory workers, and child care facilities were no longer considered necessary. But where did that leave her, and others like her?

The small boy was now in the throes of a huge tantrum, drumming his heels on the floor in a sound fit to wake the dead, while Sarah Jane wept in sympathy. Polly was struggling to instruct a confused Big Flo on how to pull back an old blue and white cardigan, on the grounds that if she could keep the old woman occupied, she might not wander off again. She'd seemed even more vague since the incident.

Benny looked upon the scene in despair. 'It's bloody pandemonium in here. Can't a chap find a bit of peace in his own home? Isn't somebody going to shut that child up?'

'Will you mind your language please,' Polly tutted, casting a nervous glance at Big Flo who, in her better days, would have clipped him round the ears for defying her Methodist morals so blatantly. 'Let the child be. He'll shut up when he runs out of steam,' she finished, in a tone even Benny didn't dare to argue with. He tried a different tack, by complaining that he was hungry but nobody heard, or troubled to answer if they did.

'I said I've had no tea.' He addressed this directly to his sister. 'Or any dinner either for that matter.'

'You'll have to get it yourself for once.'

Benny looked appalled, as if she'd asked him to build Blackpool tower in their front parlour. 'Make it myself?' Polly set down the ball of wool she was winding with a sigh and got wearily to her feet. 'We thought you would've got something while you were out. I'll make you some dried scrambled egg.'

Lucy protested. 'Mam, you've done enough. You look fair worn out. He can surely get it himself for once. There's some cold sausage in the larder.'

Benny felt as if he was still being punished for his mistake over Big Flo. 'Cold sausage? Dried scrambled egg? Don't I deserve a proper meal? *I've* fought in this war, not *you*? *I'm* the one the Germans have been taking pot shots at.'

Lucy pulled a warmed night-dress over Sarah Jane's head, thankfully noticing that at least the arrival of Benny, Sean's idol, had stopped his screaming and he was listening with interest to the growing argument. 'Don't exaggerate. You never went overseas, not like my Tom. You had it soft. You worked in the stores for ages, and the most trouble you had was finding the right size of uniform.'

Benny was incensed by his sister's casual assessment of his war effort. 'Stores is a responsible job I'll have you know, and that were only my first job anyroad. I went on to others, training men to fire machine guns for one. I may not have been sent overseas but there were planes going over all the time, firing at the base.'

'We've had a few bombs dropped on Manchester,' Lucy hotly protested, determined not to let her brother have it all his own way. Hadn't they all enough to worry over, without him adding to it. Oh, she could see how it was going to be, now he'd come home for good, arguing the whole time, selfishly thinking he could be waited on hand, foot and finger. Well, he had another thing coming.

Benny, embittered by the keenness of his disappointment over Belinda, couldn't allow his sister to belittle his war career. 'I was wounded once, in me leg, when the roof of our billet caved in. And you can't even be bothered get me a bite to eat, you bl—'

Big Flo suddenly lifted her great head and fixed him with a glare. 'Tha's been told once. Watch thee language, lad, if tha knows what's good for thee. Tha's not too old to have thy mouth washed out wi' carbolic soap.'

They were so stunned at the old woman's return to the fighting talk they'd once taken for granted, that they all burst out laughing.

'Listen to your gran. Doesn't she talk sense?'

Ashamed now, Benny went meekly to the larder and made himself a sandwich with the cold sausage. Polly placed a brimming mug of scalding tea on the kitchen table before him, and another beside Big Flo. 'There you are, Ma. You deserve it after sorting that lad o' mine out.'

But Big Flo shook her head. 'Nay, I couldn't face one. I'm feeling a bit peculiar. I reckon I'll go and have a lie down.' They all tensed, ready to block the back door when she attempted, as was her wont, to go down the yard back to the shelter. Instead she opened the stair's door and climbed wearily up to bed. They were all so startled that both Lucy and Polly ran to fill the stone hot water bottle, realising she must indeed feel poorly.

'Don't fuss, I'll be wick as a snig tomorrow,' she tartly informed Polly as the bottle, carefully wrapped in a flannel cloth, was slid in beside her feet.

Polly expressed doubts on her mother-in-law wriggling like any eel the following morning, no matter how much she might protest to the contrary. 'You're all clammy and cold. Couldn't I just leather our Benny for losing you. I'll fetch you some Fenning's Fever Cure, in case you're getting a temperature., and you'll stay right here, with your feet up tomorrow and no argument.'

Big Flo gave a weak smile as Polly tucked the covers tight. 'Thee allus manages to have yer own way, lass. Always did, I seem to recall, even against our Josh. Only one I know who ever dared to stand up to him.'

Polly was startled. This was the first time in years that the old woman had spoken of her favourite son in the past tense. She'd grown used to hearing Joshua Pride referred to as if he were still with them, as if Big Flo expected him to walk in at any moment. And with such conviction that there were times when Polly would glance over her shoulder and shiver. She hated to be reminded of her brother-in-law's malice, thankful only that she'd beaten him in the end, if at a price. He'd ended his days in an institution for the mentally insane and his mother had never quite recovered from the shame of it.

Polly made up a fire in the bedroom, then piled extra blankets on the big high bed.

'Don't forget the blackout,' came the forceful voice and realising there was little point in arguing that the war was over, Polly dutifully pulled down the black paper blind and drew the curtains over it, but she didn't return to the kitchen. Instead, she sat with her mother-in-law, sipping quietly at her tea, her eyes on Big Flo's face, remembering a time when the pair of them had been constantly at odds. They'd been forever at each other's throats, just as Benny and Lucy were now. Polly could hear them continuing their quarrel down below. 'Will you listen to the pair of them. You'd think they'd be sick of war and want a bit of peace, wouldn't you?' Polly said with a sigh, but the only answer was a heavy snore and she smiled, letting her own eyes close. Wasn't it grand to have a minute's peace herself?

After a while she heard Benny go out and Lucy climb the stairs to put the children to bed. The house was filled to bursting so it was. Oh, but she didn't mind a bit. Didn't she love having her family about her?

It was a good house, for all she'd have preferred to stay on at Cheetham Hill had they been able to afford. But they'd three bedrooms which was one more than most in Pansy Street, save for Minnie Hopkins at the top house with seven. Even so Benny was forced to sleep in the alcove bed downstairs since Lucy and the children were crowded into one, and Big Flo had this little box room. Downstairs, the front door might open directly onto the street but the long lobby led the way to a living room as well as a front parlour. At the back was the kitchen with a few steps leading down into a backyard which they shared with no one, and wasn't that a treat? They even possessed a good sized cellar, which was where they'd spent much of the war, though Big Flo had always favoured the Anderson Shelter. One day soon, when Polly was feeling brave, she'd have the dratted thing pulled to pieces.

She smiled down at her mother-in-law, sleeping peacefully, like an old war-horse herself. She thought how different things would have been if Matthew had lived. Not that she didn't love Charlie. She'd been fortunate to have two good husbands in her life. She and Matthew had enjoyed many happy years together, not like poor Lucy who'd lost her own husband far too young. Yet somehow, Polly knew she'd manage. Didn't you always, when you'd no choice in the matter? This reminded Polly that her first task tomorrow was to help Lucy find someone to mind Sean after the nursery closed, otherwise wouldn't she be landed with the job herself? And much as she loved the little tyke, she needed to get her business going and not spend her days baby minding. But it needed to be someone trustworthy and reliable to take care of her grandson. She worried a long time over this.

Charlie came in, urging her to go to bed and get a bit of rest but still she refused to leave Big Flo. Much later Polly heard the front door bang when Benny came back from the pub, and the sound of his stumbling feet going along the lobby. He was singing some raucous song and bumping into the furniture. Wouldn't she clip him one if he woke the poor old soul up, not to mention those children in the next room. Polly had changed into her old dressing gown by this time and she pulled it close about her before tiptoeing downstairs, ready to give him a piece of her mind.

In the dim light of the kitchen fire, she saw him slumped in a chair, head flung back, loud snores emanating from his wide open mouth. A stink of vomit filled the tiny kitchen. Polly punched her son in the chest.

'Will ye wake up, you good-for-nothing lout. Is it come to this, that you defile your own mam's hearth?'

Benny woke with a start, mumbling apologies that he'd only been celebrating his own homecoming, though he was clearly having difficulty focusing on exactly who it was he was apologising to. Polly pulled down the alcove bed that nestled in the wall by the kitchen fire, with a snap. Cramped it may be for a lad as big as Benny, yet it was warm and snug and more than he deserved, drunken sot that he was.

'See you wash your face and take off those filthy boots before you get into it, you useless tyke,' stabbing him in the chest with one finger to emphasise every word. Polly could feel her whole body begin to shake with fury. 'First you leave your poor old grandmother wandering the city like a lost soul, so is it any wonder she's sick with a temperature and possible pneumonia. Now you come home the worse for drink. Tis me Da all over again, to be sure, and see how he ended up. Dead as a nail. I'll not have it. Not in me own house. Couldn't I just batter your daft head in.'

Benny flinched as he saw her snatch up the dish cloth, but it was only to wipe the sick and spittle from his face, just as if he were a lad still. He jerked his head away, anxious to avoid her ministrations but knew better than to argue, not when she was in this frame of mind. In truth he was secretly ashamed of his drunkenness. By trying to sink his sorrows over Belinda, he'd succeeded only in worsening the poor opinion his mother already had of him. He could see her winding herself up into a fair paddy. In addition he'd made himself ill and would no doubt suffer a thick head in the morning.

Polly poured a jug of cold water over her son's head, soaking him through. 'Tomorrow you'll come to the warehouse with me and no more nonsense of being your own boss, or finding yourself a job. There's enough work there to keep us all busy and don't we need all the help we can get?'

'Aw, Mam. I've told you already. I'll not work for you in the warehouse, I'll not. I mean to make me own way.'

She could hardly believe what she was hearing; her own son still stubbornly refusing to work with her, and after the way she'd given him his first job when he was no more than a whelp. The Irish temper rose in her so fierce that a flush of red seemed to blur her vision. 'Jesus, Mary and Joseph, you'd make a saint swear, so you would. I'm thinking you're too stubborn for your own good. You'll pull your weight as I tell you to, or it's out on the streets for you, ye daft galoot.'

Benny drew himself up in the chair to his not inconsiderable size, concentrating hard so that he didn't fall off it while he put this very important point, enunciating each word as slowly and carefully as he could. 'I'll please myself. I'm warning you, Mam, I've had enough of folk tellin' me what to do. I'm going to pleashe meshelf in future.'

'Oh, is that so, to be sure. Then it's a bill you'll be getting every week for your bed and board,' and swinging on her heels Polly strode from the room, ignoring his pleas of 'Aw, Mam, you can't do that. I've no money yet.'

At the door she stopped and the finger wagged one last time. 'Then you'd best earn some pretty quickly, or it's the warehouse for you, like it or no. I don't want to spend every day doing battle with me own son, but if it's a war you want, then it's a war you'll get. Only *I'll* win.'

-

After an achingly long and uncomfortable night, necessitating frequent trips to the privy down the yard, Benny felt worse rather than better as daylight approached. He couldn't believe what he was doing. How did he imagine he could take on his mother? Wasn't she notorious for getting her own way? Why couldn't he just agree and accept the miserable job? What was so marvellous about independence anyway? He never did find the answer to this one before merciful oblivion took over.

At some time during her long vigil, Polly must have closed her eyes and slept too, for when she next woke with a start, it was to find the night-light had guttered, the fire gone out and the room felt strangely cold for early summer.

Polly drew back the curtains and lifted the paper blackout blind a fraction so she could see to find a match to relight a candle. The moon still hung in a pale grey sky, sending a shaft of pale light into the bedroom, eerily encircling the figure which lay so still in the high brass bed. That was the moment in which Polly realised her mother-in-law was dead.

For once in her life, without making any fuss, Big Flo had slipped quietly away when no one was looking.

-

Polly sat on the polished seat of the pew, her family gathered silently about her and tried to take in the words of the minister as he droned on about Florence Pride, our dear departed sister.

The small chapel was almost filled with family and friends, some in severe black, others wearing well-used arm bands over their ordinary coats. Aunt Ida was there, almost as stoic as Big Flo herself had been in a lifetime of troubles. Uncle Nobby, looking pale and solemn and smelling faintly of the manure he'd put on his rhubarb patch that morning. Lily Gantry putting her hand on Polly's arm. 'Eeh lass, I'm sorry. She were a grand woman in her day.' Minnie Hopkins dressed in a funereal black coat that had a greenish cast to it from long disuse but her shoes were well polished, and she'd put her teeth in for the occasion. The two women sat together like a pair of old crows.

Behind them came other neighbours. The Taylors and Beckworths, Maggie Stubbs, Maisie Wright, Harry Entwistle the joiner and Mrs Shaw from the end house. Then of course there was Doris-from-next-door and Gladys and Vera Benson, the two sisters who ran the corner shop for all they too, like Polly, were Catholics and would have some explaining to do for even being present in a Methodist chapel. The sisters had managed to find a bit of ham and pickles from 'under t'counter', for those who wished to go back to the house for a bite of refreshment afterwards.

Every now and then Polly would sniff into her hanky and Charlie pat her shoulder, or Sarah Jane would feed her little brother a toffee to still his chattering tongue. He'd surely be sick if he had many more, Polly thought, watching them. Benny was looking unusually sombre in his drab demob suit, as if the bomb Big Flo had been expecting for so long, had finally fallen and he'd been the one to bring it. And so he should.

Polly could hardly believe she was sitting here, calmly taking part in Big Flo's funeral. The old woman had seemed indestructible, larger than life itself. Now, all because of Benny's neglect, she was gone. She swallowed the lump of tears that blocked her throat. Sure and she'd be hard pushed to forgive Benny for his carelessness, so she would.

Michael Hopkins, occupying the pew immediately behind the diminutive figure of his aunt, leaned over to whisper a few sympathetic words and while Polly nodded vaguely, Lucy turned her head to smile a radiant response.

'Look at that little madam,' came the hissing voice of Lily Gantry to her companion Minnie Hopkins, overriding the muted tones of tuning-up from the organ. 'Making eyes at that nephew o' thine at her own grandmother's funeral. You'd happen think her a merry widow instead of a good Catholic wife to a soldier declared missing.'

Polly felt as if someone had struck her. *How dare they!* If she weren't in chapel, she'd give them a piece of her mind for uttering such blasphemy. She cast a sideways glance at Lucy, who was using her hymn book to hide her scarlet cheeks.

'Blethering idiots,' Polly whispered.

The minister was asking them to rise, hymn books were being opened, throats cleared and the organ straining to find the right notes. Then good Methodist voices soared up to the gallery, *The Day Thou Gavest Lord is Ended,* and Polly felt the tears roll unchecked down her cheeks, to make little splashes on the blurred words in the book. Oh, but she'd miss the old dragon, so she would.

Chapter Six

Outside the chapel Michael Hopkins hovered at Lucy's elbow. 'Will you be coming to work tomorrow, as usual?' he asked.

'Of course.' Lucy sounded her surprise for didn't she have her living to earn?

'Only I'd like a word.' He meant about the whispers they'd all clearly heard in chapel but even as he disappeared amongst the crowd she didn't dare watch him go, too keenly aware of his aunt's all-seeing eye fixed upon her and her evil tongue still wagging. Lucy contented herself with tugging Sean's collar into place and hustling Sarah Jane into the waiting car to cover her embarrassment.

The cortege of two funeral cars, hired by Polly to show how they could still hold their heads high, unemployed or not, carried the entire Stockton and Pride family and various close friends along Lower Byrom Street on its way back to Pansy Street.

Benny took no part in the polite attempts at conversation around him, too concerned with his own troubles. He'd loved Big Flo. Hadn't she spoiled him rotten as a boy for all her sharp tongue, and he'd never meant her any harm. Yet he could sense that everyone blamed him, just as if he'd deliberately left her sitting on that bench in the hope she'd catch pneumonia. Coming home seemed to have been something of an anticlimax. There'd been no welcome home banner for him. Arriving at the same moment as the telegram bringing news of Tom's fate had scuppered any chance of that. The longed for freedom in Civvy Street was, in reality, a bleak and lonely place. He still hadn't sorted out his future and he'd even messed up his chances with a wonderful girl called Belinda.

It was as the cars turned into Liverpool Road that he saw her. For a moment he thought his eyes were deceiving him, that he'd conjured her out of a battered and overworked imagination. He couldn't think what she might be doing here, at Castlefield, but he would have recognised her anywhere, even in a large floppy red beret that hid half her lovely face from his view. She was standing at the corner of Fenton Chemicals, talking to a young man. Wearing a light grey costume that seemed to mould itself to her slender figure, Benny thought she looked even more beautiful than he remembered.

'Stop the car.' He was shouting at the driver and Lucy was slapping his arm, telling him to be quiet and show more respect. But the car did indeed stop and within seconds he was beside her, grinning from ear to ear.

She looked startled, as well she might, to have him appear out of nowhere. There was a slight puckering between her straight brows as she gazed at him with those mesmerisingly wide blue eyes. Perhaps, he worried, she didn't even remember him. Benny was about to remind her who he was when the brow cleared and she laughed.

'Of course, you're the chap who got me served in the Rating Office.'

Benny beamed. 'You remember me.'

'How could I forget?'

She introduced him to her companion, Frank Fenton no less, the son of the owner. He was thin, not very tall, with light brown hair and eyes, pale pockmarked skin and a faintly sulky expression on his boyish face. A nondescript in Benny's opinion and he took pleasure in paying the fellow scant attention. 'I'm glad I caught you. I must've missed you the other day.'

Benny couldn't take his eyes off her, saying the first thing that came into his head, foolishly asking how she came to be here in Liverpool Road, as if it mattered so long as he'd found her again. She told him that her father had business interests in the area and they were soon chatting twenty to the dozen until Lucy shouted to him to hurry up. He turned and yelled back, to tell her he'd be along later and she slammed the funeral car's door in a most inappropriate fashion. Benny hastily explained how he couldn't hang around for long as he was at this very moment on his way back from his grandmother's funeral, earning himself a softening of those dazzling blue eyes as a result.

'I'm so sorry. Don't let us hold you up,' Belinda murmured, in that wonderful humming voice she had.

'You could come and have a bite with us, if you wanted. There's plenty.' He'd no idea whether there was or not, but he was anxious to hang on to her, wishing Fenton would take the hint and vamoose. Instead, the man simply stood there, foursquare, as if he owned the flippin' road as well as the factory.

'Oh, we wouldn't dream of intruding, would we, Frank?'

The young man shook his head. 'Indeed not. Our commiserations to your family,' taking hold of Belinda's arm as if he had a right to it. Benny longed to shove him away and take hold of her himself, but she wasn't the sort of girl to appreciate a tug of war between two warring suitors.

Panic struck. Benny knew he must do something to delay her, to make sure they met again. Then he was pulling out his pocket book, asking her to write her name and address in it, and she was laughing up at him, in just the way he remembered.

'And my telephone number too, I suppose?'

She had a telephone? Hadn't he known she had class. 'Of course,' he casually agreed and watched with satisfaction a frown mar Frank Fenton's brow as she carefully noted the details down, closed the book and handed it back to him.

'Good to see you again,' she said quite lightly but, he was sure, with absolute sincerity.

'Happen you'll be seeing me sooner than you think.' He saluted, and then remembering he wasn't in uniform, held out his hands by way of apology, making her giggle. How he loved her chuckling laughter.

Benny strode away at such a cracking pace it took him a moment or two to realise he was going in quite the wrong direction, so was forced to double back and march past them both again, making her hoot with laughter all the more, Frank Fenton smirk, and his own neck and cheeks to fire up. Still, he was beyond caring, he was so pleased with his good fortune. Benny would never have thought such a bit of luck could come out of such a sad day. If it wasn't disrespectful to say so, happen his grandmother had fixed it for him, from the other side, to show that she at least had forgiven him. Benny rather hoped so.

–

At seven o'clock that evening he was kicking his heels outside a certain house in Cherry Crescent, plucking up the courage to make his presence known. Feeling surprisingly nervous, yet determined not to show it, he finally pressed his thumb on the bell. A portly, red-faced man came to the door, looking down his bulbous nose at Benny as if he were a beetle that had crawled out from under a stone.

'I've called to see Miss Belinda Clarke. Would she be in?' Benny politely enquired, somewhat overdoing the carefully practised phrases.

'Indeed she wouldn't,' came the brusque reply. Not to the likes of you anyway, he might have added were he not interrupted at that moment by Belinda herself.

'Yes I am, Father. Don't be silly. Oh, hello, Benny. Wait there, I'll get my coat.'

And as Benny stood grinning with pleasure, Councillor Hubert Clarke fidgeted on his own front doorstep as if he itched to give the young soldier a piece of his mind for the impudence of calling without an appointment. 'I thought you were stopping in tonight,' he tried, as his daughter brushed past him. 'Frank will be round, don't forget.'

'No, he won't,' she said, tucking her arm into Benny's. 'I told him not to bother. Don't wait up, I might be late,' and the pair strolled off, Belinda smiling, Benny looking as if he'd swallowed a whole dish of cream. Hubert Clarke looked as if he'd been given a lemon to suck.

Benny took Belinda to the Gaumont, which was the most expensive cinema he could afford, to see *Meet Me in St Louis*. He curbed his natural impatience by contenting himself with holding her hand and she didn't seem to object. They came out dancing and singing the *Trolley Song* all along the tramlines, just as if Belinda were Judy Garland and to Benny's mind she was every bit as fabulous as any film star. She must have enjoyed herself too for she agreed to see him the next afternoon. Benny took her for tea at Lewis's because he thought that was what classy young women liked to do. Two weeks and several dates later he was beginning to worry that at this rate he'd spend all his demob money in no time, so risked making a suggestion.

'I'd take you home to meet Mam and Charlie and our Lucy, only you'd happen think us a bit – well – a bit humble like. Clean and honest but ordinary folk, us.' He'd chosen his words with care, so that she felt obliged to agree. And she did.

'Don't be silly. I'm ordinary too. I'd love to meet them,' she said, with genuine warmth in her voice, exactly as he'd hoped.

Beaming, Benny tucked her arm in his. 'That's settled then. Lucy'll be back from her cleaning job by now, and she'll make us a cuppa.'

'I wouldn't want to get in her way though, if she's busy.'

'You won't be. She likes a bit of company does our Lucy.' He was anxious for the two girls to meet for, if they got on, Belinda might take to calling while he was away. He hadn't much cared for the red-faced old geezer who'd opened the door that first evening, though the house had been a real eye-opener, much bigger and grander than he'd expected, and with a garden front and back, no doubt. But if Belinda didn't think much of her father, then she'd happen take to coming round to his house regular like, and he'd be more sure of her. He was almost certain she and Lucy would hit it off.

In the event he was proved right. Lucy and Belinda liked each other on sight, the two girls were soon laughing and talking as if they'd known each other for years. The children climbed all over Belinda's knee, vying for her attention, and when it was time for her to go, Lucy went with them to the door.

'You must call any time. I'd be glad of your company.'

'Me too.' They smiled at each other. 'You could come to the pictures with us some time,' Belinda added.

Lucy glanced at her brother's face, noted the quick frown and chuckled. 'I wouldn't want to play gooseberry.' Belinda laughed, making it clear she was perfectly capable of choosing for herself, sometimes she would go with Benny, sometimes with Lucy or all together. And so it was agreed.

The two girls became firm friends. Belinda would call regularly and, if Polly was working, Doris-next-door would baby-sit for Lucy and off they would go, shop window gazing along Deansgate or, if they were a bit flush, a trip to the pictures. On these occasions they were two young lasses again, not a wife worrying about a missing husband, or somebody's daughter trying to hang on to a battered independence. They cheered when Dane Clark won the war, stamped their feet when the cavalry chased the Indians, and wept unashamedly when Ingrid Bergman lost her man.

On other occasions, like today, Benny was with them, and the three of them would walk arm in arm, laughing and joking, their young voices soaring out, singing songs from the movies, making up fantasies of how it felt to live in a vast Hollywood mansion. Afterwards they'd treat themselves to a fish supper, or walk along Liverpool Road eating a meat and potato pie, hot and succulent, giggling as the gravy dribbled from their chins. There was nothing better on a cool autumn evening.

'Wait till I get my own business going,' Benny announced, swaggering a little in front of Belinda. 'Then I'll buy myself a car and drive you somewhere smarter than the Gaumont. Mebbe all the way to the seaside for a day.'

'What about Mam?' Lucy queried, bringing him back to reality. 'I thought you were helping her with the carpets?' Benny flushed, for he had done a bit of work for his mam, since so far he'd been unable to find premises or a job to suit him. 'I can do better than that, Luce, see if I can't. I mean to set up on me own, you know I do.'

Smiling fondly at him Belinda said, 'I remember you telling me how good you are with your hands, that you'd like to try joinering and make your own furniture to sell.'

'Aye, happen so,' Benny agreed, with not too much conviction in his tone. He could feel himself becoming more and more embroiled in this lie, surely only a white one since he had done quite well in woodwork at school, yet seemed unable to do anything to extricate himself from it. 'There's going to be a great call for good furniture. That's certainly true.'

Lucy snorted her disbelief but, smiling to herself, left him to his harmless fantasies.

Belinda chipped in, 'I think you're ever so brave but wise too, to start up on your own, now peace is here. The best way to make money is to work for yourself, or so Pops tells me, and judging from his success I have to believe him. Of course, you'd need premises,' and so flattered was he by her interest in contrast to his sister's negative attitude, that Benny couldn't resist expanding on his theme.

'Oh, I'm keeping an eye open for summat suitable, though they're hard to come by these days, shop premises. Once I find a place I'll set it all up with a bench and tools and everything. Then customers will flock to my door for whatever I produce.'

'I could help you look.'

'Really? Well, why not?' He felt almost breathless with hope. She *liked* him. She really did. Happen he was in with a chance after all.

Lucy had heard enough of his foolish bragging and sought for a way to change the conversation. They were walking past the Co-op which was still open and doing a brisk trade, for all it was late, the shop's bright lights spilling out on to the wet pavements. They could see Lily Gantry barging her way to the front of the queue. Lucy shook her head in despair. 'What a woman! D'you remember what she said at Big Flo's funeral?' and related the words that had caused her such hurt at the time.

'The old witch,' Belinda said, and put her arm around her friend's waist, giving her a comforting squeeze. 'Take no notice. She's only jealous of your lovely youth.'

'Aye,' Benny said. 'Who'd fancy her, an old goat with whiskers on her chin.'

Belinda gave a merry chuckling laugh. 'Who is this Michael Hopkins? What's he like?'

'A rather private, reliable sort of man. He's my employer, and a good friend,' Lucy explained, telling how he helped her keep her job when his aunt would have sacked her. 'He's rather nice actually, a sort of Trevor Howard type.'

'And our Luce is panting for him,' Benny said with a snort.

'Ooh, I never am.'

'You make his dinner every day for nowt. That sounds pretty keen to me.'

'I'd no choice in the matter. His dragon of an aunt, Minnie Hopkins, insisted I did it if I wanted my job back.'

'Why don't you invite him to come to the flicks with us?' Belinda suggested.

'Then you can canoodle on the back row,' Benny teased, thinking this a good idea as it would leave him more free to do the same with Belinda. Having his sister tag along too often hadn't been the plan at all. Lucy's response however, was to knock him over the head with her rolled up umbrella.

Belinda laughed as the pair of them tussled together in a play fight. 'Mind you don't drop your pie, Lucy.'

'Quite right. Let's keep our priorities in order. Eat first and I'll batter his brains in later.'

Over the next weeks as the days shortened, Belinda continued to see almost as much of Lucy as she did of Benny and seemed content to have it that way. Not that they weren't pretty inseparable as a couple and, in a way, Lucy envied them that contentment. Yet within the family, disagreement rumbled on. Benny seemed determined to be independent, refusing any sort of commitment beyond a bit of temporary employment now and then with his mother. Polly was clearly upset by his continued stubbornness and went about tight-lipped. Knowing her mother as she did, Lucy could see the situation exploding in Benny's face if he didn't make a move to find himself a proper job soon. Much as she adored him, Polly's patience with her one and only son would surely only stretch so far.

But Lucy was happy for him, she was really. Belinda was a lovely girl, though what she saw in her head-in-the-clouds brother, she really couldn't imagine. Maybe she was jealous in a way for wouldn't she just love a man of her own; a life other than one with herself and two children packed in the spare room of her mother's house.

That Christmas the Ministry of Food handed out free Christmas puddings and one was given to Lucy, since she was bringing a family up alone. A part of her resented this act of charity even as she gladly accepted it. Every day she was forced to remind herself that Tom was only *missing,* as if she needed to drum this fact into her head. Yet however much she might do so, deep down she held no hope that he would ever return, which left her feeling like a widow with all the problems that brought. But what if she wasn't? Others, besides Lily Gantry and Minnie Hopkins, didn't see her as such, so how could she ever rebuild her life, ever start again with another man until she knew for certain one way or the other.

She missed having someone to confide in, to chat with, to open her heart to as she'd used to be able to do with Tom. She didn't always see eye to eye with her mother though it was admittedly true that Polly had never been one to interfere and when she offered advice, it was usually wise. Like the time she'd urged her to apologise to her employer for those telling sharp words. Nevertheless even a loving mother or a friend like Belinda, however valuable, couldn't make up for the loss of a soul mate, a husband and lover.

As always Lucy took refuge from her troubles in hard work. It was the only way she could cope with her grief. Every morning she went to the end of the street and cleaned number 179, keeping a well buttoned lip despite much provocation from Minnie Hopkins. Lucy still couldn't stand her but at least she'd kept her job, one she needed and enjoyed, and they both became reconciled to a state of what might be called an armed truce between them. Generally speaking they managed to keep out of each other's way, circling each other whenever they met, like a pair of sparring dogs.

Lucy enjoyed looking after Michael. He was a kind and gentle man, had even stood up for her when she'd asked if she could have Sean with her while she worked, since the day nursery had closed. Minnie had been vehemently opposed to the idea, but Michael very reasonably pointed out that if Sean didn't come, neither would his mother. And by that time, even Minnie had come to appreciate the excellent meals the young woman cooked for them, so had grudgingly accepted the situation.

To Lucy this was a huge relief as it eased the pressure on her over-full day. Sean, though curious about the big house, was no trouble and seemed to benefit from spending more time with his mother. He played either in the long back yard or safely in the small front garden. Little bigger than a pocket handkerchief with a few stalwart marigolds surrounded by a privet hedge, the little boy seemed content with his chalks and slate, toy soldiers, or bowl of soapy water for blowing bubbles, and Lucy could keep an eye on him from out of the many windows as she rubbed them clean.

Yet she was aware, as Michael returned each dinner time from the haulage depot where he worked as foreman, of how he watched her with concern, often remarking that she worked too hard, that she'd lost weight and looked worn out.

One day when Lucy made a delicious mutton hot pot, he insisted she sit and share it with them. Minnie looked outraged but for once, wisely perhaps, kept her opinions to herself. Lucy was equally opposed to the idea but the more she protested, the more Michael insisted. Cushions were placed on a chair for Sean and, finally succumbing to the mouth-watering aroma of good meat, the like of which Polly could rarely afford since all her spare cash was being poured into restarting the business, Lucy urged the small boy to be on his best behaviour and seated herself beside him. She was aware, throughout the meal of Minnie Hopkins's grim silence, apart from the clicking of her false teeth as she sucked on the mutton bones.

After the meal Michael walked the length of the street with her, while Sean skipped and hopped along in front, riding his imaginary cowboy horse. As they approached number 32 among the more tightly packed terraces where Lucy lived, Michael said, 'You still look tired. What you need is a rest, a day off.'

Lucy laughed out loud at that. 'What chance do I get for a rest? Today, I have to pick up our Sarah Jane on her way home from school, then make a bite of dinner for everyone. That's my job, d'you see? Mam, or sometimes Charlie, usually cook supper. Then I'm off to Taylors this afternoon to do their weekly clean through. That's after I've washed the dishes and dropped our Sean off next door and Sarah Jane back at school. Pick the kids up again at four. Then there's only all the washing, ironing and mending to do, which never stops with two children, plus my share of the housework. After that my time is my own!'

'You do too much,' he said as she finished on another laugh, tucking her brown curls behind her ears.

'When you come up with a way of earning brass without having to work for it, do let me know.'

Michael was thoughtful for a while as they walked, before returning to his argument. 'I still think you need a day off, a day all to yourself, and by heck I'll see you get one.' He was gripping her arms now, swinging her round to face him and the heat of his touch was doing peculiar things to her insides. 'You could have a day trip to Belle Vue, or Blackpool. I'll take you myself, Lucy Shackleton.'

'Belle Vue? Blackpool?' She stared at him in wonder, as if he had suggested a trip to the moon. 'And who'd take care of the children, if I did?'

'They'd come with us, of course.'

A day in Blackpool. A ride in a tramcar, a dance in the tower ballroom, sucking on a stick of rock and paddling her feet in the sea. Ooh, it sounded grand. She couldn't remember the last time she'd enjoyed such a day. Ah, yes, with Aunt Ida and Uncle Nobby just before the war. They were no more than courtesy titles, them being old friends of Charlie's, but they'd always been good to Lucy. They'd stayed at a boarding house in York Street for a full week, in one of those tall terraced houses with stairs that seemed to reach all the way up to heaven. But she wouldn't say no to another visit, nor to an afternoon at Belle Vue. Near as it was to her home, she'd rarely visited this magical place, as she'd scarcely had the money since the children were born. A few hours with nothing to do but gawp at exotic animals, lick candy floss like a big kid and whizz on a whirligig. Wouldn't that be grand?

For a moment as his big broad hands gripped hers she felt dizzy at the prospect of such heady joys. The temptation was so great, happiness so nearly in her grasp that she almost flung her arms about his neck and said yes, she'd love to, before reality drenched the madness.

She couldn't let Michael pay for them. That wouldn't be right. Both the children needed new shoes, and hadn't she enough trouble finding money to pay the bills, let alone to waste on whirligigs and candy floss. She was supposed to be saving hard for a place of their own; her children deserved a bit of space and privacy, even if they no longer had a dad. So she laughingly refused his kind offer. 'You must be soft in the head. I've no time to take a day off. Anyroad, it'll be too cold now. Maybe next year?'

'Is that a promise?'

Lucy could hardly meet the intentness of his gaze. It seemed to be burning her up. 'Barring accidents, as they say,' she commented brightly. Yet it stayed in her mind, this foolish dream, and Lucy couldn't help but wonder what Michael Hopkins would look like dressed up all smart, instead of in his blue work overalls.

Chapter Seven

Lucy was keenly aware that Sean missed the nursery and that he also missed his dad. For all he had never known him, she'd made sure that he kissed Tom's photo every night and he'd got it into his head that this father would one day come home, play football with him and teach him how to fish. It was surely all her fault if the little boy now felt let down, as if a promise had been broken.

'When is Dad coming home? He hasn't forgotten me, has he?' and Lucy would explain that he might never come back, that she didn't know the first thing about fishing or football, and he should ask Uncle Benny. But Uncle Benny was always too busy with his own affairs these days, looking for the shop of his dreams and taking Belinda out. When Sarah Jane had gone back to school at the beginning of the autumn term, it was hard for the little boy to accept that he couldn't go too. It made him feel even more left out of things.

'You can go next year, perhaps by next summer, if the teacher will let you. You'll be four and a half by then, love,' she'd told him.

'Dad'll be home soon, won't he?'

'No, love. I don't think so.' In a little tantrum he'd picked the photo up from where it stood on the dresser and flung it to the stone floor where the glass had shattered into a dozen pieces. Sean was a child with a determined nature. Lucy tried to explain this to Michael one morning after he'd found her weeping as she swept the endless stairs in his aunt's house.

'I can't bear to see you cry, Lucy.' He laid a hand on her shoulder and something inside of her seemed to unfold at his touch, as if her body were reaching out to him.

'It's our Sean. I'm that worried about him.'

'Don't be, you're a wonderful mother to him.' And to her surprise he reached over and placed his lips very gently upon her cheek. It was nothing more than the sweetest breath of a kiss but it left her with a strange sensation of anticipation, not to mention a trembling breathlessness in the pit of her stomach. The next minute his mouth was seeking hers, then his arms were tight about her, holding her against him and offering her such wonderfully solid comfort and her heart was thumping like an express train.

Afterwards, she swore to Polly that she hadn't been distracted at all, that of course she'd been keeping a proper eye on Sean. He'd asked to go down into the front garden to play and she'd thought it perfectly safe, with the small green gate fast shut and the sneck tied up, since she was aware how resourceful he was. But while she stood in the dark intimacy of the stairs with Michael's arms about her, out in the garden Sean dealt quite easily with the bit of string that held it fast and was soon marching smartly up Pansy Street straight as a soldier, just like Uncle Benny.

He knew where the school was. Hadn't he walked with Mam and Sarah Jane often enough? He turned the corner quickly and kept on marching, trying not to look at the round things at the crest of the hill that looked like bogeymen's heads, but which Mam had once told him were chimney pots. He wasn't sure he could believe her. Grown-ups didn't always tell the truth. Mam had said his dad was coming home. Now he wasn't.

The school yard was empty when he arrived, which threw him for a minute. Then he realised that the children would be in their classrooms having lessons, and all he had to do was walk down the long corridor to find Sarah Jane's room, and she'd tell him which was the right class for him. But first he had to cross this busy road.

Lucy and Michael leapt apart when Minnie came to find her. Lucy began to sweep for all she was worth, brandishing the stiff hand brush with vigour while Michael attempted to adopt an air of casual interest. She wondered if her lipstick was smeared and that was why Minnie glared at her so fiercely.

'Do you realise you left the front gate open? Anybody could have walked in, perfect strangers who might have murdered me in my bed, if I'd still been in it, that is.'

Lucy stopped sweeping, a small cloud of dust settling upon her head as she froze and stared up at Minnie Hopkins. 'What did you say?'

'I said I could've been murdered...'

'No, no, about the gate.'

'I've told you, it were wide open and—'

Lucy dropped the brush and scrambling to her feet almost fell down the stairs in her haste, heart racing. She saw the gate swinging open and stood transfixed before turning and flying back through the house, calling his name, 'Sean. Are you there, Sean? *Sean!* Oh, my God, where is he?'

Minnie, puffing down the stairs after her, caught some of Lucy's alarm and her beady black eyes shot wide. 'I never thought of t'lad. He's probably hiding somewhere. Playing some sort of daft game.' Michael dashed out to the back yard, flinging open the doors of various outhouses. None of them contained a small boy.

Panicking quite out of control, Lucy couldn't begin to think. 'Oh please God, not the canal. He's kept pestering me to take him fishing but I always put him off. What do I know about fishing?'

'He can't have got far,' Michael said, trying to calm her but she was running now, and Minnie wasn't far behind, her short legs having a hard time to keep pace. Michael caught her up easily. 'I'll search down by the wharfs and the canal.'

While Minnie scoured the length of Pansy Street from top to bottom, Lucy tackled the wasteland where the abandoned air-raid shelters were. It was just like Big Flo all over again, only this was a small boy who could wriggle his way into all sorts of tiny, fear-filled places. Heart in mouth, Lucy searched every place she could think of, yet could find no sign of him. She was considering calling the police when she suddenly saw Sarah Jane and her teacher walking down Duke Street beneath the railway bridge and clutching tightly to Sarah Jane's hand was Sean, his tears making grubby tracks down his chubby face.

–

'I didn't know whether to hug him or smack him,' Lucy told Michael that evening as she sat sipping a welcome sherry in the Dog and Duck on the corner of Pansy Street. He'd decided that she deserved one, for the shock. Polly had disapproved strongly of her going out, giving her a hard time and accusing Lucy of the kind of carelessness she'd expected only to find in Benny. Lucy couldn't for the world have refused Michael's invitation, even if it were only out of kindness. She had to see him, to be with him, however innocently. It made her feel good just to see him smiling at her. 'I've no doubt you did both. Mothers usually do.'

Still pale to the lips, Lucy sighed. 'The teacher was very kind. She told him that if he was a good boy and didn't run away again, she'd let him start half time in the nursery class next Easter, when he's four. I could've kissed her.'

'Some good came out of it then.'

Her face clouded as she recalled the scene putting the small tearful boy to bed. 'It still sounds a long time off to Sean. Trouble is, he won't believe that Tom is dead. He can't picture it, you see. Death I mean. He was so looking forward to having a dad.'

Michael said nothing and a small silence fell between them. 'He won't be the only child without a dad, not these days. Or the only dad without a child for that matter.'

'I know that but does he? He finds it hard to understand. He's so very little.'

'Perhaps the little boy is right and Tom isn't dead. The telegram did say missing, *presumed* killed.'

Lucy shook her head so vigorously the brown curls bounced. 'I'm not going down that road. He's dead. I'd know inside of me if he was still alive. Aunt Ida agrees, she thinks I should be wearing black, grieve for him properly and be miserable all the time.'

'How do you feel about that?'

'She's not one to cross isn't Aunt Ida, for all she's not really my aunt at all, besides...' Lucy flushed and hid her embarrassment with a sip of sherry. 'There are times when I find it hard to remember what Tom looked like. It's so long since I saw him. Does that sound awful?'

'No. We all suffer from that problem, it's fairly normal. We don't want to remember, that's why. Memories bring fresh pain.'

Lucy looked into his gaunt face but didn't think this was so in her case yet she realised, for the first time, how little she knew about him. Unlike her, Michael Hopkins had not lived in this street all his life. He was a newcomer, having moved in shortly after he was invalided out of the RAF. 'You sound as if you speak from experience. What sort of pain did this dreadful war bring you?' She asked the question gently, but hastily added, 'it's all right if you don't wish to speak of it.'

He answered directly, without any prevarication. 'It killed my wife. Blasted her and our small son out of existence.'

'Oh, Michael,' she breathed, and he told her in one further crisp sentence about the bomb that had flattened his house. She asked no further questions about the woman he had loved and lost, or of his beloved child. It seemed far too intrusive upon such a private man. Instead, she found herself saying, 'Enough of this gloom, the war's over. This is supposed to be a new beginning. What about that day out you promised us? Is it still on?'

'It certainly is. We could take young Sean on that fishing trip he's so desperate for? Or maybe that trip to Belle Vue if the good weather holds. Please say yes. I want to see you smile again.' For a long moment he looked into her eyes and Lucy did not flinch away. Then as if by some compulsion over which neither had any control they drew closer till they were a mere breath apart. This time when Michael placed his mouth against hers, capturing it completely, she instinctively opened her lips to his, just as if she longed for him to invade and explore her thoroughly.

She only vaguely heard what he said after that, some details of tram times and picnic baskets, fishing rods and umbrellas. She was staring at him entranced, feeling bubbles of unexpected excitement starting up somewhere deep inside her. Feelings she'd never thought to experience again, the kind a woman with a missing husband had no right to be feeling. No right at all.

–

Lucy, Michael and the children embarked from the tram at Belle Vue bursting with excitement. Sean had been sick before they'd even reached the end of Quay Street, filling Lucy with embarrassment, though why she really couldn't imagine. Michael was charm itself, holding the little boy on his knee for the rest of the journey so he could see out of the window. He'd already taken him down to the canal and given him a short lesson on how to catch fish with a rod and a net, while giving stern lectures on how he mustn't go anywhere near either the canal or the River Medlock by himself. Michael had also promised to teach the little boy how to swim and the two were now fast friends.

So here they were, at Belle Vue.

This was the place beloved by all Mancunians with its zoological gardens and amusement park, the dirt track racing, various exhibitions, dancing and even a circus at certain times of the year. Folk were attracted to its pleasures like bees round a honey pot.

'Can I go on the caterpillar?' Sean wanted to know, jumping up and down with excitement.

'And be sick again, no fear,' Lucy told him.

'I want to go on an elephant,' Sarah Jane put in.

So many dangers. The thought of her children let loose amongst all these rides filled Lucy with terror but Michael swiftly put an end to her concerns. 'They'll be safe enough with me,' he assured her and she cast him a shy glance of gratitude as they went through the turnstiles, for of course they would, in more ways than one. But then she had to strictly remind herself not to read too much into his kindness. It was one thing to spend time with this man as her employer, even out with him on a Saturday afternoon all dressed in their best, quite another to look upon him as anything more than that. Even so, she felt a bit sick with excitement herself, and wondered how they would get on.

She needn't have worried. The day was a great success.

They giggled at the monkeys climbing all over their rocky mountain. Sean and Sarah Jane rode on the Bug and the Bobs and of course the miniature railway. They all went on the caterpillar and squealed when the green hood came over and made it all dark. Then it was time for the elephant ride. The elephants were famous at Belle Vue. There were three of them there today. Mary, Annie and of course Lil, the most famous of all. These were led by a dark-faced man in oriental robes who went by the even more exotic name of Fernandez. Perched high in a precarious swaying chair, the children squealed with delight. Lucy could hardly believe that outside of the turnstiles lay Gorton with its factories, rows of dark red brick houses, shops and pubs. Here, inside Belle Vue, was a magical kingdom, a wonderland of fun and entertainment.

The elephant ride was so popular that Michael paid for the children to go again, which gave the two adults another few precious moments to themselves. And somehow this seemed to be particularly important, possibly because summer was almost over and this soft September day was an unexpected treat.

'Are you happy now?' he asked, brushing the words softly against her ear and she could hardly bear to look at him as she whispered her agreement, flushing like a schoolgirl.

After the elephant rides came far more candy floss and vanilla ice cream than was good for them. Sean demanded to see the fireworks which he'd seen illustrated on a poster and Michael had to explain how they'd been cancelled because of the war. Both children groaned, Sarah Jane looking as if she was about to cry.

'Why does the war spoil everything?'

'Good question, but they'll start again soon, when things get back to normal,' Michael promised.

'Can we come again?' Sarah Jane asked and Michael smilingly agreed, glancing quickly across at Lucy.

'We'll make that a date, eh?'

'Yes!' both children squealed so loud that Lucy decided it was time to take control.

'How about something to eat. Fish and chips all round?'

'Sausages, sausages,' yelled Sean, jumping up and down so violently that Michael picked him up and swung him round in the air like an aeroplane, leaving the little boy gasping for breath and giggling so much Lucy had to calm him down all over again. She scolded Michael for encouraging him even while her eyes sparkled with laughter.

'If you're very good,' Michael solemnly warned, wagging a calming finger in the children's eager faces. 'We'll go and watch the dirt track racing after we've eaten.'

Lucy gave a mock groan. 'Now I'll never have a moment's peace whenever he goes out on his bike. He'll think he's a speedway star rider.'

Both children did indeed love the race track on the corner of Hyde Road and Hunter's Lane, the roar of the engines filling their ears as they watched in breathless excitement the bikes tearing around the track, frequently overtaking and sometimes slipping and sliding in a perilously dangerous manner. Michael told them about how he used to come often before the war to watch the riders, Frank Varey, known as the Red Devil, being a particular favourite on his Scott motorbike, and he tried to imitate the noise it made, making them all laugh.

Later, while the children were more restfully building castles in the sand pit, the two adults took a breather by renting a couple of deck chairs to enjoy the last of the sunshine.

'You look all flushed and sun-kissed,' he said, and Lucy laughed.

'I'll be red as a turkey-cock tomorrow with my fair skin, but I don't care. I'm having a lovely time.'

'I'm glad.' She opened her eyes to look at him and something shifted and lurched inside of her, as if her small world had turned upside down. 'I am right about what passed between us the other day when I kissed you, aren't I?' he asked, very softly, and she could only manage a small nod.

'Then I wouldn't mind repeating it.' When he leaned across the short gap between the deck chairs to pull her close with one arm, she did not resist, did not even glance in the children's direction, hoping against hope they were happily playing with the sand. His mouth closed over hers and she gave herself up to the pleasure of it, soft and warm, smelling sweetly of sunshine and something indescribably masculine. It had been so long since she'd felt like this with a man, she could hardly believe it was happening. Then his warm breath was against her ear and he was kissing that too, murmuring her name against the pulse-beat in her throat, telling her how much he had longed to touch her in this way, and in other ways too. Pleasure soared through her, making her heart beat like a mad thing against her breast.

'It must be a sin to feel this happy,' she said, unable to tear herself from his hold.

'Happiness is never a sin, but even if it was, I'd very much like to sin some more with you, Lucy.'

'Me too.' She gave him her lips again, shamelessly opening them, aching to be rid of the dratted chairs and savour the hardness of his body against hers. And why not? Her mind was telling her that Tom was dead, that they'd barely had any sort of marriage in any case because of the war, and now she was a widow and free to do as she pleased. 'Mam, look at our sand castle. It's got two towers. Look!' The spell was broken. Riddled with guilt and confusion, Lucy rummaged in her bag for a comb and powder compact, trying to avoid his smiling eyes before admiring the children's creative efforts.

They had to be back at Lake Entrance Corner by six and it was a tired and happy little group that climbed back on to the homeward bound tram. Sarah Jane couldn't stop chattering about the delights of the day, her one regret being that there hadn't been time to try out the boating lake. Michael carried a sleepy Sean, still making vrrm–vrrm noises following the thrills of the speedway, aloft on his shoulder.

The tram swung into view as it curved around the loop by Gorton Town Hall. Then while the driver walked through the tram, the trolley-boy used a long pole to reconnect the wire with the opposite end of the tram. Only then was everyone allowed on board and Lucy, Michael and the children collapsed on to a seat with a sigh of relief.

'I'm worn out,' Lucy complained, cheeks rosy with happiness.

It had been a good day, and as Sarah Jane and Sean slept all the way home, it gave the two adults ample opportunity for some serious conversation, even to try out one or two more of those delightful kisses.

–

Polly stared at her daughter as if she'd gone mad. 'Marry Michael Hopkins? May the saints preserve us, are you not already married?' She was sitting at the kitchen table, little piles of money set out before her on its scratched wooden surface, a task she did every week. One heap of coins was for the gas man, another for the coal, one for the rent, a few bob for the electricity meter and whatever was left would feed them. For all money wasn't as tight as it had once been, she couldn't get out of the habit of careful budgeting.

'Tom is dead,' Lucy stubbornly pointed out.

'*Presumed* dead. Michael's a lovely man, I'll grant you, but you can't marry again until you know for sure, one way or the other. You know that's true, in your heart?' A pile of coins fell with a clatter, as if echoing the hollow destruction of dreams.

Lucy sat gazing into her mother's sympathetic eyes and as Polly talked, explaining the reality of her situation very clearly and concisely, all the excitement of the day drained out of her, even the sunshine on her cheeks seemed to stiffen the rosy skin.

'I know it's too soon,' Michael had said. 'That it's wicked to even think this way but one day, when you're good and ready, I want you to know that I'll be here. Waiting.'

But by the time Polly was done, she knew her mother was right. It had been no more than a dream, a foolish fantasy. And for the first time, Lucy felt some sympathy for her brother and his own fanciful ambitions.

—

The next day Lucy could hardly bear to look at Michael when she repeated the conversation to him. Even the weather had changed from brilliant September sunshine to a solid sheet of rain, entirely in keeping with her mood. She watched it swirl down the gutter, washing away the last of her hopes while she stood on his doorstop, her hands thrust deep in her raincoat pockets.

'Why?' he asked. 'Why won't you marry me?'

'I didn't say won't, I said *can't*. Because I'm still married to Tom.'

'Come in, for goodness' sake. You're soaked through.'

So they stood in the narrow hall because she refused to go any further in case his aunt should overhear, and Lucy repeated what she had already told him. She explained how the magic of a sun-filled day at Belle Vue must have gone to her head to make her forget such an important fact. 'I'm ashamed at even considering such a thing so soon, with Tom posted missing only a few short months ago, even though it seems longer. But that's only because it's years since I last heard from him. Mam says I'll have to wait seven years, before I can get a death certificate.'

'Seven years?' Michael looked aghast for a moment but then had to admit that he should have known, if only he'd stopped to think. 'I must have been carried away too, by your sweetness and your beauty.' He kissed the tip of her nose, and she flapped a hand at him in agitation.

'Don't. What if your aunt should come?'

'She's in the parlour listening to *Band Wagon* on the wireless. I can't help but want to kiss you.' Lucy was suffering from much the same problem. Her hands were clenched into tight fists in her pockets so they couldn't sneak out and betray her. Almost to her disappointment, Michael made no attempt to touch her again. They both stood for a long moment, looking deeply into each other's eyes, not daring to reach out for each knew they might never let go.

'Seven years is a long time,' Lucy said at last, her voice barely above a whisper. 'I can't expect you to wait for me that long. I'll be thirty-five.'

'Mercy, quite old, and I'll be thirty-eight. Even older.'

'Don't tease me. This is awful. I shouldn't even be thinking this way, not with Tom only just… I have to go.'

'I'll wait, Lucy.' He was earnest suddenly, his eyes unnervingly solemn. 'I don't care how long.'

She turned quickly away, not trusting herself, making a great business of pulling up her head scarf and tying it in a businesslike fashion. 'I've left the children with Doris-next-door, I must go.'

Michael attempted to rally them both. 'Don't worry, Lucy. We'll sort something out. All isn't lost yet. We can at least still be friends. I'll wait, I tell you. I love you.' Then he did kiss her, pulling her into his arms with a fierceness that robbed her of the last breath in her body, just as if by holding her so tightly he could make it a part of his own.

Chapter Eight

By the end of May 1946 everyone began to fear the country might be on the verge of bankruptcy which meant they all had to pinch and scrape more than ever. The ration book Polly guarded with her life wouldn't buy nearly as much as it used to. Butter, margarine and other cooking fats had been cut from eight to seven ounces a week. Even bread was rationed now and pretty awful it was too. Greyer and tougher than the Victory Loaf due to a lack of wheat. Folk were now queuing to get divorced as well as buy sausages. What a sad mess of people's lives war made, Polly thought.

Even so, she was pleased with the way things were going. The warehouse she'd found was large and spacious, even if the windows were still mostly boarded up and you needed to keep your coat, scarf and gloves on against the cold of a late spring.

She'd had a gas fire installed in the two offices where she and Charlie worked, which meant the pains in his joints had eased somewhat but she hoped to put proper heating in the rest of the building eventually. In the meantime she'd purchased a few paraffin heaters and urged her employees, mainly women, to wear plenty of clothes and keep moving, allowing them to take regular tea breaks in the warmth of the main office.

Polly had installed new machinery for steaming and cleaning carpets but still had plans to expand one day. Folk seemed to be itching to spend money on brightening up their homes now the war was over, and a new fashion for fitted carpets was taking hold, one she hoped to take advantage of one day. Polly dreamed of buying one or two looms to make new rugs. The problem, as always, was capital.

She'd used every penny to get the business set up again, and was reluctant to borrow from the bank until she knew how successful it would be. Nevertheless she intended to think positive. Polly believed the future to be bright. The warehouse had a good location with easy access to Castle Quay which meant transport was not a problem, so long as they acquired a van to deliver the carpets to customers. She bought a large green one and had Polly Pride Carpets painted on the side. One evening over supper she suggested it be Benny's task to drive it. He refused.

'Jesus, Mary and Joseph, what'll I have to do to persuade you to see sense?' She slammed his supper down on the table in front of him, hoping he'd take the hint that someone had to pay for it.

'Leave me be, Mam. I'll sort my own life out.'

'And would that include getting a permanent job, d'you reckon?'

'Only if I must,' Benny said. 'I'd rather have a shop.'

'I'll swing for him, so I will.'

Lucy, washing her hair in the sink, kept her head down, not wishing to get involved with the argument. She wished her mother would say that living on the dole and lounging about the streets all day looking for shop premises in King Street and other places he couldn't afford, as he'd been doing for months, wouldn't get him anywhere. It was time her brother pulled his weight as the rest of them had to. In Lucy's opinion Mam was far too soft with him.

Polly did indeed feel a strong urge to remind her son of how tough life had been when they were in Ancoats, how she'd sold all their worldly goods and chattels in order to start her own little business in the first place. That if she was cautious it was because she remembered those days of poverty so clearly, and had no wish to return to them. She'd imagined that life would get easier now the war was over and she could get back to what she most loved doing. But she wanted Benny with her in these exciting new plans of hers.

She glanced across at Charlie, one eyebrow raised in a plea for his support, but he picked up his knife and fork and just winked at her, grinning broadly. 'Why should you imagine that Benny would always agree with you. Isn't he as independent-minded as his mother, a real chip off the old block? Give the lad time to find his feet.'

Polly gave a wry smile, because of course he was and she wouldn't have him any other way. A determined young man with a mind of his own. 'Or enough rope to hang himself?' she suggested, starting to laugh. Charlie was right, she should be encouraging Benny in his desire to start his own business, not putting him down all the time. Hadn't she had a similar reckless belief in herself when she was young? She certainly had no intention of fracturing family relations purely over business matters. 'Go on then, lad, make your own way.'

Lucy, frantically scrubbing at her hair with the towel, could have wept.

–

Councillor Hubert Clarke was not without influence, largely due to his prominence in business and local council affairs. It was gratifying to see how eager people were to keep friendly with him, even willing to perform small tasks or favours on his behalf. Look at the way George Fenton was as anxious as he to encourage his son to court Belinda, despite her obstinate lack of interest. Yet all too often, she wasn't even in the house when the poor boy called.

This morning they'd had their usual exchange of heated words, Belinda refusing to eat her breakfast and going off in a huff, with much slamming of doors. She'd got herself a job in an insurance office, which he thought quite unnecessary and she still stubbornly insisted on wearing those hideous trousers on her days off. Today, however, they'd returned to their favourite sparring topic: why she was spending so much time with that unemployed squaddie. He'd let her go in the end since her stubbornness was making him late for the office, which really was insupportable.

When she was gone, Hubert sliced the top off his egg as if he wished it were Benny's head and decided it was time to start exercising some of that influence. He'd shilly-shallied long enough, which was most unlike him.

He glanced across the table to where Ron, his only son and heir sat noisily crunching toast, the sports pages of the morning paper collecting smears of jam and butter from the dishes it was propped against. A surge of irritation soared through his veins but he had the common sense to curb the impulse to insist he remove it. If he fell out with Ron who could he depend on then? The boy's tall, rangy body was flung out with equal abandon, as if he had no pressures on him at all, unlike Hubert who felt every burden like a lead weight on his chest. At least Ron did as he was told without argument. Hubert got little if any support from anyone else, not even from his own wife, who usually hid in the kitchen during these spats. Anyone would think he was the villain, simply by striving to save their daughter from rushing disastrously into the arms of her working-class lover. 'What do you know about this chap?'

Without taking his eyes from the paper, Ron took another bite of toast and shook his head. 'Nothing.'

Again the hot flood of fury in his veins. Hubert drew in a steadying breath, knowing it was bad for his heart to get too excited. But he could not allow his only daughter to ruin her life, ruin all their lives by making a fool of herself. What on earth did she see in this common jack-me-laddo from the worst part of town, when she could have Frank Fenton, a chemical dye works that served a good third of the textile trade in Manchester if not all of Lancashire, a large house close to Heaton Park and access to huge family wealth?

And there was no denying that such an alliance would do his own credit trading company no harm at all.

As if on cue, the young man himself appeared at the door of the breakfast room and Hubert stifled a groan. He really didn't have the strength for any more thwarted love, not this morning.

It was Ron who spoke, again without lifting his dark head from the paper. 'You've missed her. She's just left.'

'Oh!' Frank looked thoroughly nonplussed. 'I–it's usually the other way around. You've both gone by now and Belinda just starting her breakfast. That's why I popped in. It's often a good time to catch her,' he explained, rather lengthily.

Hubert spooned egg into his mouth, catching dribbles of yolk on his moustache. 'I'm surprised you can spare the time. I'm in a bit of a rush myself.'

'Er, I've got the day off.'

Joanna came out of the kitchen, neat in twin-set and pearls, a pink floral apron tied about her waist. She started stacking cups and plates on to a tray. 'Hello, Frank. Belinda's gone, I'm afraid. You can come and talk to me while I wash up the breakfast dishes. I expect she'll be back later.' And like a lamb, he followed her into the kitchen.

Hubert dabbed at his mouth with a folded napkin and grunted. The boy was too weak for his own good. Faint heart never won fair lady. He really couldn't sit back and do nothing while his own daughter scuppered his chances of advancement on the City Council by going about with a chap from Castlefield, mebbe even marrying him, or getting herself into bother. At this thought, his heart began to pound and the heat in the room became utterly intolerable. Reaching across the table, Hubert snatched the newspaper from his son and tossed it aside. 'Shift yourself. We've work to do.'

'What?' Pale blue eyes narrowed enquiringly. He knew Ron was always interested in his plans. They usually involved putting the skids under some poor fool who owed him money. Before they'd finished paying for one item, a coat maybe, they'd usually been persuaded by Ron to buy shoes to go with it, or some item of furniture for their home.

Inevitably their greed led to too much debt, which Hubert never tolerated. Then it was up to Ron to sort it out, which always gave the boy a surprising amount of satisfaction. But then they hadn't got where they were today by being overgenerous to layabouts. Quite the opposite. 'Someone being difficult?'

'You might say so. Fetch the car to the front.'

Hubert watched him leap up to bring the Wolsley to the door. It spent most of its time in the garage, highly polished and taken out only when there was no sign of rain. He placed his folded napkin precisely by his plate, walked from the breakfast room to collect his greatcoat, bowler hat and briefcase and, standing by the kitchen door, (he never set foot in this female domain) called out to his wife.

'Tell Frank I'll have the matter in hand by next week at the latest. She'll see him in quite a different light by then, mark my words.'

Then he left the house without demanding the usual farewell on the front doorstep, largely performed for the benefit of the neighbours. Joanna stood transfixed, with her hands in the sudsy water and her eyes on Frank. She looked oddly bleak, not at all the happy expression you would expect from a mother who'd been told her daughter would soon see sense.

–

The family argument rumbled on at odd intervals throughout the day and the one after that and in the days following, with Benny constantly propounding his theories on how the second-hand carpet business was a dead duck. 'Finished. Caput. Don't waste your time on it,' he would say whenever he could get Polly to listen.

Not that she had much time to listen, what with working long hours at the warehouse as well as looking after Charlie. Osteo-arthritis had finally been diagnosed, inflamed by a desperately cold winter, so working in the freezing warehouse had done him no good at all. Sometimes the pain was that bad he couldn't even get up but lay in his bed moaning in agony. Polly could hardly bear to see him suffer so, and when she came home she spent hours rubbing his shoulders, back and knees with embrocation, which brought little more than a momentary relief from the crippling pain.

All of this put more pressure on her as the bread winner. She spent night after night with her little piles of coins, juggling finances, robbing Peter to pay Paul. She'd heard of a loom going cheap, out Hebden Bridge way and she meant to have it. She was determined to break into manufacturing as the best way forward. Perhaps then Benny would come in with her. She knew that a business either expanded or died, and she wasn't prepared to let that happen.

Never short on courage yet this seemed an enormous risk. And buying the loom was only the beginning. She'd need more than one, lots more, and there were bobbins, spools, work benches and fitted shelving called cribs needed to hold the raw wool, a machine to wash the wool, and maybe another to dye it. Money would need to be found for all of this. Polly wondered if perhaps she was getting too old to face the risks involved but then would chide herself for such self pity. She could do anything she wanted to do, she told herself. Always had.

But tired as she was, how could she find the patience to deal with an obstinate son blocking her plans, on top of everything else?

Today the argument had blown up again because she'd insisted Benny stand in for Charlie whose knees had swollen up so much he could barely stand, let alone deliver carpets. It was true that Benny had done the work, as asked, but Polly wasn't in the mood to listen to him blathering on about his dreams and fantasies. She felt only irritation that this young whippersnapper could stand in her own office after a single day's shift and think himself an expert on a business she'd devoted her life to. Now he was saying he might come in with her after all, if she made him a full partner and let him have an equal say.

Polly pooh-poohed this ridiculous notion and told him in her no-nonsense way that he could start at the bottom like everyone else. But Benny had a chip on his shoulder after six years of being told what to do, and absolutely refused this option.

'You'd soon learn and move up the ladder,' Polly snapped. 'I mean to get into manufacturing one day, once we have some money coming in and can afford to buy looms and equipment. Second-hand carpets are what got us started in the first place. It's what we do best. Cleaning and steaming is our bread and butter, as it was for a number of years before the war.'

Benny pulled a face, still not satisfied. 'The war's over and done with, Mam. It's history. Now it's time to move on. You shouldn't wait too long. After all, you could always borrow on the house.'

'I don't like to borrow.' Polly was loathe to abandon the skills she'd acquired through those hard early years, insisting that it was surely not impossible to move forward with new ideas while hanging on to the old. 'I don't want to take any risks till I can find the capital.'

Benny scoffed at this. 'Everyone borrows in business. Anyroad, there are other things that'll make more money without buying looms and taking on too much labour. We could sell furniture and household goods for instance. Belinda's father makes a fortune out of stuff like that.'

Polly put back her head and laughed at him. 'So now we're to become a grand furniture store are we, or is it a huge joinery factory you've a mind for?' She clicked her tongue with annoyance. 'Tush! And where do ye imagine we'd find the capital to expand the business in such a way?'

Benny's voice took on a sense of urgency as he leaned across her desk, eagerness lighting his young face. 'Listen to me for a minute, Mam. If you're short of capital, you shouldn't be wasting it on second-hand stuff, or on all these workers you have to employ to deal with old carpets.' He waved a dismissive hand in the direction of the humming work room. 'All that expensive labour. Is it worth it? You'd do better lending your money to me. I'm young. I'm the future. With enough capital behind me I could buy a proper shop, in the city centre, and really make my way. All you have to do is back me.'

Polly gaped at him. 'So now my carpet business is as dead as the dodo is it, and I should give all my money to you? I don't think so.'

Benny scowled. 'You'll do nowt for me, will you?'

'I've done *everything* for you, ye daft galoot, if only you'd the sense to see it. One minute partnerships, the next a fancy shop. I'm thinking ye should get your feet planted back on this earth with all speed.' She didn't mention that the last time he'd had his head in the clouds, he'd mislaid his grandmother who later died, but it was there somehow, in her face as she confronted him.

Benny's greeny-grey eyes, so like Polly's own, flashed with anger at his mother's intransigence. 'And I reckon it's time you came out of the ark, time you listened to someone else's ideas besides your own.'

Polly was shocked to the core. She was on her feet, fists planted on the desk in front of her as she glared across at him. 'Will you listen to his divil tongue? I'm old and past it am I? Out of the ark, am I? Haven't I paid a high enough price for this business in the past?' She certainly had no intention of giving it up because her son had taken some daft notion into his head to sell furniture from a fancy shop in the centre of the city. She shook a fist in his startled face. 'Find the money some other way. I'll not finance your crack-brained schemes. Leave me out of it.'

He was shouting at her in his desperation. 'Watch me then, and don't think for one minute that I won't succeed.' And with this parting shot he tossed the van keys on to his mother's desk and strode out of her office, slamming the door behind him.

–

Benny was tired and in a foul mood as he marched home. He hated quarrelling with his mother in that way. Why had he done it? He knew the reason. Because he was keen to have his own business then he could ask Belinda to marry him. Hadn't he bragged from the start how he was going to be his own man?

What would she think of him if he failed? What chance would he have with her then?

He might've agreed to go in with Mam if she'd let him have some say, been a full partner. But no, everything had to be done her way, the way things had always been done. Why couldn't she understand that he needed to make his mark, not be an underling. He'd no time for starting at the bottom, even if being part of an expanding business like Pride Carpets might win him a bit more credibility with Belinda's family. He wasn't totally against the idea, but nobody would listen to *his*. And he knew why. It was because of Big Flo. The whole family still blamed him for his grandmother's death, and it mortified him.

His first call as he turned into Pansy Street was to Benson's Corner Shop for more cigarettes. He usually had plenty of fags but he'd finished the packet during that boring delivery run. He was wasted driving a van. If only he could make Mam listen. Benny swaggered out again and strode off, looking about him with the air of a man who knew he was on his way up in spite of an ill-fitting suit and pathetically few quid in his pocket.

Since it was a Saturday he expected Lucy to be at home, perhaps even Belinda as well if the two girls had been to a matinee. They'd have his tea ready for him and a bottle of stout to go with it. Benny rather enjoyed this sort of attention after six years of war and NAAFI food, particularly if he could share it with Belinda.

He'd promised to take her out for a drink tonight, or to the flicks. He could hardly wait to see her again, but then he was always like this before one of their meetings, all tense and sick feeling inside. He wondered if she felt the same when she was waiting to see him. He really must convince her that he was going all the way to the top. It was his only chance. If she thought he was a no-hoper, she'd drop him like a stone.

He found the door locked and the house in darkness. Women, he thought. Completely unreliable. The silent, empty house seemed to echo the awfulness of his day, convincing Benny that not a soul cared. In a fit of pique he took himself off to the Crown on Byrom Street. Here he downed a couple of pints, relating at length his plans for the future to anyone who cared to listen. This cheered him a little and at half past seven he decided the girls must have arrived home by now and be wondering where he was. He liked the idea of Belinda worrying about him but he couldn't bear to wait any longer, besides he was feeling a bit peckish, ready for his supper.

He was passing the end of Camp Street when a dark figure suddenly lurched out of the shadows. The next minute he was flat on the ground with his nose pressed hard into the pavement.

'Were you wanting your thumbs cut off?'

Benny tried to speak, to say that he didn't but couldn't seem to manage it. His teeth were grinding into the paving stones and an elbow was applying painful pressure on the back of his neck, which was having a disastrous effect on his windpipe. Then he felt his head lifted by a hand grasping a fistful of hair and shaken vigorously from side to side.

'Is that a no?'

'Yes,' he croaked. 'No. Yes.' He was growing confused, could feel the wet dribble of blood on his chin and he wondered how many teeth he'd broken.

'I'm glad to see you're paying attention,' The voice was calm, controlled and entirely unfamiliar. Benny had terrible memories of being bullied as a boy and wasn't taking kindly to this treatment. He'd thought himself past all of that and could feel a terrible rage gathering in his veins.

'Get your bleedin' hands off me before…'

'Before what? I don't reckon you're in any position to make threats, do you?' The face came down close, the voice hissing in his ear, so soft and melodious it sounded like rushing water. 'I'm here to ask – nay – to *inform* you to leave Belinda alone. Right? Lay one finger on her, or try to see her again, and I'll chop them fingers and thumbs of yours right off, followed by your chattering tongue. Do you understand that, soldier boy?'

Benny might have grunted a response, had he been able. Fury was soaring through his rigid limbs, his vision blurred with a haze of red fury but his position, face down on the hard unyielding pavement with the weight of the man on top left him helpless. If he could just break free he'd paste the floor with the bastard.

'The message comes from her father. He doesn't like to be crossed, doesn't our dad.' Benny's head was jerked upwards for one last neck-crunching twist before being smashed down on to the pavement. He never heard the terrible ringing sound it made, as blackness crashed in.

Chapter Nine

Lucy had indeed gone to the Saturday afternoon matinee with Belinda. They didn't hurry home because they knew that the children were with Doris-next-door, and that Polly would still be at the warehouse, trying to cope with a pile of paperwork and worrying over how she should develop the business. For once Benny would be there too, helping with deliveries. Do him good to put in a full day's work, Lucy thought.

It had started to rain and they were sheltering in a doorway when they saw the shop.

'Look at this.' Belinda was staring through the filthy windows. 'What did this used to be?'

'This used to be Netta Abram's tripe shop. She sold the best pig's trotters I've ever tasted. What a delicacy.'

'What happened to her?'

'She died.' Lucy filled her mouth with hot fish cake, spitting bread crumbs as she talked. 'She was reluctant to go, mind, her only being ninety-eight at the time.'

They were both now peering through the dirt-encrusted glass but someone had painted it on the inside so it was impossible to see in. 'Wouldn't this be just the thing for Benny?' Belinda said.

'Our Benny? I thought he was looking for summat grander.' Lucy rubbed at the filthy glass, aghast at the very idea.

Belinda pointed out that the best thing the shop had to recommend it was its position. Situated as it was so close to the Co-op it would never be short of customers, assuming it had something of interest to sell. She sounded optimistic, almost excited. 'Why not? It's what he wants, to make furniture. He talks about it often.'

'Aye, that's the way he is. All talk. He'd never have the gumption to actually do it.' Lucy wiped her mouth and looked at Belinda with curiosity. 'I can't make you out, a girl from Cherry Crescent going with a chap like our Benny. He's a bit of a rough diamond, you know. Harmless enough but not the brightest creature on two legs.'

Belinda smiled. 'Perhaps I find him a refreshing change after the hypocrisy and snobbiness in my own family, not to mention the endless machinations of my father to find me a husband.'

Lucy gave a snort of laughter. 'Well you're safe enough there with our Benny. He'd run a mile at sign of a wedding ring.' She popped a chip in her mouth. 'What about your own brother? What does he do?' Lucy had noticed that Belinda rarely spoke of her own family.

'Ron managed to spend the duration working part time for the post office delivering mail, and the rest feathering his own nest, as you might say.' Belinda frowned as she wondered, not for the first time, just how he'd managed to evade the call up. 'He's in the business with Pops. Bit of a yes man, to be honest, which suits my father down to the ground.'

'And you're the opposite?'

'Seems so.'

'Well, don't expect our Benny to follow in your father's footsteps. He couldn't win an argument, let alone run his own business. Forget it.'

Belinda wasn't listening. 'Let's look inside, for goodness sake. I'm soaked through,' giving a push that made the door swing open.

'Hey, what you doing?' Lucy had exactly twenty minutes to spare, then she must collect the children from Doris-next-door, and she'd promised to peel some potatoes for Polly and Charlie's supper. Both girls stepped inside and at once put their hands to their noses in disgust.

'Cats!'

'Better than dry rot,' Belinda said, shaking the rain from her mackintosh and hair.

'It might have that an' all.'

The room, lit by a single electric light bulb, was not large but adequate for Benny's purpose, she decided. Belinda pointed out how the work bench could sit under the window, for maximum light. 'Tools could be hooked along the wall and there would still be enough space to store furniture as it was made.'

'What does our Benny know about joinering? Nowt.' Lucy kicked aside bundles of newspapers and other unspeakable rubbish. 'Besides, it's filthy.'

Belinda had gone through into a small back kitchen where she found a large stone sink and a small rusted gas cooker. The windows were encrusted with so much grime, hardly any daylight filtered through. She slapped the sink with a delighted grin. 'Somewhere to make the necessary brew of tea. Basic but definitely promising. It's perfect.'

That was not the word on Lucy's tongue.

Upstairs there were, as expected, two sizeable empty rooms. The paint was a nauseous brown and wallpaper hung from damp walls, behind which no doubt lived a multitude of wildlife.

'No bathroom?' Belinda enquired, showing her ignorance of this style of property.

'Oh aye, it'll be down t'yard. There's probably a bath next to the lavvy with gold-plated taps.' Lucy began to giggle and then stopped as she noted the intent expression on her friend's face. 'You weren't thinking of actually living here?'

Belinda hadn't but it didn't seem quite appropriate to say so. After all, Lucy's family lived in a fairly humble back-to-back themselves, if nowhere near as bad as this. Nothing quite so reckless had entered her mind, despite the fact that meal times at Cherry Crescent continued to operate very like a war zone. She tactfully explained how she saw Benny living up here, over his own shop. 'It could be cleaned, scrubbed out and whitewashed with lime to kill the bugs. Isn't that what you do?'

Lucy pursed her lips before replying. 'We don't have bugs, so I wouldn't know.'

Belinda looked stricken. 'Sorry, I didn't think. It's just that I'm so thrilled, so excited to have found it. This is the first decent empty shop we've seen in months. Like gold they are. It's too good an opportunity to miss.'

'It must be,' Lucy drily commented, feeling bound to point out that her brother might be less enthusiastic.

Belinda was so keen to tell him about it there and then that she rushed Lucy straight back to number 32 Pansy Street, only to find the house empty. 'He would be late today, of all days,' she moaned, dropping into a chair quite out of breath.

'He'll be downing a jar with his mates,' Lucy agreed, shaking the rain off her coat and putting the kettle on. She'd just get it going then nip next door for those two tearaways. 'You'll not clap eyes on him again till closing time.'

'But the shop could be gone by tomorrow.'

'That's his loss, not yours.'

Belinda's eyes suddenly lit up and she grasped Lucy's hands. 'We'll keep it a secret. You're right anyway. He'll be much more enthusiastic once we've given the place a thorough clean, and a lick of paint.'

Lucy gaped. '*We?*' But there was no gainsaying Belinda. Within half an hour she'd found the landlord, beaten him down from a pound to seventeen shillings and sixpence a week rent and paid the first month's in advance. The deal was done.

'Won't Benny be pleased?' she said.

'Over the moon,' Lucy agreed, but with less conviction in her voice.

-

Polly stood, arms akimbo, and looked pityingly at her son. 'Ye great daft galoot, you'll sober up before you sit at my table.'

'I'm not drunk. I swear I'm not.'

Any defence he might have uttered dissolved under her critical glare and while Charlie hid behind his paper and Sarah Jane stood by giggling, she made him stick his head in the sink while she poured cold water over it. Benny yelled like a banshee but she paid him no need. 'Hush your wailing. If ye didn't pour ale down your throat then you wouldn't get into these scraps, now would you? You've only yourself to blame.'

Benny tried to protest his innocence, that he'd only had two pints but Polly scrubbed his raw wounds with a loofah daubed with carbolic soap, a mimic of the kind of sympathetic nursing he'd been used to receive from his grandmother.

'Hush, ye big babby. Isn't Belinda upstairs with our Lucy putting young Sean to bed. Do you want her to find you the worse for wear?'

This sobered him somewhat and Benny began anxiously worrying over whether or not he should tell Belinda that it'd been her own brother Ron who'd done him over. He worried whether Ron was, at this very moment, watching number 32, knowing Belinda was here and would set on him again the minute he stepped out the door.

Yet why the hell should he give her up? He liked her. Loved her in fact. Belinda was special. He couldn't risk losing her. Surely it was not beyond the bounds of possibility for him to keep her in the manner to which she was accustomed. It worried him a bit how he might manage such an enormous task since his mam was proving so uncooperative and he still hadn't found the right sort of premises, but he was determined to hold on to his dreams. Mebbe Polly would reconsider her offer if she knew he was seriously contemplating matrimony. Or was he rushing it a bit? Would Belinda be more likely to accept a proposal if he got a business going first? It was so much more difficult in real life to think and plan than it was in the army, where all decisions were made for you.

When Belinda came downstairs with Lucy, Benny was washed, shaved and changed into a clean shirt even if there were still signs of bruising around his nose and mouth. Painful bruising as it turned out, that would put paid to any kissing and canoodling this evening. Benny expected her to lay into him for getting himself into a punch-up but to his great surprise she ran to him and threw her arms about his neck. 'Benny, how lovely to see you.'

He winced slightly as she planted a hearty kiss on his cheek, but was thankful that she made no mention of the bruises. 'By heck, its good to see someone who cares,' he said, preening himself with pleasure at her fervour.

She didn't scold him for looking like a prize fighter, or even complain about the stink of beer on his breath which she usually hated. He was so relieved to be let off the hook that he never noticed she didn't tell him where she'd been either. Both girls were acting a bit daft and giggly but he put that down to normal behaviour following an afternoon out together at the flicks. It was quite plain he had her eating out of his hand, so her brother could go hang. No bully boy was going to make him give up his lovely girl.

–

Hubert was late for the auction so had to stand at the back, which he hated. Today it was largely second-hand goods which were going under the hammer. He preferred bankrupt stock, new and modern, but he wasn't too fussy, so long as he got what he wanted at the price he was prepared to pay. He and his cronies had come to their usual agreement before the auctioneer had even lifted his gavel. None of the dealers present believed in pushing up prices unnecessarily, certainly not Hubert.

He'd laid his mark on some rolls of barbed wire, evidently no longer required by the authorities but which he was certain he could sell on at an interesting profit in the right quarters. There was also a sizeable dinner service, amounting to over five hundred items from cups and saucers to tea, breakfast and dinner plates. They bore a crest marking them as His Majesty's Royal Navy but Hubert wasn't fussy. He'd make a killing out of them, split up into smaller sets.

The auctioneer was calling for order, wanting to make a start. He'd deal with the smaller items first, Hubert guessed, to keep everyone hanging on for the best items later and this was confirmed when the auction began with a collection of cast iron cobbler's lasts. After that the auctioneer moved on to other ironmongery goods, ladders and various tools.

It was then that he saw Belinda. Hubert jerked to attention, itching to push through the crowds and go over to demand what she was doing here. He strained to see over shoulders, pushed people aside, earning some fierce glares which he ignored, wishing he could tell what it was exactly she was bidding for. He saw her hand go up once or twice and knew something had been knocked down to her. If it had anything to do with that no-good piece of dross he'd give her what for. He would really.

He saw her make her way up the crowded room to a table where she handed over some notes, then turn and quietly leave the building.

Hubert forgot all about the barbed wire and the dinner plates as he followed his daughter out into the street, keeping a safe distance so she didn't spot him. Where was she going? To arrange transport for whatever it was she'd bought? Damnation but he wished Ron was here. He'd be much less conspicuous. Despite the risk, he continued to follow her, maintaining what he hoped was a safe distance. Hubert saw her turn into Pansy Street and thought she was going to the blighter's house, but then she peeled off down Nelson's ginnel, which threw him completely.

By the time he'd reached it and rushed through to its opposite end, he was thoroughly blown for breath and his daughter was nowhere in sight. By heck but he knew where to watch for her though, now. He'd set Ron on the task first thing tomorrow.

–

It was the second Saturday in June that Belinda told Benny she had some marvellous news. 'Come with me. I can't wait to see your face.'

'Me neither,' said Lucy, with a wry smile.

Benny stood looking at the shop utterly dumbfounded, wondering why on earth she'd brought him here. Chuckling, Belinda took a key from her pocket, unlocked the door and led the way inside. To Lucy it looked even worse without the last fading rays of afternoon sunshine to lift the gloom, for all it had been cleaned and scrubbed and painted inside and out. It was also fully equipped with a work bench and a battery of tools which any good joiner might need. A glance at her brother's face told Lucy that all her fears had been justified.

'Good lord, whoever owns this dump? What a load of junk. I wouldn't give 'em tuppence for the lot,' he said with brutal frankness.

Belinda went white. Lucy, seeing she was too upset to speak, was the first to find her voice. 'Benny Pride, sometimes I could swing for you, I could really.'

'Why? What've I said?'

Belinda quickly interceded, 'It's all right, Lucy. If I've made a mistake, the fault is entirely mine. I thought Benny wanted a shop. Obviously I was wrong.' There was a betraying tremor in her voice, despite her brave words. She was thinking of all the effort she'd put in, the money she'd spent, not simply on things like wallpaper and furniture for the two rooms upstairs, which she still had to show to him but on the equipment to get him started. 'I thought you'd be pleased. It's position is excellent, right next to the Co-op and close to the main road. What more could you ask for?'

'My permission for a start.'

'But you *said* you wanted your own joinery business, that you were looking for premises. You *agreed* I should keep an eye out too. We've been looking for months. I thought you'd be pleased.'

This was undeniably true. But then he hadn't expected her to take him quite so literally, let alone actually rent a place and do it up so that he was committed without the chance to say yea or nay. 'You should've told me,' he grunted, unable to think of anything else to say.

'It was meant as a surprise.'

'Shock, more like,' Benny pouted, feeling cornered. Had he been wrong to fall so badly for Belinda? The Clarke family must all be a bit queer in the head. On the one hand there was brother Ron bringing messages from *Pops* to keep out of his precious daughter's life, and on the other Belinda herself taking over his life, lock, stock and barrel. Much as he was desperate to have her, the cheek of it left him momentarily breathless. 'What the hell do you know about joinery tools anyroad?'

'Don't use foul language on me, *Sergeant*.'

'And don't you dare organise my blasted life, *Corporal*,' he shouted back.

Belinda had never felt more angry and exasperated and yes, disappointed, in her life. Tears smarted the backs of her eyelids though not for a moment would she allow them to fall. *'Drat you,'* she yelled, as if joining in the slanging match made everything better. 'You were right, Lucy. I should've listened to you.'

Lucy didn't answer, merely backed away, not wishing to get involved.

Belinda was struggling against a ridiculous urge to cry. She'd been so certain he would be as thrilled as she was by the way the shop had turned out. A rough diamond he may be, but she liked Benny Pride. He was cheerful, considerate and quite good looking in a roguish sort of way, and there was something about him that excited her. Perhaps his hunger to make something of himself, his youthful arrogance, so certain he could do anything he wanted in life, now he was out of the army. Let's face it, she fancied him like crazy though she certainly had no intention of giving him the satisfaction of telling him so.

She gathered up an armful of tools and flung them at his feet with a resounding clatter. 'There. Be a bloody joiner. That's what you said you wanted.' She was panting with the effort of controlling her emotions, which made her breasts heave, a phenomenon which Benny didn't fail to notice. 'Don't think I care one way or the other what you do. You're not at all the sort of man my father would choose for me, nowhere near as eligible as Frank Fenton for instance but...'

'A damn sight more exciting,' Benny finished for her.

'I didn't say that.' She was furious with him and didn't quite know why. What did she want from Benny Pride anyway? For him to sweep her into his arms and promise to spend his life building a business and a home for them? Or did she just want a bit of fun before moving on to something more suitable? She had the strangest feeling that unsuitable or not, she was already more than half committed to this man so he could at least show some gratitude for her efforts on his behalf. What was wrong with the fool? Just because he didn't find the shop himself, she supposed. Wounded male ego.

She bit her lip, looking up at him from under her lids. 'I bought this lot at auction. At a good price, but don't worry. If it's no good, I can get rid of the stuff in exactly the same way.' She flung the words at him with such force he could taste the warmth of her breath before she flounced away to stand at the window with her arms folded. When he didn't come after her but remained sunk in a silent pout, she added in a voice tight with anger, 'At least it's my own money I've wasted.'

'Oh aye, and you've money to burn, of course.' His tone mocked her.

All the heat and fury drained out of Belinda, to be replaced with a rush of sympathy as she suddenly understood. She'd insulted Lucy over bugs she didn't have, now she'd insulted Benny over money. She turned and ran to him, grasping him by the arms. 'That's it, isn't it? I've hurt you by using *my* money. Is that all? Why didn't you say?' She put back her head and gave her full rich laugh and, unable to help himself, Benny found his eyes drawn to the slender whiteness of her throat, moving down to where it dipped into the open vee of her shirt and swelled into full firm breasts.

'I've money of me own, if you want to know,' he said, thinking that perhaps he should go on letting her think this was the reason, so he could perhaps salvage the ruin of their promising friendship before it was too late. Benny was beginning to appreciate that he might have shot his mouth off a bit too loud, and all because she'd called his bluff. What he knew about joinery could be written on the back of a chisel.

He could try it anyway, he thought, reckless with need, for if he didn't have her soon he'd go mad. Maybe she was worth the sacrifice of his other dreams.

But if she ever told her father that she'd loaned her 'soldier-boy' money to get started up in business, he'd really be in hot water then. Benny didn't care to think just how hot that might be. 'I'd pay back every penny, and it would have to be our secret,' he said, just to be on the safe side. Lord, he thought, what am I saying? Why am I agreeing? This was all a terrible mistake. Her lips were moist, full and sweet and the pain in his loins was growing so that he was certain he'd shame himself soon. He wondered desperately if there were something else he could do with the place other than joinery and despite the workbench and array of tools. It certainly wasn't big enough for a furniture store.

'What does money matter?' She was smiling at him again, and it was as if the sun had come out, warming him, searing him with new heat. 'You can pay me back when you get going. Oh, Benny, you silly man.' Then she had her arms about him, pressing that ripe luscious body against his and he thought he might burst with pain. She was kissing his cheek, his mouth, saying something about not letting pride stand in the way of what could be a good future for them, though her voice came from such a far distance he wasn't too sure.

From the corner of his eye he saw Lucy quietly closing the shop door as she slipped away. Belinda was telling him she had yet another surprise, waiting upstairs and he made no further protest for Benny knew now that he must go along with the plan whatever the cost. He was lost completely.

Chapter Ten

Hubert made up his mind that it was long past time he cracked the whip and brought his recalcitrant daughter to heel. He set out his shaving brush, soap mug and cut-throat razor on the bathroom shelf with painstaking care while his mind buzzed with plans. Ron was supposed to have seen off soldier-boy but she was still mooning over the young whippersnapper.

It wasn't like him to fail. The one good thing about his son was that he had very little brain and even less imagination, therefore was always willing to carry out whatever task his father set him. What he lacked in the brain department he more than made up for in native cunning. If a child told him her mam wasn't in, he'd wait round the back of the house till the woman emerged and squeeze a bob or two out of her even if she did claim her family to be starving. And if it were a chap who refused to pay, Ron usually found a way to make him regret that daft notion.

So why hadn't it worked with young Benny Pride?

Hubert began to lather his chin with his best badger bristle brush. This was the cause of half his problems at the moment. Folk weren't listening any more, and weren't paying up. The world had gone haywire and everyone thought they could avoid unpleasant responsibilities just because the war was over. As well, some of the returning servicemen objected to coming home and finding their wives in debt. As if it were *his* fault that they couldn't find a job.

He had an appointment today with Eric Wilnshaw, his accountant, and he didn't expect the news to be particularly good. He'd made a lot of money over the past few years but sadly had spent a good deal of it almost as fast. But then he did have a lot of commitments, some of them quite delightful ones, which brought a smile to his face as he applied the soap with greater care. He needed to look his best today. After the accountant he had another meeting, a much more interesting one.

Myra was the kind of woman any man would hock his soul for. Unlike his wife, for whom he had every respect, naturally, as the mother of his children. But Myra knew how to excite a man. She knew how to peel off her stockings in the most tantalising way imaginable, how to carry out a chap's every fantasy while adding a few of her own. Her imagination had provided them with countless sensual diversions and she knew better than any of the many women he had enjoyed over the years, how to bring him to a fierce climax and still leave him panting for more. Myra was a bad girl, in the best possible sense of the word.

So if he'd been a touch too generous with her in his gratitude of late, didn't she deserve it? This slight cash flow crisis could be quite easily rectified, given time and energy, of which he still had plenty. Credit trading was suffering just at present. The firms who supplied his clients with goods were getting greedier, cutting their discounts, demanding payment up front. And the bank was squeezing him to reduce his loans, fearing the change of government might damage trade, that the coming of peace had bequeathed them all as many problems as it had solved. But he was impatient to further his ambitions and move ever upward in the city of Manchester, without sacrificing these pleasant diversions which surely any hard working businessman deserved.

Hubert slid his cut-throat razor over his throat, the scraping sound it made on his rough skin echoing in the stark Victorian bathroom. A liaison with Fenton Chemicals would have fitted the bill nicely, providing him with the extra kudos he craved, would perhaps have led to himself and George Fenton fixing up some sort of partnership deal. Hubert was not averse to having his fingers in many pies.

He nicked himself and cursed, sticking a piece of tissue paper on it to stop the bleeding. Myra preferred a close shave which wasn't always easy to achieve. But then nothing worth having came easy. Despite the difficulties there was no question that he would survive. The answer, surely, was to increase his holdings and therefore his profits.

His accountant, at their lunchtime meeting held at the Rising Sun, confirmed this diagnosis, adding that Hubert's latest set of tax returns were even now in the process of being prepared. They in no way revealed the true picture of his affairs, for what the Inland Revenue didn't know, couldn't hurt either them or Hubert. Much of his trading was done on a cash only basis (Hubert never referred to it as the black market) with no invoices or paperwork of any kind to show that it had taken place. All those details were in his head with the money carefully deposited in obscure places, saved for a rainy day and his old age.

'The difficulty is, Hubert, that this kind of trading will gradually disappear,' Eric informed him. 'So you need to look in other directions to expand.'

'There'll always be those who prefer to deal in cash.'

'True, but opportunities will be reduced once the allocation of materials are relaxed. Nothing lasts for ever, Hubert old chap. You need to be thinking more creatively.'

Hubert puffed on his excellent cigar and smiled through a swirl of smoke. Creative thinking, when it came to business, had never been a problem. 'Right then, let's order another malt and put our brains to steep.'

It was pointed out to him how, in the past, he'd often taken over a failing enterprise in lieu of debt. That this was, in fact, a useful way of building an empire and there was really no reason why he shouldn't do more of that in the future. The secret was to latch on to a business that was new and overstretched, suffering from insufficient capital or some other problem such as an unsettled workforce or division between the partners. There were a surprising number, once you started to look. Hubert judged this idea a fruitful one to pursue.

Tactics and planning were, of course, of the essence. He couldn't simply go barging in but must carefully manoeuvre and manipulate his target into just the right weakened state ripe for a take-over, rather like a cat battering a mouse. Fortunately he was strong on patience and could devise all manner of interesting tactics to bring this happy situation about. All he had to do now, was keep his eye open for a likely victim.

–

Yet another awkward breakfast was over. Belinda had taken a week's holiday from her job as she hadn't been feeling too well lately, though it wasn't turning into quite the rest she'd imagined as there was still a great deal of work to be done on the upstairs rooms at the shop. She packed sandwiches and a flask of tea into the bag she took with her each day.

She'd never intended to let things go so far the day she'd taken Benny upstairs to the rooms above the shop. She'd meant only to try to explain to him how much better the rooms would look once she'd finished the painting and decorating, and that with one or two bits of furniture he could enjoy the independence he'd so craved. But somehow the explanations had been lost in their need to touch, to kiss, to express the burning passion they felt for each other. Within moments he'd had her backed up against a wall, her legs up around his solid waist while he thrust into her, her cries sounding embarrassingly loud in the empty room.

Now, it seemed, she must rue the consequences and she still hadn't got round to telling him – or her father. Belinda hadn't even allowed herself to dwell on the problem, preferring to push it to the back of her mind. Time, she was only too aware, was fast running out. The problem could no longer be ignored.

'Frank's called here regularly, most days in fact, and you're never in,' Hubert was saying, sounding peeved.

Belinda reached for a couple of apples and stuffed those into the bag too, studiously refusing to allow him to rile her. 'I've already told him that it isn't on, that whatever there was between us before the war, if anything, is well and truly over. We were little more than children, which we definitely are not now. He understands. Why don't you?'

Her calmness inflamed him. 'Don't take that tone of voice to me, young lady. Show some respect when you're living in my house. Who do you think you are, running wild, not helping your mother properly, wearing trousers, not to mention refusing to have anything to do with a fine young man from a good family. You're so determined to make yourself cheap, you can't even be civil. Are you listening to me, madam?'

'No, Father. There's really nothing more to be said and I don't have to stand here and listen to anything.' Belinda picked up her bag and swung it on to her shoulder.

'You will if I say you must. You'll marry who I tell you to marry and be thankful someone is prepared to have you, plain lump of codfish that you are.'

Belinda froze and whatever remnant of pity she had left for her father, finally snapped. 'As a matter of fact I doubt Frank would have me now that I'm expecting Benny's child.' She strode towards the door.

Hubert could feel the blood pounding in his ears, a haze of red growing before his eyes. 'What did you say?'

'Oh, I think you heard. I'm just on my way to break the happy news to Benny.'

'You whore!'

She'd taken no more than two steps when, in one swift movement, Councillor Hubert Clarke wrenched the bag from her shoulder and flung it across the room. It hit the sideboard, smashing the thermos flask on impact and sending a vase of roses crashing to the floor, spraying water and flowers everywhere.

'Oh Hubert, what have you done?' Joanna, rushing in from the kitchen, gasped in distress and instantly went down on her hands and knees to gather up shards of glass and broken stems.

'Stop it, Mother.' Belinda, aghast by what had happened, ran to help. 'Stop it, you'll cut yourself. Let me get the dustpan and brush.' Hubert, colour coming and going in his flaccid face, thrust past them both and without a backward glance, carefully extracted his coat, bowler hat and briefcase from the hall stand and walked from the house as if it were a perfectly normal day.

'It's all my fault,' Joanna sobbed, when they were alone. 'All my fault.'

Belinda, feeling she really couldn't cope with her mother's hysterics on top of her father's display of temper, briskly began to sweep up the debris. 'Don't be ridiculous, Mother. How can it be your fault? Pops simply won't come to terms with the fact I can make my own decisions now. As a matter of fact...'

She might very well have broken the news to her mother at this point, except that Joanna, still kneeling on the carpet, interrupted. 'No, I mean about Frank. He doesn't come here to see you. That's just a ploy, an excuse. He comes here to see *me*. We're having an affair.'

Within three weeks Belinda and Benny were married. They had a small reception at the Co-op, then moved in to the two rooms over the shop. It wasn't at all what either of them had planned but there didn't seem to be any sensible alternative.

—

Having his daughter elope with a ne'er do well was, to Hubert, an unmitigated disaster, not at all what he'd planned for her. Where was the benefit in such a marriage for him, he asked Myra, watching greedily as she lazily unhooked her skirt. But as she slid beneath him and he pounded out his frustrations into her warm yielding body, he knew that he mustn't give up too easily. There had to be some way he could turn the situation to his advantage, some way to bring his daughter to heel.

The next day he put this very point to Ron. 'Who do we know that can put a spoke in his wheel?'

'What would be the point?' Ron commented, picking his teeth with the blade of his penknife. 'They're wed now, aren't they? What's done is done. Anyroad, I gave him a thorough dustup like you said, but it didn't work.'

'Everything can be mended, you daft lout. It has to be. I'll not be made a laughing stock. You've heard of divorce I suppose, or an annulment. We must find some way to prove the marriage wasn't legal, or to make certain that lass o' mine has learned her lesson and is ready to come home with her tail between her legs.'

He'd already cut off her allowance. Now he would drive her almost to the brink of starvation if necessary to make her see the folly of her ways. Once hunger and desperation set in, she'd come home fast enough, chastened but wiser. Didn't she appreciate that he wasn't a man to cross? He'd certainly proved this point to Joanna years ago, about how he wouldn't stand for his name to be sullied, not at any price. His wife had learned to toe the line if she was to continue to enjoy the comforts in life which she so craved, and so must Belinda.

He let his mind range through the people he knew, the contacts he'd made, like a file flicking through his head. Then he smiled. Of course, John Riley, Secretary of the local branch of the Board of Trade. Riley owed him a favour or two and Hubert had always been good at calling in those. Soldier-boy might find it less easy than he imagined to get himself the necessary licences, once he'd had a quiet word in Riley's ear, shop or no shop.

–

Belinda was beginning to discover that nothing had turned out quite as she'd expected either. Without question, life with Benny during that first wonderful week was fun, exciting and wildly unpredictable and there was an undoubted fizz between them. She loved his looks, his physique, the way he clearly adored her and paid her so much attention. But most of all, she loved his ambition, the way he wouldn't let anything stand in the way of it.

Every morning he'd bring her tea and toast in bed, which was just as well since she felt horrendously nauseous. Even then she could spend a good twenty minutes throwing up. Having babies clearly wasn't as much fun as she'd been led to believe.

If she were honest, marrying Benny had been not only expedient but an escape, and a crazy form of retribution. The relief of being released from the machinations of her father had felt glorious. To build a new future with a man of whom Councillor Hubert Clarke did not approve seemed like a marvellous way of expressing that freedom.

Yet she was fond of Benny, and anxious that their marriage be a success. She meant to be a good wife and help him rise in the world. But as she huddled shivering beneath the covers in their sparsely furnished bedroom she began, for the first time, to experience doubts. The shop seemed smaller than she remembered and the two rooms over it, where they must live, positively poky. They were also perishing cold despite it being early summer. God knows what would happen when winter came.

On the Monday of their second week together Belinda got up first for once and cooked porridge on the old gas stove. They'd had it brought upstairs into the other room which they used as a living-kitchen. Benny watched, giving instructions, for he was surprisingly good at cooking himself, his hands and lips teasing her so much she could hardly work for laughing. They ate the porridge, which was dreadful, at the small table, the only piece of furniture they possessed save for the cooker, a small sink and one armchair. Afterwards she expected him to start sawing wood or whatever must be done to make furniture but he didn't even get dressed, being still in his pyjamas. Instead he began pushing her back into bed.

'Here, what are you doing?'

'I need to recover after eating your lumpy porridge. Anyroad, there's plenty of time.' *They were on honeymoon after all, weren't they?* he reminded her and she protested no further. Besides, bed was the warmest place.

As they rolled about in the tumbled sheets, laughing and giggling, the silk of her blouse ripping slightly in his eagerness to drag it off her, it dawned on Belinda that it would be her task to cook and clear away breakfast every morning, and tidy through when he'd started work.

'I've never done much cooking before,' she gasped, for he was kissing her now and she could barely think while he busied himself with the buttons on her skirt.

'You'll have to learn lots of new skills then, won't you,' sliding off her silk French knickers with a practised hand. 'Though we could always employ a chef if you like.'

Her giggles changed into gasps of excitement as his fingers explored her, even as that tiny voice at the back of her mind reminded her that fun as it may seem now, they couldn't spend their entire lives eating fish and chips in bed, or making love. She didn't even know if she could cook anything more complicated than porridge. She'd never had to do it. There'd always been her mother, or the NAAFI to take care of such matters.

The next day she was again up first while Benny lay sprawled on his stomach and the silence of early morning folded around her. Outside the narrow, grimy window she could hear the rattle of milk churns, the sound of cart wheels on cobbles and somewhere in the distance a church clock started to chime. Seven o'clock. She'd wake Benny in a minute, persuade him to find something to do in his workshop, or better still, go down to the council offices and sort out the delay over the issuing of an allocation licence. Without that, apparently, he couldn't buy any wood.

On slippered feet she padded downstairs to collect the post and seeing a brown envelope lying on the mat, thought it might have come. Excitement bit into her and she'd barely paused long enough to scoop it up, slip it in her dressing gown pocket preparatory to taking it up to him, before the shop door bell jangled, making her jump. She turned the big rusty key and opened it a crack.

Frank stood on the doorstep, a sheepish grin on his face. Without waiting for an invitation, he pushed open the door and walked in. 'Sorry to barge in but I wondered if you could spare me a minute.'

'I'd rather you didn't come round here at all. I don't think we have anything to say to each other.' She had no sense of betrayal by Frank. Had she been in love with him, she supposed his and Joanna's behaviour would have been the ultimate betrayal. Even though this was not the case, she still felt used and certainly saw no reason to be civil to him. 'I'd really prefer you to go.'

'I won't take a moment of your precious time,' Frank said, closing the door behind him as if he owned the place. 'There's trouble.'

She didn't want to hear. Whether her father suspected his wife of having an affair or if her parents' marriage would survive Belinda had no idea, nor any intention of investigating. It was really up to them. 'I've told you, Frank, I really don't want to know.'

'Are you deaf or summat?' She hadn't heard Benny come up behind her, but clearly irritated to find his one-time rival stepping uninvited over his own front doorstep, he told Frank to leave this instant if he didn't want his head battered in.

Frank looked slightly taken aback by this, as well he might though he steadfastly stood his ground. 'It's about your mother, Belinda.'

Belinda looked from one to other of these two young men and for all Benny's undoubted sexual attraction, wondered if she would have been quite so ready to marry him, baby or no baby, had her mother not confessed to an affair with Frank Fenton, or her father hadn't tried to bully her into submission. Impossible to say. Nor was it a question she cared to examine too closely. Despite her qualms, she invited Frank upstairs for coffee, more to compensate for her husband's ungraciousness rather than any concern for Joanna. It was her own dash into matrimony which was now beginning to seem like madness, a dangerous impulse made in a crazy fit of pique.

–

Belinda served tea since she didn't have any coffee, and listened with what patience she could muster to how her mother was sorry for the upset caused, how she needed her lovely daughter home, how it wasn't too late to save the situation.

'On the contrary, I think it is. Much too late.'

'Aye, and time you flung your hook,' Benny interrupted, feeling he'd been ignored long enough and noting with pleasure the surprise on Frank Fenton's face. 'This is *my* shop, if you haven't noticed and it isn't even open yet. So hop it! You're upsetting my wife and we've work to do, right?' Belinda spun about, excitement lighting her face. 'You mean that letter I gave you is your licence for the allocation of materials?'

Cornered by this small lie, Benny shuffled his feet in discomfort. 'When I say work, I mean paperwork, sorting out this bureaucratic muddle for one thing.'

'Oh!' Belinda looked disappointed, as if it were his fault in some way that he couldn't get the dratted licence.

'It'll be here any day, I'm sure of it.' He fingered the envelope in his pocket, wondering how she would react when she learned that it brought further trouble. 'Besides, I've tools to sharpen, a vice to set up, workshop to clean and...' He ran out of ideas. '...other jobs that don't do themselves. So, if you wouldn't mind?' He opened the stair door and shouldered Fenton towards it. The gesture had a hint of military aggression in it, which Frank Fenton didn't miss. Nevertheless, for all Benny's bullish attitude, he made a valiant attempt to hold his ground.

'I haven't finished speaking with Belinda yet.'

'Oh, I think you have, mate. She don't look too pleased to see you, from where I'm standing. So be off with you before you feel my boot make contact with your backside. This is *my* property and you're trespassing.'

Belinda, watching this small skirmish, was at first amused and then, belatedly, incensed. She'd spent the last half-hour forcibly putting forward her arguments that what Frank and Joanna did in their private moments was of no concern to her. She'd called him a liar and a cheat, accused him of using her but had assured him, at length, that he hadn't broken her heart. Throughout her discourse, he'd calmly stood there and smiled, exactly as her father might have done when she was a child in the midst of a tantrum. Infuriating. Now, perversely, she swung to his defence.

'Hold on a minute. I live here too and pay my whack, so I've as much right as you to decide who comes calling.' In point of fact, Belinda paid more than her whack. She'd paid all of the rent so far, but didn't think reminding Benny of that fact right now would be entirely tactful.

As if aware of these unspoken words, Benny glowered at her. 'I'm your husband, so you should ask my permission before you invite another chap into my property.'

Arms folded, she tossed her head back in disgust and the sunlight glinted on the golden sheen of her hair. It was growing now, forming sleek wings of colour against each cheek. 'Damn you, Benny Pride. I've just told you. It isn't *your* shop. It's *ours*. And don't you try telling me what to do. I've had enough of that at home to last a lifetime, thanks very much.'

The dressing gown was embroidered silk, dark brown in colour and clinging to her pale skin like chocolate. Benny would like to have licked it off her there and then. He cleared his throat. 'The lease is in *my* name, don't forget.'

'Look, I didn't mean…' Frank began but Belinda didn't hear, she was far too occupied prodding a finger into Benny's broad chest as the argument descended into one of their more passionate and all too familiar rows.

'I've agreed to stand at your counter, brew your tea, look after our home, even deliver whatever you sell or repair, if you want me to. But *I'm* in charge of my own life, and nobody else. Not you, not my parents. I'll not be bossed about by anyone. Is that clear? To both of you?' Blue eyes sparked like polished steel, magnificent in her anger, making both men fall silent as they stared at her mesmerised, enthralled by her beauty. She was shaking with fury but her voice rang out clearly, echoing eerily in the half-empty rooms. 'I've been in the army too, in case you'd forgotten. I've fought in this bloody war, suffered agonies, lost good friends, grieved. So I feel I've earned the right to have some say in how I spend my peace time. Being someone's daughter, or even your wife, Benny Pride, doesn't take away that right. OK?'

Benny's face was set tight and an angry dark red, for all he itched to rip that liquid dressing gown off her. He always fancied her more when she was all fired up like this. 'The women's army has certainly taught you how to swear, corporal. But I outrank you. I'm the bloody sergeant here.' For one long furious moment each outfaced the other and then, to Frank Fenton's complete bafflement, as one they burst out laughing and almost fell into each other's arms.

Chapter Eleven

It wasn't till long after Fenton had gone and they'd reestablished good relations to their joint satisfaction that Benny remembered the envelope in his trouser pocket. Lying back comfortably on the pillows with Belinda's head warm against his shoulder, this, he thought, is as good a time as any. He handed it to her and watched as she read it with dawning disbelief.

Belinda sat up. 'It's from a Harry Entwistle, says he has a shop on Collier Street and that all the other carpenters in the district have signed a petition to stop us opening.'

Benny took the letter from her hand and tore it up, letting the pieces fall over the floor. 'Aye, trade's bad, he says, and they can't afford the competition. Says we might as well pack up and go somewhere else.'

Belinda stared at him, devastated. 'Move? After all the work we've put in here. We can't do that. Where would we move to? I've searched the area with a fine tooth-comb and there are no other shops to let anywhere. None that we can afford.'

'We're staying put,' Benny said, perversely determined to hang on to the shop he'd so despised, now that it was under threat. 'Nobody pushes me about, not if I've owt to do wi' the matter.'

Had Benny been aware that he owed this particular piece of misfortune to his father-in-law, he might have known better how to fight it. Yet weeks later the shop remained closed for the allocation licence had still not been issued. Benny sweated with worry, earning little more than a pittance from whatever part-time labouring jobs he could pick up on the docks or wharfs, yet was no nearer to achieving his dream of becoming his own boss.

He'd have taken a permanent job if he could've found one, but work of any kind wasn't easy to come by and he refused to go cap in hand to his mother, for that would have been admitting failure.

At least he and Belinda were happy, despite everything. She believed utterly in every one of his many boasts including his competence as a craftsman. She promised to treasure him, to support him utterly in everything he did and, once he got going, to save every penny she could so that within no time at all they'd move out of the two squalid rooms and rent, or maybe even buy a proper house of their own. This was Benny's dream too and they would spend most evenings talking over how it might be achieved.

'This is but the beginning,' she would say. 'You can do it, I know you can. Big clever boy like you.'

Trouble was, they couldn't even make a start without the materials, and they couldn't get those without an allocation licence. Time and time again Benny called at the various council offices asking about the forms, stoking up his failing belief in himself that if he could only get his hands on that essential bit of paper, no petition on earth would prevent him from opening. He really couldn't understand what the hold-up was. Despite countless promises by countless different officials, no licence materialised. He was tired, he was hungry, and just when he least needed reminding, Belinda pointed out how she would have to give up her own job soon, how expensive babies were and how the pair of them couldn't live on lumpy porridge indefinitely.

'Talk to your family then,' Benny bitterly responded as they sat huddled in bed eating yet another dreaded bowlful of the stuff on yet another drizzly wet morning. The day ahead, rather like his life, stretched out before him, grey and dull and completely without hope. 'They're the ones with brass. Why don't they help us? They could lend me a bob or two. I'm their son-in-law after all.'

'I'd rather starve than ask them,' Belinda coldly responded, stiff-lipped with pride.

'Aye, well, we can arrange that easily enough.' Anger flared in him so strong that he broke out into a cold sweat and out of sheer frustration, picked up the bowl and flung it right across the room. It hit the bedroom wall and slid down it, leaving a trail of sticky porridge over Belinda's pretty pale blue paint. Stunned by his own violence Benny was shocked into silence for a whole half minute before murmuring, 'Sorry, love. Don't worry. I'll scrub it clean.'

'You certainly will. It's a shocking waste of good food. I should make you lick it off,' and she gave a throaty chuckle. 'Though perhaps we're not quite that starving hungry yet.'

'Well I'm certainly not licking that mucky wall,' Benny scoffed, grinning sideways at her and then they were both laughing, the outburst seeming to have done them both good. Happy, silly nonsense, two young lovers squabbling and enjoying each other, trying not to take life too seriously despite its being very serious indeed.

They made love, tenderly, and with all due care for their coming child but with undoubted passion. Afterwards they lay warmly entwined and reverted to their favourite pastime of planning a solid future, a prosperous business, a loving home life for their child. This was the dream, but how to bring it about?

'What will you do if you never get the licence?' Belinda murmured from the warm hollow where she'd settled herself beneath his chin. 'Would you change your mind about taking your mother's offer?'

His reply was a long time in coming but she didn't hurry him. Belinda knew it had to be his decision.

'I might think about it,' he conceded at last. 'But I'd want my ideas to be listened to. I'd want a proper say in the running of the business. It all depends what she's offering.'

Again a long thoughtful pause, this time on Belinda's part. She stirred softly in his arms. 'Why don't we ask her and Charlie to tea on Sunday and find out?' She'd been seeking the right moment to broach this suggestion for some time and even now held her breath in case it brought a stormy response.

127

Instead he gently disentangled himself and shrugging into his jacket, declared his intention of trying one more time at the council offices, taking no nonsense this time. He wrapped his muffler round his neck, tied the laces of his boots and just when she thought he wasn't going to mention it, said, 'You'd have to include our Luce and those two tearaways.' Benny spoke with affection for he adored his nephew and niece.

'You'd trust my cooking then?'

'Reckon our constitutions are tough enough to take the risk. But tidy this place up, Corporal, or it's jankers for you.' She was kneeling on the bed, her hands caressing the swell of her stomach, lips twitching upwards into her famously bewitching smile. Benny only had to look at her to agree to whatever she asked. Giving her belly a quick kiss while pinching her bottom at the same time, he swung out quickly through the door before she could land him a four-penny one in return.

She scrambled from the bed to blow kisses to him through the window, now cleaned of its grime and shining bright. With one hand still on her stomach as if by this simple gesture she could protect the baby growing inside her, she waved to him lovingly with the other, knowing that the next few months would be even more testing, particularly after the little one was born. Perhaps Sunday would give her an opportunity to speak to Polly on the quiet, to talk about whether Benny was right to stick out for a shop of his own, or whether he should go into business with her after all.

Belinda understood his need for independence but she also knew how vital it was for them to get a regular income coming in soon. If they were ever to successfully adapt to civilian life again, build a home and a marriage together, then there had to be give and take on both sides.

And if sometimes she thought with nostalgia of the more intellectually challenging and less domestic life in the forces, then that was something she must put aside as over and done with. She pressed her forehead against the cold glass so she could catch a last glimpse of his retreating figure. She did love the stupid tyke, dreamer or no.

–

Benny issued the invitation on his way back from yet another fruitless argument with officialdom and found Polly up to her elbows in machine oil, struggling to get one of her fancy new machines working properly. Laughing at her hopeless efforts he took off his jacket, rolled up his sleeves and set to work.

'How's Charlie, any better?' he asked, frowning as he soon had the steam rollers moving again.

Polly's voice thickened with the emotion that suddenly blocked her throat. 'He's up and down. There must be something else wrong with him, Benny. I'm that worried. I'm trying to persuade him to see the doctor again, but he accuses me of fussing. Stubborn as a mule, so he is.'

Benny refused her request for him to hang around long enough to help with the next delivery run, insisting he had his own fish to fry. She even tried telling him that Charlie was working too hard and could do with a break but he marched off, head high, to nowhere in particular. Polly stood at the door of the warehouse and shouted after him.

'Now who's stubborn? Sure and aren't I surrounded by fools and idiots?'

'Come to your dinner on Sunday,' he yelled back. 'We'll be expecting you.'

Polly shook a furious fist after his rapidly retreating figure. 'Wouldn't I grab at any opportunity to put a flea in your stupid ear.'

When he'd gone she strode back into her office buzzing with irritation. Where in heaven's name he got such obstinacy from she really couldn't imagine, and then gave a shout of laughter for of course she knew only too well. Well, at least he'd fixed the machine for her, bless his kind heart.

Benny also called at number 179, to issue a similar invitation to Lucy. He thought she took an unconscionable length of time to come to the door and then wouldn't let him over the threshold, saying both her employers were out and it wouldn't be right to let him in when the house was empty. Then after they'd spoken, which took less than a half minute, she quickly closed the door in his face and he could've sworn, as he turned to go, that he heard a man's voice. Yet how could he have when she'd said the house was empty?

He instantly dismissed the puzzle from his mind as he hurried on home, anxious to return to his lovely Belinda.

–

When Sunday came, Belinda's determination to be considered an equal partner in the whole of Benny's life and not just on the domestic front led her slap-bang into their most serious marital discord to date. Benny informed her that he was off down to the Dog and Duck for a quick pint while she cooked the dinner.

Her first reaction as he reached for his jacket was to ask how he could afford a pint when he hadn't had much in the way of regular work lately due to bad weather. She guessed he probably had some of his demob money left, and wouldn't be above accepting drinks from his mates. Even so, she pointed out that what with money being tight, and his family coming over, he could perhaps stay and help her in the kitchen instead. Benny looked askance at this suggestion, insisting he'd only get under her feet and there was loads of time.

Belinda gave in, smiled and said, 'OK, why not? A drink sounds a good idea. I've got the roast already in the oven. Give me a minute to put in the potatoes, then I can come with you.'

Benny's jaw dropped and his mouth fell open. 'Come with me? You can't do that?'

'Don't be silly. If there's loads of time, as you say, then why shouldn't I come too?' Paying no attention to his spluttering excuses, she slipped the piece of brisket, circled by potatoes, back into the warm oven. The piece of meat was one of the cheaper cuts. Even so, Belinda hadn't realised it could cost quite so much. For the first time in her life she'd begun to worry about money, wondering how long her savings would last since there was precious little left in her account and no more allowance coming from her father. Still, Benny would surely have the business up and running long before she ran out of funds. She put on her coat and beret and took his arm with a proud smile. 'We must be back by half-twelve in time to have everything ready for one o'clock, when your family arrive.'

It was only as she walked through the double doors of the Dog and Duck that Belinda realised what a very big mistake she'd made. A hush fell as she entered, there not being another woman in the place, and every eye turned upon her.

She'd been used to dealing with prickly male egos on many occasions in the past, but this was something else. You could have cut the atmosphere with a knife. It was so oppressive that she very nearly turned tail and ran. It might have been the done thing for Belinda Clarke to share a pint with fellow soldiers, male and female but this wasn't the army, this was Pansy Street, and these were not fellow soldiers. These people had a set pattern to their lives, certain customs and traditions, and she had just broken the holiest of them all.

On Sundays women must cook while men must drink.

Well, she was here now, so she'd have to stick it out. The next hour was the most difficult Belinda could ever remember. Every word and gesture told her that she'd no right to be here, that she'd overstepped an invisible line. Her place was in the kitchen, seeing to her man's dinner, as their own wives were at this very moment. She certainly shouldn't be standing at her husband's side in the vault room of a public house.

'She's got the shackles on you now, lad,' said one old codger, winking at Benny and making him go red with embarrassment and anger.

'Aye, watch out, she'll have you clocking in and out next.'

Belinda went home alone well before the allotted time simply because Benny refused to come with her. She was relieved to find that the joint was only slightly overcooked, and the potatoes nicely crisp. Not bad for a first effort. She'd already made an apple pie which stood cooling on the window sill.

Lucy arrived with the children moments later, along with Polly and Charlie, and they all ate the meal in a silence which might have been called companionable. Polly offered high praise on her Yorkshire puddings despite their being a touch leathery while Belinda gave an entertaining account of her visit to the pub. No comments were made upon this, and no one enquired where Benny was. She quite lost her nerve to ask whether there was still a place for him in Polly's business. When Charlie politely enquired how they were managing, she assured them that Benny had been getting plenty of work on the wharfs in recent weeks and had the matter of the licence all in hand. Then she offered them a slice of apple pie and the subject was dropped.

–

By the time Benny deigned to come home his family were long gone. He'd made sure that they would be, having no wish to have his mother again picking over the ragbag of his life. It also left him free to play the heavy husband, as his mates had insisted he should, getting him tanked up so that he could do it right. He swaggered in, tossed his cap and coat on the back of a chair and demanded Belinda fetch him his dinner, good and hot. 'And that's the last time you'll shame me in such a way, woman,' he announced, quite spoiling the ferocity in his voice by hiccuping loudly at the end.

Belinda cast him a withering glance as she placed the dried remains of his dinner on the table before him with commendable control. She'd never seen him in such a filthy temper but had no intention of being cowed by it. 'I accept that perhaps my coming with you to the pub was a mistake, though by rights it shouldn't be. I'm your wife, and entitled to the same relaxation as you.

Besides, I'm used to such places, having been in the army myself, remember.'

'You shouldn't be drinking anyway, being pregnant,' he muttered, rather self-righteously.

'I only had a half shandy. However, I offer my sincere apologies if I embarrassed you.'

Benny subsided into an aggrieved silence, not quite knowing how to proceed now that she had so quickly capitulated. His advisers had been quite certain that she wouldn't, that he'd need to throw his weight about. They'd said she'd be in a mood because this was the first Sunday lunch she'd ever cooked for his family but she wasn't behaving as he'd expected at all, even her apology sounded genuine. Which made it feel as if he was in the wrong.

As he chewed on the dry tough meat, half wishing he'd had the pleasure of eating it when it was still hot and tender, Benny stubbornly offered no forgiveness, no soft words of reconciliation. A man, his advisors had assured him, must make a stand. Start as you mean to go on. Show who has the iron fist. He regretted having to treat Belinda in this way, but they were clearly right. He couldn't have a woman dictating his life, as if she owned him. It wasn't the way things were done round here.

Belinda seated herself at the opposite end of the table and started to tell him about the lunch, about how Charlie had looked much better, and how relaxed and happy Lucy seemed to be, almost glowing with health these days.

He gazed at her, growing increasingly annoyed that he'd missed this happy family occasion, yet justifying his anger by insisting that she still hadn't got the point. 'Have you heard a word I've said? I'll not be made a fool of in front of my mates.' His carefully nurtured reputation would vanish like fog in sunshine, if she did anything half so daft again, he told her. 'Then where would we be? Up Queer Street.'

Belinda gave him that crooked smile of hers, which made the blood pound where it did most damage. 'Oh, I heard all right, but I'm a lady of determination as well as great talent, Benny. Make no mistake about that. I've already apologised for embarrassing you but we're equal partners, remember. Isn't that what we agreed? And I'd really like to be treated as such.'

While Benny swallowed his anger with his rapidly cooling dinner, Belinda went back to discussing bits of gossip and the funny things the children had done, as if the problem were settled. 'Sarah Jane is a sweetheart, but young Sean is a little devil. He must've been downstairs for an age playing with those sharp tools of yours before anyone missed him.'

As she chattered on, Benny ceased to properly take any of it in. The beer and whisky were fuddling his head and doing a war dance with the food in his stomach, making him feel decidedly queasy. He ruefully contemplated a whole list of worries that tormented him, not least his lack of success in his business venture. He'd spent the afternoon in a rebellious, and illegal, game of black jack that he could ill afford, in an attempt to recover some of his lost pride and credibility. All he needed was that licence, though how he would explain to Belinda when he finally did get hold of some new wood, that he wasn't quite the skilled carpenter she imagined, nor had the first idea how to make a chair, he wasn't quite sure.

He felt himself starting to panic, overwhelmed by his own fantasies which had somehow turned into barefaced lies without his meaning them to. He now bitterly regretted treating his mother's offer with such contempt. But how had he known that he'd be making this headlong dash into matrimony? That's what had done for him. In his present mood of maudlin self-pity, Benny felt tempted to put the entire blame on Belinda. She'd been the one to take on this white elephant of a shop, after all, without even a by-your-leave.

If only he had more capital then it wouldn't matter. He could change direction, do something other than joinery. But how could he even buy stock for the shop in his current state of penury? He'd asked Polly for help in this direction and she'd refused. There was only one more avenue worth exploring.

'We'll have to go and talk to your dad,' he found himself saying, the words popping unbidden out of his mouth. 'If we put it to him straight, I'm sure he'll help.'

'With the licence?' Belinda laughed. 'Like hell he would. It could well be him who's putting the block on it.'

Benny stared at her, stunned by this new insight into Hubert Clarke, never having considered such a possibility. He tried insisting that she must be mistaken, that he'd surely be prepared to help since she was his only daughter after all, perhaps with a loan so they could buy stock, for instance. Belinda calmly refused to even consider the possibility.

'I've already told you, I won't ask for help. I'm done with them. We'll make it on our own in the end, I know we will. However,' she continued, in that low, sexy voice of hers and running her fingers through his hair, 'returning to our earlier conversation, I'd prefer it if you did not address me as "woman" and don't ever shout at me again, Benny Pride. I won't stand for it.' She rubbed noses with him, gazing intently right into his greeny-grey eyes. 'I deserve some respect as the mother of your child, for all I may be making a few mistakes. You should've been here for lunch with your family. It was your duty to me, as well as to them.'

Weak with fresh love for her, Benny could do nothing but agree. And his mam would give him gyp next time she saw him.

While Belinda went to put the kettle on to make him a fresh pot of tea, Benny pushed aside the half-eaten meal, a bleak expression tightening his jaw, bitterly aware that for all their undoubted love for each other, the marriage was equal only in the sense that they occupied the same flat and the same bed. Apart from that, Belinda supplied the money and he spent it.

–

Hubert sat back in his chair and steepled the tips of his fingers together. His smile, if you could call it that, beneath the crisp moustache showed a row of pearly teeth, but did not reach the narrowed eyes beneath the beetle brow. He'd unnerved the lad, or so his sources reliably informed him. Stubborn as Belinda herself, Benny Pride still hadn't given up, so which card should he play next? Hubert never liked to lose.

It took very little effort to discover the name of Benny's landlord. The handing over of a few paltry pounds elicited an agreement to evict the pair from the premises at the first opportunity, on the grounds that they'd never opened the shop.

Chapter Twelve

Summer changed into a damp autumn when the rains never seemed to stop and as the days shortened and winter approached Belinda was forced to give up her part-time job at the insurance office because of her advanced pregnancy. Several local cotton mills had closed and there was talk of a coming coal shortage, not that they could afford much in any case. Benny was more worried about the threat to nationalise ports and road haulage as these were the only areas where he was finding work. Permanent employment now seemed an impossible dream, and he'd lost all hope of ever getting an allocation licence so he bought a few bits of second-hand wood from a mate and set about fashioning a stool. He thought this would be easier than a chair but somehow memories of woodwork at school had grown surprisingly hazy and after hitting his thumb with the hammer several times and almost slicing a finger off, he announced that he'd changed his mind about being a joiner. The dream was dead.

He stuck an advert up in the fish shop window and sold off the work bench together with all the tools to the first half decent offer he received.

'Something will turn up,' he told Belinda with a confidence he didn't quite feel. 'Just wait and see.'

What did turn up was the eviction notice. Benny stared at it horror-struck. It seemed like the last straw. How were they going to manage without even a roof over their heads? The prospect of going back home to number 32 and the pair of them squeezing into Big Flo's single bed seemed too much of a defeat for Benny to swallow. There'd been severe flooding in September when the

River Irwell burst its banks in neighbouring Salford and Benny knew they were lucky to have a roof over their heads at all. Housing was in short supply and the floods hadn't made it any easier. The last thing he wanted was to have to take Belinda to a municipal lodging house. He'd die sooner.

Desperate not to upset her, since she'd spent most of the morning feeling ill and all afternoon sleeping, he tucked the eviction notice into his pocket, hoping for some inspiration before it was taken into effect. He'd have a word with Percy Sympkin, the landlord, and make it clear they were up to date with their rent, though how much longer that state of affairs would last, he couldn't say. Surely no one would be so cruel as to turn a pregnant woman out on the streets?

–

Polly was keeping a close eye on the goings on of her son and daughter-in-law. She'd enjoyed the Sunday roast Belinda had made for them, the meat a touch overdone perhaps and the potatoes a mite greasy but then it was the girl's first effort. That Benny hadn't turned up to eat it had troubled her somewhat at the time, but the fact there'd been no invitation since concerned her even more, seeming to indicate that there were problems the young couple weren't owning up to. Polly was so worried she could barely stop talking about them.

'It's nowt to do with us,' Charlie constantly warned her. 'Don't interfere.'

'I'm not,' Polly protested, even as she wondered what she could do to put matters right. She could guess what it was. Benny hadn't found work and was too proud to crawl back and accept her offer. She'd grown tired of trying, deciding to let him stew in his own juices in the hope that would bring him round quicker. It didn't seem to be working. Perhaps a quiet word with Belinda wouldn't go amiss, woman to woman, as it were.

She saw Belinda rarely but once or twice caught sight of her out shopping and felt again that nudge of worry as the girl quickly hurried out of sight, as if not wanting to be seen. But then she wasn't exactly blooming. Pregnancy didn't seem to be sitting well on her and so far as Polly was aware, Benny was still stubbornly waiting for that dratted licence.

Christmas came and went, dull and damp, the shortages seeming to bite ever deeper. Lucy was having a hard time finding the money for presents for young Sean and Sarah Jane. Michael Hopkins managed it though, buying Sean a fire engine and Sarah Jane a high chair for her dolly of which Polly didn't entirely approve. After all, as she constantly reminded Lucy, Tom was only *missing*.

One Monday morning in early January, Polly decided to pop round to Belinda's for a quick cuppa. Uncle Nobby and Aunt Ida were keen for them all to attend a New Year Coffee and Bun Social at the Methodist Church. Not being a strong Catholic, Polly had no problem with this, particularly since Big Flo had been strong chapel throughout her long life. Maybe she could persuade Benny to bring Belinda along. It would certainly make a good enough reason for Polly to call on the grounds it might do the lass good to have a night out.

She was appalled to find the little flat freezing cold despite the haze of steam coming from the wash tub in the small back scullery. The swollen figure of her daughter-in-law was propped on a kitchen chair, evidently trying to catch her breath before starting the mangling. Mindful of Charlie's warning, Polly tried not to show the shock and concern she felt at sight of her. There were dark patches under the girl's eyes and she looked far too thin for so late a stage in her pregnancy. 'And how are you this fine day, me lovely girl?'

'Fine, apart from feeling a bit sick, as usual,' Belinda confessed. 'It never seems to get any better.'

'Then it's a cuppa you're needing, and one of these lovely custard tarts I've brought you.' Polly helped Belinda up the narrow stairs to the small living room, insisting she take a short rest. While she waited for the kettle to boil she went in search of a few scraps of wood and coal to light a fire, and found none. The coal man,

Belinda told her when she tentatively enquired, had forgotten to come this week.

Polly managed to bite her tongue though she felt sure it was more likely her dozy son had forgotten to pay the last coal bill. She couldn't think what had got into the daft eejit. She put a shilling in the meter and switched on the small electric fire instead, more expensive but there seemed no alternative. Something would have to be done, of that she was certain. 'Sickness is common enough,' she said brightly. 'And you've nought to be afeared of, a fine healthy girl like yourself.'

'I'm not frightened, just over-tired, that's all. This little monster keeps me awake half the night kicking and churning inside of me. I'm lucky if I sleep a wink.' Belinda rubbed at the burning stitch that ran down the inside of her right leg but Polly didn't notice as she was brewing the tea.

While she poured out, Polly told her about the Coffee and Bun Social and watched with increasing concern as Belinda quickly took a scalding sip and then bit deep into the custard tart as if she hadn't eaten a square meal in days. 'Wait till the baby comes,' Polly consoled her with a cheery grin. 'You won't sleep at all then.'

'Thanks,' but Belinda did see the funny side and gave a little smile. 'I'm sorry you've found me in a bit of a state. I got up late this morning so now the dolly tub will be under our feet all day.' It took ages because she found it hard bending over the galvanised washtub, not to mention operating the heavy, copper-bottomed posser. Even so, when they'd finished their tea and enjoyed a bit of a crack, as Polly called it, Belinda insisted on returning to the washing. Polly took hold of the posser, a long wooden stick with a disk of copper on the bottom and started swirling and thumping the sheets.

'Where is your husband, the lazy tyke? If he's no work on, he should be giving you a hand.'

Benny had brought the tub in from the yard and helped her to fill it but then had dashed off on important business, or so he'd claimed. Belinda chuckled, easing herself into a more comfortable position, feeling better already at having eaten the delicious tart. She couldn't remember the last time she'd tasted anything as good. 'Benny's very good and tidy about the house, army training you know, but that'll be the day when a man helps to wash grubby sheets, eh?'

'Aye, the sky will fall on our heads, and that's the truth.'

'According to him, having a baby is a perfectly normal state, which doesn't prevent washing being on the line by nine, ten at the latest.' He'd grown surprisingly critical of her lately, an attitude which was not going down too well. Belinda knew why of course, all because she wouldn't ask Hubert for help. But since he refused to work for his mother, you'd think he'd understand.

Polly frowned, wisely refraining from enquiring what it was that had got her son into such a lather. He'd never shown any interest in when the washing was done before. There had to be something more important on his mind than that. 'Well, tis certainly true that having a baby is a perfectly natural state of affairs, but that doesn't mean you shouldn't pander yourself with a bit more rest. I'm sorry you're having all this sickness, lass, I'd no trouble at all with either of mine.'

'Are you saying it's all in the mind?'

'Indeed I'm not. I'm thinking it's in your belly,' Polly said with a grin and, startled by her mother-in-law's flippancy, Belinda burst out laughing. She realised at once that it was the first time she'd laughed properly in days, and it felt good.

'Aw, now that's brought a bit of colour into your cheeks. You're looking better already.' Polly returned to her mission with increased vigour. 'It would do you both good to have a night out. And wouldn't I welcome the chance to have a word with the daft galoot and give him a piece of my mind for neglecting you so. If ever you should feel poorly again, send our Benny over, won't me or Lucy be glad to come and sit with you for a while.'

A rush of tears came into Belinda's eyes, in gratitude for the warmth in Polly's voice. 'There's really no need. It's just getting me down I suppose, being stuck in this place every day.' Pregnancy, so far as Belinda was concerned, was proving to be a far from a joyful experience. Her legs throbbed, the sickness lingered, her blood pressure was up and her spirits were sinking lower by the day. And although Benny continued to get some casual work which just about kept the wolf from the door, she'd begun to despair whether he'd ever get a business off the ground. But how could she admit this failure to his own mother.

As if reading her thoughts Polly asked, 'So what about the shop? Has any progress been made?'

Belinda shook her head. 'You've seen that the work bench and everything have gone?'

'I did notice.' Polly sounded grim.

'No demand, apparently. He's looking for something better, and I'm sure he'll find it – eventually.' Belinda rubbed a hand down the inside of her thigh, then quickly stopped when she saw Polly glance at her with an anxious frown. 'We're just running out of time.' She gave a rueful smile. 'This baby seems to be growing bigger by the day.'

Polly dragged a soaking wet pillow sheet from out the dolly tub, and insisting Belinda remain seated, began to wring it between her hands for all the world as if it were her son's neck. Sweat was pouring off her by the time she was done. 'Sure and I'll have a word with him about that too.' Tight-lipped, Polly handed Belinda one end of the wet sheet and as they folded it and set it ready to go through the mangle, her mind was racing. She'd have a word with the lad all right and some decisions would have to be made, like it or not. Independence was one thing, sheer pigheadedness was another matter entirely.

–

Never short on courage, Polly wasted no time in calling on Hubert Clarke, eager to confront him with the reality of his daughter's situation. She watched as his lips thinned into a rigid line of disapproval even as he offered her a seat in the plushness of his mahogany and leather study, after sending his wife scurrying for coffee.

'I don't believe in interfering in young folk's business,' he sanctimoniously and falsely announced. He looked as if he'd been knocked a bit off balance by Polly's bluntness. 'It's up to them what they make of their lives. Not my problem.'

'Oh I do agree, but there are times, like this current situation with Belinda pregnant and in need of good food and care, when no one but a heartless beast would ignore the poor girl's plight. Which I know you aren't, Councillor Clarke.' She gave him the benefit of her fine Irish smile so that even Hubert was slightly mollified.

'Aye well,' he blustered. 'She's her husband's responsibility now, by my reckoning.'

'And hasn't Benny done his best? Couldn't he have had a fine job with me in the carpet warehouse, had he not wanted to prove himself and be independent, the daft galoot.' Polly slanted her greeny-grey eyes up at him, hoping her charms hadn't quite faded, and again offered the benefit of her soft smile. 'Couldn't you find it in that great heart of yours to give your son-in-law a first foot on the ladder? He'd mebbe take it from you, rather than his mam.'

Hubert's mind had been working overtime through all of this embarrassing conversation. Not until Polly had mentioned the carpets did he make the connection. Of course! What a blind fool he'd been not to realise before. Pride Carpets, an up-and-coming firm which his accountant had mentioned to him more than once. Now that little gem of information, Hubert thought, put an entirely different complexion on the matter and would demand most careful thought, maybe even some revision to his plans. Funny thing about life, it could often throw up a wild card that turned out to be the very one you were seeking.

He was saved from answering by the door opening. Joanna appeared, looking flustered and precariously balancing a silver tray loaded with coffee jug, cups and saucers and tiny petit fours. Hubert got briskly to his feet and took the tray from her in a gesture of good will which left her standing with empty arms and mouth open in an 'Oh' of surprise.

'Now then,' Hubert said, as he magnanimously started to pour coffee. 'What are we going to do then, for these youngsters of ours?'

'Whatever it is,' Polly said, agreeably pleased by his unexpectedly positive response, 'it must look as if it has come about through their own efforts. Not a sniff of interference on our part, d'you not agree?'

Hubert took a slurp of coffee before beaming upon his guest. 'Indeed I do, my good lady. Indeed I do.'

They talked for some time over the delicious coffee and cakes. When he had showed his visitor out Hubert returned to his study, closed the door and lit one of his best Havana cigars, to consider the implications. In his unswerving opinion, poverty was the fault of the individual. The fact that Benny wasn't alone in failing to find full-time employment or get a business going in post-war Britain cut no ice with him. Hubert didn't hold with this newly created Ministry of National Insurance or the Family Allowances Bill, which only encouraged laziness. If a couple were bringing a child into the world, they should be entirely responsible for it. The lad must be daft if he'd had a good job offered him by his mother, and refused it.

And wasn't Pride Carpets exactly the sort of enterprise that he enjoyed swallowing up with his own greedy empire. This one would be a particular pleasure.

–

Lucy sat in the corner of the school hall where she could watch Sarah Jane and Sean sliding up and down the polished floor with their friends. Everyone seemed to be dancing and laughing and having a good time, except her, which made her sense of anticipation bite even deeper. At least from here she could keep an eye on the door. She longed for Michael to come, yet worried over how she could possibly face him in front of her family and friends without showing plainly how she felt about him.

The slightest inkling of the way they felt about each other, and the matriarchs of Pansy Street would tear the pair of them apart with their gnashing teeth and malicious tongues. Lucy had seen the groups of women gather, heard the scrape of chairs as they pulled closer together at their front doors to exchange salacious gossip.

At least Belinda and Benny seemed happy. Lucy could see them now, dancing a quickstep, the skirts of Belinda's dress, clearly silk and a beautiful peacock blue, swirling about her legs with a grace that seemed to defy she was only a matter of two months from giving birth. She might well complain it looked untidy with its let-out seams and her bump making the hem lift at the front, but to Lucy she looked marvellous, about as out of place in this room as a butterfly would in an Anderson shelter.

Sitting on the hard Sunday School chair watching everyone dance and laugh, Lucy felt quite old and dowdy in her navy two-piece, its plainness relieved only by a double row of buttons down the front, and a touch of white at the collar and cuffs. But then she supposed it was perfectly appropriate for a widow, and if nobody asked her out on to the floor, what did it matter? There was only one person she wished to dance with.

'Please may I have the pleasure of this dance?' She started, but it was only Johnny Parkinson grinning down at her. Determined not to show her blushing disappointment, she grinned back. 'Hey up, chuck, eaten t'dictionary for thy tea, have you?' she teased, using dialect to make him laugh. Grasping the blushing young man's hand she let him lead her out on to the dance floor, then wrapped his arm tight about her slim waist and pressed herself close against him, making him go bright red to the tips of his ears. 'Pity it isn't a tango. Very passionate dance, a tango.'

Belinda, seeing this pantomime, laughed at her sister-in-law making herself out to be a vamp. Nobody could make fun of themselves quite so effectively as a Lancastrian and Lucy was incorrigible. She looked pretty and relaxed with her light brown hair curled into soft victory rolls on the top of her neat head, as if a glow lit her from within. Nor did Belinda miss the many glances she cast throughout the hilarious dance, in the direction of the door. A woman with a secret perhaps?

–

It was past nine o'clock and still he hadn't come. Perhaps he wouldn't come at all and Lucy's heart sank at the bleakness of sitting like a wallflower all night. She could see Johnny Parkinson had gone over to ask Belinda to dance now, the pair tripping about the floor in some fancy two-step. Poor boy, he looked bewildered by his good fortune before being grabbed by his own mother and waltzed away clutched tightly to her bosom. She thought Belinda looked slightly relieved as she quickly returned to her seat.

'Would it be too much to ask a lovely young lady to dance with an old man?'

Lucy beamed. 'Uncle Nobby.'

'I've two left feet, but they're starting a slow waltz so I might manage that as I can count to three.'

Laughing, Lucy readily got up to join her favourite courtesy uncle on the dance floor. Nobby did a little reverse turn, spinning her round in a manner so accomplished, it quite belied his modest statement about his two left feet.

'Methodist or no, you've been dancing before,' she teased.

'Oh aye, it's true,' he said in his low, rasping Lancashire tones. 'I learned, like many another, in the Tower Ballroom, Blackpool, when I were nobbut a lad. We're not all po-faced and miserable, tha knows. Even your Aunt Ida can tread the light fantastic, if she's a mind. But don't let on I told you. That's where I met her, in Blackpool. As you well know, we went every year after that, staying at Mrs Nelson's guest house on York Street. Eeh, them were the days.'

Lucy burst out laughing. 'Oh, I do remember. I loved those holidays. Uncle Nobby, you're as good as a tonic.'

'Now that's another thing your Aunt Ida likes, a bit of tonic wine. What a sinner she is, on the quiet. Not that she wants it bruited abroad, you understand, her being so strong in the Chapel department. She says she's too old fer dancing and only come to this do tonight because she's on the committee. She's on a committee for everything is our Ida. But she'd not've missed this daft fandango for owt. I'll persuade her up later, see if I don't.' He grinned, swirling Lucy round in such intricate steps that she had to struggle against her giggles in order to keep up with him.

'Did you have a dance when you went with that Michael Hopkins to Belle Vue?'

The quick change of subject startled her so much Lucy very nearly missed her step. But before she could find any sort of answer, she saw that Michael had at last arrived. He was leaning against the doorjamb as if he'd been there an age, watching her, when she knew he must only have walked through the door a minute ago. Wouldn't she have seen him otherwise, since she'd been watching the door all night? He smiled at her and now she did lose her step and trod on Uncle Nobby's foot. 'Oh, I'm so sorry. I lost my concentration.'

Nobby too glanced across the hall. 'Aye, I'm not surprised. Nice chap.'

'Yes.'

'Widowed?'

'I believe so.'

'They say he's a conchie?'

'*What?* That's not true.' She was so upset, Lucy stopped dancing and Uncle Nobby led her back to her chair, one arm about her waist, his eyes kind.

'I want only the best for thee, love. Since Charlie's not well enough to think on these matters himself these days, I thought it my place to put in a quiet word. If I've overstepped the mark you'll have to put it down to nosy old age. It's just that folk are talking.'

'Folk are always talking. I don't listen.'

'Sometimes you can't help but hear.'

'Then if that's what they're saying, they couldn't be more wrong. He was in the RAF, invalided out in 1942 after his plane went down.'

'You've only his word for that. He arrives here in civvies, in the middle of a war, so folk are bound to gossip. We know nowt about him, so he makes up some yarn to shut the gossips up. Who can blame him? Nay, don't take on, just think before you make any snap decisions, that's all I ask. Your husband might well have died fighting for his country. Or he might still be alive some place, trying to get back home to thee.' And having said his piece, the old man walked away, leaving Lucy desolate.

'Hello!'

She felt her heart constrict. 'Hello,' she said, outwardly demure, inwardly on fire. Sickness was invading her fluttering stomach. Could she possibly be going down with flu, or something far more serious? He didn't ask if she wished to dance. He simply took her hand as if he knew she'd been waiting for him to do that very thing, and led her into it. It was a 'Paul Jones' and soon they were galloping round with the rest to the music *Here We Go Gathering Nuts in May*.

'You look lovely,' he whispered into her ear. For a whole five seconds she was in his arms, feeling the exciting closeness of him. Then the music changed and they were back into the circle again. Yet it was astonishing how many times when the two circles of dancers stopped, Lucy found herself opposite him.

'What a coincidence. You again,' she'd say, amused and highly flattered by his swift detours across the floor to be by her side.

'Fancy that.'

Neither of them noticed the interest they were causing, not least among Lucy's own family. Benny's face, as he watched Michael's antics, grew dark as thunder. When the dance finished, it seemed quite natural for them to collect their suppers and sit together.

'Just as well,' Lucy said. 'I'm fair starving,' and giggled as she tucked in to the food. She wasn't really very hungry but had noticed he'd started limping again on his bad leg and didn't like to mention it, but a rest would probably do it good. And she was looking forward to a quiet chat. Then Minnie arrived, bearing down upon them with a loaded plate in her hand. 'Ah, there y'are, lad. Thought I'd lost thee. Hutch up a bit lass and make room for a little 'un'. So saying, she plonked herself down between them.

They exchanged a glance of pure anguish but could say nothing, only concentrate on eating their supper in silence while Minnie demolished hers with several refills, and never stopped talking once.

Chapter Thirteen

Later in the evening they managed to escape. Lucy complained about being hot and Michael led her outside, when he thought no one was paying them any attention. It felt cold in the school yard for the air was sparkling and fresh, with a clear view of a myriad of stars glittering high in the heavens. Lucy slid her hand into his, revelling in this moment alone. Even so she kept looking back, imagining shadowed figures watching them. 'We must be careful.'

'It's all right,' he urged. 'There's no one here.'

Standing under the shelter in the school playground, he rubbed her bare arms, slid her inside the warmth of his jacket, urging her not to get cold. She didn't feel cold, despite the crispness of the night air. Every nerve ending was on fire, her limbs glowing with the heat of the passion she felt for him, her lips burning for his kiss. Unable to resist, Lucy could feel her body growing languorous with desire.

When the kiss came she melted into him, became a part of his soul, grafted on to the hard planes of his body. He slid the buttons of her little navy jacket apart and when he struggled with the last one, she helped him. His hand on her breast was icy but that only added to her excitement. She could never remember feeling this way before. Certainly not with Tom.

'We could go home.' His voice rasped with a low passion. 'No one would notice, they're all busy dancing. Our house is empty. We could be alone for once.' How could she resist? 'The children,' she murmured against his hot kisses, still desperately trying to.

'We could be back in half an hour. Thirty whole precious minutes.' Enough to make her his for all time. Dare he risk it?

His mouth teased hers open, his exploring tongue only making her want him all the more. 'They'll never miss us. I love you so much, Lucy.'

She kissed him again. Oh, she loved him too. The thought of his naked body hard against her own, of his exploring hands gently urging her to a climax were tempting beyond endurance. She even found herself shamefully glorying in the fact she was wearing her best underwear, handmade from parachute silk. What she wouldn't do with him, given chance. 'Maybe…' she began.

'*Lucy*. Are you taking a breath of fresh air, m'cushla?'

They broke hastily apart, Lucy hastily doing up buttons with clumsy fingers, desperate not to be found anywhere near Michael Hopkins. 'Lord, it's Mam. She'll flay me alive. Quick, hide.'

By the time Polly crossed the dark playground and reached her, Michael had ducked into the boy's lavatory and Lucy was alone, leaning against the stone wall in her little navy two-piece as if it wasn't actually starting to snow and she now freezing cold.

'Saints preserve us, is it pneumonia you're wanting to catch?'

'No, just a bit of peace, Mam.'

'Aw, is it that you're missing Tom, m'cushla?' and Polly put sympathetic arms about her daughter, holding her tight, urging her to have faith and patience and her husband would be home in no time, so he would. Lucy despaired of ever making her understand.

—

Michael slowly emerged from his hiding place. He loved Lucy. He wanted her. He didn't care if the world knew it. Lucy, however, did care and had a reputation to protect.

Making his way around the perimeter of the yard, his bad leg ached from the cold, dragging a little. He really shouldn't have done so much dancing, then stumbled across a group of men huddled together, obviously a card school; not unusual in these parts. Michael heard the clink of coin, a few choice words uttered in anger. He tried to avoid them but a scuffle broke out.

One man was on the ground, another on top and in seconds fists were flying. He hesitated, wondering if he should get involved. They were grown men after all and it wasn't his quarrel. Everyone else seemed to be standing back in a wide circle, egging the combatants on.

'Come on, Benny lad. Hit him hard.'

There was no question then. Benny Pride, the young fool, fists and feet flying, blood streaming from his nose, no doubt thinking a bit of fisticuffs could solve everything. Michael ploughed into the melee, knowing he could hardly stand by while Lucy's brother was being pulverised.

A hand grabbed his lapel and shoved him away. 'What's it got to do wi' you, mate. They're just sorting out a bit of family business, right?'

Michael could see now who the other combatant was. Ron Clarke, Benny's brother-in-law. Perhaps it wasn't any of his business. Or should he call for help? It could all become very nasty if they turned on him. Then Benny was struck square in the jaw and flung sprawling all over Michael's feet. Reaching down and neatly avoiding a flying fist, Michael hauled Benny to his feet. Ron was back on him in a second, clinging like a leech but Michael wasn't for letting go, not this time. 'Stop it, the pair of you, or somebody will get seriously hurt.'

Fortunately, others had reached a similar conclusion and the pair were finally dragged apart, though not without protest. Ron vanished in a trice but Benny, raring to go after him had to be held back, far from the grateful for the rescue.

'Leave it. Let him go,' Michael urged, anxious to put an end to this dispute so he could get back to Lucy and enjoy the evening.

'What the hell has it got to do wi' you?'

'Nothing.' Michael started dusting him down but Benny shook him off. 'Except that I thought Belinda might object if you were killed, but perhaps I'm wrong. Not very sensible though is it, to fall out with your in-laws when you're trying to get started in a new business?'

If there was one thing Benny didn't need, it was to be reminded that after six years away fighting for his country, he was unemployed and on the dung heap. This wasn't the way it was meant to be. Ron Clarke had just taken great pleasure in explaining why he couldn't get a licence or permission to open his shop, and never would if Hubert had anything to do with it. Benny could hardly believe his father-in-law could be so vindictive and certainly had no wish to explain any of this to Michael Hopkins, or his lack of success in keeping his lovely wife in the manner to which she was accustomed. It was far too shaming. He'd no idea what he could do about the situation but Benny knew that he was in dead trouble. He'd even lost his latest job on Castle Quay, Ron Clarke claiming credit for that as well by telling his employer that Benny was a rabble-rouser, and a unionite.

And there was still the eviction notice hanging over his head. The landlord had given him a month's grace but where next month's rent would come from he hadn't the first idea. Worse, Belinda had no money either. Benny knew it was up to him to save them, though how he was to manage it, he hadn't a clue. Frustration and anger roared in his head. What was he supposed to do? Why was everyone against him?

'It's none o' your goddamned business,' he shouted, and threw off his two restrainers to snatch up his jacket and shrug it back on. He straightened his tie, slicked down his hair and dabbed at the blood on his chin. Apart from a slight bruise on the left cheek bone, no one would know he'd been in a fight. At least he hoped Belinda wouldn't. If Michael Hopkins hadn't interfered he might have succeeded in settling his score with Ron-interfering-Clarke. They were married for God's sake. Why couldn't Hubert accept the fact?

He pushed his face up close to Michael's. 'I'll settle up wi' Ron Clarke another time, make no mistake, when there's nobody to save his cowardly skin. But then you'd understand about cowards wouldn't you, being one yourself.'

Michael said nothing though his jaw tightened and a nerve flickered at the corner of his mouth.

'In the meantime, you keep your nose out of my affairs, *conchie,* and your wandering hands off our Lucy. Don't think I didn't see you slobbering all over her when you were dancing. It may not seem like it but she's still a married woman, and *my* sister. If you come anywhere near her again, you'll be sorry, very sorry.'

'Will I indeed?'

'Aye, you will.' Confidence restored by this show of aggression in front of his pals, Benny dusted off his hands as if he had soiled them by touching Michael Hopkins and thrust back his shoulders with a cocky arrogance. As he strolled away, his mates smacked him on the back, as if he'd won a great victory.

–

For the rest of the evening Lucy tried to go nowhere near Michael, yet it seemed she couldn't avoid him. Too frequently, as if by instinct, their glances met and held for a fraction of a second before hastily turning away in case anyone should notice.

When everyone got together to do a progressive barn dance, the Hokey-Cokey or the Teddy Bear's Picnic, she made a point of dancing with anyone but him, even so it was difficult to avoid him without making it look obvious. She would quake with anticipation whenever he came near. It was pure torture as his fingers would link possessively into hers for the merest second, or more agonising still if he put his hand to her waist while he whirled her round. Her anguish as he moved on with another partner was almost more than she could bear. She very nearly called him back.

At one point Benny waylaid her as she made her way on to the dance floor. 'You're making an exhibition of yourself. Remember you are a married woman.'

Lucy snatched her arm away. 'And *you* remember it's none of your damn business.'

At the end of the evening she collected her coat and made her way outside with Benny and Belinda, Polly and Charlie. They were all tired but happy, little Sean and Sarah Jane half asleep already, for it was well past their bedtime. But what did it matter once in a while, she thought, hugging them to her. And she'd enjoyed the dancing, for all she'd longed to spend more time with Michael.

Then Sean realised he'd left his cap in the Sunday school cloakroom and she called out to the others not to wait for them while she ran back to fetch it. After a hasty search Sarah Jane found the cap fallen into a corner.

'Here it is, Mam.'

'Dozy,' Lucy teased, pulling it on to the little boy's head where it nodded against her shoulder. After sitting down a moment to tie his shoe laces which had worked loose they set off again, Sean in her arms and Sarah Jane holding her hand, singing *Here We Go Round the Mulberry Bush*.

It happened so suddenly. One minute Michael had appeared out of the darkness to wish her and the children goodnight, the next he was falling, blood spurting everywhere. Lucy screamed, watching in appalled horror as he hit the ground as if in slow motion.

'Conchie! Conchie! Bloody conchie!'

There was a hissing voice she heard without quite registering as she fell to her knees beside him, desperately trying to staunch the blood with her scarf, her handkerchief, whatever she could find. She could hear Sean starting to cry. Sarah Jane shouting Michael's name. Where did all this blood come from? And she must have been shouting for help too, for it came in the form of running feet and noisy shouts, yet no one came to kneel beside her. When she finally glanced up it was to find themselves surrounded by a small group of curious onlookers.

'Whoever it were, hit him wi' that brick, love,' said one.

'It'll need stitching,' agreed another.

'Aye, proper mess, eh?'

Lucy looked into their faces and knew that for all they were happy to gawp, not one of them was willing to offer help. She'd always believed this to be a neighbourly district with the kind of people who, despite their predilection for gossip, would rally round if someone was in trouble. Salt-of-the-earth types. They'd bring food to the sick, wash bed-linen, mind a woman's family while she was occupied delivering yet another mouth to feed. They'd make sure the old folk had coal in their buckets in winter and always found time to stop for a bit of a natter on a front doorstep. But these same people had lost sons, husbands, lovers in the war and not one was prepared to lift a finger for an accused conchie. Lucy struggled to lift him, feeling as if her fury might choke her. At least he was awake now, thank God, and then Minnie Hopkins came galloping out of the darkness, her skinny legs and arms pumping like pistons and together they helped Michael to his feet. There was no sign of Polly, or Benny or Belinda.

'Thanks for nothing,' Lucy shouted to the gathered crowd as she pulled her children close and offered her own shoulder for Michael to lean on. 'Thanks for bloody nowt.'

Later, when she'd got the children safely tucked up in bed she marched straight round to the shop and accused Benny of throwing the brick. He vehemently denied it, saying he might be a bit of a loud mouth but violence wasn't his style.

'And what's that then?' Lucy mocked, pointing to the bruise on his chin. Benny rubbed it, looking shamefaced and privately thanking his lucky stars that Belinda was in bed.

'I had a straight and fair fight with someone, but I don't go in for those sort of tactics. I don't hit folk behind their backs, or on their head wi' a brick. What d'you take me for? Anyroad, I've enough troubles of my own, without taking on yours as well.' He looked so hurt by her lack of belief in him and so sincere in his protestations of innocence that Lucy felt half inclined to believe him. But then if Benny hadn't thrown the brick, who had?

-

The next day, calmly shredding lettuce in Minnie Hopkins's kitchen, Lucy rehearsed how she would explain to Michael that they must never see each other alone again, not till she'd got things sorted out. She was thankful that no real hurt had come to him beyond a cut on his head that Minnie's nursing skills would soon mend, but those stolen moments together in the shelter had made her think.

Lucy made up her mind to write to the army, to ask them if it was true that she had to wait seven years for Tom to be declared officially dead. Seven years sounded like forever. She knew in her heart that no one could hold on that long, not loving each other as much as she and Michael did.

There came a rat-tat on the door knocker. She wiped her hands and went down the hall to find Lily Gantry standing on the clean doorstep with an expression like sour milk on her face.

'Thee's to come home at once.'

'Has something happened? Is it Sarah Jane? Sean?' There was panic in her voice. Aunt Ida had promised to collect them both from school, now fear flooded through her even as the old woman shook her grizzled head.

'Nay, nowt like that. But you're to come quick.'

Minnie appeared, scowling with disapproval at this interruption of the morning's work, wanting to know what was going on but Lucy was already reaching for her coat. She was quite certain something terrible must have happened and the old besom was trying to break it to her gently.

Minnie interrupted her. 'Thee can't run off wi'out a by-your-leave. You're not done yet. What about dinner? Our Michael'll be home and wanting his tea in half an hour.'

'I'll be back by then,' Lucy said, wrapping a scarf about her head and, since she could hear rain pattering on the windows, starting a search for an umbrella. If Sean had run off again he'd be wet through by the time she found him. Oh lord, where would he have gone this time? The air-raid shelters where Gran was found? She really must hurry. She half ran along the passage to the front door where Lily Gantry stood watching events with interest. Minnie gave chase and brought her up short.

'But what if you're not? What'll I give 'im?'

Lucy paused long enough to think and draw breath. 'Uncle Nobby brought us some fresh vegetables yesterday so I was in the middle of doing a nice salad, and I've already made the Californian Meat cakes from the recipe Aunt Ida left me.'

'Californian Meat cakes?'

'Yes, I know. Aunt Ida has been as close to California as I've been to the Sahara Desert but all they are is corned beef, chopped onion and mashed potato, mixed together with beaten egg and formed into patties. I've done all of that, even rolled them in bread crumbs, all you have to do is fry them and prepare the salad. You can manage that surely?'

Minnie was about to remark that with her standard of cooking, they could turn into Lancashire Coal Mine meat cakes but the front door knocker rattled again.

'What is it this time? If something's happened to our Sean, I'll kill him,' Lucy gasped, rather contrarily. The last thing she needed right now was trouble with her son. Wasn't it difficult enough hanging on to this job? Pushing passed both Lily Gantry and Minnie, she flew to the door and flung it open.

But it wasn't young Sean standing in the small front garden, nor Sarah Jane but a stranger, his coat collar turned up almost to the brim of his trilby hat against a brisk wind that had blown up.

'If you're wanting Michael,' Lucy began, irritated by this interruption. 'I'm afraid he isn't home from work yet.'

'Lucy. Don't you recognise me? Benny told me I'd find you here. Don't scowl at me, lass. All I ask is a friendly welcome,' and the stranger took off his hat so that she could see him properly. At which point, for the first time in her life, Lucy fainted.

Chapter Fourteen

Minnie had galloped off for Michael the moment she realised who their unexpected visitor was. Now he'd arrived, out of breath and clearly in torment at this stunning realisation of his worst nightmare. He focused on Tom's lopsided smile and decided instantly that he couldn't compete.

'They told me you were dead.' Lucy sat in the kitchen facing her husband, hands clenched tight in her lap. Michael could see she was shaking, her face ashen as if she were sickening for something. 'At least,' she remembered the exact wording of the telegram. 'Missing, presumed killed in action.'

'They presumed too much. Here I am, fit and well. Never better.'

She looked at him oddly for a moment, then said a strange thing. 'I'd forgotten how full of confidence you always were.'

Michael called it arrogance.

He was also tall, admittedly thin but with light brown hair cut close to the head. His shoulders were broad, his skin tanned as if from years in the sun, not at all the yellowish tinge usually seen on POWs. He had the kind of good looks and easy smile that any woman would fall for. Michael had no difficulty in seeing why Lucy had fallen in love and married him. It was a wonder she saw anything in himself to love at all, after living with such a demigod.

Now she'd fallen silent, seemed struck dumb by events, overwhelmed perhaps by her good fortune at Tom's return from the dead or too dazed to deal with the reality of it, let alone work out all the implications. It was up to him, Michael decided, to ask the relevant questions about where Tom had been stationed and where he'd been since the war ended, which he proceeded to do, at length. He heard a convoluted story of how Tom had escaped from prisoner-of-war camp some time before the end of the war, crossed the Italian Alps, been sick and nursed back to health by a generous and kind French family.

'So where, exactly, were you imprisoned and how did you manage to escape?' Michael persisted, still puzzled. 'Were you alone? I mean, why didn't you let Lucy know you were safe?'

Tom seemed to be searching his heads for facts, dragging them out reluctantly, one by one. 'I had malaria. All sorts of wounds and sores, barely alive for months.'

'Malaria? How could you catch that in Italy, or France?'

Tom answered sharply, as if with a simmering anger. 'I was also stationed in Africa and Egypt for a while. Anyway, I was too ill to write.'

'You could have got someone else to write for you.'

Lucy interrupted, putting out a hand as if she couldn't bear any more questioning, the appeal in her eyes almost breaking Michael's heart in two. 'It's all right. I'm sure Tom would have let me know, if he could.'

'Course I would. Later it seemed a better idea to come and surprise you.'

'You've done that all right,' Michael said, hearing the sour note in his own voice and hating himself for it.

Lucy was actually shaking. 'It's been such a sh-shock. I'd best get off home, speak to Mam and Charlie. And find you somewhere to sleep tonight.'

'I rather thought I'd be sleeping with my wife.'

A small silence in which Lucy put a hand to her head, as if it had suddenly started to ache. Michael felt his jaw tense and sweat break out on his brow but managed to address his rival with perfect calm for all there was deep bitterness in his tone. 'I should think patience is called for here. Can't you see how stunned she is. Give her time for God's sake.'

'When I want advice on my marriage, I'll ask for it,' Tom coldly responded, and taking hold of Lucy's arm, propelled her towards the door. Michael instantly stepped in front of them, blocking the way to speak softly to Lucy. 'Go home and get a good night's rest. You look worn out. We'll talk tomorrow.' And then to Tom, 'You can stop here tonight, if you want. We've plenty of spare bedrooms – till you've time to sort something out.' He issued the invitation like a challenge which, for one awful moment he thought Tom Shackleton was about to refuse. But then he turned to Lucy with that winning smile.

'Why not? It has been a shock, I dare say. And there'll be plenty of time, the rest of our lives after all.' And he met Michael's glare with what could only be described as triumph.

–

After what seemed an endless afternoon of family talk and excitement, Tom did indeed go up the street to number 179 when darkness came, though he made it clear it was only to give Lucy time to make more satisfactory arrangements, insisting he would be back for his breakfast, sharp at eight.

Lucy didn't sleep a wink. She couldn't stop shaking as she lay flat on her back in bed, with her children for once cuddled beside her, even though liquid fire seemed to be coursing through her veins. Her brain couldn't seem to digest all the facts, or work out what she should do about them.

Sean and Sarah Jane had been by turn delirious with delight and oddly shy and bemused. It had taken hours to settle them so that in the end she'd relented and let them into bed with her. Lucy lay with her arms about them, breathing in their sweet fragrance, feeling calmed by the rhythm of their breathing and thinking what it meant to them, to have their dad back home. Sean in particular was beside himself with excitement. All the little boy could talk about was going fishing.

'Of course I'll take you,' Tom had promised, tickling the little boy under his chin and making him giggle. Sarah Jane had hung back, shyly clinging to her mother while Tom had laughed and patted his knee, asking her to come and sit on it.

'Do I have to?' she'd softly asked and Lucy had leaned down to kiss her cheek and whisper in her ear that she didn't have to do anything she didn't want to.

But the implications of Tom's return were far wider ranging than Sean and his fishing. Where would he sleep tomorrow? The idea of having him in bed with her so haunted Lucy that she couldn't settle either. It seemed a longer, even more agonising night in many ways than the one following the news of his death. Perhaps on that day it hadn't been quite such a shock as it might have been because it was so long since she'd seen or heard from him. Since then, she'd never, not for one moment, expected him to return. She'd been absolutely certain he was dead.

Not that she was sorry he was alive, how could she be? Once she would have given her life for this man. She'd loved him from being a young girl but her feelings had changed, there was no denying that fact. She loved Michael now, wholly and completely, for all they'd never actually become lovers in the true sense of the word. Oh, but that wasn't through lack of desire. How she loved him, as if he were a part of her very soul. How could she go back to a marriage she'd thought was over for good?

On the other hand, how could she begin to explain all of this to Tom, poor man, or turn him out on the street? A soldier returned from the front, an escaped POW, her own husband and the father of her children. It was clear that he'd nowhere to go. No job, no home even, since she'd been forced to give that up years ago and move back in with Polly. And more important perhaps, he no longer had a wife. Only when the first cold rays of dawn poked fingers of pale light into the room, did exhaustion finally overwhelm her and she slept.

What seemed only moments later, she opened her eyes to find Polly, clearly delighted by the return of her son-in-law, bringing her a cup of tea in bed as a treat and volunteering to take the children to school for once. Lucy expressed her gratitude. It would give her time to talk to Tom, to explain before the Lily Gantrys of this world did the job for her, and to make some decisions.

Lucy meant to be firm and she was, though it took more courage than she'd expected. In one way it seemed perfectly normal that they should be sitting together at the kitchen table with a pot of tea between them as once they had done years ago. Yet in another they were like polite strangers, unsure of each other and afraid of saying the wrong thing. She kept to her resolution. 'As you see, Tom, things have changed. I genuinely believed you to be dead.'

'So I gather. Didn't take you long to find compensation, did it?' His voice was hard, caustic and critical, jaw rigid.

'That's not fair. If you'd written, I would have known you were all right, wouldn't I?'

'So it's my fault is it?'

'Don't be ridiculous.' She got up from the table, disguising her distress by fetching a pan and fresh kippers from the pantry, busying herself preparing breakfast for him as she tried to explain. 'It's just that I've no wish to deceive you. I feel you have the right to hear the truth.'

He pointed out that she was still his wife, that he had a right to expect her to wait for him and all Lucy could do was keep repeating how she'd thought him dead, how she hadn't planned on falling in love with Michael, and it had taken them both by surprise.

Her cheeks flushed with embarrassment, her slender body wrapped in a long white apron with her hair tied up in a turban, she looked like a young girl still. Tom watched her small neat hands flip the kippers over in the frying pan as he listened to her halting tale and asked himself why he had stayed away so long. She was far more attractive, this young wife of his, than he'd remembered. He should have come home months ago. Years. He could have written. Why hadn't he?

He knew why. She'd become almost a stranger to him during the long years of war, a distant figure whose face he could barely recall. Even his children hadn't seemed quite real. And there were other reasons, some best not spoken about. He'd found his new life exciting and been reluctant to give it up, might never have done so if things hadn't got tricky. But what she didn't know wouldn't hurt either of them, particularly himself.

She was asking him a question. 'What about you? Didn't you meet anyone else in all these years you've been away? What stopped you from writing? A letter would have eased the shock, Tom. It would have given me hope, something to live for. Why didn't you?'

He felt the familiar surge of anger. Questions, questions, he was sick of bloody questions. People never left him alone. Everyone he met always had the same questions. Where had he been? Why? When? What? Who was he with? He was mightily sick of it. He certainly wasn't going to take being interrogated by an unfaithful wife so he dismissed her curiosity with a snort of laughter. 'What are you accusing me of? Are you implying that I deliberately didn't write? I've told you, I was ill. I'm the injured party here.'

Lucy cringed with shame as she slid a pair of kippers on to his plate. 'Whatever Michael and I feel for each other and I don't – can't – deny that I'm very fond of him, we've done nothing about it.'

'So you say.'

'It's true.' But watching her husband tuck in to his breakfast, for the first time Lucy almost wished that it weren't.

–

The newspapers the following day were saying that 50,000 couples were waiting for a divorce. They spoke of too-lengthy separations and too-hasty marriages at the start of the war, of infidelity, and of wives waking up and finding themselves married to a stranger. Lucy knew just how they felt. The Archbishop of Canterbury, however, spoke of the serious lifelong obligations of marriage. Lucy didn't want obligations. She wanted love.

The next few days were difficult. Lucy made up the alcove bed that Benny had used to sleep in and desperately tried to come to terms with being a wife again while Tom just wanted to sit in the kitchen or in the front parlour watching the world go by through the window. He had no wish, he said, to step outside the door, or start looking up old friends. Not yet. He certainly wasn't ready to even think about finding a job. Lucy accepted all of this with a calm equilibrium. What she found harder to accept was the fact that he expected her to stay in too.

'I can't stop at home. I've a living to earn,' she told him, but he insisted she owed him a few days of her time at least, so they could get to know each other again.

'I'm not sure I want you working up at 179, not with that Michael Hopkins around.'

'Don't be silly. He isn't around anyway, only after he's finished work. Besides, we need the money.'

'Now I'm back everything must change,' he pointedly reminded her.

It was a bleak thought for she liked things the way they were. Lucy realised that she had no wish for her life to change, not in this way. But perhaps he had a point. A little time together wouldn't be a bad thing, so long as he remained in that alcove bed. It might give them time to sort things out in a civilised fashion, without harming the children. Reluctantly she sent word to her clients, including Minnie Hopkins, that she was taking a few days off to spend with her husband.

That week seemed endless. Both Polly and Charlie tried to talk to Tom but few more facts emerged. Any hopes Lucy might have had for a heart to heart with her mother about her worries, or to admit that she didn't feel the same about her husband, died in her throat as the warnings came thick and fast that she must be patient, and give him time to adjust. Besides, Polly was busy with her own concerns over Charlie and the warehouse and once she recognised her daughter was depressed, she assumed it to be because Tom wasn't yet sharing her bed. Somehow Lucy never seemed to find quite the right moment to explain that she'd much rather sleep with her lover.

The children soon lost interest in him, maintaining a shy distance. This man, who was supposedly their father, felt like a stranger to them and they found it difficult to accept him as anything more at this stage. Even Sean began to avoid him, saying only, 'You never took me fishing.'

'I could take you now.'

'It don't matter. Michael took me down the canal.'

Lucy made a decision not to interfere. If he wished to get to know his children, he must set about the task himself. Despite her feelings of guilt at her own apparent betrayal, she still harboured resentment that Tom had sent no word that he was safe, nor warned her that he was coming home. Even the authorities seemed to have let her down. There'd been no letter from his commanding officer either, not a word to indicate that he was alive and well. Tom insisted that it was not uncommon for it to take six or even twelve months before relatives were informed a man had been found. A fact she found hard to believe, but without hard evidence couldn't dispute.

Only Benny seemed enthusiastic over his brother-in-law's return, 'Great to see you again, old chap. We'll go for a pint or two one night, eh?' And he flashed Lucy a challenging glare, as if saying that he'd warned her all along that Tom would be back. Wasn't that why he'd disapproved of her friendship with Michael Hopkins?

'Did you ever discover who threw that brick at Michael?' Lucy asked, without thinking that it might seem as if she were defending him.

Benny's eyes flashed dangerously, the natural rivalry between brother and sister instantly sparking into action. 'You're not still blaming me? I wasn't even there. Belinda and me were well on our way home by that time. Anyroad, he deserved it.'

'Was that because he's a conscientious objector?' Tom asked.

Lucy instinctively opened her mouth to deny this but then the thought flashed into her mind that Tom couldn't possibly know the rumours circulating about Michael. Not unless he'd arrived home a good deal sooner than he claimed and had overheard someone talking. She gazed thoughtfully at her husband's placid expression of interested enquiry and wondered if it were genuine. Wisely she decided not to pursue the matter, resolving to think about it later, when she'd recovered from the shock of his unexpected return. Instead she changed the subject, reminding Benny that Tom wasn't well enough to start drinking yet. 'Hasn't he only just arrived home.'

Perversely, Tom said, 'How about tonight? We could go to the Dog and Duck, if you like.'

'But I thought you were ill and didn't want to go out?' she protested, surprised by this contrariness.

'It's only to the pub. I can manage to go there, for God's sake.'

He was often contrary, she discovered in the days following. Once, she offered to put his things away and he went mad, snatching the shirt she'd picked up right out of her hands. He always insisted on folding them himself, personally stowing away each item with painstaking care. He would put his cufflinks in a box and lock it away in a drawer with other items he never showed her, almost as if he expected her to steal them when he wasn't looking. On one occasion she caught a glimpse of shining metal and asked if he'd brought home a German gun. She knew many soldiers did, as a memento. He was furious, shouting and raving at her, asking if she thought he was a madman. She never went near his things after that.

Benny explained that it was because he'd spent so much time as a POW. 'Affects 'em that way. Makes them very possessive because of the terrible living conditions they had to endure. Give him time.'

If anyone else told her to give him time, Lucy thought she might scream. What about her? Who was going to give her time? How was she supposed to adjust? She had no desire to coax him into her bed, as everyone seemed to think. She was hoping and praying he would never ask, that he'd be content to stay in the alcove bed in the kitchen for a long, long time. Or at least until she had found a way out of this nightmare.

On Sunday night, thankful that her days of being confined in the house with Tom were nearing an end, Lucy put on her coat and announced that she was just popping up to see Minnie Hopkins and her other customers, to let them know she'd be back at work the next day as usual. 'We need some money coming in, and I don't want you starting work till you feel ready.' She felt stifled, desperate to get out, as well as to see Michael again. She prayed he'd be in.

'Don't be long,' Tom warned. 'I want you back within the hour.'

'You what?' She laughed in disbelief that he should attempt to give her orders. 'I'm used to coming and going as I please. I'll not be dictated to.'

Tom picked up the newspaper, shook it open and began to read. 'I've told you. Things have changed.'

Lucy felt a quick surge of anger well up within her but he merely glanced at her over the rim of his paper with that odd, disconnected sort of expression in his eyes and she remembered Polly's warnings to give him more time, Benny cautioning her about ex-POWs being difficult. Tom wasn't himself. She must remember that. This man had almost died for his country, might well have endured torture and inhumanity that he couldn't even bear to talk about, and all for his wife and children. She bit back the protest. Perhaps if she didn't argue he'd get over his jealousy quicker and in time they'd sort everything out in a sensible fashion without hurting anyone.

'I'll do my best.'

As she went out through the door, his voice followed her. 'You'll do more than your best, Lucy. You'll learn to do as I say. And you won't talk to that Michael Hopkins ever again. Is that clear?'

Lucy mumbled something unintelligible as she hurried out into the night.

Minnie was alone when she arrived, surprisingly sympathetic and avid for news. The old woman explained that Michael had gone to bed early for once, since he hadn't been sleeping well lately, which Lucy didn't wonder at. But Minnie did offer her a cup of tea in the kitchen, admitting to being captivated by the whole situation and clearly itching to know more. 'What a pretty pickle, eh?'

'Upsetting and confusing, yes.'

'It would be. You fancy our Michael then?'

Startled by the older woman's bluntness, Lucy realised she'd led herself up this dangerous path by spending too much time with him at the Coffee and Bun Social. Well, she'd already made the situation clear to Tom, so there was no turning back now. What did she have to hide? She stood up, walked to the sink to fetch a dish cloth to wipe up a spill of tea, anything to avoid direct eye contact. 'I do, yes, as a matter of fact. And he fancies me. If you've anything to say against that, you'd best say it now.'

'He allus has had a soft spot for thee, lass.' Her calmness surprised Lucy, as if she didn't mind that her son was 'bothering with a married woman,' which was how the self-righteous gossip-mongers would see it. 'Thee has more than thy fair share now, eh?'

'Of trouble? You're right, I have. The whole street will be talking about it by tomorrow, I've no doubt.'

'Aye, trying to choose the right one for you, lass. Fellas, two a Penny, eh?'

Lucy tried to smile, used to Minnie's droll sense of humour, then leaned across the table, her face serious again. 'At least I stick up for Michael. They've already had a go at him.'

'"Sticks and stones may break my bones but calling never hurt me." Isn't that what kids say?'

'The *gossips* say he's a conchie. That's why someone threw that brick at him. Didn't he tell you?'

Minnie looked startled, her mouth curling in upon itself till her lips had almost disappeared. '*Conchie?* Where the hecky thump did they get that from?'

'You know what folk are like. All because they've never seen him in uniform.'

Minnie was silent for a whole half minute, quite a long time for her. 'Come on, and don't make a sound. I want to show thee summat. Summat tha'd best see if that's the way the wind blows.'

—

Back at number 32 Tom Shackleton took the opportunity of an empty house to visit his wife's bedroom. Polly and Charlie were down at the warehouse and Sarah Jane and Sean were fast asleep, curled up like a pair of spoons in the single bed they shared in the corner. The brass double bed which had once stood in a bedroom in his own home, occupied most of the rest of the floor.

Tom resented the fact that they had to share a house with Lucy's family though he could see how it had made sense for Lucy, while he was away in the war. But a man should have his own place. He also bitterly resented only being offered the alcove bed downstairs when there was this big one here, which he should be sharing with his own wife. He'd certainly no intention of sharing her with that conchie. It amused him that Lucy had no idea that he'd seen them together, kissing and canoodling in the school yard. Bit of luck that was. He chuckled now to think how Benny had got it in the neck for something he didn't do. If she knew that it'd been he who'd thrown that brick, she might not even offer him the alcove bed.

But he meant to start asserting his rights soon. It wasn't that he meant to hang around longer than was necessary. Once she'd had time to get used to the idea and accepted him back in a proper fashion as a good obedient wife should, they'd be off, out of this dratted street and this drab city. He'd never shared Lucy's love for Manchester and he'd taken a big risk in coming home, back like a rat to its hole, he thought to himself with a smile. One he had to make worth his while.

For now he turned his attention to quietly opening and closing drawers in the chest which stood beside the bed. After some

odd sort of kinship with her, as if she understood. Perhaps, some time in her own youth, Minnie Hopkins had loved and lost. 'Yes, you're right. It wouldn't be fair to bombard him with demands when he's only just arrived. Oh, Minnie,' and the old woman gathered her up in her skinny arms while Lucy lay her head on the flat chest, breathing in the scent of violets and pear drops, thinking that this cantankerous old dragon suddenly seemed to be her only friend.

Later, as Minnie showed her to the door they found an envelope on the mat that someone had pushed through the letterbox. Inside were three white feathers.

Chapter Fifteen

Coming home to find her small son in a lather of distress and Sarah Jane in a flood of tears, not knowing where to find either of her parents, inflamed Lucy with the kind of anger she'd never experienced in her life before. Perhaps it was just as well that her negligent husband didn't come home till the early hours, far too late to discuss the matter then. She'd also discovered the near empty tin which she used to save up for her share of the household expenses. It wasn't difficult to guess what had happened to that either.

But it wasn't until after supper the next day that the subject was raised. She'd been quietly fuming all day and as Lucy ladled out meat and potato pie, everyone ate in a subdued silence, as if aware of a storm brewing. Even the children were quieter than usual and as soon as the meal was over, Polly offered to put them to bed while Charlie did the clearing away, shooing the pair off into the front parlour.

The minute the door was closed Lucy calmly enquired where, exactly, he'd spent the previous evening. 'And don't say you went for a swift half because you didn't come home until after two in the morning. No doubt spending the money you stole from my tin.'

'I won't even bother to answer, since you seem to know everything.'

Lucy had vowed that she would remain calm, now she almost screamed at him. 'How could you leave the children alone like that?'

His response was cold to the point of icy. Turning from her, he picked up the paper as he always did when he needed a barrier between them. 'They were perfectly safe. Many kids have been left in worse places during this war. In any case, you're their mother. You shouldn't have left them either.'

'But I left them with *you*, their *father*, while I tried to hang on to my job.'

'I've decided I don't want you working for the Hopkins any more. You won't be going there again, or on any other cleaning jobs for that matter. You'll stop at home in future and look after me and the children.' He didn't even glance up from the paper, the tone of his voice hard and unyielding, as if the matter were settled and there was really no necessity for further discussion.

Lucy's eyes widened in disbelief, half laughing at his obstinacy. 'You can't be serious. Of course I'll be going again. It's a good job, that pays well. How would we manage without it?'

'I shall find a job. No problem. Till then, we can go on the dole, or benefits.'

'Don't be ridiculous.'

He flung the paper aside so violently Lucy took a quick step back, startled by his quick anger. 'Do you need it spelling out? I thought I made it clear last night. I'll not have you seeing Michael Hopkins, and lusting after him.'

Lucy wrapped her arms about herself in a half-defensive gesture and drew in a trembling breath, trying to keep steady and composed. 'I've already explained, Tom, nothing ever happened between us and it won't while you and me are still man and wife, so there's no reason for you to be jealous. But you can't expect things not to have changed. I'm prepared for you to stay here for a bit, till you've time to sort yourself but...'

His hand snaked out to grasp her by the hair and push her back against the wall, making her squeal with surprise, quickly stifled as she didn't wish to alarm the children upstairs. Tom's face was less than an inch from her own, his rage spraying her with spittle. 'Listen! You're *my* wife, not his. And always will be. I've no intention of giving you up. Not to anyone, and certainly not to a bloody conchie.'

Lucy felt the first nudge of fear, a worm of unease that wriggled like a maggot at the back of her mind. 'It was *you*, wasn't it? You put those feathers through his letter box.'

'What if I did? I threw the bloody brick an' all. I saw him kissing and fondling you in that disgusting way in the school yard, so thought I had the right. He deserved everything he got – interfering with my wife.'

A wave of sickness hit her. Hadn't she felt as if someone were watching them from the shadows? Now she knew it must have been Tom. She felt fury more than shame, disgust and loathing at his cunning. 'So why didn't you speak? Why didn't you let me know you were there?'

'Because it was far more interesting to find out what you were up to while I was away.'

'*I've told you, nothing happened!*' She thrust him away, breathing heavily as she resolutely outfaced him. 'I'll have you know that Michael Hopkins is no more a conchie than you are, just not so lucky, and I have proof.' She told him then about Michael's false foot, watching with satisfaction as astonishment dawned on Tom's face, making him look rather like a foolish child.

'Poor man.' Polly's voice from the door, which had quietly opened without either of them hearing it. 'A proud one too by the sound of it.' She walked in bearing a tray of tea cups and a plate of biscuits. 'Something to wet your whistle, eh? Sure and I thought I heard a funny noise. But then you could hear bread being buttered in this house, the walls are that thin.' Polly shrewdly considered her daughter as she set the tray down.

Lucy was shaking too much to answer the question, her eyes riveted on her husband.

Tom stroked a lock of brown curls back from Lucy's face, the tone of his voice now surprisingly soft. 'I was just persuading her round to my way of thinking. Necessary, I think, don't you? The man is obviously taking advantage of her, and since I'm home now, it wouldn't be proper for Lucy to work there any more. I'd prefer her to give in her notice. Don't you agree, Polly?'

'It's true there has been a bit of gossip,' Polly agreed, looking uncomfortable and backing quickly out of the room as if regretting having ventured into this private argument between husband and wife.

Lucy was incensed that Tom should use her own mother against her and very nearly flung the tea at him but, determined to stay in control of herself at least, she quietly sat down and sipped it, for all it was scalding hot and the cup clattered against her teeth. 'I think that decision is up to me, wouldn't you say?'

'I'll not have my wife gossiped about.'

Lucy pressed her lips together, praying for patience. 'If the vindictive old hags in this street choose to be malicious, that's up to them. I don't need to ask anyone's permission about what I do.'

'You need to ask *me*.'

Lucy slammed the cup back in the saucer and was on her feet, shaking with temper, her fury overwhelming her efforts to remain cool, calm and collected. She was quite uncaring of her mother hovering at the other side of the door, probably listening to every word. 'Over my dead body!' she yelled at him. 'You don't rule me, Tom Shackleton, husband or no. I'll make up my own mind what's proper and what isn't.' Whereupon she flew from the room, tears of rage and distress streaming down her face.

Hearing her run upstairs, Polly turned to Charlie in distress. 'It's not working, them living here with us. They need a place of their own.'

–

Fifteen minutes later Polly found her daughter half packed, two sleepy children brought from their beds and already dressed.

'You're not going to him, this fancy man of yours, not because of a silly argument?'

Lucy turned to her children. 'Go on, go and get yourselves downstairs and wait by the front door. Sarah Jane, don't you dare open it till I come.'

After the children had gone, each clutching the soft toy Benny had given them, Lucy confronted her mother, face set with stubborn resolve. 'I've done my best but I don't love Tom any more, for all he's still me husband. And I'll not have him lording it over me, ordering me about as if he alone can decide what I can and cannot do. He left our Sean and Sarah Jane on their own for hours yesterday evening when I went up to Minnie's about my job. That wasn't right. *And* he admits to attacking Michael with a brick, and sending him three white feathers, which is unforgivable.'

'That was jealousy.'

'Whatever the reason, it was a wicked thing to do. Michael's a brave man who fought for his country like the rest, and lost his foot in doing so.'

Polly sat down on the bed while Lucy continued to stuff clothes into a bag, not bothering to fold them. 'You love him don't you?'

She didn't attempt to deny it. 'And he loves me.'

'So you'll risk the vindictive old hags, of being ostracised by everyone?' Polly quietly watched her daughter.

'If he'll have me, which I believe he will, yes. I'd be his wife in the eyes of God, at least, if not the law of the land. Like it or lump it.'

Polly was shaking her head. 'Aw Lucy, m'cushla. If only life were that simple. Sure and wouldn't the shame of it drive you apart in the end. Look what the gossips are already doing to him.' She reached out a hand, but Lucy snatched up the bag and backed away.

'No, don't say anything. I've made up my mind.'

Then Polly did what she'd promised herself she would never do, and set about interfering in her daughter's life. 'Listen to your old mam for once. Haven't I warned you how Tom needs time to heal. As a prisoner of war, he knew what he had to do. Wasn't it all set out for him, plain as the nose on his face? He had to escape and so he did. If he forgot to write, or was too ill to do so, can you not find it in your heart to forgive him? He came home as soon as he could and if he's finding it hard to adjust then you must be patient. Hasn't the war damaged us all? No one said that getting back to normal would be easy, because it never is. But the poor boy is devastated. He thinks he's lost you by his clumsiness. It's a place of your own that the pair of you need, not to be crowded in our front parlour, or in separate beds. You need to give this marriage a chance, to try and make it work for the children's sake at least. Don't they love their Da? And doesn't Tom love you, bless his heart?'

Lucy was staring into her mother's soft face and tears were running unchecked down her cheeks. 'I don't know.'

'I want you to be happy, so I do, but running off with another man isn't the way, m'cushla, and it's sorry I am that you love him so. But if Tom has made mistakes, isn't it only out of jealousy and love for you? Who knows what he's suffered in the past? Ye have to give the poor man a chance.' Lucy was weeping on Polly's shoulder as if her heart were broken, for surely it was.

–

Losing her job was like losing her identity, not simply her independence. Lucy no longer had any money of her own but was entirely dependent upon what Tom handed to her each week out of his dole money. She even missed her daily sparring with the old dragon. And she rarely saw Michael. She found every excuse she could to nip out to the shops on any pretext, just on the off-chance she might see him. But she never did.

Tom wasn't an early riser and one morning, before he was even awake, Lucy slipped up the street to number 179 and waited for him to come out of his front door prompt at six-thirty. She had to see him one more time, if only to explain. He was startled to see her but his face lit up with delight. Grabbing her hand Michael pulled her into Nelson's ginnel and in seconds was covering her face with kisses. It was several moments before either of them had the breath to speak, and it was only to endlessly repeat the inevitable, Michael insisting she should leave Tom, and Lucy trying to explain why she couldn't. Not just yet anyway.

'How can I? The children. Mam. He's still not well but he's determined to make a go of things and he's trying to find us a house. It's all so difficult.'

He was kissing her again, hot fierce kisses that she couldn't get enough of. She felt herself weakening with every blistering kiss, every pulsing touch and caress. Lucy pressed herself shamelessly against him, her fingers threading through his hair, as if by moulding herself to him she could make them one.

'I want you, Lucy.'

'And I want you.' It was the most desperately difficult thing she had ever done but she finally summoned the strength to put a stop to the kisses, even if it was only to lay her hot cheek against his pounding heart.

Michael gently stroked her hair and her mind turned back to VJ Day, to the day she'd received the telegram and her world had fallen apart by the news that her husband was dead, leaving her in a state of shock and disbelief. Somehow she'd learned to accept it, to go on with her life. Yet only a few months later she'd taken a day trip to Belle Vue with her children and fallen in love with this wonderful man.

As she lifted her head and captured his mouth with her own, the sensations of joy were blurred and she felt sick with fear for the future. Nevertheless she was sure that her mother must be right; running off with Michael would only destroy their love and gain them nothing. She didn't protest when he slid open her blouse and caressed her breast, only moaned and threw back her head in an agony of pain and delight. She needed to savour every last moment with him. Did this wanton behaviour make her wicked? Did it mark her as a 'loose woman' as the self-righteous Lily Gantry would no doubt claim. How could it be wicked when it felt so wonderful, so gloriously right? It surprised her that Minnie didn't class her as such. Minnie Hopkins was a constant mystery to her, the kind of woman whose opinions you could never predict.

How full of optimism they'd all been just a few short months ago, glad that the war was over at last, that they were still young with all of life before them even if the first flush of youth had gone. Belinda doing up that old shop, buying a bench and tools for Benny to get started on his dreams, falling in love and marrying him, content to be carrying his child despite the difficulties of making ends meet and dealing with the disapproval of her parents. But Benny had somehow failed to get the allocation licence he needed so that he'd grown more and more desperate and left his new wife too much on her own. Poor Belinda. And now she had even worse problems.

They drew apart at last, Michael begging her not to abandon him completely, to at least meet him now and then whenever she could get away. Lucy was shaking her head, tears standing proud in her eyes as she backed away.

'How can I? Tom would find out. He deserves a chance, a home and a wife to come home to after what he's been through. I have to give him that chance. It's the least I owe him.'

'What about me? Us? I love you, Lucy. I need you desperately.'

She gave a little sob and turning, hurried away through the cobbled ginnel back to Pansy Street, for how could she resist such persuasive arguments when she needed him so badly?

—

Belinda stood holding open her larder door and gazed upon empty shelves. Not even a heel of bread left in the jar. Her stomach ached with hunger since she'd had little more than a bowl of vegetable broth the day before which Polly had brought them. What they would've done without her mother-in-law during these last weeks, she didn't care to consider. But even Polly didn't know the whole truth for Belinda had learned to hide their penurious state, putting on quite an act in order to give the impression all was well.

Pulling a shawl close about her head for warmth, she fished her purse out of a drawer and found that it too was empty. She dropped it back in with a heavy sigh. How much longer could she continue with this pretence? There was not a scrap of food in the house to feed herself, let alone the child growing inside her. Whatever she'd hoped for in Civvy Street, a new career, a life of purpose and meaning, a way of using her intelligence and training, this was far from those dreams.

The papers said that London only had a week of coal left. Well, she didn't have any. It was February and she was now keeping her gloves, scarf and coat on all day in order to combat the near arctic temperatures in the house. Outside, the streets were thick with snow and slush. It was said to be the worst winter on record. Thousands of people had been sent home from work in Manchester as factories closed for lack of power. There was no coal to be had anywhere, despite the fact that tons of the stuff was piled up at the pits, it couldn't be delivered as roads were apparently blocked by drifts as high as ten foot. Even the street lights had been blacked out again, as a conserving measure. She and Benny had been eating by candlelight for days now, and it wasn't in order to find romance. In fact she rarely saw him these days and when she did, he was exhausted.

He spent most of each day tramping the snow-packed streets looking for work, any sort of work. Gone were his hopes now, along with his dreams and the last vestige of pride. But even Polly wasn't able to offer him employment now as she too was laying people off, struggling to stay afloat. Not that he would ever ask her.

For Belinda it was a living nightmare. Living in these two poky rooms had proved to be more dreadful than she could ever have anticipated. Sometimes she heard the landlord hammering on the door, shouting rude words to her as he demanded she come down and pay the rent she owed. She would pull the blanket over her head, for she spent most of the time in bed as the only warm place, and shut her ears. How could she pay him? She had nothing.

Benny was doing his best. She knew that. And without question he loved her but nothing was quite the same. All the fun had gone out of life. They no longer had the energy to enjoy anything, not even their little spats which had nearly always led to lovemaking. Quite out of the question in any case, since she was due in about four weeks. God knows what would happen then. Belinda daren't even think about it except to hope that they'd keep her in the nursing home for ten days or so. The doctor told her the baby was coming along fine, all that healthy free orange juice he gave her to drink, plus cod liver oil and malt. She practically lived on the stuff and didn't dare tell him how meagre the rest of her diet had become.

Worst of all, Benny no longer believed in himself. Every night he moaned at the state he'd reduced them to, and every night she would hold him close and assure him of her continuing faith in him. For all Lucy said he was a dreamer with unrealistic ambitions, Belinda didn't for one moment believe their dire state was all his fault. Perhaps she should have gone to see her father, tackled him face to face and found out just what he was up to. Perhaps she'd been a coward not to. She hadn't done so because she still fervently believed that Benny would make something of himself in the end. Just because he'd kicked over the traces a bit after six years of grinding war service didn't make him bad, only foolish. And everyone was entitled to their independence, and to a dream.

Hunger and frustration caused tears to roll down her cheeks, making her feel giddy and light-headed. Her ankles were swollen and there was a constant stitch in her side. When he came bursting through the door late that evening, covered in snow and freezing cold, he glared at the bare table and then at her.

'Where's my dinner?'

Belinda shook her head. She knew he was at the end of his tether, that like her, he missed the jovial company of his comrades, the routine of army life, even the excitement of war. The last thing he needed right now was to listen to a nagging wife at the end of another fruitless day. But she nursed a terrible fear for her child and their future and no longer had the strength to be quite so mindful of his ego. The accusing words came out of her mouth seemingly of their own accord. 'Where's the money to pay for it?'

His round face grew so red that she thought he might explode. Then he thrust his hand in his pocket, took out a pitiful few coppers and flung them on to the wooden table. Three pennies rolled across its scratched surface, one tipped over the edge and rolled away into a corner. Belinda knew she'd hunt for it on her hands and knees later. For now she wanted only to erase the pain from his beloved face. 'Oh, Benny, what's gone wrong? Why do we quarrel?'

'If you'd stop blaming me for everything, we might not.'

'I don't blame you for anything. You know I don't.' She took her shawl and with it began to brush the snow from his hair, which lay flat to his head, dark and wet, no longer the glowing colour it had once been. She rubbed some life back into his icy cheeks, pulled off his soaking wet coat and hung it up to drip even if there was no heat to dry it. It all came out then, all his pent-up emotion, his sense of failure and hurt pride.

'I've spent days – weeks – looking for a job, a way out of this hole, anything,' he groaned. 'But there isn't one.' Just reading the disappointment in those lovely eyes filled him with guilt, for all it might be tempered by a small nudge of resentment. She'd let him down too, this woman he'd loved so much. She hadn't lifted him out of his world, only driven him deeper into it because of her dratted family. Not that he could say as much to her for he knew, in his heart, that nobody could tell Hubert what to do. Instead he said, 'I didn't ask you to take on this poky shop, did I? Look what trouble you've landed us in. I could've used my demob money for summat decent if I hadn't been saddled with this white elephant.'

Belinda wrung out the sleeves of his coat, trying not to let the words hurt her, for she knew he didn't truly mean them. He was just thrashing out at the injustice of life, as she was. 'I thought it would help.'

'Well it hasn't, has it? There's hundreds of soldiers, airmen and sailors all coming home from the war, all looking for work, and now this bleedin' weather. What am I supposed to do?' It sickened him. Six years fighting to end up on the scrap heap.

Benny flung away his chair, face tight with anger. 'I'm going down to the pub, happen I can win a bob or two on t'dominoes. I'll at least find a bit of peace,' and he stormed out, slamming the door on her sad face and his own guilt.

A voice prodded at the back of his mind as he strode through the slush and ice, *If you don't watch out you'll lose her. Then where'll you be?* He got as far as the pub door then turned on his heel and marched all the way back again, gathered Belinda in his arms and wept.

'I'll get work soon. I swear it.' That night they lay with arms wrapped about each other, as happy as they'd ever been.

The next day when he'd gone out again in search of work to carry out his promise, Belinda pulled a cardboard box out from under the bed and considered its sparse contents. Clothes had never been particularly important to her. She'd never pretended to be a fashion plate. Even so, the peacock blue dress had been special. She remembered buying it in Cairo, and all the parties and dances she'd enjoyed in it, the friends she'd made. Laughter and sunshine to hold back the shadow of fear, which was always present in war. Now she wrapped the dress carefully in newspaper and pushing it under her arm, walked down the street, head held high even as tears rolled down her cheeks.

Her humiliation was complete when the pawnbroker gave her only five shillings on it, claiming he was being generous at that. She'd bought it at Harrods for thirty pounds, in the days when she'd been young and foolish and money hadn't seemed to matter. Now she was using it to buy bread and cheese.

The invitation when it came the next day, took Belinda by surprise. Recognising her father's handwriting on the envelope she lacked the courage to open it and propped it against the teapot. It was Benny, coming in from the bedroom where he'd been shaving from a bowl of water in front of a cracked mirror, who ripped it open.

'Good lord, he wants us to come to tea. On Sunday.'

Belinda was so startled she was forced to sit down before her legs gave way. Perhaps it was because she was having a baby that she couldn't seem to deal with emotional upset quite so easily these days. She told Benny that of course they wouldn't go and an argument ensued which lasted throughout supper, though since that was only soup and bread and dripping, Belinda really didn't have the energy to fight any more, so Benny won.

Chapter Sixteen

Belinda rather hoped the buses wouldn't be running but when Sunday came they wrapped up well and caught one easily into the city centre, then changed to the number seventeen which took them up Park Road. There were heaps of dirty snow at either side of the road but at least the bus was able to get through. They got off at the end of Cherry Crescent and Belinda had never felt more nervous in her life.

'This is a bad idea.'

'They're your parents,' Benny insisted. 'It could be just the break we need. It's long past time you made it up with them.'

'But what if my father tells me *never to darken his door again!*' She adopted a humorously dramatic tone, although the sound came out hollow and foolish. Hubert Clarke was an easy man to argue with but a hard one to cross.

'He sent for us,' Benny reminded her. 'He must have a reason. Happen he wants to forgive and forget,' and since she couldn't imagine this for one minute, Belinda lapsed into a brooding silence. She would be polite, calm, non-controversial, she promised herself, for he was still her father.

They stood at the familiar door with its cracked varnish and stained glass window while Benny pressed the bell. A jangling sound echoed along the hall and up the empty stairs behind it and Belinda couldn't help remembering the day she'd arrived home, fresh and still young, brimful of confidence. Now she felt old, and beaten by life.

It was her mother who answered. Joanna stood and gazed upon her daughter and son-in-law as if she had never seen them in her life before, nor had the first idea what to say to them. Her eyes seemed to be riveted upon Belinda's voluptuous figure, as if the letter she'd received giving her this glad news months ago had not registered until this moment.

'Mother. How lovely to see you. Are you well?'

Joanna managed a half smile then stepped aside without a word, and let them precede her into the house.

—

The four of them sat in the chilly front parlour where they took tea, brought in on a tea trolley by Joanna as if they were strangers who had to be impressed with the best china, and the sight of a neatly folded fan of white paper in the empty fire grate. Belinda thought it typical of her father's pettiness that he had denied them a fire for all he might blame the state of the country. It was so cold a frost rimed the inside of the windows, and she recalled with longing the warm fug of the kitchen with its huge old fashioned Aga, where apparently they were no longer welcome.

Hubert sat ramrod straight in his wing-backed chair, glowering at them as he sipped at his tea, or pinched the tips of his moustache between finger and thumb. He swallowed whole one or two of Joanna's tiny egg sandwiches, leaving the butterfly cakes and scones untouched.

The silence threatened to become oppressive. Benny set down his cup and saucer with a snap, glad to be rid of the bother of trying to balance it while he ate, drew in a deep breath and beamed proudly as he indicated his wife. 'She's looking well, eh? Less than a month to go now.'

All eyes turned to Belinda who felt herself growing bright pink beneath the scrutiny. She hadn't wanted this meeting, had only agreed to come because the larder remained frighteningly empty, as was her savings account. She'd also realised that Benny was determined on this family reunion and nothing would change his mind until he saw for himself what a hopeless case her parents were. 'I'm simply going to have a baby, that's all,' she said. 'A perfectly normal state of affairs.'

'Bit of a shaker at first, mind,' Benny said, nudging Belinda and almost upsetting her cup. 'I was a bit stunned when I first heard. But think on it, Mr Clarke. A new offshoot to the family tree. That's summat to be proud of, eh?'

'I fail to see why, when it will bear your name and not mine.'

Benny looked nonplussed. This was the last reaction he'd expected. He had been absolutely certain that a man of Hubert Clarke's stature would be secretly delighted to welcome a new grandson, that Belinda's condition had been the reason for the offered olive branch.

Joanna saved the situation. She got up from her seat and went to her daughter, arms outstretched. 'Well I, for one, am delighted for you, darling. Having a baby is a wonderful joy. May I – may I kiss you?' And after an initial awkwardness on Belinda's part, mother and daughter were hugging each other, mopping up tears and both talking at the same time. After which display of affection they disappeared upstairs together, arm in arm.

Benny sank back in his chair with a sigh of relief, his grin stretching just about as wide as it could go. 'There we are then, all breaches healed. Don't it do your heart good to see it?' In his experience, families might fall out but they always made up in the end. Certainly his own did. No matter what cross purposes there might be at times between himself and his mam, or even with Lucy, they all pulled together in times of trouble.

'Indeed,' Hubert agreed, his tone as cold as the ice feathering the bay windows.

'Perhaps now,' Benny earnestly remarked, 'you and I should talk, man to man as it were. Get matters on a proper footing.' He was so beset by sudden nervousness that he stuffed a whole triangle of egg sandwich into his mouth, quickly followed by a slurp of tea.

Hubert grimaced. 'That might be productive.'

He'd been right all along. Wasn't a father supposed to help his daughter, and offer a helping hand to a new member of the family? Everything was going to work out fine. 'Well, you go first. Ask me anything you like, I've nothing to be ashamed of. Then I'll ask you. How would that be?'

Hubert smoothed the ends of his moustache. 'An excellent notion.'

Benny reached for another egg sandwich. They were so tiny he could eat a dozen but was managing to restrain his hunger. 'Fire away.'

'Where, and how, were you intending my grandson, or granddaughter, to be brought up?' Hubert coolly enquired and taking this interest as a good sign, Benny carefully explained that although there were no jobs to be found at present because of all the returning servicemen, the bad weather and strikes and so on, he had plans. Anxious to impress he hurried on to outline them, saying how he needed only a modest amount of capital to set himself up in business.

'Buying and selling household goods and furniture, there lies the future,' he expounded, 'as I'm sure you'll agree.' Hubert merely raised one brow, saying nothing and, beginning to relax, Benny pulled a packet of woodbine from his pocket, offered Hubert one and when he declined with a shake of the head, lit up one for himself.

'Our biggest problem, apart from the lack of capital, as I said, is where we're living. It's not good enough for Belinda.'

'I'm sure you're right.'

Pleased he was striking the right note, Benny ploughed on. 'It seems to me that a man of property such as yourself, wouldn't want his grandson to be brought up in the vicinity of Pansy Street.'

'It's a pity you didn't consider the matter more carefully before things reached this parlous state.'

Benny wasn't sure what parlous meant but doubted it was complimentary. 'There's still time,' he reasoned. 'The child isn't born yet.' Eager to explain further about his plans he shuffled forward in his seat so he could flick the ash from his cigarette into the fire grate. He missed and hit the faded Persian rug instead.

Mindful of his manners he got up and rubbed the ash in with his heel and swiftly apologised. Manfully swallowing the choking sensation that was tightening his chest, Hubert asked, 'And how much – capital – did you have in mind?'

Benny leaned back in his seat, feeling increasingly comfortable that Hubert was genuine in wanting to help. He mentioned a sum and seeing his expression of disbelief, hastened to adjust it. 'I reckon I could manage with less if you'd agree to us moving in here. Just till we get going like and can afford a place of us own. I mean, you're not short of space, are you? More bedrooms than you know what to do with, eh?' He was babbling now and Benny knew it but somehow felt himself too far down the road he'd chosen to back out of it. All he could do was hope for a good reception to his ideas, for Belinda's sake. 'We only need one, for us and the baby. Belinda's mam could help look after it. She'd enjoy that I'm sure, which would mean Belinda could get a bit of a job if she wanted one. I'm not a stuffy, old fashioned husband, like some. Belinda's a smart lass with a brain in her head. I've no objection to my wife working.'

'I'm sure you haven't. Your plans seem… substantial. You think big, I can tell.'

Benny swelled out his chest with pride. 'Oh, I'm a born enter-entpren…'

'Entrepreneur?' offered Hubert drily.

'Aye, that's it. Never short of ideas isn't Benny Pride. It runs in the family, don't you know. It'd all be above board of course. A proper loan. Only if I borrow from you instead of a bank manager, you wouldn't be likely to charge nearly so much in the way of interest, now, would you? It being all in the family as it were.'

Hubert leaned forward in his chair, hands lightly clasped, elbows resting on his knees. His tone was mild, ponderous. 'Let me see if I've got this right. You wish to live in *my* house, have *my* wife help look after your infant while borrowing money from *me* on a low rate of interest, so you can set up this business plan to be a–an entrepreneur. Is that about the size of it?'

'Got it in one.'

Hubert's voice dropped to a low whisper. 'And what's in it for me?'

'I beg your pardon?'

'What do I get out of this scheme of yours?' The question took Benny by surprise but before he could fathom a reply, Hubert continued, 'I expect you think you can have an easy ride because you've married Belinda. Well, in my view you've messed her life up completely.' His voice remained quiet, even meditative, but Benny didn't much care for what he was saying. If he said owt wrong about Belinda, he'd clock him one, father-in-law or not.

'If I were to put up the money for this… enterprise, and I haven't said that I will yet,' holding up one cautionary hand as Benny's eyes lit up, 'I reckon I deserve a favour in return. Wouldn't you say that was fair? I'd have a few terms of my own.'

Benny frowned. 'What sort of terms?'

He reached for the whisky decanter. 'Well then, let me tell you what I have in mind.'

Chapter Seventeen

Charlie had been to see the doctor again, his heart and lungs given a clean bill of health, which was a great relief. Polly had been afraid he might have angina or leukemia, or something else seriously life-threatening. When she'd expressed her relief about that, Charlie, twisted with pain, had said no, he'd definitely live – unfortunately. The pain of the arthritis got him down at times, though he was making some improvement with the tablets the doctor had given him. Sometimes he allowed Polly to rub embrocation into his muscles at night. At other times he nearly screamed when she touched him. It made her feel so helpless, so out of control. But the doctor insisted that he rest and not inflame the joints, which meant he was never going to be the fit man he'd once been. This meant it was even more important that she make a success of manufacturing.

Polly had invested heavily in washing and dyeing machines as well as the second-hand loom from the mill at Hebden Bridge. Despite the difficulties everyone was experiencing in these difficult times, they were already producing several yards of carpet a week which the girls stitched together to fit any size of room.

When Benny burst in, demanding to speak to her right away, she was helping her old mate Maisie Wright, whom she'd taken on as a spool setter, to arrange the different shades of bobbins in their correct pattern grid on a large square table.

'By heck,' Maisie said. 'The lad looks like he's just landed in a parachute,' referring to Benny's dishevelled, excited appearance.

He was so full of himself, that he was well on with his tale by the time Polly ushered him into her office and closed the door.

She regarded her son with eyes narrowed in shrewd speculation. 'Are ye saying that you've changed your mind, that you'll come into the business after all? Honest to God, I never thought to hear the day. So what brought about this change of heart?'

'I've been talking to Hubert.' Hands in pockets and rocking on his heels since he was quite unable to stand still, Benny tossed the name out as if he were quite familiar with using his father-in-law's Christian name.

'Hubert?'

'Hubert Clarke, Belinda's...'

'I know who he is. But what does Hubert Clarke have to do with your coming into the business with me, assuming I survive this terrible winter, that is.' Indeed she thought she could guess, following their earlier discussion about their respective children, and almost smiled to herself as Benny squirmed with embarrassment. How he hated to lose face.

Relieved as he was to get help, Benny had, in fact, been rather shaken by the interview with his father-in-law. Hubert had made it crystal clear that whatever he'd suffered thus far with problems over a licence, petitions and eviction notices, not forgetting being set upon in dark alleys, was nothing in comparison to what could happen if he didn't co-operate.

At first he'd almost been prepared to take the risk in order to hang on to his prized independence, rather than have his father-in-law take what seemed like complete control of his life, let alone interfere in his mam's business. But then he thought of Belinda, and the empty cupboard, not to mention imminent fatherhood, and somehow he'd managed to swallow his pride and hear him out.

After a while Benny recognised many advantages in the plan, besides providing the security they so desperately needed. He saw no reason not to go along with the idea. Wasn't it worth losing his pride and independence if he could keep his family safe? And who knew where it could all lead? The plan had the added benefit of a proper role for himself, as well as burying the hatchet as it were, and pleasing both sets of parents in one go. All of which surely had to be beneficial for everyone concerned. He just had to persuade his mother to agree. 'I thought you wanted me to come in with you.'

'I do.' Polly decided to play along, resolving not to let him see how she'd been the instigator of Hubert's sudden interest in his son-in-law. 'I just don't understand what changed your mind.'

'Because I can recognise a good idea when I see one. Just for once, Mam, hear me out without interrupting. It'd work like this...' And he set about carefully explaining the deal.

Polly's eyes narrowed thoughtfully as he talked, and sank into a chair while Benny paced back and forth in the office.

Hubert, as a credit trader and wholesaler, would supply Polly with goods at competitive wholesale prices. She must buy exclusively from him to get the best terms but could then sell the goods either at normal retail price to her own customers, or at a higher credit price to the club customers he sent her. They would bring with them a voucher to an agreed value which they paid off week by week at a shilling in the pound. Ron, Hubert's son, did the collecting, he explained, and if folk got behind in their payment or did a moonlight flit, it was Hubert who stood the loss.

This was the last thing Polly had been expecting, for Hubert to come up with a plan which included her. 'Why doesn't he sell his wholesale goods to his own customers direct?'

'Because that would turn his business into a retail operation. He'd have to take on shop premises, employ staff to display, sell and wrap the goods which all costs money. He makes his profit by selling in bulk to his suppliers, and through his credit club. He does well, Mam. There's no flies on him.'

Polly drily remarked that she didn't wonder at it since he seemed to be playing the fiddle from both ends, but Benny wasn't to be distracted. He continued with his explanation. 'You can't lose. He already has the customers waiting for somewhere to spend their money. Of course, you couldn't do all of this from the warehouse. You'd have to take on a shop, a big one, in the city centre.'

'No.'

'What?'

'I said no. The rates and rents of city centre premises are too high. They'd cripple us.'

Admittedly this had been Hubert's response too when Benny had made the suggestion to him. Now he shrugged philosophically as he conceded defeat. 'All right then, off centre, close to Castlefield, Salford or wherever you think suitable, only it must be *retail* premises. No reason why you can't keep the warehouse on for storage and your carpet manufacture,' he airily conceded, as if money were no object. Polly, her mind racing ahead, homed in on this point.

'And where is all the capital coming from for such ambitious expansion, might I enquire?'

'Oh, you don't have to worry, most of the finance is all set up. You only need find enough to take on and fit out a shop and Hubert will provide the stock on sale or return. He also says that if you need it, he can offer you ample credit on an interest free loan. He can't say fairer than that, now can he?'

'Why?' Polly's eyes glinted with suspicion. 'Why would he be so generous?'

Benny's whole body became taut, rigid with tension as he rested his knuckles on the polished desk, desperately holding on to his rapidly diminishing patience. Why were old people so over-cautious? Was it any wonder he'd refused his mother's invitation to work with her. It was an attitude which would have to change. 'Because we're family now, and it's in his interests to help the business to grow. The profit margins are high enough for us both to make a good living out of it.'

Polly insisted he explain it all over again, from start to finish, till she had it clear in her head. But she was sorely tempted by the offer of a secure customer base, most of all by the prospect of having Benny come in to the business with her. What better than to be working with her own son, just as she'd always dreamed of, with peace declared between them at last.

'I'll give it some thought,' she promised him, while deep down she wondered how she could refuse, when she was the one who'd set the whole thing in motion.

–

Tom found them a house to rent just a few doors down at number 67. It would need some attention before they could move in, but a bit of painting and decorating would work wonders, he was sure. Weren't women supposed to be expert in such matters these days? It would keep Lucy nicely occupied instead of pining over that stupid job and Michael bloody Hopkins. She was, however, less than enchanted about the whole idea.

'Can we afford it?' Whether out of guilt, or perhaps conceding much of what her mother said to be true, Lucy didn't feel able to dismiss the suggestion out of hand, despite her fears of more intimate relations with him.

'I wouldn't be taking it on if I didn't think so,' Tom snapped. 'Besides, I've an interview for a job lined up, at the dye works on Liverpool Road.'

'Fenton's place?'

'That's the one. It would be good money.' He was excited, so pleased with himself that Lucy couldn't help but feel glad for him. He'd fought in the war, been a POW for years, suffered untold horrors of which he refused to speak and escaped only to return to a wife who was having an affair with another man. No wonder he was scratchy. At times she felt nothing but shame at her own behaviour. He surely deserved better than she'd been able to offer him? And it wasn't as if she enjoyed cleaning people's houses. If it weren't for this madness of loving Michael she would surely have been delighted to have him back, have welcomed him with open arms.

Tentatively he put out a hand to stroke her hair. He rarely touched her and she felt almost flattered that he felt able to do so now, while at the same time nervous it might encourage him to go further. 'I want to make you happy, Lucy. I want us to have a chance. We need time together like a proper married couple.'

She quietly moved out of his reach, aware that here, in her mother's house, they never had a moment alone and secretly welcoming that fact. He believed this to be the main problem between them, that once he had his wife to himself he could make her fall in love with him all over again. Lucy wondered if that were true.

She remembered how she'd once waited so eagerly for him to come home, how young and excited she had been when they'd first married, believing the war would be merely a blink in their young lives, over in no time, not rob them of their youth completely. She'd been madly in love with Tom Shackleton for as long as she could remember, though perhaps she'd simply been in love with life, and youth, and the idea of marriage. He'd made it so enchantingly easy with his good looks and undoubted charm. Now she'd changed, grown up. So had Tom. Neither of them were the people they'd once been.

'I'll give it a try,' she agreed.

As they worked together, cleaning the little house, Tom's behaviour continued to trouble her. Everything had to be just so, sweeping brushes carefully washed after they'd been used and left to dry in the open, not put away dusty. The floors scrubbed over and over again. Every scrap of wood skirting or window frame had to be scoured a dozen times before he would let her anywhere near with a paint brush. Not even cleaning cloths were allowed to get soiled and if they were, he made her boil them till they were white again. It all seemed far more tiring than it need be but Lucy put it all down to the difficulties he'd experienced as a POW. He was ill and would get better, given time. Her one consolation was that he showed endless patience with the children.

Sean was enjoying having his dad around now, if behaving a bit silly and wild, always wanting to show off in front of him, which was understandable as the little boy craved his attention. Sarah Jane, on the other hand remained shy but then she'd always been a quiet, timid sort of child. She was old enough to remember the shock of losing her dad, and needed time to readjust to him being alive. As did they all. But Tom could easily tease her into blushes and giggles and very slowly she was coming round to accepting him. Polly said it was up to Lucy to encourage the relationship, for them to spend more time together as a family.

'Don't rush it, Mam,' Lucy would say, still wary. Yet when they moved, that's exactly what would happen. Lucy worried over how it would feel not to have Polly around, almost as if she needed her mother's protection, although from what, she couldn't imagine, apart from the increasing intimacy she dreaded.

She couldn't help noticing that the stories Tom told of his escape and illness varied slightly from day to day, depending on his mood. Sometimes he spoke of Italy, at other times France or even Africa, but never about conditions in the POW camp. All she knew was that he'd been taken to Germany after Italy surrendered.

But none of it quite added up and Lucy wondered just what he really had been up to during those missing years, certain he was holding something back. His letters had always been sporadic and, even allowing for the censor, oddly vague and unsatisfactory. Perhaps there was a woman in his past somewhere. A part of her rather hoped so, then she wouldn't be the only one with guilt on her conscience.

He'd walked back into her life as cool as you please and seemed to think he could pick up exactly where they'd left off. When she'd needed him he hadn't been there for her, hadn't even written. Now that she was in love with someone else, he'd come home. How unfair life could be.

Later that day, scrubbing the stone-flagged kitchen floor in the house she didn't want to live in, with a man she could no longer look upon as a husband, Lucy could see Michael's face in the swirls of soapy water. She couldn't get her need for him out of her mind, out of her aching body even as she knew that she must never seek him out again. Never! Heaven knows what would happen if one of them didn't learn to exercise some control over their emotions.

She must accept that whatever had been growing between them, was over.

Tiring of the endless chores, she flung the scrubbing brush back into the bucket, sending water spraying everywhere and wasn't quite sure whether it was tears or dirty mopping water that she wiped from her face.

Chapter Eighteen

The manufacturing of new carpets was progressing well for Polly. The wool arrived in soft, unwashed hanks from the west coast of Scotland. The washing was done in a long trough with the wool being fed around huge drums on the same principle as a mangle. As she watched the process with some degree of pride, Polly was hoping and praying that her daughter's marriage would survive and Lucy would be happy. Many didn't in these difficult times. She and Charlie had had it easy in a way, with no war to separate them and always having the family around but it had torn apart her family all the same. Soon, for the first time in their married lives there would be just the two of them. Not that she minded. Charlie might get more rest.

She walked from the washing room into the dyeing area, and became quickly embroiled in a long discussion on the varying shades of green. Customers liked a strong pattern in their carpets but not necessarily strong colours.

'This bright green didn't sell so well, Polly,' Josh, her chief dyer, told her. 'Better to soften it to more of a leaf shade don't you think?'

'And a pinky beige to go with it?'

Polly personally traced out the patterns on to squared paper, each square representing one tuft in the carpet, usually at a rate of seven to eleven tufts per inch depending on the quality of the carpet. Drawing the designs was one of her favourite tasks. Sales were buoyant and she longed to buy more looms, to expand, but was nervous of doing this too quickly and overextending herself. She'd always thought there was little point in building the business too big if her children weren't interested. Now that Benny had agreed to come in with her, the situation had changed dramatically. It would be a relief to have more help, even though she still held some reservations about Hubert Clarke and his scheme. By the time she'd finished the day's work it was past eight and she had energy to do no more than grab a meal and fall into bed.

'All this hard work,' she groaned, rubbing her aching back, 'and for what?'

'For us, sweetheart,' Charlie murmured sleepily into her ear. 'For our lovely family and to keep us in our old age.'

'And will we take the risk, as Benny wants us to?'

'Would it make you happy?'

'I think it would, Charlie.'

'Then do it. If you're happy, so am I,' and cuddling up like a pair of old spoons, they fell asleep in perfect contentment.

So Polly took the risk. She took out a small mortgage on her house, rented large shop premises at the Castlefield end of Deansgate and took delivery of a consignment of furniture from Hubert Clarke. Pride Carpets now moved in a new direction, into buying and selling, though she continued with, and even hoped to expand, the manufacturing of new carpet. Credit trading would not have been her first choice but if it made Benny happy, wasn't that something?

–

Benny felt like a real man again. From the very first morning he stayed late without complaint and put all his energies into the job. On his first pay day, he gave Belinda a bit of money to spend on a new frock, if she could find one to fit, just to cheer her up but she said it would be a waste and hoarded it away for when the baby was born. At least she was eating properly again. She queued at the butchers for a bit of steak and kidney, which she made into a steamed pudding. They ate like kings and she bloomed as a result. It was worth all the effort to see her happy again.

All family differences seemed to be resolved with what might tentatively be called a reconciliation between Belinda and her parents. Benny felt content to be working with his mother, as it was on equal terms. And this was only the beginning. As the business grew, moving ever onward and upward, nothing and no one would stand in his way. Since his father-in-law was a self-made man with an innate shrewdness and business acumen, Benny had every confidence in his judgement.

-

Being so close to her time, Belinda didn't care to spend too much time on her own, so took to spending the afternoons with Lucy. She was able to do little beyond brew tea and chat while her friend trimmed and pasted the wallpaper, and climbed ladders to hang it, nevertheless she was happy and content. There was much giggling at Lucy's mistakes, not least when Sean and Sarah Jane got themselves covered in paste as they helped to mix it.

Sometimes the two girls would wrap the children up well and take them sledging on the waste ground, or for a walk along by the Manchester Ship Canal to watch the barges go by. Lucy would talk of her hopes for Tom to heal and be like the Tom she remembered. But she never quite found the courage to mention her secret love. Belinda would say how content she was now that everything had come right for Benny at last, and how happy she was, despite missing her ATS friends.

'However, I'm sick of this huge bump, and I cry with frustration sometimes over the most simplest task.' She giggled. 'Like starching Benny's shirt collars. I made too much starch the other day and without thinking, I tipped the remains all down the yard thinking it would mix with the snow and slush, but it made such a terrible slimy mess you took your life in your hands just crossing the yard to the lavatory.' The two girls dissolved into helpless laughter, young and happy, oblivious for a short time to all their problems.

Tom did not get the job at Fenton's Chemicals because he never went for the interview. There was a problem standing in his way and, determined to find employment so that Lucy wouldn't get any fancy ideas in her head about going back to work herself, he meant to solve it.

He called upon his brother-in-law and found Benny, surprisingly enough, in the new shop sticking price labels on a set of chairs. It was already open for business and several customers were browsing among the carefully designed furniture displays. Tom leaned against the door jamb and chuckled. 'I thought your job was to run the show from a fancy office and let some chit of a girl write out price labels.'

Benny grinned. 'I don't mind doing my bit. It's all profit in the till at the end of the day. Anyroad, we're a bit short staffed.'

'Sounds like I could be the answer to your prayers then, if you can sort out a little problem for me.'

'I wouldn't have thought you had any problems, now you're back in dear old Blighty.'

'I had to make Lucy give up her job. She was seeing too much of that Michael Hopkins.' Tom was relieved to see Benny nodding wisely, as if he understood. 'But we have to live, which means work. But before I can get a job, I need papers. An identity card. Right?'

Benny frowned. 'Not if you have your AB64. Your army book will do just as well.'

'But I don't have one of those either. I lost it some place.'

'So go to…'

'Look, it's not as easy as all that. Can we talk, in private?' Benny led Tom into his office, which was cramped and not very tidy but he could at least close the door, take a bottle of Scotch from a cupboard and pour them both a nip without anyone seeing. He offered Tom a cigarette and propped himself against the desk to listen. Within seconds of Tom launching into his tale, Benny's mouth was hanging open and he'd forgotten all about the cigarette which burned to ash between his fingers. He disposed of it and lit another.

'Are you saying that you weren't a POW at all?' Benny was riveted with shock.

Tom shrugged. 'I was wounded at Salerno, as were many others in that quagmire of mud and misery, very nearly captured but I managed to get away. You see...'

'You *deserted?*' Despite himself, Benny was appalled. Admittedly he'd had a safe war, more uncomfortable than dangerous. Even so, he'd done his bit and he didn't care for deserters, not one bit. Nobody did. Couldn't stomach them at any price, as a matter of fact. Yet this was his brother-in-law, married to his sister. Even so... 'Don't say any more. I don't want to know.'

'*I* didn't say I was a deserter. *You* did. I said I lost my papers.'

'You'll never get away with it. Someone will shop you.'

'Why should they? So far as the neighbours are concerned I was a POW, escaped, lost, and now home. End of story. There's plenty of other chaps coming home daily with similar tales to tell. I thought, since you were once in the same boat, seeking official documentation that is, you'd understand my situation and be prepared to help.'

'Not me.' Benny felt relieved he could honestly wriggle out of this obligation. 'I never managed to sort out a licence. I'm having nothing more to do with either joinering nor bureaucracy. I'd be no help.'

'Yes you would, by giving me a job – here. We're family, after all, and you want your Lucy to be happy, don't you? You wouldn't want her to run out on our marriage.' Benny scowled, for this was all too true. The last thing he wanted was for her to run off with Michael Hopkins, a known conchie. 'Wouldn't you just love to get one over on them bureaucrats for once, eh, by ignoring all the niceties of paperwork?'

Benny's cigarette had again burned away to ash and he stubbed it out in his glass, sighing deeply and not bothering to light another. This all sounded very complicated and a bit worrying.

'I don't know, Tom. I would help, if I could, you know that. But I'm not on my own here. There's Mam to consider, and she always likes things above board.'

'What about Hubert Clarke? Is he quite so particular?'

Benny shrugged. 'Couldn't say. You'd have to ask him.'

'Mebbe I will. But not a word to your Lucy about this conversation, right? It's just between you and me. Man to man. One squaddie to another.' And since Benny thought it in his family's best interests for Lucy to stay with her husband, rather than go off with Michael Hopkins, he reluctantly agreed. What Lucy didn't know surely couldn't hurt her. Who was he to judge? Salerno had been a mess. Everybody said so.

Tom wasted no time in going to see Hubert Clarke who, after considering the young man with interest and some curiosity agreed to look into the problem for him. It took little more than a week to produce the paperwork he needed.

'I'm grateful.'

'I might need you to show me how much, one day,' Hubert said. In his experience it never hurt to have folk owe him the odd favour.

Polly took little persuading to put her son-in-law on the pay roll, in the firm belief that she was doing her own daughter a good turn. Lucy, on the other hand, was less delighted. She felt as if her nose had been pushed very slightly out of joint, since everyone in the family was now in the business, except herself.

The job Tom was given, however, wasn't nearly so congenial as he'd hoped, comprising chiefly of filling and emptying dye vats, and the money was poor. He grumbled about it constantly: the pay, the hours, the people he worked with.

'It's a start,' Lucy would say. 'Plenty of time to better yourself later, as you get fitter.' Sometimes, watching him work on their little house, she would be pleased and surprised at just how fit he seemed to be, for an ex-POW. He was making good progress and perhaps a part of her hoped that as soon as he was entirely fit and well and himself again, everything would either come right between them, or better still she could leave him to get on with his own life without any sense of guilt. Despite her best efforts to make this marriage work, Lucy still ached for Michael with every fibre of her being.

She tried suggesting that they'd make more progress if she too went back to work but he wouldn't hear of it. He didn't approve of her going anywhere for that matter, not even to the pictures. She felt like a prisoner now. Lucy constantly chaffed against the restrictions he imposed upon her. Even if she slipped out to the shops, or for a walk with Belinda and the children, she had to leave a note, to say where she was and what time she would be back. She understood why he didn't trust her but it didn't make for an easy life. She could only hope the tension between them would ease as his mental health improved.

And, like it or not, she was forced to spend hours searching Campfield market for bargain cuts, cheap titbits of offal or pork scratchings. Anything to add a bit of flavour to a dull meal. Lucy would queue for hours if she heard there'd been a delivery of sausages. She'd smile sweetly at Mr Shaw the grocer in his long white apron in the hope that he had a bit of bacon, or better still a pat of butter tucked under the counter somewhere. Sometimes she'd believe fortune was about to smile on her and then a man would come in and he'd always be served first, whether he marched boldly to the front or attempted to hang back. It didn't seem to matter whether he'd fought at the front or done nothing more taxing than dish up stew for the pilots, he was considered to be a war hero and would be treated as such. Sometimes, when she'd queued for hours and there was nothing left, it seemed grossly unfair, though not for a moment did she complain of any of this to Tom.

On one such occasion as she came hurrying away in triumph with half a dozen sausages, her head down because it was raining, she ran straight into Michael. She tried to back away but her heart was racing, her insides ached with need for him and her body simply wouldn't move in any direction but into his arms. He led her quickly under the railway arches where he wasted no time in kissing her, despite the rain having soaked both of them by this time.

'God, I love you. I need you so much. Why do you stay with him?'

'Because he's my husband, the father of my children,' she protested, craving more of his kisses, more caresses. She felt a crazy mix of emotion and divided loyalties swirling madly within her.

'But you don't love him.' He slid a damp hand beneath her coat to softly caress her.

'He's ill. He needs me. How could I simply turn him out on the streets? It wouldn't be right.' Lucy took his hand and pushed it inside her blouse. The sensation of his cold wet skin against hers made her gasp and she missed what he said next, something about them being happy together for ever and ever. 'I know,' she murmured, teasing his mouth open with her tongue. Then he was grasping her by the arms, thrusting her from him and glaring fiercely into her flushed face.

'We could go away together, you, me and the children. No one would ever find us. Ever.'

'I can't. I really can't.'

Then his mouth came down on hers without mercy as, crushing her to him, he half lifted her from the ground and with her arms wrapped about his neck, Lucy hung on, as if every atom of her happiness depended upon this man. Which in truth it did.

She was crying as she hurried home but nobody could tell because of the rain. She saw Tom the minute she turned the corner into Pansy Street, standing there in the pouring rain without cap or raincoat.

'You'll catch your death,' she said, but he didn't reply, only grabbed her arm and marched her smartly down the street in full view of every twitching curtain straight into her mother's house, just as if she were a naughty child. She could only feel thankful that Polly and Charlie weren't home yet. Ignoring the fearful thumping of her heart, Lucy calmly apologised for being late, explaining that she'd been chatting with Belinda and forgot the time, her fingers crossed against the lie.

'You said you'd be home by six and you weren't. See you don't let it happen again.'

'Or what?' she laughed, determined not to be intimidated.

His face as he turned towards her gave the answer. Never had she seen such hatred, such anger. Was this what jealousy did? Lord, what had she done to him? Shame bit deep and Lucy watched in silence as he pulled his soiled work shirt over his head, tossed it to the floor and reached for a clean one off the airing rack.

'Are you going out?'

'Aye. So look sharp. I'm hungry.'

Wisely saying no more, Lucy quickly made the tea, fed and washed the children and put them to bed, then sat quietly mending his socks on the darning mushroom while he shaved, tied a muffler about his neck and shrugged into his jacket.

'Don't wait up,' he told her. Lucy agreed, with some gratitude, that she wouldn't.

It was on the first night together in their new home that Tom decided the moment had come to exercise his 'rights.' The children had been put to bed after the entire family had enjoyed the treat of a bag of chips each, to celebrate this new beginning, and because with all the packing and unpacking, moving and sorting, Lucy hadn't had time to cook.

After supper she deliberately took her time fussing over her few clothes, laying the children's things away in their own drawers, interleaved with lavender mothballs to keep them fresh. They felt strange, having a bedroom of their own and she read them two stories before they settled. Even then Sean came downstairs for a glass of water the minute she left him. 'Can't I sleep with you?' he asked, confused by the constant changes in his life.

'No, love. You're a big boy now.'

'Or at Michael's house?'

Alarmed that Tom might have heard, Lucy quickly picked up the little boy and carried him back up to bed. 'Why would you want to do that when your dad's here,' she soothed. 'He might even take you fishing, if you ask him nicely.'

The little boy brightened. 'When? Tomorrow?'

Lucy tucked her son back beneath the sheets, kissing Sarah Jane again, so she didn't feel left out. 'Not another word. Go to sleep this minute,' and the pair screwed their eyes tight shut, still giggling as she slipped out of the room. At the bedroom door she paused and whispered, 'Don't forget now, I'm only in the next room if you need me.' As she rather hoped they might. Then leaving the door ajar she drew in a shuddering breath and went to wait for her husband.

She felt sick with nerves. This was worse than she'd imagined, worse than a new bride on her wedding night. At least then she'd been panting with love for him. Now here she was, lying rigid in the old sagging bed which Tom and Benny had moved from number 32 and all she felt was dread. She could hear Tom downstairs, raking the coals, sliding the bolt on the back door. He'd already had his shave while she was fussing over the children – his description, not hers – so any minute now he would climb the stairs and get in beside her, and she didn't want him to come, she really didn't.

Then he was pulling back the bedclothes, the weight of the mattress sagging still further and his body lying alongside hers, not touching, not speaking. He lifted one hand to switch off the light with the cord that hung over the bedhead. Darkness engulfed her and she could see nothing but Michael's face, luminous in her imagination. Lucy wondered if she would be able to hold on to this image during what was to follow. Too late now to regret allowing things to get this far.

She heard Tom clear his throat and took comfort from that. Perhaps he was as nervous as she. 'It's been a long time,' he said.

She agreed, her voice faint, hardly above a whisper. Then she felt him turn towards her, his hand came to rest on her stomach and she tried not to flinch away. Could he feel her heart beating?

'I'll not hurt you,' he said as he pulled up her night-dress. She wanted to put out her hand and stop him, to jump out of the bed and run but some instinct told her to hold still, that it would be less of an ordeal if she surrendered with as good a grace as possible. He was her husband. She'd promised to give their marriage a chance, for the sake of the children. He started to kiss her but Lucy felt none of the excitement in his kisses that she once had. As if sensing her lack of response, he gave up. She could feel the swollen heat of him pulsing hard against her, and the urge to push him away and escape was overwhelming. But ignoring the fact she was neither ready nor willing, he drew her resisting legs apart and thrust himself inside her. Lucy knew she was both dry and tight with resistance, but when she cried out in appalled shock, he pushed harder, pounding his frustration into her.

'Next time,' he told her when the agony was finally over and he'd withdrawn to his side of the bed, 'you'll put a bit more effort into it.'

She turned her face to the wall and lay staring into the darkness, silent tears rolling over hot cheeks, dampening her pillow. She hardly dared to breathe until she heard the even rhythm of his snores. Only then did she get up and creep downstairs to the kitchen where she bathed her sore body with warm water and a soft flannel. It was as if he were not her husband at all, as if he were a stranger who had violated her. Yet that was nonsense of course. The fault must be entirely hers as he had said, for not even making any effort.

Chapter Nineteen

If Lucy had been unhappy before, she was utterly wretched now. Every day dawned grey and empty, devoid of hope or happiness. Try as she might she could not banish Michael from her thoughts and Tom's continued criticism that he deserved better than a frigid wife after all these years away, began to seem highly justified.

It was Belinda who rescued her by suggesting they reestablish their regular trips to the cinema. It would be good for them both, she said, an opportunity to escape the confines of increasing domesticity. 'These last weeks have seemed endless for me too. This baby feels like a lump of clay in my stomach, using up all my energy and managing to govern my life completely.'

Rebelliously ignoring Tom's rules, Lucy left the children with good old Doris-from-next-door and the two girls went to their favourite cinema, the Gaumont. It was the first of many such outings. Sometimes she left them with Uncle Nobby and Aunty Ida, who were always happy to have the children they said, telling her young folk should enjoy themselves. 'Isn't that what life is all about?'

Lucy eagerly snatched the opportunity to put on her glad rags, as Uncle Nobby called them, and if the matriarchs of Pansy Street gave her fiercely censorious looks, then she paid them no heed. Anything was better than stopping in night after night, living in dread of her husband wanting sex. Let them paint her as a scarlet woman, if they'd a mind. She was young still, and life was for living. If she couldn't live it with the man she loved, at least she could have some fun going out with her friend.

Off the two would go, arm in arm, giggling like young girls again, dreaming of their celluloid heroes and a fish supper afterwards. At least the picture house was warmer than Belinda's flat, and she got to rest her swollen ankles. Celia Johnson and Trevor Howard in *Brief Encounter* proved to be one of their favourite movies. They saw it three times in two weeks and still came out of the cinema surreptitiously drying away tears.

'What a soppy pair we are,' Belinda chuckled. 'So deliciously sad. Do you think Laura meant to kill herself when she ran out to meet the express at the end?'

Lucy sighed, and it was a deeply unhappy sound. 'Rather than live without him you mean? I don't know but I'm glad she didn't. I'm glad she went back to her husband.'

'Heavens no, what a bore he was. Far better to go off with her lover and be happy.'

'But would she have been? Happy I mean,' Lucy argued, her friend's answer more important than she dared to admit. 'They were both married. How could they be so selfish? It would have destroyed their love.'

'Utter rubbish. They might have made one person happy instead of making two miserable.' Lucy couldn't help but laugh because it all sounded so simple when Belinda put it like that.

Following one such happy evening, Belinda arrived home to find her front door not only locked but with slats of wood nailed across it. The icy February weather had changed to a thin drizzle, and stacked against the rough stone wall of the shop were the few sticks of furniture which she and Benny had managed to collect: the kitchen table and two chairs, a broken box which held a few knives and forks and a blackened pan. Even the bed and mattress, once a haven for their loving, lay in shaming view for any passer-by to see. Belinda could hardly believe what her own eyes were telling her, that all her worldly goods had been thrown out on the street as, it seems, had they.

Somewhere in the next street she could hear a vendor calling 'hot peas and puddings,' and felt thankful that at least her stomach was full and warm from the fish supper she'd enjoyed with Lucy, the days of near starvation long gone. She thumped on the door again in disbelief, though she knew Benny was at the pub with Tom so there was no one to hear her. Who could have done such a thing and why? It made no sense.

She was shaking with cold and knew she couldn't stay here, on the damp pavement, railing at injustice.

Lucy would be in, of course, but Pansy Street suddenly seemed as far away as the moon. Nevertheless she set off, her back starting to ache with a vengeance from the effort it took just to walk in the chill of the increasing downpour. It was as she took a short cut through Nelson's Ginnel, that Belinda felt a rush of warm liquid between her legs. Staring down at herself in horrified fascination she saw a puddle of water forming at her feet.

She cried out in shocked surprise, then sank to the wet cobbles, sliding into a heap of dirty snow on a gasp of sudden pain. She glanced desperately about, only to discover the ginnel deserted, black dark with not a single lamp lit. Freezing rain hammered and bubbled up on the glistening setts, gushing from the broken guttering of the roofs above her head and within seconds she was soaked. Belinda neither noticed nor cared as she became swamped by pain, fierce shots of fire slicing through from her lower back to her belly, emerging as wailing screams that seemed to be swallowed up and spat out by the icy rain as it heedlessly drummed on dustbin lids and washed the scarlet stains from Benny's son. She just managed to bring the baby to her breast inside her coat before darkness overwhelmed her.

–

Benny took some comfort from the fact that he came home early from the pub that night, leaving Tom to his self-pity and his moans. Finding the shop door boarded up he realised at once that the eviction notice had still been carried out even though he'd found a solution and would have moved his family out anyway within a few weeks, business permitting.

Cold fear clamped his stomach. Ignoring the heap of new furniture getting soaked on the pavement, his one concern was for Belinda. Where the hell was she?

'Belinda? *Belinda!*' He screamed her name into the teeming rain and began to run.

He knocked on every door, asking if anyone had seen her, was she there taking shelter? When he finally found her, in Minnie Hopkins's house on Pansy Street of all places, it didn't take the presence of the officious doctor or the grimfaced midwife to tell him the news was not good. He could sense it the minute he set foot across the threshold.

'Nay, lad, don't go in there,' Minnie told him, blocking his way as he marched up the lobby. Benny thrust the old woman aside, not unkindly but with a desperate determination. He didn't care if she'd lost the baby, he wanted only to find his beloved Belinda.

She lay quite still on the sofa, in a parlour which seemed crowded with people, their anxious voices dying away to a dreadful hush as he approached. Someone had tried to light a fire and it smoked fitfully in the tiny grate. Beside it stood a bowl covered in a blood-soaked cloth. He averted his eyes from this and went at once to Belinda. A soldier's greatcoat was slung across her slender body, now showing no sign of the pregnancy which had dogged her life for months. Her face, he thought, as he kissed her, had lost its strained expression and was once again, exquisitely beautiful, the eyelids curving up and outward at each corner, the veins shadowed a translucent blue. Her lips too were smiling as they had been that very first day when he'd seen her in the rating office, but it was only when he found no response to his kisses, heard the whisper of soft tears around him that he realised what he'd lost that night. The very meaning of his existence.

Minnie placed what appeared to be a bundle of rags in Benny's arms. 'Take good care of this little mite. He's thy son, and he's needs you now more than ever.'

Benny gazed in stunned disbelief at the pink, screwed up face staring up at him from the folds of cloth. He'd assumed the baby to be dead but here he was, alive and well and in his arms. He wished with a terrible intensity that it were not so, that it had been the baby who'd died and Belinda spared. He felt his knees start to shake as the awesome weight of responsibility closed in and he sank on to a chair someone had thoughtfully provided, the soft bundle held awkwardly in his big hands. This was a living nightmare. He couldn't take in what was happening.

He felt disorientated, set apart from the real world as if he were trapped in a bubble and couldn't reach through it, back to reality. He could hear, as if from a great distance, Minnie Hopkins fussing and arranging the baby in his arms, Lily Gantry and her cronies discussing arrangements to have Belinda moved to a Chapel of Rest, hushed voices wondering whether next of kin had been informed and suddenly Benny needed his own mother.

'Mam,' he said, and Minnie gave his shoulder an awkward little pat, assuring him that Polly and Lucy had both been sent for. Nausea rose in his gullet at the pain and shock they were about to face.

He looked again upon his child.

He knew he should cry for his lovely Belinda but somehow no tears would come. Somewhere in his head he could see a gaping black mouth, hear a silent scream, and in his chest a tight sensation which felt like fear but wasn't. Then it was as if he was falling through that mouth, through a long black tunnel and a voice was shouting in his ears. *'It's not true. She isn't dead. She's not! She's not! Bloody vultures! Get out, the lot of you. Get out!'*

The baby was gone from his hands, the room emptied in seconds. All except for Minnie Hopkins, who sat with the child on her knee.

'And you can bloody go too.'

She didn't move, just sat rocking the baby without saying a word, not even when he grabbed the aspidistra pot from its tall stand and smashed it against the mahogany fire surround. Nor when he swept all the books from her shelves, including the family bible and followed this by smashing the Westminster Chime clock given to her by her beloved employer. Minnie merely commented that she'd never really liked it anyway.

It was then that he crumpled. Head bowed he sagged to his knees and great racking sobs came out of some black pit deep inside, one he couldn't reach the bottom of but somehow must in order to rid himself of this terrible pain.

'That's it, lad. Let it come.' But he really had no choice. For now that he had started, nothing would stop him. Benny put his head in his hands and gave in to his grief.

–

The entire street came to pay their respects, which took place in Polly's front parlour, more fitting than a funeral home. She set several candles around the open coffin and put a garland of flowers in Belinda's golden blonde hair. Minnie Hopkins and Lily Gantry insisted every mirror in the house be covered, so that her precious soul could not be stolen by the devil. Lucy, who spent hours sitting with her friend, thought she had never looked more beautiful.

'It's such a waste,' she sobbed, quite unable to control her distress.

Polly took care of the baby, which Benny ignored completely.

The funeral took place the following Tuesday when, for the first time, the two branches of Belinda's family came together in one place. Benny was white-faced and rigid in his grief, Lucy clinging to his arm and Polly quietly weeping. All Belinda's friends and neighbours were there, more than she would have expected, being a modest, unassuming sort of person.

Belinda would not have been surprised, however, to see her father, Councillor Hubert Clarke, in his best funereal attire, watch chain swinging over the curve of his belly, take complete charge of the service whether it be reading the lesson, singing the loudest through the hymns, or leading the mourners to the graveside and then on to a cold repast at the Tudor Cafe. Joanna's role, as a grieving mother, was relegated to second place. And Benny, as a distraught husband, was ignored completely.

–

Hubert knew where to place the blame for his daughter's death. He had completely erased from his mind the blocks he'd put on Benny's enterprise, though there was, of course, the small matter of the eviction notice. But then if Benny Pride hadn't got his daughter pregnant in the first place, she'd have been alive today, eviction or no eviction. Hubert certainly had no intention of bearing the responsibility for her death and, just to be on the safe side, had taken the precaution of ensuring that the landlord didn't shoot his mouth off about why he'd decided to put the squeeze on the young couple in that way. He was certain that his role in the matter would never be mentioned. The subject was closed.

The need for justice, however, so far as Hubert was concerned, was not. Not by a long chalk. If Benny Pride thought he could seduce his lovely daughter, get her pregnant and force her into an entirely unsuitable marriage, then keep her in abject poverty which resulted in her death, he was in for a rude awakening. Hubert meant to take his revenge for her loss. He meant to make Benny pay.

It was Hubert, however, who was in for the first surprise. When he reached his office on Potato Wharf the following morning, it was to find Tom leaning against the door-jamb, waiting for him. 'What are you after now, Shackleton? More problems with your paperwork?' Hubert's tone crackled with annoyance. He'd a busy day ahead, with no time to listen to this nincompoop begging yet more favours.

'I thought I'd do you a service,' Tom mildly replied. 'At least give you the chance before I went elsewhere.'

Hubert thrust his key in the lock, pushed open the door sufficiently to let himself slip through without giving any indication that the young man could follow. 'Give me a chance at what?' he barked, his curiosity awakened despite his better judgement.

'I was out walking, that night your Belinda copped it. Glad to be out of the house, away from a nagging wife. You know how it is. I was on my way for a drink wi' me mates and I wondered what all that pile of furniture was doing out on the pavement in the rain.'

'They were evicted. My daughter was turned out on the street because she'd married an idiot who couldn't look after her properly.'

Tom took a step closer, his voice dropping to barely a whisper. 'Or because somebody decided to apply a bit of extra pressure. Put the boot in as it were. Somebody quite close to her, in fact, with his own axe to grind. Or so Percy says. You remember Percy Simpkins? He was Belinda and Benny's landlord. Good mate o' mine is Percy. We go back a long way. Used to work alongside him when I lived in Ancoats. I believe you had a quiet word with him on the subject of eviction only recently, is that right?'

Tom's mildly enquiring gaze met the blazing fury in Hubert's bloodshot eyes, and seemed to find it amusing. The corners of his mouth tilted into his famously charming smile. 'Small world, eh? Lift up a stone and you'll always find a worm or two underneath. Or so I've found.'

'You'd best come in,' Hubert growled, and glancing up and down the empty street, allowed Tom Shackleton into his private domain.

–

The worst time for Benny came after the funeral, after Joanna had meticulously repossessed every item of her daughter's clothes and belongings, after everyone had gone home and when all practical details had been attended to. Benny was, quite literally, left holding the baby.

What, in God's name, was he going to do with it? He knew nowt about babbies.

His son lay in a crib in Polly's room, though during the day Benny wasn't sure what happened to him, and didn't greatly care.

He'd moved into his sister's old room at his mother's house, now it was free, lying alone in the big brass bed he'd once shared with Belinda. Besides this there was a small chest of drawers and a single chair. The sparse surroundings seemed to suit his mood.

Most of the time his mind seemed locked in a blessed numbness, as if unable to take in the terrible event that had occurred. He would get up, wash and shave, go to work, come home, eat, give every appearance of normal behaviour. But every so often the numbing mists would lift and disperse and he would realise with a terrible clarity that his beloved Belinda was dead. It was then that the pain started and all he could do was to sit with his head in his hands and think of Belinda, of her laughter, her teasing sense of fun, her lovemaking. No, he couldn't bear to remember her lovemaking. Not yet, for when he did, the pain became almost unbearable.

At other times he couldn't bear to think of her at all and he'd storm out, walk the streets, down several pints at the Dog and Duck where he became a frequent visitor, or occupy himself with some useless task at the shop or even in the warehouse. He'd stay all night if necessary, anything to keep occupied so that when he fell into bed, he would sleep instead of his mind going endlessly over his loss.

—

Polly found caring for a tiny baby taxing, on top of coping with a new business. If she didn't grieve for Belinda quite as intensely as Benny did, she still missed the girl sorely and felt she owed it to her to do the best she could for her poor motherless child.

'Benny will have to come round to it soon,' she groaned wearily to Charlie as she climbed from her bed for the second time one night to go in search of a warmed bottle. 'I'm too old for this caper, so I am.'

'Give the lad time,' was all Charlie would say. Perhaps he was right, but then again maybe Benny needed a bit of a push, if she could just think of the right way to give him one. In the meantime, she'd ask Lucy for a bit more help.

Perhaps helping care for Belinda's child would help with her own grieving. To her great surprise and disappointment, Tom refused to allow it.

'She has enough on her plate,' he tartly informed her, 'looking after our own two.'

'One more wouldn't be any trouble,' Lucy said, her voice thick with tears. 'He's so tiny, and he's family after all, my nephew.'

'I say you've enough to do, and I'll hear no argument on the matter.' He glared fiercely at Polly. 'You should know better than to ask, seeing as how we've only just set up home together after all this time apart.'

'It would only be during the day, while you're at work, as I am myself.'

'That's your problem, and Benny's. I've said no.' Lucy shot him an anguished glance but Polly was forced to concede defeat. She certainly wouldn't beg. It seemed every request, however simple, created bad feeling in her family.

'You should have asked me, Polly love,' Doris-next-door chided her. 'Tha knows how I loves childer, and I could do wi' the money. The little mite'll be safe enough wi' me till his da's up to taking over. What is the little lamb called?'

'Benny hasn't named him yet,' Polly said, her face sad.

'Nay, poor little sausage. No name. That's a bad show, that is.'

From the very first day after the funeral Polly drew some consolation from the fact that Benny came to work as usual, as if he realised it was even more important now for him to bring home the bacon, to try to make up to his son for the loss of a mother. Polly certainly didn't intend for the child to want for anything. Hadn't she seen enough poverty in her time? Not for this babby a jam buttie on a cold doorstep. He would have the best.

When Hubert called in sometime in the second week, claiming Joanna had asked him to enquire about the arrangements and well-being of their grandson, she was pleased to inform him that he was being well taken care of. 'Yet he lacks a mother,' Hubert rather pedantically stated. 'But he'll never lack for love,' Polly stoutly replied. 'Getting back to business, what about this new shipment of bentwood chairs you promised me. We're nearly out of stock and you know how popular they are. You can swap them for those heavy Victorian monstrosities you brought last month. I can't shift those for love nor money.'

He rocked back on his heels, thumbs in his waistcoat pockets and scowled at her. 'You need to put more ingenuity into your selling techniques then, lass.'

Polly itched to tell him that she wasn't his lass, that she could sell anything so long as it was worth buying, which those chairs were not, but managed to bite her tongue. There were enough ill feelings about already. Benny spent every evening searching for Percy Sympkins, the landlord who'd turned them out on the streets, ever since the day it happened. God help the poor creature if he ever did find him.

'Well, aren't I learning all the time,' she agreed, giving Hubert the benefit of her most winning smile. 'But we did agree sale or return, I seem to recall, so long as I took what you sent, so I'm returning them.'

'I'll make a note,' Hubert growled, making no effort to produce either paper or notebook from his pocket. Polly could only assume he meant a mental one.

'Mind you,' she told Charlie later. 'If he doesn't remember to have the chairs collected, I'll remind him again next week.'

At the end of each day Polly collected her grandson from Doris, as arranged, and took him home. Tired as she was after her long day at the warehouse, she fed him, changed him, bathed and burped him, then lay the baby safely in his crib, rocking it till he fell asleep.

'Don't I love the bones of him,' she said whenever Charlie asked if she minded the extra work.

Benny himself did nothing for his son. What could he do? he thought. Looking after babbies was women's work.

–

After three more weeks of this arduous regime, Polly was feeling the strain. 'I need a night off,' she told Benny, 'a chance to get a bit of uninterrupted sleep.' With some reluctance, he agreed to the crib being moved into his own bedroom.

'How will I manage?'

'Saints preserve us, Benny lad, you'll manage because you have to, as we all do. Wouldn't Charlie and me give a gold clock for the chance of a good night's sleep? I'm too old for this caper, so I am.' She went on to gently remind him that he was the child's da and as such, must take a share in his care and upbringing.

She showed Benny how to mix the National dried baby milk into the baby's bottle, how to hold and feed him, how to sit him up and rub the little chap's back so that he got rid of his wind. She even demonstrated how to clean his little bottom and change his nappy. Benny prayed that the baby would sleep through the night and he'd be spared the whole terrifying procedure.

It was a wish not to be granted.

He heard the first few little hiccups long before they turned into a cry. Benny lay there for some moments, only half awake, hoping the baby would shut up and go back to sleep. This proved to be unfortunate because by the time he did scramble sleepily out of bed the cry was a full-blown howl of distress. Benny hoped the noise might bring Polly running from her bed but again was disappointed. She was clearly determined that this was his shift, which seemed a bit unfair. He had to work all day too, after all.

He picked the baby up and carried him aloft down the stairs, holding him with outstretched arms some distance away, though supporting the precariously wobbly head with his fingers. He propped the child against a cushion in the corner of the old kitchen armchair while he struggled to read the directions on the tin of dried milk powder and remember Polly's instructions.

He could hardly think with the racket the baby was making, and it was some moments before he realised he hadn't even put the kettle on and then had to rush around filling it from the tap, lighting a match to the gas, by which time the infant was screwed up into a tight red ball of rage.

In that moment he hated the child. *It* had surely killed his beloved Belinda. Hadn't *it* been the bane of her life throughout the pregnancy, making her sick and tired, coming between them at the very start of their married life together. Yet *it* sat there, alive and well while *she* was dead, demanding to be fed as if by right.

He picked it up, again remembering to carefully support its tiny head as Polly had shown him. He ordered it to hush but still the scream went on, the tiny fists clenched with fury and Benny's own frustration and rage grew, his patience threatening to slip. He was exhausted; the day at the furniture shop had been long and wearing, filled with stress and problems of one sort or another. How could he be expected to care for a small child on top of getting a new business going?

The kettle began to sing and he shoved the baby back in its corner, stopping his ears to its gasping sobs. Even as he set it down Benny realised with horror that it stank. After the feed, he'd be forced to change its dirty nappy after all. He almost ran to snatch up the kettle, anxious to put some distance between himself and the cause of his anger. As he mixed the formula, he didn't hear stealthy footsteps on the stair, was unaware of the door opening a crack or of Polly's eye peering through it.

'Right, shut up, you,' he said, turning back to his son. And then he remembered Polly's warning about temperature and tested the milk on his wrist. Too hot. Thank Christ he hadn't given it to the boy. It occurred to him in that moment that the child had no name. Having a baby had always been something that would happen in the future, not now, and not without Belinda to look after it and make such decisions. They'd never talked about names. Whenever he'd brought the subject up she'd always put the decision off, saying it tempted fate to decide too soon. Now, drat it, he supposed he'd have to decide.

The baby had worked himself into a lather of hot fury and distress and was sliding down the chair. Benny didn't know whether he should run back and shove him safely back into place or keep holding the bottle under the running tap to cool it. Desperation closed in.

'*Stay still!*' he shouted, but the child didn't seem to hear or understand, behaving like a termagant of balled temper. But then of course how could it understand, it was only a babby. Benny dashed across the room and caught him long before he'd wriggled anywhere near the edge but his heart was racing with fear all the same. He held the child securely in his arms, sat himself down in the chair and offered the bottle. Blessed silence fell.

The eyes closed in a bliss of contentment and Benny looked down upon his son in wonder. He marvelled at the translucent blue of the lids, the soft down of golden fair hair with just a hint of red in it, and the vulnerable pulsing hollow on the baby's crown. Small fingers spread like tiny stars and he felt the tension ease out of the small body. As the baby pulled on the teat, Benny marvelled at his strength. He was a fighter this one. What a paddy he had on him.

'Still some Irish blood whirling in those veins eh, little chap?'

And he was a survivor. Benny thought that one day he would have to tell his son how he'd been born in a back street on a pile of mucky snow and in the pouring rain, without any assistance save that of his own brave mother. The rhythm of the baby's sucking was steady now, punctuated with contented little gasps. Benny found it immensely soothing, almost therapeutic to be sitting here with his son in the quiet of the night, as if there were just the two of them in all the world. Course, it wasn't the little chap's fault that his mam was dead. How could he even think such a thing? Neither of them had been given a choice in the matter. And he'd do well enough, that much was plain, even if he did have to make do with an amateur for a da.

'She would've loved you,' Benny said, unaware of the tears sliding down his cheeks. He'd tell him about Belinda too when the boy was old enough to understand, how lovely she was, how spirited and determined.

He chuckled softly at the memory. 'We hadn't two pennies to rub together and there were times when we fought like cat and dog but by heck, lad, we were in love. I worshipped the ground she walked on, and she never lost her faith in me, despite my fanciful notions at times. That's your ma, a survivor, like you.'

The baby's eyes opened for a brief moment, round and blue, gazing intently up at Benny as if memorising his father's face, as if he'd been taking in every word and agreed with it, before allowing the lids to droop closed again. And not once did he pause in his sucking.

Benny tucked him closer to his chest, protectively, as if shielding the baby from a harsh world. He saw, in that moment of intense emotion, how he could best pay tribute to Belinda's memory, by being the man she'd always believed him to be. All he had to do was work hard and be a success.

He thought of his own father, Matthew Pride, bravely fighting for his country then coming home and being the best dad any boy could've wished for. Benny had worshipped him.

The baby was drowsy now, sated with milk, a small bubble forming on his pursed lips as Benny withdrew the teat. He lifted his son and lay him gently against his shoulder, just as Polly had shown him. 'Come on now, Matthew love, give yer old dad a good burp.'

In the stairway, Polly slipped quietly back to bed, tears in her eyes and a soft smile on her face.

Chapter Twenty

So far as Lucy was concerned everything changed when Belinda died. Losing her dear friend felt like the end of everything of value in her life. And she was haunted by the conversations they'd had about love.

'Why make two people miserable when you can make one happy,' Belinda had said.

Life suddenly seemed very fragile, as if every day must be enjoyed to the full for you never knew when it might end. Wasting it with a man she no longer cared for, who gave no indication of truly caring for her, didn't seem the best way to spend it at all. Lucy felt as if she were living a life of pretence. Pretending she loved Tom, pretending she was happy. Yet what she truly felt was a desperate urgency to spend every possible moment with Michael. She was young still, and in love. There surely wasn't a moment to be lost. Yet how to gain her freedom, that was the problem.

She lay beside Tom night after night, longing for Michael's touch, for the excitement only he could instill in her, regretting ever having given him up simply for the sake of duty. Each morning she went about her daily routine like some sort of clockwork toy, cooking and cleaning, doing what was necessary without thought or reason, without even the chance of escape to the Gaumont with her lovely friend. Inside, her heart lay heavy and sick, robbing her of the last of her appetite.

Following their agreed parting she'd caught no more than a glimpse of Michael in the distance. Lucy convinced herself that he'd forgotten all about her, filled his life with other things, whereas she couldn't get him out of her mind. One evening she was so wrapped up in these thoughts that she put salad cream on the table instead of custard.

'I don't think this goes with rhubarb tart, Mam,' Sarah Jane giggled and Lucy dashed about, trying to remember what she'd done with the custard jug.

'How could you cope with Benny's baby, when you can't even manage a simple meal?' Tom said, his voice thick with sarcasm, as so often these days. 'Get off to bed soon tonight, then you'll be more awake tomorrow.'

'I'm not tired. I'm fine.'

'Do as I say. The children can see to themselves for once, and you can do the washing and clearing up tomorrow. Go to bed.' And she did, for it seemed easier to obey.

–

It was Whit Sunday and Polly had invited the entire family to lunch. Lucy and Tom began it with their usual morning toast and mug of tea taken largely in silence, which even so somehow led to an argument. It all started innocently enough. Tom complained about there not being enough butter on his toast and Lucy laughed, saying it was actually margarine and she couldn't remember the last time she'd even seen any butter let alone had the money to buy it. That inflamed him and he accused her of mocking him for not earning enough money to keep them.

She felt cowed by his dominance of her, by his constant carping and criticisms. Yet something of the old Lucy still remained, buried deep beneath the damaged self esteem. Now she experienced an unexpected surge of rebellion at being repeatedly bullied, even by a husband scarred by war. Benny had been bullied as a boy but he'd won through in the end. Maybe she would too, if she held her nerve. She waited until the children were upstairs getting dressed and she was tying his best tie for him. 'I was thinking of getting a job,' she announced, without giving herself time to think. 'Maybe that would help.'

'Don't talk daft.'

'I mean it. I'm bored out of my mind stuck here at home. It's not as if there's enough to do, what with our Sean now at school. I've worked for years. I like working and having a bit of money in my pocket. Besides, we could surely do with a bit extra. We could happen afford butter then, eh?' And she smiled, trying to keep what she saying light.

'There you go, accusing me of keeping you short.' Tom bridled at the implied criticism.

Lucy hastened to assure him. 'That's not what I meant at all. I like having a bit of pocket money of my own, or to spend on the kids, that's all. And as I say, I like working.' Yet as so often before Tom absolutely refused to listen to her point of view or even to discuss the matter. 'You'll stop at home, where you belong. You're not even managing the housework very well. How could you possibly cope with a job as well.'

'I've told you, it's because I'm bored. Why can't I work? I could easily get my old job back with Minnie Hopkins.'

'So that's it. You're still pining after lover-boy.'

Lucy sighed but was determined not to rise to the bait. 'All right then, maybe Mam could find me a job at the warehouse. Everyone else is working for the family business, why not me?'

'Because you have childer and a husband to look after.'

It was no good, she could feel the pointlessness of the argument in her bones and afterwards would wonder what had possessed her to battle on. She smoothed his tie into place, handed him his hat and raincoat. 'I overheard you telling Lily Gantry at the funeral, that you spent years in that prisoner-of-war camp in Germany, yet you told Michael and me that you'd crossed over the Alps into Italy *after* you escaped, and then made your way through France. Where, exactly, were you held then?' The thought had come out of nowhere, but she couldn't doubt that her words had hit home by the way he flinched.

He rubbed a hand over his face and started prowling about the kitchen, back and forth, like a lion in a cage. *'Michael and me.'* He cruelly mimicked her voice and before she could guess what was about to happen, he'd brought the flat of his hand down across her face. The blow knocked her off balance, sent her reeling across the kitchen so that she stumbled and fell, catching the side of her head on the edge of the steel fender.

He was instantly contrite. Full of apologies he hurried to fetch iodine and warm water, assuring her that he hadn't meant to lash out. It was the war that caused his temper to be so short, he explained, and jealousy of her feelings for Michael. 'All you have to do is agree to give our marriage a chance. You really shouldn't have provoked me. It's your own fault.' Lucy rather thought that it must be, for otherwise why would he have hit her?

Polly met them at the front door and, in honour of the occasion, wasn't wearing the much knitted cardigan which she'd rarely seemed to have off in six long years of war but a smart frock in navy blue with a crisp white collar. It made her look young again. She hugged and kissed her daughter, saying how pretty she looked. Lucy was wearing a lemon seersucker dress, cut on the bias and it was quite apparent to Polly that she'd lost weight since Belinda's death. Polly intended to get something inside her today. As Charlie led the way into the house, limping slightly on the stick he now used, Polly also noticed a small bruise on her daughter's face and mildly enquired how she'd come by it.

'Oh, I bumped my head on the cellar door,' Lucy said. 'Shall I set the table?'

'Now isn't that something? A pair of willing hands for once.' Aw, and wasn't she proud of the lot of them. It made her heart sing for all there was the sadness of an empty place at the table. 'And where are my two treasures?'

The children, having not long since filled their stomachs with their usual breakfast of bread and jam, were soon sprawled on the floor, flat on their stomachs playing with toy soldiers, oblivious to the appetising aroma of roast beef and Yorkshire pudding that was making all the adults salivate with hunger.

Polly watched her only son with pride as he carefully spooned cereal into baby Matt's mouth which fluttered open like a young bird for more every time the spoon was taken away. At three months, wasn't he the finest baby in the street if not the whole of Manchester? She tickled him under the chin and, thinking it was the spoon, the small mouth fastened itself upon her finger with a startling fierceness. Polly burst out laughing. 'Look at the precious soul. Isn't he the one? Won't he grow as big as his da one day and just as greedy.'

Benny grinned, taking this as a compliment.

Seated opposite Benny was Tom, looking fitter than ever. What a fine, good looking young man he was, to be sure. He'd surprised Polly by proving to be quite diligent at his work in the warehouse, for all it was little more than labouring. She'd agreed to let him drive the van occasionally as he was proving to be a useful member of the team.

She glanced across at her daughter, as if searching for clues as to her state of mind but Lucy was busily setting out knives and forks. Polly watched as Tom slid an arm about her waist, popped a kiss upon his wife's neck as she bent over and then merrily tweaked the soft brown curls on her brow. So everything must be fine and dandy between them, she thought. Lucy didn't return the gesture or even smile a response. Mebbe she'd best have another talk with the girl, just to make sure.

Serving out the meat and vegetables on every plate took an age, but nobody minded as by then they'd all consumed a fluffy slice of Yorkshire pudding topped off with onion gravy. As Polly handed out the brimming platefuls, she recalled a time when her family would think that humble dish alone would constitute a dinner fit for a king, certainly it had gone down well one Christmas back in Ancoats when there'd been no meat to follow.

'That's too much for me,' Lucy demurred, unloading half of the food on to her brother's plate.

'Nay, is that all you're having, lass? It wouldn't keep a sparrow alive,' Charlie said.

'I'm not very hungry.'

Polly gave Lucy a keen look and wondered if she'd been crying. But then losing her sister-in-law had been a blow to them all, and the pair had been as close as two slices of bread stuck together with jam. Which reminded Polly for some reason of her grandchildren. She finally managed to drag them away from their toys and placed a small plate of dinner before each of them, all the while advising Lucy as if she was a girl still and Polly's responsibility as a mother were as strong as ever, to take better care of herself.

'Ye definitely look a bit peaky. Starvin' yourself will do no good at all. Belinda would hate to see you make yerself ill, wouldn't she so?'

Benny, returning from putting Matt down in his crib asked what it was Belinda would hate and Lucy irritably told him that it was only Mam nagging.

Tom chipped in, 'I'm at her all the time to rest more but will she listen? Stubborn to a fault she is. All she has to do is settle back and enjoy her children, instead of which she's again fussing about going back to work.'

Perhaps these words rekindled her rebellion, or maybe it was being in the heart of her family with a mother who had always worked outside of the home, which gave Lucy the courage to make one more stand. 'And why not? I don't have to spend my entire life wiping children's mucky faces, cleaning other folk's doorsteps. There might very well be something more interesting and demanding I could do.'

'Well said,' Polly laughed, applauding vigorously. 'Couldn't we use all the help we can get at the warehouse, if you'd a mind.'

Tom scowled at this apparent show of feminine solidarity. 'Leave her be, Polly. Don't encourage her day dreams. A wife's place is in the home.'

Polly might have protested against this damning indictment of womanhood but Lucy, her dander up now, returned to the subject which had been exercising her mind more and more these days, wagging her fork at him across the table. 'Tell me, when you were wounded at Salerno, there was presumably a roll call.'

Tom looked startled by this abrupt change of subject, as did the rest of the family while Polly clicked her tongue in annoyance.

'Sunday dinner is not the place to discuss the war, m'cushla. Besides, haven't we put all of that behind us?' 'I'd like to know.'

'It's all right,' Tom said with a patient smile, as if he were used to humouring his wife. 'Aye, there always is a roll call after a battle. That's very shrewd of you to guess.'

She hadn't guessed of course. Michael had mentioned it once and somehow the question had stuck in her mind. 'And later, when they'd collected in all the wounded, they'd check again, wouldn't they? Scour the site for bodies, for instance.' A nerve by the corner of Tom's eye twitched, and though he appeared to be searching for an answer, or even a way out of the conversation, could apparently find none. 'Your mam's right. This isn't a fit subject for dinner. Can we get on with it in peace?' Then bent his head to the task without bothering to answer the question at all.

Lucy set down her knife and fork and leaned across the table towards him. 'But how come they didn't find *you*? Why did they rescue all the other wounded, and not you? Why were *you* left behind to be captured and nobody else?'

'How should I know? I was unconscious. That was a bad winter. The mud was dreadful. By the time I was well enough to walk about or ask questions, my battalion had moved on.'

'So *where* did you spend that first winter? And who found you? When were you taken to that POW camp? How?'

No one else at the table spoke a word, or even moved; every eye was upon Tom, every ear listening to the exchange, waiting for the reply which came eventually in a soft monotone.

'It – wasn't quite then I was captured. It was later. An Italian family found me. They were very kind. Can we forget the war, please? This beef is delicious,' he added, turning deliberately to Polly who smiled sympathetically at him, not quite understanding what was going on but clearly troubled by it.

Lucy pushed her plate aside, despite protests from her mother. She'd always been able to tell when he lied, and she knew he was lying now, without question.

When the family had gone, Polly toed off her shoes and sank into an easy chair to rub her aching feet with a sigh of relief. 'What a mystery they all are to me these days,' she groaned. 'I thought they were hard enough work as children, but there's still never a moment but what I'm worrying about one or other of them. There's our Benny upstairs, widowed and alone, poor soul, thankfully turning into a devoted father.'

'You should be pleased about the latter, at least,' Charlie smiled.

'Oh I am. Though I'm none too chuffed to be tied up so tight with that father-in-law of his. He's a cold fish is Councillor Hubert Clarke.'

'But substantial. A self-made man.'

'Aw, he's substantial all right. Too many beef dinners there, for sure.' Polly's chuckle soon changed into a frown. 'It's odd but whenever we reorder anything for the shop, he's nearly always out of stock. And when I ring and ask him to send the van to collect unsold stock as we agreed, the van's always occupied somewhere else and I have to keep reminding him. I've been waiting for over a week now to be rid of a consignment of bookcases. Like cardboard they are. I'll never sell them.'

'Ring him again,' Charlie said, only half listening with his eyes closed.

But Polly's thoughts had moved on. 'Our Lucy is another worry. Is she happy d'you think?'

Charlie met her gaze with the frankness she'd come to expect from him over the years. 'No, I don't think she is in the least bit happy. I'd say, if I didn't know better, that someone put pressure on her to stay in that marriage against her will. I hope, Polly my girl, that it wasn't you.'

Polly's eyes rounded with false innocence as she felt a nudge of guilt. 'Now would I do such a thing?'

'You just might, by your own twisted sense of loyalty.'

'Twisted is it, to want me family to thrive?'

'Yes, it is, if you interfere too much. A person must make their own way in the world, not follow a path set by someone else. The only way a marriage can thrive is with love, and no one can order that to be present, not even a loving mother. I reckon you should have a word with your Lucy, and tell her that whatever she decides to do about it, we'll give her our full support. There's not much wrong with Michael Hopkins, and if he makes her happy, isn't that what you want too?'

Tears standing proud in her fine eyes, Polly dragged herself out of the chair to kiss her husband full on his lips. 'Sure and what would I do without you. Aren't you the wisest man in all of Castlefield.'

'Not Manchester?'

'That too. The whole world. Come on. I'm whacked. Take me to bed.'

'Only if you hand me my stick first,' and they both burst out laughing.

–

At that moment Lucy was attempting to explain to her husband why she had asked all those probing questions, desperately striving to calm his irascible temper. She'd certainly had ample opportunity to regret such impetuosity as she put the children to bed and read them a story, delaying the moment she too must go to bed till the last possible moment.

'You questioned my honesty in front of your family,' he kept repeating, over and over. 'You'd no bloody right.'

'I wanted to understand, that's all. I need to know what you went through,' she prevaricated. 'How you managed to survive through all the humiliation and torture you suffered. That way I can perhaps better help with your problems. I *want* you to tell me, Tom. I feel that if this marriage of ours is to survive, then I need to know everything.'

'Why?'

She decided to take the risk and make her feelings plain. 'Because of the way you make love, and speak to me. So harsh and unfeeling, even unkind. Perhaps it's because of what happened to you back then. But if we could talk about it, maybe it would go away, this anger which seems to be gobbling you up.'

Tom strode over to the fire where he took down a pack of cigarettes from the mantle shelf and shook one out of the packet, as if he were an American GI. Lighting it, he inhaled deeply. 'And you're an expert on war veterans, are you?'

'I care about you. Despite everything that's gone wrong between us, I'd like to help put it right. Yes, I've been guilty of fond feelings for another man, but only because I thought you were dead. Nothing physical happened between us.'

He snorted his disbelief. 'So you say.'

'It didn't, I swear it. In any case, forgiveness of my supposed infidelity isn't enough. We have to be happy together. If we can't, then there's little point in carrying on, is there?'

Having gone this far, Lucy was determined to speak her mind. She smiled reassuringly up at him, hands clenching with nervousness. 'So let's talk, shall we? Properly. You can start by explaining what life was like in that camp, then how you managed to escape. Did you dig a tunnel, or sneak under a fence? It must have been an incredibly dangerous thing to do. Were you alone, or with comrades?'

He was still pacing about the kitchen, unable to settle, his voice high-pitched and taut with anger. 'Of course I was with comrades. I've told you, we got separated.' He bent over the fire, stabbed at the coals with the poker to bring the flames back to life and Lucy could see his neck growing red. She wondered if it was with the heat he was producing or with annoyance. Whatever the reason, she couldn't curb her curiosity.

'Why? Were you chased?'

He turned upon her, brandishing the poker, his eyes matching it with a glowing fury. 'For God's sake, how many times do I have to tell you? *I don't like talking about it!*' Heart racing, Lucy saw that she'd pushed him too far.

'I'm sorry,' she murmured. Going to him she took the poker from his shaking hand and slid it back in the stand, then rested a soft hand upon his shoulder. 'Perhaps we should leave it for now.' He'd clearly suffered far more than she realised. Tom turned to her with a tight little sob and sank into her arms, burying his face into her shoulder. The raw vulnerability of his despair shook her and she helplessly smoothed his shoulder, patted his back, trying to share his pain as he gulped on his sobs.

Later, as he sat sipping the tea she made him, he talked a little and Lucy listened in shamed gratitude. 'You've no idea what we suffered in those camps. Starvation, torture, locked in solitary if we stepped out of line,' he fabricated, remembering what he'd read about such places in the newspaper reports he devoured every day. 'After I'd got away, I could've been recaptured at any time, tortured, killed. Can you imagine how that sort of terror feels?'

Lucy felt hot with shame and pity at having interrogated him so hard. 'Oh, Tom, I should keep my nagging tongue still, I really should. It was just that I wanted to understand what you've been through, so that I know how to help you.'

He put down the cup, looked her straight in the eyes and there was such sorrow in his face, such an aching sadness that a knot of agony rose in her throat. 'You can help me best, Lucy, by giving the final heave-ho to that Michael Hopkins, to getting him out of our lives for good.' Then firmly and possessively he pulled her close into his arms and kissed her while Lucy, as so many times before, did her utmost to respond.

The scent of the cigarette he'd smoked, the warmth and closeness of him, rekindled memories of long forgotten pleasures they'd once enjoyed together. He was still an attractive man and even if she couldn't love him quite as she did Michael, she was still fond of Tom and felt guilty at having let him down, and of causing him to mistrust her. Didn't he deserve some happiness at least, after suffering such untold horrors that he couldn't even bear to speak of them? Now she'd forced him to recall those painful memories, and caused him to break down, her guilt intensified.

'How about that day's fishing you keep promising our Sean. It's Whit Monday tomorrow, a holiday. I'll put up a picnic and we'll have a day out, as a family. See how we get on.' He really didn't deserve to be hurt any more, not after everything he'd been through. She should remember that.

He seemed pleased by the suggestion and Lucy asked no more questions, nor gave him any further arguments. She allowed him to take her to bed, hoping against hope that this time when he made love to her, he would be patient. She laid her head against his chest, let him stroke her hair, her buttocks, her breasts, steadfastly setting the image of Michael aside but, as always, he was as selfish and clumsy as ever. He turned her on to her back and took her as if he were barely aware of her as a person, simply using her to satisfy his lust. Valiantly she fought against the tears that brimmed in her eyes. The only relief being that, as usual, it was over mercifully quickly, then he lay with his back to her on the far side of the bed.

'Goodnight, Tom,' she said. He didn't reply, nor did he trouble her again that night, for which she was unutterably grateful as she nursed her soreness.

Chapter Twenty-One

It was a gold and emerald spring day, the sky a bright blue with fluffy white clouds as fat as pillows and a light breeze to take the edge off the intense heat. They caught a bus along Oldham Road and walked down Ashton Road to Woodhouses. From here they followed the path down by the cricket club which led to the River Medlock where they were deep in the countryside and the air was sweet yet just moments from the city centre. What a wonder it all seemed. Birds sang, dragonflies skated on the quiet waters, and the grass verge was starred with oxeye daisies, red campion and stitch-wort. The children ran ahead, constantly chastised by Lucy not to go too far, or too near the water.

'What a worry children are. It's a wonder you decided to return, knowing all this responsibility was waiting for you.' She slanted a glance at Tom, half hoping he would snatch the opportunity she offered to admit he hadn't returned out of love for her but only because of a sense of duty to his children. Would knowing that fact release her from any sense of duty to him? Lucy found herself holding her breath while Tom stopped, as if needing time to consider, letting his gaze travel slowly over her.

Lucy felt herself grow hot beneath his scrutiny. Because she'd felt so down lately, much of the time she looked as if she'd dressed herself from the rag bag, a far cry from the Lucy of old; her hair too often fastened up, as wartime fashion had dictated, in a scarf which she wore like a turban with the tails tucked in. Today she'd let her hair fly loose in the breeze and she could feel her cheeks flushed pink by the breeze, knew his gaze lingered on her lips, rosy with the lipstick she'd applied, as if inviting kisses. She wished, in that moment, she hadn't indulged her vanity quite so recklessly, when the last thing she wanted was to attract his attentions.

He drew her close to his side. 'Remembering the children was what kept me going. They're a part of you, so how could I wish to be without them?'

She felt strangely moved by his words, tears springing readily to her eyes. 'Oh Tom, what a lovely thing to say.'

'Besides, I flatter myself that Sean and I are getting along better these days.'

'Which is the reason you are loaded down with fishing rod, nets and jam-jars,' she said, laughing.

'Exactly.'

'I'm going to catch a big whopper,' Sean announced, running back to them at the sound of his own name.

'Are you? Well that'll solve what we have for our tea.' Lucy's eyes were dancing as she walked along beside her husband, almost as if they were a normal family, and she wondered if her foolish suspicions had made her misjudge him. Perhaps he was jumpy because he was finding it hard to settle, and not because he'd lied at all.

It was indeed a delightful afternoon. Lucy's worries that he might try to kiss her dissolved as they ate a huge picnic from the basket she'd brought then lay about on the grass, content to watch the children play and giggle at silly jokes. Sarah Jane took great delight in waving to all the passing barges, declaring her earnest intention to live on one because she loved all those pretty flowers they had painted on them. Lucy said her daughter would be better suited to a coal barge, considering the state of her frock, while Sean was in his element fishing. He cast his line like an expert, after Michael's careful tuition, without any fear of his ending up in the water himself. He even caught two fish, admittedly small, due largely to the patient assistance of his father. He didn't stop talking about his prize all day. Today Lucy saw a different Tom Shackleton, one who seemed quite his old self, cheerful, joking and relaxed as if anxious to re-establish himself with his family, and with his wife.

After lunch they picked bluebells in the Clough then walked on, following the path by the river to Daisy Nook.

'For years I thought of nothing but getting back home to you, wanting to make things right.' He turned his face away, his gaze fixed with a melancholy sadness upon the rickety bridge ahead of them, so that she wasn't able to judge whether he truly meant what he said. When he did turn to her, she saw a strangeness in his eyes, as if he were in some distant place where she couldn't quite reach him. 'But you're right. It has been hard coming back. I lived in a village in the Italian mountains for a long time. It was an unusual sort of life but I grew used to it.'

Lucy held her breath. Would he reveal more? She waited and hoped but he seemed to snap back to the present, a dreadful bleakness in his gaze.

'Don't *you* ever leave me, Lucy. How would I manage without you?'

'I do appreciate how hard it's been for you, Tom,' she said, alarmed by his plea and she could have sworn there were tears in his eyes, not for a moment considering they might be manufactured by self-pity. 'Really I do. Perhaps if you talked about it more, it would make it easier?'

He didn't seem to hear her. 'I want us to be happy, to be safe. I want to make up for the time we've lost. I've got myself a good job, found us a house, even put a bit by for a rainy day. What else should I do? Tell me, Lucy, and I'll do it.'

She felt close to panic, almost as if she were being suffocated. She'd meant to break free, now she felt more entangled than ever. How could she leave him without seeming as if she was letting him down when he needed her the most? 'I don't know, I really don't know what to say.' She was thankfully saved from her dilemma by Sean who came running pell-mell back to her. 'Mam, Mam. There's a lake, and boats. Can we go on one. Can we?'

They'd reached Crime Lake about which there were a multitude of yarns about its bottomless state, legends of ghosties and ghoulies, no doubt all intended to keep curious children from venturing too near the water. Tom hired a boat and took them all out in it. Lucy lay back, trailing her fingers in the cool water and felt a new confidence flow through her veins. They were at least getting along better. Today had been good for them both and perhaps in future he would relax more and not feel the need to bully her in his typical army fashion. He'd opened up a little this weekend. Perhaps that too was a good sign, one she could encourage.

It was after she'd put the children to bed, both near dead on their feet from tiredness and the excitement of the day, and she was preparing vegetables for a quick stew, that it all started to go wrong. He began by saying what a lovely day they'd enjoyed and Lucy agreed.

'We could move if you like,' he suggested, quite out of the blue and in his most reasonable tone. 'We could leave this house, this city and go somewhere fresh. Just you, me, and the childer. I'd like that.'

Lucy felt a jolt of panic. 'Why would I want to? Manchester is my home.'

'There are plenty places just as good. Better, in fact,' he smilingly told her. 'I could buy us a little business of us own. Why not? Then you could work for me. Some place abroad where the weather's better, far away from the grubby wharves of Castlefield and nosy old Pansy Street. Like I said, I've a bit put by.'

Lucy picked up a carrot and began to scrape it clean. What was he saying? She wondered how he could have come by any money. He surely didn't earn enough labouring for Polly to have much in the way of saving. She longed to summon enough courage to tell him that it was all over between them, that she'd no wish to work in a little business with him, that it was Michael she loved with all her heart and soul, with every ounce of her being. But she daren't take the risk. He was so volatile, with such mercurial changes of mood. Heavens, she couldn't deal with him like this, she really couldn't.

As if reading her thoughts, he hissed, 'Michael Hopkins isn't right for you. He's a weak fool. A bloody conchie.'

'He isn't,' Lucy retorted, instantly on the defensive and going all hot and flustered. 'He's a fine man and I love him.'

'No you don't.' Tom lurched towards her with such violence that she jumped back, startled by this burst of ferocity. The knife she'd been holding fell with a clatter to the floor and he snatched it up. Holding it in his fist, he stabbed the table in front of her, over and over in a ferocious outburst of temper, punctuating every word. *'You only-went-with-him-because-you-were-missing-me.'*

She was stunned by this outburst. Shocked by his violence.

'Lots of women have had affairs during this war, but when their husbands came home, they gave their lover-boys up.'

Lucy could only gaze in horror at the row of holes in her table, a tremor of fear crawling up her spine.

Seeing her expression Tom let his shoulders droop and he placed the knife down on the table, straightening it meticulously then grinned up at her, shamefaced. 'Sorry. I didn't mean to alarm you. I get carried away sometimes.' Very gently he reached out a hand to stroke her cheek and she managed not to flinch as his voice dropped to a soft whisper. 'But it's all right. I've forgiven you, Lucy. You should be grateful I'm prepared to let the past go. I can't say fairer than that, now can I? You wouldn't want me to have to defend my honour, as it were? Or for anything nasty to happen to lover-boy, now would you?'

She gave a tiny shake of her head, anxious to appease him, to put an end to this appalling conversation before his temper flared again. What did he mean about something nasty happening to Michael? This day, this marriage, was all going terribly wrong, sliding out of her control.

But he was still smiling at her, saying what a lovely day they'd had and must repeat it some time soon. 'Now, is this dinner ever going to be ready? I'm sick of waiting.' Reaching for a potato he began to peel it, taking painstaking care to bring off the peel in long thin slivers. With shaking hands, Lucy picked up a carrot.

That night he cried in her arms, whimpering that he might have hurt her through his ungovernable temper and all because of what the war had done to him. He begged her again not to leave him and Lucy felt that the fragility of his mind was such that if she did, he might break down completely. Goodness knows what would happen then. She knew she should leave, run far, far away, but couldn't quite summon up the courage to do so. But how could she possibly escape? And if she did, he might hurt himself. He might hurt her, or even the children? There seemed no help for it but to continue to live as a dutiful and loyal wife.

Yet Lucy also knew that neither could she give Michael up. The sacrifice would be too great. Since Belinda's death, she needed him more than ever. Life was too short.

–

Lucy invented a new friend, named Sally, and claimed she lived in the next street. She persuaded Tom to allow her to continue having one evening out a week with her 'new friend' to go to the flicks. In truth she would be seeing Michael but Tom agreed without demur, making no comment as he sat quietly watching her apply lipstick, sweep her hair into bangs and select a pretty frock to wear. It renewed her hope that he was becoming more reasonable, that he deeply regretted his outburst.

Michael was more than willing to meet and they took a bus as far from the twitching lace curtains of Pansy Street and the bustling wharves of Castlefield as they could. They would hold hands and talk, relishing this time together. Week after week they met in this way. Sometimes they'd sit and cuddle on park benches, in dreary little cafes, or on the back row of anonymous picture houses, never noticing what was on screen. Once, Michael took her for lunch to a seedy hotel out in Ashton-in-Makerfield.

'You're mad,' she told him, excitement cascading through her.

'I'm in love.'

They sat in a drab dining room that smelled of stale cabbage and endless fry-ups yet barely recognised the fact. They paid even less attention to the curiosity and amusement in the eyes of the landlady who served them fatty pork and jam rolypoly pudding. All they wanted, all they needed, was each other.

'Will you be wanting to use the facilities?' the woman enquired when the meal was over, not quite with a wink but plainly enough for them both to understood that she was not discussing the bathroom arrangements.

Lucy gazed across at Michael and, embarrassed by what she read there, dropped her eyes to the grubby tablecloth, blushing furiously. Then somehow, without any conscious thought she was smiling up at the woman and saying thank you, that would be splendid.

Michael handed over the money to buy them an afternoon of privacy, an hour or two away from reality.

No time was wasted in preliminaries. They were tearing at each other's clothes the moment the bedroom door was closed, Lucy shivering with a new intensity of longing when Michael caressed her breast. The excitement of warm naked flesh meeting for the first time was too overwhelming for either to spare a glance at their surroundings. Neither noticed the fly-spotted wallpaper or the dingy curtains. They were too absorbed with tasting, sharing, loving, becoming one with the other, lost in a private world of their own where they could express the pent-up emotion and passion that they felt. Afterwards, lying with arms wrapped tight about each other, they could hardly bear to get up and dress and return to cold reality.

'You realise this is wicked. It should never have happened,' Lucy whispered, nuzzling close against the warmth of his body.

'Ask him for a divorce. Explain how you believe there is no hope for the marriage.'

'I did try, but failed. It's too soon.' Lucy related parts of their conversation but made no mention of the knife. She believed Tom regretted that moment of lost control, that he would never do it again.

'Try one more time. Please, Lucy.'

'I will, as soon as he's more settled in his new job, more used to civilian life and has come to terms with whatever is eating him up about his past.'

'I can't bear to give you up.' Michael was rolling her over onto her back, placing feathery light kisses over her throat and breasts, making her gasp with new desire. How could she resist, when she needed him so?

Over the following weeks the dingy hotel in Ashton-in-Makerfield became a favourite haunt for the two lovers. The landlady came to welcome them as old friends, asked no questions, simply took their cash and left them alone. It felt to them both as if it were only here, in this grubby little room that they truly became alive.

It amazed Lucy to find how adept she became at lying. She returned home that first evening, as on every other following and smiled at her husband, asked how the children had been. She behaved as if they were a normal, happy family and she had not just betrayed him with another man. But Lucy knew in her heart that what she was doing was wrong, and it couldn't go on like this.

Decisions needed to be made.

She was afraid that if she asked for a divorce she might lose the children for wouldn't she, in theory, be classed as the guilty party? Not for a moment did she consider giving Michael up. She'd felt suffocated, trapped in a marriage without love. She gloried in the love she found with Michael, bloomed with the wonder of it so that her hair shone, her face glowed and her eyes sparkled with happiness. Yet she continued to shy away from making any decision. Much better to leave things as they were. Tom didn't suspect. How could he? They were very careful. No one was getting hurt, she told herself Tom was reasonably content, and she could deal with her mother if she started interfering again.

'But I want more than this, Lucy, more than a hole-in-the-corner affair,' Michael would protest. 'I want us to be together all the time. For us to be man and wife.'

'I know love, so do I. Oh, what are we going to do?' And her heart would melt with need for him, so that they would have to make love all over again.

–

Polly, still keeping a close eye on the goings on of her family, was surprised one evening in late June to find young Sean walk into the warehouse, bold as you please. 'Heaven help me, where did you spring from? Where's your mam?' She quickly peered out through the door on to an empty street.

Sean grinned, jumping up and down on one foot with excitement. 'I came all by meself, Nan.'

'What, all the way, on your own, across the canal basin? Even under the railway arches and over the canal bridges?'

Sean nodded vigorously, evidently proud of this feat.

'Glory, isn't that a brave thing to do,' Polly said, trying not to alarm the child while hugging him tightly to her breast. Later, when she'd taken him back home and found the house empty save for Sarah Jane who was going frantic with worry, she fed them both and gave a stern lecture about strangers who ran off with small children, and Jinny Greenteeth who lived down by the water and ate them if they wandered off alone. Then having thoroughly frightened her beloved grandchildren into staying safely at home in future, Polly read them two cheering stories and tucked them up in bed. After that she sat in the kitchen and waited impatiently for Lucy to come home. Within seconds of her daughter crossing the threshold, Polly laid into her, determined to frighten her witless for her neglect of the children, using words such as irresponsible, dangerous, wanton, lazy and hair brained eejit.

It made no impression on Polly that Lucy insisted this was her one evening out a week, or that Tom had agreed to stay in and mind them. Polly had been too frightened by the little boy's adventure and told Lucy in no uncertain terms that the task of child minding was, first and foremost, a mother's responsibility. 'Did you even remember to ask Tom? If you had he would surely have been here with them.'

'Oh, so he's innocent and I'm guilty without even the benefit of a fair trial, is that it?'

'Where was it ye had to go that was so urgent? And don't try and lie, for you know I can allus tell.' Polly watched the tell-tale signs of guilt wash up her daughter's throat to mantle her cheeks with pink. 'So that's the way of it. I might've guessed. Aw, Lucy, have ye no sense?'

Any hopes Polly might have had of talking sense into her daughter were demolished as Lucy flounced out of the room, refusing to answer any more questions. Undeterred Polly went instead to see Minnie Hopkins and demanded she tell her what was going on between Michael and Lucy.

The old woman folded her arms across her skinny breast and sucked on her teeth, which for once she had in, and shook her head. 'I know nowt. Not my business.' Nor yours neither, her expression seemed to say.

'Saints preserve us, of course it is. Isn't he your nephew and Lucy a married woman. It's a sin for sure. Aren't they committing adultery, apart from the unholy mess they're getting them poor kids into.'

'Don't tell me you've turned to religion in your old age, Polly lass, and after all tha suffered from it in the past by way of bigotry from that brother-in-law of yours.'

Polly had the grace to blush but persisted with her concern for Lucy. 'No good can come of it. They'll all end up getting hurt.'

'Don't be too hard on t'lass. She's doing her wifely duty and sticking with Tom, po-faced and shifty though he is, just as you asked her to.'

Polly was startled. 'Shifty, who says so?'

'I do. Never looks you straight in the eye. There's allus summat suspicious when folk won't do that. And don't try telling me how much he's suffered. We know about suffering in this house, and he looks pretty fit to me.'

'Lucy is neglecting her children, going out night after night.'

'Nay, only one night a week, so far as I'm aware. Surely any woman has a right to that? But if yon lass is doing summat she shouldn't then it's for her and that husband of hers to sort out, not thee. You're her mother, but you don't rule her life.'

Minnie terminated the discussion by firmly changing the subject to the coming Bring and Buy in the church hall. Polly was forced to make a tactical withdrawal if not an absolute surrender.

–

The following Thursday, Lucy was late leaving as Sean had been fractious, trying to persuade her to take him with her to the pictures. She'd had to run to catch the bus and could hardly believe her eyes when, the moment she jumped on board, there was Polly, large as life in her tweed coat and head scarf, seated next to some toothless old dear in a rain hood. 'Hello, m'cushla, and where are you off to?' She might very well have added 'at this time of night' for it was writ plain in her bright enquiring eyes that she'd caught the bus on purpose to check on her.

Lucy took a moment to answer while she found a seat opposite her mother, fumbling in her pocket for some loose change for the conductor. Thrusting a collection of carefully hoarded half-pennies into his hand, he jiggled them and wisecracked, 'Carol singing started early this year, has it?' He gave her a broad wink as he clipped her ticket. Lucy tried to smile, her brain whirling.

'I'm going out with a friend,' she said at last, unable to find a better excuse.

'Who might that be?' Polly softly enquired. Her neighbour removed the rain hood so that she could better hear the reply, shaking drops over everyone seated nearby. 'I thought they all lived in Castlefield. This bus is going to the city centre. Now who d'you know who lives there? No one at all, I'm thinking.'

Lucy met her mother's shrewd, probing gaze and surrendered, mainly because a friend was the one thing she needed most in all the world. There were times, like now, when she ached to have Belinda to talk to, but her dear sister-in-law was gone. 'All right. I'll tell you, but you mustn't blame me too much. We couldn't help it.' Lucy became embarrassingly aware of how a bus full of prattling chatter seemed to grow oddly silent as ears positively twitched in their eagerness to listen in to this fascinating discussion. While Lucy hesitated, Polly pressed on with her interrogation.

'I suppose you're going to tell me that you love him.'

'I suppose I am.'

Polly's neighbour sucked on her gums and gave a brisk nod of her grizzled head. 'God makes 'em and the devil pairs 'em.'

Lucy shot the woman a fierce glare. The bell pinged and the bus lurched to a halt, the conductor calling out to mind the step. There was the usual jostling crowd waiting at the bus stop, anxious to get on before people had time to alight. Lucy waited until the conductor ping-pinged for the bus to start again then was on her feet in a second and jumped off the moving vehicle.

She waved cheekily at Polly as it roared away, her mother's face tight with annoyance.

Chapter Twenty-Two

During the long hot summer of that year, Lucy struggled to cope with her difficult and loveless marriage. How she envied the young Princess Elizabeth as her romance progressed smoothly towards what would undoubtedly be a happy one. The young couple were so clearly in love. But then Lucy's too had once seemed equally full of hope and promise until the war had changed everything, destroying the Tom Shackleton she'd once known and loved. In his place had come this hard, unfeeling person.

Despite his protestations to the contrary it was as if Tom was barely aware of her as a person. He would sit mute through family meals, barely register her presence as she went about her household chores. To her enormous relief his lovemaking, if you could call it that, became less frequent, though it remained as rushed and insensitive as ever. Lucy could barely bring herself to tolerate the intimacy let alone respond. But fearful of arousing his irascible temper, she never refused him. Afterwards she would stare up into the darkness and silently nurse her despair.

With Michael it was entirely different. She only had to see his smile, look into his eyes for her to burst with love for him. He would stroke her with such a loving tenderness it made her cry. He would kiss her warm eager mouth and groan with desire as he pressed against the soft silkiness of her skin, their bodies melded together as if created for that sole purpose.

And if she ever suffered a pang of guilt for acting upon their love then Lucy would remind herself of how cold and unfeeling Tom was, of how he could have written and told her that he lived, yet had chosen not to do so. Lucy was utterly convinced that he was lying to her about whatever happened to him back then, that there was much he could tell her if had he a mind to. If she could but discover the truth of those missing years, then she would be free.

She watched with some envy as Benny slowly rebuilt his life, caring for his son, working with his mother in an easy and friendly fashion. Her own relations with Polly remained distant following her shameful behaviour on the bus. On two occasions Lucy had plucked up the courage to go round to Polly's house specifically to apologise and talk about the problem. She longed to unburden herself and ask advice on what she should do, or rather ask how she could leave her husband without suffering guilt, a seemingly impossible quest. The first time Polly wasn't in. On the second she found her putting a cold compress on Charlie's knee which, as well as being swollen with painful arthritis, sported a massive purple bruise.

'I was only weeding the marigolds along the back yard wall,' he ruefully admitted.

'You're supposed to be resting, not gardening,' Polly scolded.

'I'm tired of resting and it isn't doing any good. Trouble is the knee doesn't always behave as I tell it,' Charlie joked. But this incident, not the first by any means, had so clearly upset Polly it somehow didn't seem the right moment to impose further worries upon her mother.

Lucy brewed tea for them all and sat for an hour listening and sympathising over the agonies Charlie suffered, the various treatments and 'cures' they'd tried, not to mention the pressures of Polly's business. Then she went home without even mentioning her own troubles.

When the precious Thursday came round again, Lucy put on a new frock, one she'd made herself, finding the money for it by pinching a penny here and there out of the housekeeping. But for once, Michael failed to notice for his distress over their situation was growing. Lucy strived to placate him, to make him understand that however much they might want to be together, Tom needed her more, for now. But his pleas grew so heated they came close to quarrelling.

'And what about *my* needs?'

'We must be patient.'

'For how much longer? I love you, Lucy, and want to spend the rest of my life with you, not simply snatched moments in this seedy hotel.' Looking out through the smeared glass of their bedroom retreat onto a dingy back street piled high with rubbish and rust-caked dustbins, Lucy couldn't help but agree.

She unbuttoned her dress, let it fall to the floor in a soft whisper, heard Michael's stifled gasp as she stood before him in her brassiere and French knickers, his eyes riveted to the outline of her nipples pressing against the flesh coloured silk. His voice, when he found it, was hoarse with longing. 'It's marriage I want, Lucy, not just sex. A proper life for us both.'

Lucy put her hands to her cheeks and began to cry.

'Don't. Oh lord, how I want you.' He went to her then, smoothed back her hair and cupped her small face in his hands. 'You know that I love you. I used to think we could run off and live together. But much as I want to be with you, it's no good pretending that would be an easy decision, because it wouldn't. In the eyes of the whole world we'd be living in sin.'

She slid a hand up about his neck and kissed his chin, his mouth, the roughness of his cheek. 'I don't call it a sin to love someone as we do.'

'Folk like Lily Gantry would have a field day.'

'I don't care. Let them do their worst, we'd be happy at least.' She felt desperate suddenly to get away from Tom, to feel safe and start life anew with the man she truly loved, yet knew she lacked the courage to leave, or ask Tom for a divorce. Perhaps living together was the only way out for them. What was so shocking about that? She pressed closer, pushing the softness of her breasts against the hardness of his chest, teasing him and bringing a smile at last to his lips with her display of wantonness. 'Maybe Tom would give up the fight to hold on to me, if he saw how happy we were together.'

His face was in her hair, breathing in the sweet, exciting scent of her. 'What about the children? How would they feel about it? They'd be ostracised at school, all their mates teasing them.' He asked this in such a quiet, sensitive way that Lucy dropped her gaze so that he couldn't read the fear in her eyes. If they didn't solve this problem would she lose him? She hardly dared think of that.

'It wouldn't matter. They both adore you, you know they do.'

'Try talking to Tom first, Lucy, sensibly and honestly. I'd come and speak to him myself, only that would be more likely to inflame him. Tell him you've done your best but that we need to be together, no matter what. Ask him for a divorce. I'll find the money to pay for it somehow.'

He stroked her cheek and meeting the loving urgency of his gaze, for the first time in months Lucy felt a surge of hope for the future, a new sense of freedom. 'All right. I'll try once more, I promise.'

'Be firm this time,' Michael insisted, pulling her down beside him on to the grubby sheets so he could remove these last silken impediments to their loving with his own eager hands. 'Be firm but kind. Show him you mean it this time.'

'I will.' Lucy was drowning in her need for him, helping him with the buttons and hooks. 'I shall be absolutely determined. Believe me.'

–

The next week passed in an agony of indecision. Time after time Lucy attempted to summon up the courage to broach the subject. But life was going along quite smoothly for once and she felt a reluctance, a fear almost, to spoil it. Tom even allowed her to have little Matt one afternoon, to give Doris-next-door a rest, which was lovely.

So the following week when they met, she admitted to Michael she hadn't yet found the right moment to mention divorce. He looked so hurt and disappointed that she struggled to explain her reluctance. 'Tom is working hard, settling in nicely at his new job. I'm afraid to risk upsetting him. It isn't easy for me, Michael. He can be up one minute and down the next. Life is so much better when he's calm, as he seems to be at the moment.'

'Better for *you* maybe,' Michael grunted, disappointment causing an uncharacteristic bitterness to curl his lips. 'Not for me.'

'Are you suggesting that I didn't really try?'

'How would I know? What proof do I have? I'm just your *fancy man.*'

'Don't say such a thing. You know it's not like that. You know that I love you, and want to be with you.' Not for the world did she want Michael to suspect this foolish fear that was growing inside her that Tom was only too aware of where she went every Thursday evening, yet chose not to mention it. Why she thought that, she couldn't say but if she was right, then it somehow made her extra wary of raising the subject of leaving him. It was as if one word from her might topple him from this pinpoint of patience upon which he balanced.

As summer progressed and the country talked of little else but the hope of a Royal wedding it became ever harder to keep Michael happy. Even Lucy began to shudder at the stained sheets they must lie on, the cobwebs festooning the cracked lamp shade above their heads and the fly-spotted mirror as she replaced her lipstick after their lovemaking. It all began to feel cheap and sordid as they furtively made sure they caught different buses back to Castlefield. Yet she couldn't quite bring herself to walk out on a husband who was clearly unstable, damaged by a war he'd never asked to be a part of, and would allow his wife and children to live in a free world.

-

By August Lucy knew she had fallen pregnant. She was quite certain that Michael must be the father, perhaps because she wanted him to be. Tom had bothered her less lately so it seemed likely, but how could she be sure? How could she go to either her lover or her husband and say with any conviction or sense of joy that she bore his child? She decided to say nothing to either. After all, it might prove to be a false alarm, and the delay would give her time to think.

Delay, in fact, only made Lucy worry more. She felt herself shrink a little whenever she felt Tom's eyes upon her, almost as if he knew what was happening inside her own body.

Afraid she might start to show, she took to wearing a corset whenever she was at home with Tom or out and about where people would see her, pulling the pink laces in quite tight. Only when she was with Michael did she leave it off, half hoping he would notice the slight thickening of her waistline and then she might at last find the courage to tell him of her suspicions.

It shamed and troubled her to discover how indecisive and weak she was becoming, as if she'd forgotten who she was and had lost all faith in herself. Why didn't she just come out with it and tell Michael she was pregnant with his child? Tell Tom she was leaving him. Tell Polly... Oh, lord, she couldn't.

What she dreaded most was what her mother would say.

Not that Polly would have noticed anyway, she was too caught up in her own business. Perhaps she didn't even care, Lucy thought, uncharitable in her misery.

While little Matt struggled to shake off a summer cold, Benny grew increasingly harassed trying to cope with a fractious baby all night while maintaining a full day's work at the shop. Despite his own concerns, even he realised Lucy wasn't herself when he again asked if she'd mind baby Matt for an afternoon, and she sadly refused.

'Where's that bright rebel of a sister I once had?' he teased. 'I know you're missing Belinda. I am too, for Christ's sake, but life goes on. We can't stop in bed and grieve for ever, much as we might want to.' He had to pause here to compose himself before continuing. 'Couldn't you have the babby now and then, Luce. I feel awful putting on good old Doris all the time.'

'It's not that. It's... it's Tom. He doesn't like me working. He thinks I have enough to do.'

'Ask him again,' Benny argued. 'Use your feminine charms.' Lucy merely looked at him and knew, deep in her heart, that the longer she put off confronting Tom about anything, the less likely she would ever to find the courage.

–

In the first week of September, Lucy called upon her mother at the warehouse. Polly showed her usual pleasure at seeing her daughter but barely paused in her labours of setting up a new loom with her mate, Maisie Wright, except to ask if she wanted a job as a spool setter, as she'd be needing another.

Lucy thanked her for the offer, wishing fervently she could accept but knowing Tom would never agree. Besides, if it was true and there was a baby on the way, what would be the point? She felt desperate to share the agony of her suspicions with someone who cared, but Polly was too busy explaining the process to listen.

'See here, each square on the pattern sheet has been given a number relating to the particular shade of wool to be used, a total of two hundred and fifty-two for the pattern width. Then we set out the correct shade of bobbins on to this spool table, in rows of colours which correspond to the pattern of squares. Clever eh?'

'Mam, can I just have a word.'

''Course you can, m'cushla. Then these threads see, will be wound in short lengths on to spools and then taken over to the loom for weaving into carpet. Isn't that clever? You'd learn it in no time.' Polly seemed oblivious to her daughter's distress. When Lucy didn't respond, she glanced up, perhaps noticing for the first time her daughter's pale cheeks and pinched expression. Polly's shrewd gaze narrowed in that familiar way. 'I was forgetting Tom's views on women working. You'll have to take that husband of yours in hand. He's living in the past, so he is. The war has changed all that nonsense. Talk to him, Lucy. Getting a job would do you good, instead of being cooped up in the house all day. It might put a bit of colour in your cheeks. Explain that to him.'

'I've tried. The thing is, it isn't simply Tom. Actually I'm...'

'Aw, give me the right thread for goodness' sake, Maisie. This job's difficult enough as it is.' Polly wiped the sweat off her brow. 'It's number 37 not 34. The pale blue. Keep your mind on the job and not on your new chap,' Polly teased her friend. 'Sorry, love, what were your saying?'

'The problem is...'

'Aw, Maisie, will ye keep hold of it. Hadn't I just threaded it through the flippin' hole.'

Lucy suddenly yelled at Polly. '*You* talk to him. I can't. He just won't listen. Matter of fact, nobody ever listens to a word I have to say.' Whereupon she turned on her heel and stalked away, head in the air. Polly stopped threading wool to gaze after her daughter in startled surprise.

'What can be eating her? Did she get out of bed the wrong side?' Polly shook her head in despair, pushing back a lock of hair with a tired hand before picking up the wool again and threading it through the correct slot. She longed to rush after Lucy, to ask what was wrong but this task couldn't wait. It was desperately important that they get the loom running. Knowing it was essential that the business prosper, she'd invested heavily in this third new loom, stretching herself to the limit in order to meet the orders she had waiting. She wouldn't be so strapped for cash if so much money wasn't tied up in dratted furniture that wasn't selling near fast enough for Polly's liking. 'What a trial life is at times.'

'It is indeed, and then you die,' Maisie agreed.

—

Polly made it her business to keep up to scratch on everything that was going on in her family and, in spite of Charlie's advice not to interfere, could rarely resist doing so. She was always ready to take up the cudgels on their behalf and fight all corners. But now she took note of his wise words and left well alone.

If Lucy had got herself into some sort of a muddle then she must, as both Minnie and Charlie insisted, get herself out of it. What could she do to help the daft eejit anyway? Benny had a battle of his own to fight and was waging it well. She admired him for the care he took of his son, and for the work he was putting into the business. Shouldn't she be the happiest woman in the whole world to have him here with her at last? Yet she felt swamped by worry.

Although some of their customers came into the new shop by chance while out and about in the street, most came via the credit club operated by Hubert. In many ways this was an advantage. It was a sure market, necessitating very little in the way of advertising. They were paid within thirty days for every sale, no matter how long it might take the customer to pay Hubert on a weekly basis. And if customers got behind in their payments, or did a moonlight flit, which was common enough in these parts, this would be dealt with by the ubiquitous Ron. Polly suffered no financial loss at all. In addition, the profit margins were excellent. It was largely because of this side of the business that she was able to expand her carpet manufacturing side quite so rapidly.

Because of these benefits, Polly was reluctant to complain to Hubert when she experienced difficulties. Inevitably some items moved less quickly than others, while some wouldn't shift at all. Right at the start he'd assured her that he had other outlets in the city as well as in Rochdale, Stockport and Bolton, so could easily move goods on to there. Unfortunately, he consistently failed to do so and Polly became increasingly frustrated and finally infuriated by the delays.

'You'll have to tackle him about it,' she curtly told Benny one day, after counting sixteen unsold balloon-backed chairs. 'Nobody wants these Victorian monstrosities. Haven't I told him so a dozen times.'

'He's asked us to give them a proper chance.'

'So we have. Far longer than any other shop would tolerate.' She smoothed a hand over the chair seats. 'Feel that leather. It's cracking already. Cheap, that's what they are, just like those dratted book shelves which are coming apart at the seams. Tell him I'm still waiting for compensation on losses there too. No wonder we aren't selling these chairs. Manchester folk have too much sense than to buy outdated rubbish. See you get rid of them. If you don't talk to Hubert, I will.'

She could tell by the way Benny's mouth folded into a tight line that he didn't care for her blackmail tactics.

'Don't sulk, laddie. Business is business. Sale or return means exactly what it says – if they don't sell you return them. Have 'em packed up this minute and Tom can drive them to Hubert's warehouse this very afternoon.'

The next morning on her way to work Polly called again at the shop and there the chairs still were, all lined up against the wall as if they were at a ball waiting for some Victorian young ladies to recline upon them. She felt a tide of hot-blooded Irish fury bubble through her veins as Benny patiently explained how Ron Clarke, in charge at the time Tom had called, had absolutely refused to unlock the stockroom doors so he'd been forced to bring the chairs back again. 'Something about the proper paperwork not being done.'

'Proper paperwork? Sure and won't I give the pair of them proper paperwork indeed.'

Benny wagged a placating finger. 'Mam, don't interfere. This is my part of the business remember, and Hubert Clarke is my father-in-law, er... ex father-in-law. I'll deal with the matter.'

'Then see that you do,' Polly warned him tartly. Jesus, Mary and Joseph, if it wasn't one of her children creating havoc in her life, it was the other.

Chapter Twenty-Three

Once the new loom had been set up to her satisfaction Polly spent a quiet morning in the office poring over the accounts, which were becoming a real source of concern. She wished now that she'd waited a bit longer before taking on a third loom, even if the manufacturing side of her business was doing well. It was the retail part which troubled her.

Charlie was perking up, insisting on getting out and about more as the pain subsided a little and Polly was glad about that. But the responsibility of being the main bread winner in the family still lay heavy upon her.

After a quick sandwich lunch, the first of several young girls answering the advertisement for spool setters began to arrive and she went to interview them. This took an hour of her valuable time and even when she'd set two girls on, neither of them much over thirteen since they'd just left school, Polly wished with all her heart that Lucy too would come into the business. She would have made more of the job than the pair put together. What an old stick-in-the-mud Tom was, to be sure. *Should she have a word with him herself?* she wondered.

Charlie was against the idea. 'So how would you speak to him, as his employer or his mother-in-law? Leave well alone or you'll make things worse for Lucy.'

That was hard to do as Polly was only too aware she'd neglected the girl lately, fussing about her own affairs when all the time she might need her. Something was wrong. She could sense it. What had Minnie said about Tom? Shifty! Polly promised herself a private word with Lucy, at the very first opportunity.

The next morning she put one of the young girls with Maisie to learn about spool setting, the other she took over to Joyce, who checked faults in the newly woven carpets; created because the hessian hadn't properly been woven in or gaps had been left where they shouldn't, or the warp had broken.

'Show her how to mark the faults, Joyce. If she cottons on to that in six or seven weeks and watches you carefully, I'll mebbe let her have a go at mending them. Work hard and you'll be happy enough here, lass. Though the pay's terrible, isn't it, Joyce?'

'Crippling,' Joyce agreed, and took the young girl under her wing, grinning widely.

It was half past seven by the time Polly got home. Charlie was trying to read the paper and complaining his eyes weren't focusing properly. 'I think I need specs.'

'You've already got some. Put them on.'

'They don't work any more. I need new ones. New eyes too,' he cheerfully told her.

Polly sighed, wondering if he'd given any thought to what they might eat. Her stomach felt as if it were full of razor blades, all sawing at each other, yet she felt too exhausted to do anything about it. 'No part of your old body seems to work as it should according to you. I'd ask for a complete refit if I wasn't so fond of the old one,' and she kissed him on the nose.

'How's it gone at the warehouse today?' he enquired, setting down his newspaper and fetching a dish of hot pot from the stove.

The steaming aroma made her juices run as he spooned it out. Polly mumbled a reply as she gratefully forked the first load into her hungry mouth, the meat so tender he'd clearly had it in the oven for half the day. 'Ooh bless ye, this is good. Unlucky in business but lucky in love, eh?'

Charlie chuckled. 'Shop not going too well then?'

'Don't ask.' Steam issued forth on her breath and it wasn't till she'd half emptied her plate and sated some of her hunger that Polly addressed the question properly. 'I'm going to see Hubert Clarke first thing tomorrow to tackle him about this furniture, whether our Benny likes it or not. A deal's a deal and if he promises sale or return, that's what I mean to have.'

–

Polly and Charlie spent all that evening going over the accounts yet again – bank statements, petty cash books, details of loan payments and profit ratios – and their worst fears were confirmed. If the business was to prosper and all payments were to be met, drastic action was called for. But the next day, faced with Hubert Clarke's solid figure, he proved to be as arrogant and unruffled as ever, setting out to pacify and urge Polly not to panic, to show faith and courage in the enterprise.

'It's not courage I lack, it's money,' she bluntly informed him, planting herself in his office as if she'd taken root there. 'If you don't stand by your promises, Councillor Clarke, then I'll be forced to take my business elsewhere.'

He smiled at her, moustache twitching, only the dark eyes beneath the ridge of bushy eyebrows giving any indication of his irritation. 'Nay Polly lass. Don't get in a lather. It'll all come out in the wash as they say.' He chortled good-humouredly at his own silly joke.

Polly frowned. 'It'll have to come out somewhere for sure. I'm not going on like this. Haven't I shown the patience of a saint, to be sure? Over twelve months I've had those chairs and sold only two. You promised me faithfully that you'd take 'em back, yet still I'm waiting and still you're delivering more stuff each and every week. Incidentally, that sideboard Benny ordered the other week never arrived, and we've a customer waiting.'

'I think you must be mistaken. That lad of yours must've got in another muddle over paperwork. Ron delivered it personally.' He smiled benignly at her, his expression seeming to challenge her to deny it, which Polly most certainly did.

'I don't think so. We're very particular with our invoicing and docketing. I've too much money tied up in stock and some of it must go.'

'Go?'

'Don't you deliver stuff whether we order it or not? We'll have furniture coming out of our ears soon, so we will. It's not good enough, Hubert.'

'There's no need to worry, lass,' he assured her, coming from behind his great desk to pat her shoulder with a placating hand. He went on to promise that Ron would persuade one or two of their better off customers to take the balloon chairs or, failing that, he'd mebbe agree to her returning half a dozen. When Polly insisted he should take the lot, due to the state of the leather seats he instantly backtracked, saying he couldn't take defective goods, not at any price.

'But they were in that state when you delivered them,' Polly insisted, shocked by his attitude. 'And what about those book-cases? Like cardboard they are, coming apart at the joints.'

'Happen they've had careless handling in your shop,' Hubert gently scolded, as if she were a naughty schoolgirl. Polly felt a strong urge to smack his arrogant face but managed to curb her temper and leave without doing any such thing. She did bang the door rather louder than she should on her way out. Later, she gritted her teeth with frustration when she told Benny that the chairs would need to be reduced in price and sold off at whatever they could get for them.

'And next time you take a new delivery check every single item. We take nothing that isn't perfect. Check your paperwork. Check everything.'

Benny resented being taken to task over paperwork which was, in his opinion, perfectly correct. He insisted she was fussing, that there was little wrong with the chairs and he would sell them given time and a bit of luck. 'You just have to fix the right price and find the right customer.'

'And not go bankrupt in the meantime,' she tartly informed her son. This wasn't what she'd expected, not at all. Something smelled fishy to her. Polly believed that trust was essential in any business partnership. It seemed to be sadly missing in this one and she'd have to keep an even closer eye on Hubert Clarke in future, and his so-called bargain furniture.

–

Within two weeks she was knocking on his office door again complaining that she'd ordered a batch of kitchen tables and chairs that had never arrived, nor the sideboard that they were still waiting for. Hubert called in Ron, who insisted he'd delivered them personally. 'If you don't know what stock you do have, Polly lass, how can you hope to succeed?'

Polly returned to Benny in a lather of embarrassment but despite searching the entire shop and stock rooms from top to bottom the consignment remained elusive, as did the paperwork.

'No invoice or delivery note,' Benny insisted. 'How can they have been delivered?' There was a copy of the orders, plain as day. Unfortunately it proved to be their word against his.

Polly next asked to return two dining room suites. 'They're in good condition but everybody passes them by. Too expensive for our neck of the woods. You'd do better sending them Cheshire way. I'll have them brought round tomorrow.'

Hubert refused point blank to take the suites back and also denied ever having agreed to a sale or return arrangement in the first place. Polly gaped at him open mouthed. 'Will ye say that again. I reckon me hearing has gone on the blink.'

'Whatever you take, you keep, Polly lass. I should've thought that was obvious. It's usual business practice, after all. However, I'll be generous on this occasion, since it's you.' He rocked back and forth on his booted heels, as if considering the matter then offered the now familiar placating pat on the head. It was such a patronising gesture that in different circumstances she might very well have slapped his hand away. Just the way he called her *lass* all the time, set her hackles rising.

'I tell you what I'll do for you, lass. I'll take back the two suites in question and swap them for four good sofas. How about that?

Fair enough deal, wouldn't you say?' Polly found herself forced to agree.

'Your father-in-law changes his mind with the wind,' she told Benny as she strode through the shop half an hour later, blind with rage and only too ready to land one on anyone who happened to be handy. 'The divil take the man but I'll have his guts for garters if those sofas don't sell. I'll cancel the whole deal, so I will, but I'll not be put upon.'

The four sofas sold within two weeks and, mollified, Polly grudgingly agreed to allow Benny to take a further consignment, covered in a lovely blue velvet-like fabric this time. It wasn't till several days later that she found time to examine them closely. The fabric showed clear signs of mould.

'Jesus, Mary and Joseph. What has he sent us this time?'

Benny, who admitted that he possibly hadn't checked them thoroughly enough when they were delivered, since he'd believed his mother to be making a fuss over nothing, said that he would deal with the matter himself this time. But even he returned from the fruitless visit white-faced and angry. 'Hubert says there must be damp in our shop. The fault is ours, he says, and he'll not offer credit for faulty goods. We're stuck with them, Mam. No one will buy them.'

'How can they have got damp in this shop? We've had them no time at all. Drat the man, I've had enough. No one is going to get the better over me. Certainly not Hubert Clarke.'

Oblivious to the squalls of rain misting the air, she marched down Castle Street, past the old Merchant's warehouse where a couple of barges were unloading at the shipping holes, across the iron foot bridge and on to Potato Wharf with such a fierce look in her eye and such a determined spring in her step, people turned to watch as she passed by.

She found Hubert superintending the unloading of a shipment of wooden crates, no doubt containing more of his rubbish. 'I've had enough, so I have,' she announced, silver knives of fire sparking in her greeny-grey eyes. Several of the men involved in the unloading hesitated momentarily to look at her in shocked surprise. It was unheard of to confront Councillor Hubert Clarke in that way, let alone beard him in his den, as it were.

Hubert grabbed her elbow and propelled her towards his offices. 'We'll save this for a more private place, if you don't mind.'

The minute the door was closed, Polly wrenched her arm free to face him with the kind of expression that proclaimed she would stand no more of his bullying. 'I'm sure I've nought to be ashamed of. Have you, Councillor?' she challenged him. 'Haven't I only come to tell ye that I'll be happy to supply your credit customers with *quality* goods. Unfortunately, yours are anything but, so I mean to find a different supplier, one who doesn't sell faulty merchandise, who delivers what we order and nothing more, and whose word is worth a good deal more than yours.'

It was several chilling seconds before Hubert deigned to respond. His face gave the impression that he'd like to throw her into the circular sluice that gushed and swirled in the canal just outside his window. Yet his voice, when he spoke, was studiously quiet as he leaned closer in a conspiratorial fashion.

'I've no wish to quibble nor deny you your rights, Polly lass, but you seem to be in a rather delicate situation. Don't you owe me rather a lot of money?' He smiled his beatific smile into Polly's shocked face. 'If you were to try such a manoeuvre, I'd let it be known, in the appropriate quarters, that you aren't to be trusted. So far as I can see, your credit rating as it stands now, is not good, not good at all.' Hubert clicked his tongue, accompanied by a sad shake of his head.

She could smell the tobacco on his tainted breath, hear her own heart beating a loud warning to remain calm. 'Isn't that only because you pile stock on me that I don't want, and diddle me left, right and centre.'

'I'd take care what charges you make about me, lass. Not unless you can make 'em stick.' Hubert flexed his shoulders, took out his watch, studied it carefully and dropped it back into his waistcoat pocket. 'It's a changing world, Polly lass,' almost as if the watch itself had told him so. 'There's no room in it for sentiment. Pay up what you owe and you can use whichever supplier you please. Till then, you'd best take care. You don't want no nasty whispers going the rounds questioning your credit standing, now do you? That wouldn't do your business any good at all.'

Polly was so furious her feet scarcely touched the ground as she sped home. But undeterred she did indeed set about finding a new supplier. She'd been in tighter corners in her life, she told herself crossly, and she sure as hell meant to get out of this one.

-

It proved to be more difficult than she'd expected but finally she succeeded in discovering a firm out Salford way who could provide her with good, non-utility quality furniture at a reasonable price.

'It won't be easy,' she told Benny who, not unnaturally, objected to this decision. 'But I mean to become independent again. It was a mistake to tie ourselves so closely with Hubert. It'll be a struggle but if we pull our horns in a bit, we can soon pay off what we owe him, then we'll be free.'

They were seated in the front parlour at number 32, relaxing after a substantial Sunday lunch and, while Charlie took his usual nap, Polly was happily dangling her grandson on her lap. Baby Matt had his mother's lovely cornflower blue eyes which had not darkened at all, coupled with his father's light brown hair and sturdy build. He'd break hearts for sure one day. Polly tickled the baby under his chin, making him erupt into happy giggles.

Benny was shaking his head. 'What if he sends his credit custom elsewhere? How would we manage then? Take on another supplier if you must, Mam, but don't sack Hubert.'

Polly felt a warm happiness despite her worries over the business, because her son had seemed more content of late, much more settled and mature. She touched the baby's nose with her own, making him gurgle with fresh laughter. 'Mebbe I'll look for a new credit trader an' all. Hubert Clarke isn't the only one.'

'No, but he's the one with power in this neck of the woods. Make no mistake about that.' Benny lifted his son from Polly, deciding it was time for his afternoon nap and perhaps too much excitement would prevent him from sleeping.

'You're a good father,' Polly told him fondly as he changed the child's nappy, preparatory to putting him down.

'Aye, that's because he's all I've got, which is why I want to have summat to leave him one day.' Benny stuck the nappy pin in place, taking care to keep one hand protectively against the baby's plump tummy. 'I'm not sure I trust Hubert any more than you do, but don't push him too far, that's all I'm saying. For now, at least, we need his business.'

Much as it might grieve her to admit it, the point was valid.

–

When Hubert heard of Polly's new supplier, he got out his Wolsey car and had Ron drive the mile or two to Salford to see him, just for a quiet word. The next day a van drove up in front of Benny's shop and the goods which had been so recently delivered, were all collected up again and taken away. Polly was furious.

'If this is war, won't I be the one to win it,' she cried, pounding her clenched fists on a brand new mahogany table so that Benny had to grasp her hands before she marked it.

'Just remember we're in this together. He did Belinda few favours in the past, and she was his daughter.' Mother and son exchanged glances locked in a grim promise of unity.

Polly found another supplier, in Ordsall this time, one who seemed only too keen to deliver a shipment of kitchen tables and chairs. Two weeks later he called at the shop on Deansgate personally and asked for them to be returned. Benny ranted and raved at the man but was told their credit rating had not come up to scratch, that the word had been put about that Polly was in hock to Councillor Clarke. Like it or not, they were stuck with Hubert and she'd have to accept that.

Desperate to find a solution to the problem, Polly went again to her bank manager to explain how well her carpet manufacturing was doing. It was admittedly new and still with a long way to go before it did anything more than break even. More importantly, she explained how the retail side of the business was draining away all her resources through overstocking she couldn't control, poor quality furniture they couldn't sell, and an exclusive contract she had no way to get out of except with hard cash. 'Councillor Clarke seems to think he can deliver what he likes, when he likes, and refuses to take the stuff back when it doesn't sell, despite our initial agreement that he would. I've called a halt to payments but he's turned nasty.'

After some hours of tough negotiating, the manager agreed to lend her the sum she required, though not a penny more.

'There you are,' Polly announced with no small degree of triumph as she slapped the cheque of settlement down on Hubert's polished desk. He barely glanced at it, made no move to pick it up, then smiled up at her. 'So where's the interest?'

Polly stared at him, dumbfounded. 'Interest? What interest?'

'On the loan. You surely don't imagine that I gave you free rein on my money for nothing?'

'You told me the loan was interest free.'

'Have you got that in writing?' Of course she hadn't. Hubert Clarke, Polly realised, had been very clever, taking full advantage of their family links and grief over Belinda, which had distracted them. She snatched back her cheque and left his office before she did actual physical violence.

–

Some few weeks later, Hubert was driving home in his Wolsley. The smell of coal dust was strong on the night air as he drove along Liverpool Road, but within the confines of his motor he inhaled with satisfaction the aroma of leather and a good cigar. He didn't usually indulge while he was driving but he was feeling particularly in need of its solace this evening. He'd already spent an hour with Myra but that hadn't helped calm him as it usually did, his mind not quite on the task in hand. Perhaps he was growing a little bored with Myra. She never seemed as welcoming as she used to, always asking awkward questions, like if Joanna was missing Belinda. Ridiculous woman.

Nor was he satisfied with the way his business affairs were progressing. Ron, seated beside him in the front passenger seat, had just informed him that Polly was now going round the Manchester hotels trying to win a contract to supply them with carpets. She was canny that one. Never missed a trick.

The Pride family should have buckled long since beneath the pressure he was applying. He'd made sure he sent them nothing but rubbish, as well as stuff that had failed to sell anywhere else, yet still the blasted woman hung on. Maybe she was making more brass out of her carpet manufacturing than he realised. If so, it might be a good idea to put a few spokes in that wheel as well.

He rubbed the cigar between finger and thumb, enjoying the expensive aroma as he turned various ideas over in his head, then clamped it between his teeth as he changed gear and negotiated the corner into Deansgate. The simplest plans were always the best.

'Could you get inside that warehouse of hers?'

Ron gave a snort of contempt. 'I can get in anywhere, me.'

Hubert smiled. 'Funny thing about the weaving industry. It never learns, does it? Spends a fortune on fancy new looms, but no matter how well they weave, whether it be coats or carpets, they still make a lot of waste. Makes you wonder don't it, if the folk who run these places, knows just how dangerous it is to leave oily waste lying about in a weaving shed. Or even in an old warehouse.'

Ron swivelled his head round to consider his father for a long moment in silence. Then his narrow lips split into what might be called a grin, making him look rather like a lizard after it's caught its dinner. 'Aye,' he said. 'Dangerous stuff, oily waste. Owt can happen to it.'

Chapter Twenty-Four

The papers were full of the Royal Wedding. They spoke of the princess's beautiful ivory gown, her radiant loveliness, the rose petals which showered the bride and groom. They described the cheering crowds who gathered along the route and waited at the gates of Broadlands to welcome them on honeymoon. Everyone in the whole country seemed to have something to cheer about so far as Lucy was concerned. She even caught some of the excitement herself for hadn't she too found romance and, given half a chance, could be as radiant as any royal princess, even if she was obliged to meet her 'prince' in a seedy hotel.

Lucy's 'prince' didn't agree with her. She'd never seen Michael so upset and no amount of seduction or teasing on her part would mollify him. On this night when all the country was celebrating with parties and fireworks, they had their worst quarrel yet. His voice rose to such an alarming pitch that Lucy felt quite certain half the hotel must be listening to their squabble.

'You say that you love me, that you can hardly bear for Tom to touch you. Yet you stay with him, day after day, week after week, month after month. If you loved me half as much as you say, then you'd tell him so, and ask for a divorce and leave him. Then we could be wed.'

'You know I'd leave him if I could, Michael. I do love you only...'

'Show me! Prove it.' Distress lined his face, in that instant making him look almost old. 'By next Thursday when you come, I'll expect you to have made it plain to him that your marriage is over. I've said I'll wait for you, Lucy, but not forever. I've had enough. If I can't have you right and decent, then I don't want you at all.'

It nearly broke her heart to see him so upset and two huge tears squeezed out from beneath her lashes. 'You don't mean that.'

'I do mean it, Lucy. I've had enough of this hole and corner affair.' And she saw that he had.

'All right. I'll think about it. I promise.' She longed suddenly to tell him about the baby, might well have done so had his next words not robbed her of the fragile remnants of her courage.

'This is the end, Lucy. It's time for you to choose. That's all I ask. It's him or me. Make your mind up one way or the other.'

–

When the day for their usual meeting came round, Lucy woke with fresh determination in her heart. All week the fever of excitement had been growing in her. Michael was right. They couldn't go on like this. She felt a new resolve to put her life in order once and for all. She would first of all tell Michael about the baby and then the pair of them would go to Tom and explain the whole situation. She couldn't think why they hadn't thought of doing this before. It would be so much easier to face him together. Of course if she'd ever properly explained about Tom's violent mood swings, then he might well have offered. Tom surely wouldn't attempt to bully her if Michael were there.

The two of them might have to go away of course, somewhere other than Castlefield, or even Manchester. But she no longer cared where she went so long as she had her children with her, and Michael. The decision had been made.

She put on her prettiest pink dress, the one cut on the cross which so enhanced the neatness of her figure. She was three and a half months gone and there was as yet little alteration to her slender waist or the firm flatness of her stomach despite her worries and fussing with a corset. For the first time since realising she was pregnant Lucy felt happy, which only added to

273

the surge of excitement she always felt when she was going to meet Michael.

'Where are you going tonight, Mam?' Sarah Jane asked, coming into the bedroom as Lucy was getting ready, Sean trailing behind her, thumb in mouth.

'I'm off out with my friend Joan,' Lucy fibbed, not meeting her children's collective gaze through the mirror. She tapped Sean's hand and the thumb came out with a loud sucking noise.

'I thought she was called Sally.'

'I've more than one friend.' Lucy made a mental note to be more careful. She understood now why they said liars should have good memories.

Sarah Jane flung herself on to her parents' bed, chin propped in hand and watched with interest as Lucy applied Hollywood red lipstick to her rosebud mouth. Sean scrambled up beside her, sliding the thumb back in, eyes wide. 'Do you ever see Michael?' Sarah Jane innocently enquired, a wistful expression on her pale face.

The lipstick slipped from Lucy's fingers, leaving a trail of crimson extending over the corner of her mouth and she began to scrub at it with a licked finger. 'Why would I?'

'He never comes to see us any more. I thought he was our friend.'

'He used to take me fishing,' Sean said, speaking around the thumb. Lucy again removed it and worried about why he'd recently taken up this babyish habit. She tucked her children up in bed, read them the story of the Gingerbread Man and then, acutely aware she was late, half ran downstairs. As usual Tom was in his chair by the fire, reading the sport's pages. He made no move as she shrugged on her best brown coat and carefully pinned an evidently new and very perky little scarlet hat atop her curled bangs.

'I'm off out then,' she said, kissing the air an inch above the top of his head. Tom neither moved nor spoke. Lucy took a step back towards the door. She wanted to call and speak to Polly first and if she didn't hurry she'd miss the seven o'clock bus and then Michael would think she wasn't coming. 'I won't be late. It's the first house pictures we're going to. You'll mind the kids?' No response. 'Are you listening?' And when he still didn't respond, she turned and left the house.

Only then did Tom fold his paper and get up from his seat. He hovered in the shadow of the front door while he watched Lucy hurry up the street and go into her mother's house. She was barely in there more than a second or two before she was out again, half running this time, in the direction of the canal basin and maybe the warehouse. Tom collected his jacket and followed her, maintaining a safe distance.

–

Lucy hurried down Pansy Street, scarlet hat askew, coat flying open in her haste to put her decision into effect. She skirted Potato Wharf, barely glancing at the rushing sluice and clattered over the iron foot bridge on her way to Polly's warehouse near Knott's Mill. Ahead of her were the railway bridges and viaduct that spanned the canal basin, a section she loved during the day when she could watch the comings and goings of brightly painted barges and folk about their business but now, with dusk falling, she kept up a brisk pace, the thunder of train wheels going over just at the moment she passed beneath, seeming to rattle the teeth in her head.

'Spare a penny luv, or an 'appenny'll do.' A voice from the shadows beneath the arches made her jump and she hurried on, drawing her coat close, starting to button it. The November night was cold and dank and she wished, not for the first time, that Polly spent more time at home and less at the warehouse. A drunk with a whiskery chin lurched out from behind a pillar so that by the time she reached Castle Street Lucy was running flat out, arriving at the side door of the warehouse, built into the filled-in arch, quite out of breath.

It was unlocked and she wrenched it open, the shadows seeming to leap out at her as she stepped inside. She heard a sound, a rustling whisper and Lucy halted in her tracks, staring about from eyes grown wide with fright. The entire warehouse was shrouded in darkness, the only light coming from Polly's office. She glanced back over her shoulder, thinking the noise must have come from outside and quickly pulled the door shut behind her. The darkness became even more intense and the looms reared like black apparitions in the dusty shafts of moonlight that seeped in from semicircular windows set high in the walls. Lucy shuddered, then took a step out into the void. As she hesitantly negotiated the crossing of a room littered with obstacles at every step, though now empty of its workers at the end of the day, the sound of her heels echoed hollowly on the wooden flooring. So loud were they, that had there been any other sound, she would not have heard it.

Polly set down the wad of papers she'd been studying when Lucy entered the office and stood, arms akimbo, to consider her daughter. Lucy saw at once that she wore her most disapproving frown, not at all what she'd hoped for.

'Saints preserve us, what is it now? I can see something terrible has happened by the look on your face.'

It took no time at all for Lucy to pour out her guilty secret, for the burden of it had grown heavy of late. In order to quench any expressions of joy or attempts at congratulations she quickly added that it was Michael who was the father and not Tom. Polly showed her disapproval only by a slight widening of her eyes.

'And what does Tom think of all this?'

'He doesn't know, and you mustn't tell him.'

'He needs to be told.'

'I know and I'll tell him myself, as soon as I've spoken to Michael. He doesn't know either.' She let it all pour out then, all her disappointment in the marriage, her efforts to please Tom in the beginning, quickly stifled by his selfish and cold attitude towards her. Polly responded as Lucy would have expected, with exhortations for her to show more patience, to allow for the fact that this man had spent years as a POW so how could he be expected to behave normally? Guilt cascaded through Lucy, making her feel small and cheap. She could see that her mother was doing her best to hide her shock, but Lucy could sense her disapproval in the stiff way Polly's head moved on her neck, the pursing of the lips and the way her hands were folded tightly together.

'You neglect your children because of this foolish passion with your fancy man. Running wild they are. And have ye thought of the babby? You'd be making it into a bastard if you choose Michael as the father and, to my way of thinking, that's what ye would be doing – choosing. For how can ye be sure?'

Lucy hung her head, saying nothing, unable to deny the truth of that. What proof did she have either way?

'Shame on ye lass, for such wickedness. I'm disappointed in you. Didn't I think you'd show more sense and be kind to your poor husband when he comes home to ye at last.' Somewhere in the depths of the building there came a scraping sound, as if a door or window had blown shut in a draught. For an instant Lucy was aware of it and then forgot it in her distress.

Tears ran down her cheeks at her mother's lack of under-standing. Nobody did but then how could she explain the misery of living with Tom, the long accusing silences, his volatile moods and his episodes of violence. He exerted an almost dehumanising control over her which assumed that he alone was capable of making decisions, treating her as if she were an idiot with no mind of her own. And then there was the callous way he used her body which made her shudder whenever she thought of it. How could she face the embarrassment of telling her own mother all of that?

'If ye take my advice you'll kiss goodbye to Michael Hopkins, however lovely a man he might be, for it wouldn't be right. Don't tell him about the babby. What good would it do, except to bring more pain? You've not been with Tom a year yet. Give him a proper chance. Wouldn't he just love the chance to be a dad, a proper one this time, there every day to watch the child grow up? Ye owe him that at least, do ye not?'

Lucy felt herself driven almost to the limits of her endurance. Why couldn't somebody be on her side, instead of always taking Tom's? It was perfectly clear Mam wasn't going to find it easy to accept a daughter who'd given up on her marriage. But then having been fortunate in both her husbands, how could Polly ever hope to understand? To all outward appearances Tom was an impeccable and caring husband, always smartly turned out and mindful of his family's needs. Only Lucy, as his wife, was aware of his darker side, of a simmering anger that nothing seemed to mellow, and how he too often seemed poised on the brink of explosion.

She pushed her face up close to Polly's. 'I owe him nothing. You don't understand. Tom *lies!* All right, I've no proof but I know he lies all the same. I've only his word that he was anywhere near a POW camp. Who knows where he was or what he's been up to all those years. Half the war he was missing and more than a year after it ended with not a single word. Nothing but silence. Michael is good to me. He's kind and gentle, and I can hardly bear for Tom to touch me. It's no good. It won't work.' Her voice broke on a hiccuping sob. 'However long I stay with him, I'll never feel the same about him as I should.'

She began to sob in earnest now and, seeing her distress, Polly put her arms about Lucy, a tide of sympathy and love for her daughter breaking down the barriers of disapproval.

'Aw m'cushla, don't I know what it is to be in love, to have no other thought in your head.' This surge of sympathy might have brought forth more details about the dark side of her marriage, and of Lucy's secret fears, were it not for the crack of erupting flames as they shot through the open doors opposite, and the smell of dense smoke suddenly alarmingly evident to them both.

–

Lucy arrived home in the early hours in great distress. Tom was waiting in the kitchen with the kettle simmering on the hob despite it being past two o'clock in the morning, almost as if he'd expected her to walk in at any minute. But then he'd probably been half out of his mind with worry over why she was out so late. It was a wonder he wasn't standing at the door with his sleeves rolled up and fists at the ready. Instead, he was surprisingly kind to her when he heard about the fire, and as tears of shock rained down her smoke-blackened cheeks, Lucy told more than she had meant to.

It was Tom who helped her out of her soot-blackened clothes, washed her face and limbs and dressed her in a warmed night-gown, just as if she were Sarah Jane. Then he assisted her up the stairs to bed, all the while explaining how he'd known all along about the coming baby. Hadn't he heard her throwing up in the sink each morning? He was glad, he told her. He'd always wanted another child. They stood at the top of the stairs and he told her how delighted he was of this chance to be a proper father at last. He made no mention of Michael Hopkins, and neither did she. His only reference to her evening out was to mildly enquire if she'd ever got to the pictures and Lucy dolefully shook her head, then put her hand to it for it throbbed horribly. 'Sally wouldn't mind. She'd go in and see it anyway.'

His fingers closed about her arm, 'I thought you were going with Joan. Forgotten your friend's name already?'

'No, both Sally and Joan were hoping to go, but at the last minute Sally had to cry off,' Lucy hastily fabricated. 'So poor Joan would be on her own?'

'Yes, yes – that's right. Joan would be on her own. God, I'm tired.' She made to move towards the bedroom but he was still holding her arm.

'You'll have to go round tomorrow and explain.'

'Yes, I will. We'll talk then, shall we?'

'And no one else was expected to be there, at the pictures?'

'No, no one. Just the – three of us.'

279

It was as she turned to step thankfully into the bedroom and the oblivion of sleep, that it happened. His attitude suddenly changed. One moment he was stroking her arm and smiling sympathetically at her, the next he was spitting his fury directly into her face. '*You're a liar!* I don't believe a bloody *word!*' Then she was falling, over and over back down the narrow stairs. She had time only to wrap her arms instinctively about herself to protect the coming child as her hips and knees bumped and jarred on every step.

Seconds later she lay shaken and crying, having cracked her head on the door post. Tom was beside her, cradling her in his arms, murmuring words of remorse and sympathy, stroking her bleeding head and saying how he'd never meant to hurt her. 'Something just comes over me, Lucy. I can't seem to help myself.' Then somehow her tears had dried and it was she who was comforting him. Yet in that moment everything changed, a turning point had been reached in her mind.

'I know it was an accident, that you never meant me any real harm. Nevertheless, I think I'll sleep with the children tonight. My head is aching so badly I might disturb you with my restlessness.'

For once Tom did not argue.

In truth, only the warmth of her children's loving bodies were able to ease the horrors of the night's events. Exhausted as she was, sleep deserted her the moment she lay down. Tom was a consummate liar. She felt his behaviour tonight had proved that. He'd given every impression that he believed this to be his child with his soft words and caring gestures, yet his actions, by deliberately thrusting her down the stairs, proved he didn't believe that at all.

Lucy was shaking with emotion, shivering with shock yet not for a moment dare she venture downstairs for a cup of tea or a warm by the embers of the kitchen fire. She was too afraid. Eyes wide open, she lay staring up into the darkness, her thoughts turning to Michael like an angel of light in her head.

He would have been disappointed, of course, that she hadn't managed to get away but he'd understand, and soon it wouldn't matter for they'd be together always. Thinking of his love made the shock ebb slowly away and a warm sensation to flow through her veins as she came to a decision. She realised now that she could never find the courage to tell Tom she was leaving him, not face to face. She saw that there was only one recourse open to her. Tomorrow, while he was at work, she'd pack her things, hers and the children's and go to Michael. Then they would indeed run away together. Far away from Pansy Street and the gossips of Castlefield.

She didn't expect to sleep but she must have done, for it seemed no more than a matter of moments before morning came and she was dragging herself out of bed, searching for fresh clothes. Tom was already seated at the kitchen table by the time she reached it, waiting for his breakfast as he scanned the morning paper, just as if it were any normal day.

'There's nothing in here about any fire,' he said, as if she'd made it all up.

'It happened too late for them to print anything.' Lucy crossed to the sink to fill the kettle. Every muscle screamed with pain, even her bones ached as if she'd fought the fire herself instead of simply helping Polly carry out as much stock as they could before it took a proper hold. Sadly, they'd managed to save precious little as it had spread frighteningly fast. Lucy guessed she must be covered with bruises. 'It'll be in the Evening News. I'll go and see Mam this morning. She'll be in a terrible state.'

Exhaustion dragged at her, fogging her mind so that she couldn't think properly, making her eyes feel like burned holes in her head.

Lucy cooked kippers for Tom's breakfast, handed him his hat and coat, even let him kiss her cheek as usual when he left the house. He made no mention of the baby, or her 'accidental' fall down the stairs. Neither did she. They simply kept up the pretence of normality, which had become second nature to them.

When he'd gone she forced herself into action, hastily packed bags with clumsy fingers, stuffed clothes in anyhow, ironed or not, and instead of taking the children to school she walked and dragged and hustled them to the end of the street where she knocked on Minnie Hopkins's door. Michael, she knew, would be delighted to look after all three of them.

It was Minnie who opened the door, holding a handkerchief to her face. Lucy saw at once that the old woman had been crying. Her first thought was that she'd heard about the fire but then how could she, it surely wasn't generally known yet and why would that make her cry? Nobody had been hurt, but then inside of her a creeping fear swelled and began to fill her entire body.

'What is it? Where's Michael? Dear God, *no!*' Somehow it came as no surprise to hear Minnie Hopkins open her toothless mouth and wail that he had gone, vowing never to return.

–

They all four crowded into Minnie Hopkins's tiny kitchen to listen to her sad tale. 'He was all I had. To be honest, he weren't really my nephew at all. He were me son,' she confessed on a great gulping sob. 'My mam and dad were so ashamed of my fall from grace they were going to send me to a home for wayward girls. So I up and run away. Never went back.'

'Oh, Minnie, I didn't know.' Lucy could hardly take in Minnie's story, as she sat in a state of disbelief. This couldn't be happening to her. Michael wouldn't go off and leave her. Yet she knew that he had. Hadn't he told her to choose? That this was her last chance. Last night, the very date when she was to give him her decision, she'd missed their date completely because of the fire. He wouldn't have known why she'd failed to turn up, of course. He would simply assume that she'd made her choice, and that it wasn't him. Oh, dear God, why hadn't she gone to him last night, however late it was.

'It was nobody's business but mine,' Minnie was saying. 'Least said, soonest mended.'

'But how did you survive, a young girl on her own?' Lucy now found her sluggish mind racing, half of it listening to Minnie's tale, the rest of it desperately seeking a solution to her own tragedy.

'Oh, it was hard at first. I near starved. Lived rough for a year or two but I weren't the only one in t'same pickle. I met other girls. We helped each other. Then I found a job working on the wharves packing, and Michael used to help me. He were only small like but he were a right little Trojan. Wife of my gaffer spotted him and told me it was no place for a child. She were the woman what owned this house. Come down in t'world she had, but still had a bob or two. She took me on as housemaid and told me I could fetch him wi' me. I said he were me sister's child, though I never had no sister. For my lad's sake it seemed better if I made out I were his aunt. Saves all that nasty name-calling. But he were t'best thing that ever happened to me.' Despite her tough words, Minnie's faded eyes again filled with tears which she quickly stifled with a large white handkerchief, blowing her nose vigorously.

'Oh, Minnie, I'm so sorry.'

'He said you and him had quarrelled last time you were together, that you'd refused to...' She ran out of words, of breath even as choking sobs finally doused her control.

Filled with a new, deeper shame and guilt for robbing this old woman of her one and only joy in life, Lucy put her arms about her. Sensing the rigid shoulders, the unyielding spine, she went instead to grab the kettle and began to issue orders, as if someone had been taken ill and they must all rally round to deal with the emergency.

'Sarah Jane, fetch the cups. Sean, get the biscuit barrel.' Something sweet for shock, wasn't that right? But it was only the children, bewildered and exchanging anxious glances, who dipped into it. At least the treat kept them quiet and happy while she strove to think. Poor Minnie didn't even have the heart to suck one of her favourite pear drops.

She'd no idea where Michael might have gone, but no, she didn't think it would be back in the army, because of the missing foot. 'They wouldn't have him, would they?' Nor did she know the names of any of his friends outside of Castlefield, or even Pansy Street for that matter. The rumours of his being a conchie had done their worst. And she didn't expect him to go back to his old house either since it'd been flattened by a bomb. It was as they talked that the true reality of her situation finally hit Lucy as the tears slid down her cheeks. Michael was gone, she knew not where. She was carrying his child, of that she was quite certain, and since she'd no intention of ever returning to her husband, she knew she must bear it alone, just as Minnie had done.

Chapter Twenty-Five

Hubert was satisfied that events were swinging his way. He could feel his tide of luck turning. His own financial situation was growing stronger by the day, greatly assisted by having taken over a small but significant clothing manufacturer which had stubbornly evaded making proper payments on a loan. Taking control of the company would make him a far greater profit in the long run which had been his object from the start. Yet another case of someone else's grey cloud providing him with a silver lining. All most satisfactory. Some people collected works of art. Hubert preferred more substantial artefacts, like property or businesses. With his next victim already picked out, he lit a cigar and sat back in his smart leather chair with a smile to wait for events to unfold.

He was interrupted in his reverie by the strident clang of the door bell. Hubert waited, one ear cocked for Joanna to answer it as she always used to. The door bell clanged again.

'Damnation. What was wrong with the woman?' True, losing Belinda had proved to be a severe blow to his wife and she hadn't been the same since. Never in the darned house for one thing, her excuse being that where was the point in making a fuss about meals and her garden when there were only the two of them, a state of affairs which would now never change.

He clamped the cigar between his teeth and strode to the door, flinging it open with a growling, 'Well?'

He was mildly surprised to find his son-in-law standing on the doorstep, a gurgling baby propped on one hip as if he were some gypsy who couldn't afford a pram, and despite the fact it must be well past the child's bedtime. Class, Hubert decided, always revealed itself unless properly trained.

'I've come to ask if you'd anything to do wi' that fire,' Benny bluntly announced. 'Because if you had, I'd like to know why, since it damages your grandson as much as anybody.'

Hubert was momentarily startled. By heck but Ron had been quick off the mark. He hoped it had been a bad one. He covered his confusion by studying the child which seemed to be surprisingly well cared for, all smartly dressed in a blue knitted jacket and balaclava. Joanna had dreamed of grandchildren, yet couldn't quite bring herself to accept Belinda had actually given her one. Nor more could he. It came to Hubert in that moment that there was one obvious way he could curb his wife's restlessness and make her happy for once.

'Why would I harm this little chap, Benny lad. Or the business he might inherit? All I can do now that I've lost Belinda, is to ensure her son gets what would've been hers by right.'

Hubert really had no wish to be harangued by this ruffian, whom he'd never liked. Nor had he any intention of allowing the Pride family to keep either their business or his grandson. Little Matthew's inheritance would come from quite a different source. He'd easily get custody of the child, for Joanna's sake, when the moment came. Once he'd won his revenge over what this rogue had done to his beloved Belinda.

Time, it seemed, had warped Hubert's memory of his relationship with his only daughter and he now viewed it as a close one, spoiled only by Benny and not by his own machinations. He'd conveniently forgotten his part in her eviction from the shop, the very reason she'd given birth in a freezing back street with no medical assistance until it was too late. The fault, in his mind, lay entirely with this no-good piece of dross who was cluttering up his doorstep.

Benny was still glowering, as if trying to decide whether to believe his father-in-law or not. 'If you had any hand in what went on last night, don't think I won't find out, and do summat about it.'

286

'What right have thee to threaten me?' Hubert's carefully practised diction always deserted him under stress, revealing that self-made man though he may be, underneath he was no more than a step removed from his lowly origins in Quay Street. His mother had taken in washing to earn an honest crust, her one ambition to buy a better life for her only son. And hadn't he clawed and cheated his way up the ladder of success ever since, right to the bloody top, if only to prove she hadn't wasted her efforts. He certainly had no intention of being knocked off his perch by this piece of dirt. 'I'll thank you to take your mucky boots off my doorstep. It's a pity, to my mind, that I ever let them stand on it at all. I should've knocked your clock off the first time I clapped eyes on thee. Then my Belinda might still be alive today instead of...'

He got no further. Snapping to attention, Benny took a step forward to shake a furious fist less than an inch from Hubert's nose. 'Damn you to hell, Hubert Clarke. Mam's right. You *are* the lowest of the low whether you set that fire or not.' In that moment he was very much the soldier with a power he wasn't above using. The ferocity of the action so startled Hubert that he instinctively backed away while Matt, alarmed by the anger in his dad's voice, started to howl. 'Make no mistake. Our family sticks together. Take on one, you take on the lot.' Then as the baby's cries rose to a higher pitch, Benny smoothed his son's head with a gentling hand, swung on his heel and marched away.

–

It took till the middle of the next day before the fire brigade was satisfied the fire was completely out. When they'd finally gone, all Polly's pent-up fury erupted in a tide of temper almost as hot as the flames themselves. 'Will ye look at this mess? What the fire hasn't ruined, the water has.' She began to cry, hands outstretched, encompassing the awful scene. The new looms were a mass of charred metal while almost every scrap of wool, every bobbin and shuttle, every yard of carefully woven carpet was destroyed. Over the whole building hung a stinking pall of smoke. It looked as if the Luftwaffe had been over and dropped their last bomb. Polly stood in puddles of water and looked about her in desperation for someone to blame. Her gaze fell upon poor Benny and she at once laid into him for not having removed the waste as he was supposed to do.

'We were lucky I happened to be there at the time, dealing with some bills,' she ranted. 'Otherwise, saints preserve us, the whole building would have come down. Have you no sense in that head of yours?'

She regretted the words almost as soon as they were out of her mouth. The accusation was unfair and they both knew it. Benny wasn't the only one responsible for clearing away the waste wool. He worked as hard as she did on the business, sometimes even harder for, apart from little Matt, it was his only solace. She knew that he was desperate to fill every moment of his day with work, even if it meant carrying the baby about on his hip while he did it. This was the only way, he'd admitted to her in one unguarded moment, that when night came he could lay his head on his pillow and sleep, instead of thinking about Belinda till the pain swelled in his chest so that he could scarce breathe.

Polly quickly apologised, putting her arms about his great shoulders and hugging him, for wasn't he her lovely boy. But the accusation left a sour taste in both their mouths. To justify her anger and prove the reason for her flash of temper, she showed him the parlous state of the accounts. 'We're over-borrowed and overstocked and don't I know full well whose fault that is. No matter what I do to try to get out of this awful mess, Hubert Clarke sticks his oar in and stops me.'

She could see by the thin white line above tightly compressed lips that Benny might be beginning to share her lack of trust in his father-in-law. Yet still he stepped in to defend him. 'It's certainly true that he's an awkward old sod. He and Belinda didn't get on at all well. But he's lost her, for God's sake! Now he insists that he wants to help provide a sound business to pass on to his only grandson. He told me so himself.' Benny picked up a hunk of scorched wool and crumbled it in his hand. 'Some heritage.'

Polly was about to express her doubts that Hubert was capable of such a sentiment when a voice from the door interrupted her thoughts. 'The boy's right. My grandson is more important to me than you might imagine. Isn't all of this partly your own fault, Polly Pride, for buying those looms.'

'I would say you're right there,' she agreed, turning to face her accuser. 'And my fault for getting involved with you, Hubert Clarke, in the first place. But like the phoenix, we'll rise from the ashes, see if we don't.'

'What with? Are you properly insured, lass?'

'I am.'

'But will that be enough? Insurance folk can be a touch choosy how much they cough up in a case like this. By heck,' he said, walking about and poking at charred beams with the point of his stick, coughing when he caused a shower of sparks and soot to fall all about him. 'Proper mess, eh? I thought I'd come over and express my sympathy. But I can see that even when you've cleaned up, you'll have to re-equip and restock. Cost a mint, that will. Then there's the lost income while the business is closed. Never rains but it pours, eh? Of course, if there's any way I can help,' he offered, smoothing the dust from his fine worsted suit. 'You have only to say the word.'

'We'll manage, thanks all the same.' Polly suffered Hubert's gloating presence for the longest half hour she could imagine before he finally took his leave, coldly refusing his offer of the services of Ron, his odious son, to help with the clearing up. Benny was itching to give Ron a 'good seeing to' but Polly managed to persuade him against such a reckless act.

Hubert had no sooner gone than Lucy arrived, looking wan and slightly dishevelled, as no doubt they all were. Polly went to her at once and mother and daughter put their arms about each other for a comforting hug, indulging in a quiet weep. But it was Lucy who was the first to rally.

'Come on, Mam. You tell us what to do and we'll do it. We won't be beaten by this.' She'd come to help clean up along with Polly's stalwart band of workers, all eager to do their bit. There'd be plenty of time later to think about her own problems. Minnie Hopkins was at the ready with her sweeping brush, even Uncle Nobby and Aunt Ida were there with mopping buckets and mops, 'to swill out t'muck,' as they kept repeating. Polly could only smile with gratitude at this rallying of support.

Charlie too had come along to help, which caused her to huff and puff some more, telling her husband he wasn't fit enough to be out and about, let alone working in a burned out shell of a warehouse. But Charlie was adamant he was perfectly capable of helping to root through the mess and spot anything of value which might have survived.

They worked all day and the best they could salvage were a dozen or so bobbins of singed wool.

'At least it's a popular colour,' Maisie joked. 'Your favourite pink beige.'

Benny flung down the pile of spindles he'd just been sorting, not a decent one amongst them and rubbed a tired hand over his face, blackening it even more. 'Let's go and have a jar. I reckon we all need one. Mebbe things won't look so bad in the morning.'

But when the insurance assessor arrived the following day, his verdict was far from reassuring. The site had been examined by both the firemen and the police, he said and without doubt, arson was suspected. Without actually accusing her point blank, the steely quality of his stare made it clear to Polly who he considered had set the match.

'Saints alive, you don't think… You can't imagine that I'd set light to me own warehouse.'

The inspector cleared his throat, somewhat noisily. 'I understand you're suffering a slight financial embarrassment at present?' His expression bore a mask of professional sympathy, as if inviting her to confess all.

'Who the hell has told you that?'

'It's generally bruited abroad that you've been chopping and changing suppliers, yet not settling outstanding bills. Your credit status at present, Mrs Pride, is, I believe, in a sorry state.'

'Stockton. The name is Mrs Charlie Stockton. Polly Pride is only the name I use for my business.'

'Ah, as you wish.' He managed a smile which did not reach his eyes. 'Nevertheless, I am correct, am I not?'

Drat him and drat the man who'd put her in this mess in the first place but Polly could not deny it. By going about seeking new suppliers while still in debt to Hubert Clarke, she'd made herself appear to be the guilty party.

The insurance company couldn't pay out, he explained, until after a more intensive investigation had taken place which might, he admitted, take months. The authorities still had a great deal of work on their hands assessing bomb damage and which houses could be made fit for occupation. Civilian fires were given some-what lower priority. It was made plain to Polly that although they may not have sufficient evidence to prosecute, they were deeply suspicious, their doubts such that they could delay payment for as long as they wished.

Certainly long enough to leave her business in ruins.

No matter how many hours Polly and Benny might pore over the accounts which they did every night in the kitchen of number 32, Charlie putting in his twopennorth, nor however fervently she might plead her case with the bank manager, the truth of the matter was that Polly had more debts than she could handle, more stock than she could sell and the only successful part of her operation, the manufacturing of carpets, was now defunct. Even her carpet cleaning and beating machines were gone, reduced to rubble in the fire. The result was indisputable. Pride Carpets was no more, and all her workers were now without jobs.

'You mean we're all on the cob'n coal?' Maisie asked.

Polly admitted that yes, they would indeed have to collect the dole, if they couldn't find other work. 'But you'll all get your jobs back, just as soon as I'm up and running again.' Didn't she know how hard it was to get work? Hadn't she suffered the indignity of unemployment herself back in the thirties, not to mention the endless worry of where the next shilling was coming from to put in the gas meter.

'A hungry sow won't follow an empty bucket.' This from Joyce, ever blunt, and revealing the doubts they all felt that Pride Carpets would ever rise again from the ashes.

'What about us?' Charlie asked, when Polly expressed these concerns to him. 'Where will we find the next bob or two for the meter?' The question silenced her completely.

So it was that when Hubert Clarke came round with his proposal, she was in no position to argue.

'You might as well admit, Polly lass, that you're done for,' he cheerfully informed her. 'But I'll not see you go bankrupt.' He smiled magnanimously, going on to outline in painstaking detail how he would be willing to take over the company, generously agreeing to keep both herself and Benny on, as employed managers. 'Admittedly the wages I could offer would be much less than you are getting now. But there'll always be a place for you both in Clarke Enterprises.'

Polly felt not the slightest degree of gratitude and made no bones about telling him so, which caused him to smile all the more as he took out his pocket book and reminded her of the sum still outstanding.

'Take the blasted furniture back, why don't you? That'll more than cover the debt, surely to God,' she said.

Hubert sadly shook his head, agreeing that he must of course take possession of the stock. 'But with the added interest, even if some of the furniture wasn't damaged from standing in your damp shop, it would barely cover a fraction of the debt.' He also pointed out that she had no other choice, since she couldn't afford to re-equip or restore the warehouse following the fire, nor any longer pay the rent on the shop premises.

So saying, he took over her business, lock, stock and balloon backed chairs. Polly refused his paltry offer of a job, thereby leaving the building for the last time with nothing but her pride.

Chapter Twenty-Six

When the knock came to the door, instinct told Lucy who it would be.

'If that's our Michael...' Minnie cried, jumping up from the table where she'd been peeling potatoes.

Lucy pressed the older woman gently down again. 'More likely Tom.' She was surprised that it had taken him this long to come round. The children had not been sent to school for three days and she'd been grateful for Minnie's offer of accommodation for them all until she'd made up her mind what she wanted to do. Much of that time Lucy had spent with Polly down at the warehouse, where all she'd built up over the last two or three years seemed to be unravelling.

She too felt as if she was living on borrowed time, for any day now the truant officer would be sure to come round. But then if the children went back to school, Tom could easily steal them, just to spite her. Perhaps he'd already been watching and waiting at the school gates. Her stomach churned at the thought, yet Lucy knew they couldn't hide forever.

'Tha doesn't have to see him,' Minnie told her.

'Best if I get it over with. Put things on a proper footing. I can't spend my life hiding behind corners just because I've left my husband.' Lucy marched to the door with head held high and a determined spring in her step. Tom stood on the doorstep, as expected, hands in pockets, trilby hat pulled well down over his eyes as if he were Humphrey Bogart on a spying mission. Lucy experienced a frantic urge to laugh but managed to calm her hysteria and face him with some degree of control.

'I reckoned I'd find you here.' There was a purr of satisfaction in the flint-like tones.

'I'm sorry, Tom. I don't care what you say but I'm not coming home.' There, that would show him she could stand up for herself at last.

'You'll do as I say.'

She felt her cheeks grow red with annoyance. 'I will not.'

'Get your coat on. You're coming home with me.' He reached out to grab her but Lucy backed away, cringing from his touch.

'Never.'

Tom's lip curled upwards into a sneer. It made him look even more like a stranger, one she couldn't believe she'd ever loved. 'So where's lover-boy then? Hiding under the stairs, is he? Still playing the coward we know him to be. I'm aware he's not even shown up at work.'

If Lucy had been hot with anger before, now she felt herself go cold with a new fear. 'How do you know he's not been in to work? Have you been looking for him? Leave Michael alone, d'you hear? What he does, where he goes, is his affair, not yours. *Leave him be!*'

Tom only laughed, an odious sound that chilled her all the more, while Lucy fought to steady her breathing, and keep a grip on her frayed nerves. 'I did my best to be a good wife to you. If you'd thought of me once during the days of your escape, just long enough to let me know you were alive, then I might well have waited for you. It wasn't my fault I fell in love with Michael. That's what lonely women do during wartime when they think their husband is dead, they turn to someone else. And when you did come home were you kind to me? No. Did you make love to me with any sign of gentleness or affection? *No!* Did you ever consider my feelings for one minute, on whether I wanted to go out, have friends, or carry on working? *No, no, and again no!* You attempted to control my every thought and movement. Now Michael's gone and I've lost him. All because of *you.*'

'Stop your hysterics and get on home this minute. That's my child you're carrying and I don't want it harmed.'

'You speak as if I was a piece of merchandise and you own me. Well, you *don't*. I pray every day that this child isn't yours. I want you out of my life, Tom Shackleton. *Leave me alone, drat you!*' She became aware of Minnie standing beside her, gently touching her arm. She must have been shouting, for neighbours in the street had started to gather to listen and stare.

'That's enough, lass. Tha's made your point. Go home lad. Best leave her alone for now.' Minnie drew the sobbing Lucy back into the house and shut the door.

Tom did not go home. He strode along Pansy Street, knocked loudly on number 32 and asked to see Polly. When she came to the door, anxiety clouding her eyes at sight of him, Tom burst into noisy tears. 'You'll never guess what she's gone and done now.'

Never having seen a grown man cry before, Polly was appalled. 'Aw, Tom, whatever is it? Ye poor lamb. Come in, lad, come in.' And she took her weeping son-in-law into the warm heart of her home.

–

Polly came round to number 179 hot foot, wishing her children would just get on and live a quiet, orderly life instead of being such a trial to her. She seemed to be fighting a war with them worse than the one they'd all come through. Minnie, having made them a pot of tea, quietly withdrew. 'If it isn't one of you, it's the other, so it is,' she accused Lucy. 'What's got into ye, leaving your husband? Have you run mad? They'll carry you off to Prestwich, so they will.'

'I'm not staying with a brute of a husband just to make life simpler for you,' Lucy quietly responded, her patience exhausted.

'A brute is he now, poor man? You've not shown near enough patience, nor given him time to settle and after all he's…'

Lucy flapped a hand wildly in the air to shut her mother up. 'Don't tell me again how much *he's* suffered. What about me? Do you want to know how much *I've* suffered? How Tom has slapped me? How he frequently loses his temper and the other night actually pushed me down the stairs? You don't know what it's like living with that man. It's hell on earth, I tell you,' Lucy cried, tears brimming over despite her best efforts to prevent them.

Polly folded her arms and shook her head in disbelief. 'Tom tells a different tale.' Her voice changed to her soft Irish brogue. 'It's sorry I am that it's come to this between the pair of you, but didn't I warn you, m'cushla. No man will tolerate a cheating wife for long, war or no war. Is it any wonder if he loses his temper now and then?' She reached out to take her daughter's hand but Lucy snatched it away before she even touched it.

'What's he been saying?'

Polly sighed. 'He says you confessed about the babby and that he forgave you. More credit to him for his generosity for there's many wouldn't be so understanding. He apparently asked you again to give up your fancy man and you refused, throwing yourself down the stairs in a fit of hysteria.'

Lucy stared at her mother out of eyes grown black with shock as the pupils dilated. 'So you believe everything he tells you but nothing I say. I'm just an hysterical adulterer. Is that the way of it? Right, so we know where we stand don't we?' She marched to the front door and pulled it open, clearly prepared to throw her own mother out in the street. 'I think you'd best go before you say something you might afterwards regret. We'll talk another time when we're both calmer.'

Determined to have her say, Polly refused to simply walk away. 'Lucy love, I'm only thinking of you.'

'No, you aren't. You're thinking of yourself, and what the gossips will have to say.'

Entirely oblivious of how she too had been the unwitting victim of Tom's lies every bit as much as her daughter Polly warned her of loneliness, of the difficulties of trying to bring up a family alone. Hadn't she gone through all of that herself until she'd been lucky enough to meet Charlie? 'It serves you right if Michael has gone for ever. Having played fast and loose with both the men in your life, you've now lost the pair of them.'

Finally recognising the fierce flash of fury in her daughter's eyes, she quietly took her leave.

-

Minnie was waiting for Lucy in the kitchen with a pan of milk warming on the gas stove. She made her a mug of hot cocoa and watched while Lucy drank every drop. 'Your eyes look like two lumps of black coal in a snow drift. So it's your turn to be up the spout, eh? Is it our Michael's? I reckoned it must be. Does he know?'

Lucy shook her head.

'Thought not. It isn't like our Michael to run from responsibility. Well don't worry about that daft husband of yours. He couldn't knock t'skin off a custard.'

Lucy wiped the tears from her face with the flat of her hand, starting to laugh despite the fact her eyes were welling up with fresh tears all over again. 'What am I to do, Minnie?'

'We'll think o' summat, but not now eh, chuck? Here, have a pear drop.' And she popped one in Lucy's mouth, making her smile all the more. 'I'll be gone no more'n twenty minutes or so but I must go and see your mam. She was upset too and she's got other problems right now, has Polly. Tha should stop sharpening swords on each other and start counting your blessings. Will you come round yon wi' me, and apologise?' When Lucy shook her head, Minnie heaved a sigh and pulling her old brown shawl over her head, got to her feet. 'Well, I'll just pop round and see if she's all right. She should know she has friends in time of trouble.' Then turning to the children, said, 'I'll bring a bag or two of chips back wi' me, eh? How would that be? And a nice bit of haddock. But only if you two have washed behind your ears and have got into your jammies on by the time I get back.'

'Ooh yes,' cried Sarah Jane and Sean, jumping up and down with excitement, then charged out, racing each other to the bathroom. They didn't have a bathroom at number 32, so this was still something of a treat.

Lucy followed them at a slower pace, going through the nightly ritual of scrubbing mucky knees with a stiff loofah, inspecting ears and brushing hair in a somewhat distracted frame of mind. She was filled with guilt over this latest quarrel with her mother, but why couldn't she leave well alone? Why did she always have to stick her oar in? Lucy was half listening with some trepidation for the sound of Minnie's returning footsteps, fearing a heavier tread on the stair. Surely Tom wouldn't be so stupid as to attempt to break into Minnie's house, though so far as he was concerned it was Michael's, and if he thought she was here alone, with him, would that drive him to some stupidly reckless act?

Sean inserted the thumb in his mouth. 'Where's me dad? Is he coming to stay at Aunty Minnie's as well?'

'No, love. We're having a bit of a holiday on our own, for a change.' She took the thumb out again. 'Come on, I'll read you a story till Minnie gets back. Then you can eat your chips in bed for a treat.'

This proposal went down well but once installed in the high bed which sagged alarmingly in the middle, Sarah Jane peered over the great brass bed rail. Shadows lurked in the corners of the gloomy room, large enough to house an army with its heavy mahogany furniture, and the night light on the bedside table flickering scary fingers across the high ceiling. 'Have we to sleep with you every night in this big room?'

Lucy thought of all the empty bedrooms in the old house and spoke without thinking, as if unwilling to acknowledge that she'd made a decision. 'No, you don't, love. You can both choose a room of your own tomorrow afternoon, if you like, when you get back from school. Nice small cosy ones. How would that be?'

'Ooh, yes please!' The children squealed with excitement, bouncing up and down on the feather mattress with delight at this unexpected turn of events. Life seemed full of them at the moment.

If only everyone could be so easily pleased, Lucy thought, then stifling a sigh cuddled her beloved children warmly beside her and began to read 'The Three Little Pigs' in hope of a quiet night's sleep ahead. But the calmness didn't last long. Soon they were all huffing and puffing and rolling about the bed in an ecstasy of giggling hysteria. After that Minnie arrived and was soon doling out chip butties which kept the children quiet for at least five minutes before they were up and bouncing again on the old sagging bed. For once Lucy let them play while she and Minnie talked, for wouldn't life become serious enough for them soon.

–

The following morning Lucy took the children to school at their usual time, making excuses that they'd both had bad colds. The teacher said nothing about the fact they seemed to be positively glowing with health now, and chattering twenty to the dozen about how they'd moved house and were to have new bedrooms, with their own bathroom. On the way back down Lower Byrom Street, keeping a wary eye open for Tom at every corner, Lucy started to worry over how Minnie would react to a more permanent arrangement, and how she could pay for their keep. But before she could open her mouth to ask, Minnie said, 'I've had a word wi' Poll and it's all sorted.'

'What is?'

She set a mug of tea down in front of Lucy. 'Eeh, I reckon we make more pots of tea in this house than they do at Lyons. You're to stay here, with me.'

'But what happens when the baby comes?'

'We'll cross that bridge when we come to it. Let's see how we get on, shall we?'

Lucy was so grateful she began to weep.

'Nay, don't start. I'll not throw thee out on t'street,' Minnie Hopkins said, thrusting a spanking clean handkerchief brusquely into her hand. 'Anyroad, I'd rattle round this big old house like a pea on a drum on me own.'

'You could always sell it,' Lucy suggested, wondering for the first time how Minnie came to be living in this grand house, all by herself. 'Buy something smaller.'

'Nay, I'm not allowed to do that. It isn't mine, d'you see. But I've the right to live in it, me and Michael, fer the length of my lifetime. After that it goes back into the estate. My lady was cast out too by her family, so they get nothing till I'm gone. She left me enough to get by, so why not share a bit? Money's made round to go round eh? Isn't that what they say?' The old woman actually winked, chortling with delight at the old joke, her toothless mouth a wide open chasm of pink gums.

'Oh, Minnie, I don't know how to thank you.'

'You can start by going to see thy mam.'

Lucy was thoughtful. Having found a stable home for her children, Minnie was right, this wasn't the time to be at odds. They had to stick together or they'd go under for sure. 'Where is she?'

'Down at the warehouse, clearing up.'

Lucy snatched up her coat, yanked on a woollen beret and Minnie, claiming to be at a loose end, insisted on coming with her. 'I can shove a yard brush round that mucky floor if nowt else,' she said.

Lucy gazed in wonder at her one-time employer who had turned into such a treasured friend. 'Minnie,' she said, respect and gratitude warm in her voice. 'What would I do without you?'

Minnie laughed again. 'Tha'd be buggered.'

–

Hubert was interrogating his son. Ron, however, denied all knowledge of the fire. He was, in fact, equally stunned by events, agreeing that although this had been their intention, he hadn't actually got around to making all the necessary arrangements, like laying his hands on a bit of petrol to get it started.

'Then who set it?' Hubert asked, wondering if it could have been an accident after all. Not that he concerned himself too greatly over the matter. Accident or design the fire had served his purpose very nicely, causing Polly Pride to shut up shop and her business to fall neatly into his lap. So pleased with himself was he, that he made a date with a young widow he'd met at the auction, taking her out for a meal as a special treat. He did make sure they met in a place far removed from the twitching curtains of Castlefield. Not because he cared about his wife's sensibilities, but because he really didn't care for any whiff of scandal to affect his business.

She proved to be particularly accommodating, so much so that Hubert didn't get home until the early hours. It was fortunate that he and Joanna now occupied separate quarters. Far more convenient. He slipped quietly up the stairs to his own room without hearing a sound from hers. It made him smile to think of her so innocently asleep.

The next day he paid a visit to Colin Wilnshaw, his accountant, who outlined the particular advantages of this new acquisition. The debt would not now be paid, admittedly, but having regained possession of the entire stock of furniture for which he'd paid a mere fraction of what he charged Polly for it, he'd regain some of his losses by selling it himself. He'd send the rubbish on to other dealers, of course.

It was a pity, the accountant pointed out, that the looms and carpets had been completely destroyed. Hubert too was privately irritated that he hadn't been able to take over the machinery and name of the company, Pride Carpets. 'I can't say I'm particularly interested in carpets and have no use for a rented warehouse. However, the big new shop will come in handy.' There were, of course, more important reasons to be pleased at seeing an end to the Pride family's business venture. 'They'll never get it going again, not in a million years.'

Wilnshaw smoothed his chin in a thoughtful gesture before offering his opinion that a little care should perhaps be exercised before Hubert attempted to take over any further enterprises. 'We can't have you become too successful. I mean, we've no wish to arouse suspicion in more bureaucratic quarters, such as the tax office for instance. It might be a disadvantage to arouse their curiosity over your affairs.' Hubert paid lip service to this excellent advice whilst privately keeping his options open. Opportunities, he'd discovered, came when you least expected them and often had to be snatched or they were lost for ever. But he was still puzzled about that fire. If it was arson, why would Polly risk such a thing since she'd realise that it would be bound to make her insurance policy void.

The answer was supplied to him a day or two later when he had yet another visitor, one who'd called regularly over recent months, costing Hubert a great deal of money as a result and now claimed credit for the entire shebang. Tom Shackleton calmly informed Hubert that he'd done him a favour in his scheming against the Pride family, by bringing the matter to a swift conclusion. He asked for a final payoff, promising that would be the last Hubert heard from him.

'You didn't do it out of the goodness of your heart then?' Hubert drily remarked to which Tom merely smiled. 'And how do I know that'd be the end of it, if I did pay up?'

Tom shrugged. 'I've lost my wife and family, so why would I want to stop on in Castlefield? I've always fancied moving on and mean to do so, soon as I've completed one other bit of business. All I need is the wherewithal.' He named a sum which made Hubert wince.

'You set a fire and ask me to pay for it? Don't push it, lad. I'm the one who has to pick up the pieces and make a go of that furniture shop. I'll admit you've got a hold over me with what you know, but don't take me for a fool. In any case, what other bit of business would this be?'

'Nothing that need concern you. A domestic matter, you might say.' Again there was that smile which, charming and handsome as it might outwardly seem, appeared strangely disconnected from the rest of his face. 'I could always throw in a bit more information by way of a bonus, so you know you're getting a good deal,' Tom added.

Hubert's eyes narrowed. 'Meaning what exactly?'

For a moment Tom didn't speak, but when Hubert walked over to his safe, opened it and took out a metal box, he began to talk fast while his greedy eyes fixed on the crisp notes Hubert was counting. 'I was in Polly's house the other night. Took a shufty at a few papers she'd left lying around while she cooked me a good supper. Very trusting of me is my mother-in-law.'

Hubert was instantly alert as he flicked the notes with his thumb, inches from Tom's nose. 'Go on, I'm listening.'

'She's just about used up all her spare cash, as you know, from starting the carpet warehouse up again and going into manufacturing. The problems she had with you, finished her.'

'I know all of that.' Hubert sounded irritated. 'Get on with it. Have you something more or not?'

'Only that she took out a mortgage on her house in Pansy Street in order to fit out the shop and come in with you.'

'Normal business practice,' Hubert said, rubbing his chin between finger and thumb. 'A cheap way of borrowing money. I've done the same myself.'

'Then there was the bank loan. Not huge, you understand, but enough to help tide her over when things got sticky and she found herself over-committed.'

Hubert smiled. 'You mean when I overstocked her and started manipulating new rules of play.'

'I wouldn't know about that but I saw a letter from her bank manager. He's not too happy now and is asking how she means to make the payments. She's a bit behind, do y'see?' Tom's face was a picture of innocence. 'Not that I would repeat such sensitive information to anyone outside the family, you understand? But then you are family, are you not? By marriage like.'

'So I am,' Hubert agreed, his tone quietly thoughtful as he counted the notes into the outstretched palm. 'You could say that.'

–

Polly wasn't in the warehouse when Lucy found her, because she no longer had any right to use it. She was sitting on a bollard watching the barges load in the canal basin. Lucy came to sit beside her mother on a nearby step and without even glancing up, Polly said, 'Hubert Clarke has won. I've to start all over again, m'cushla, from scratch.'

'I know. Minnie told me last night.' She half glanced back at her newly found friend, who was pretending to feed the pigeons with bits of bread crust, keeping a discreet distance.

'I've lost count of the number of times I've done that already. Remember when I sold every scrap of furniture we had in the house, just to buy second hand carpet. Your dad thought I'd run mad, so he did.'

'You were wonderful.'

'I'm not sure I've the energy to start again.'

Moved to tears, Lucy put her arms about her mother and held her close. For all their differences at times, she was still her mam and in that moment as they clung to each other they were as one, together again, all differences forgiven and forgotten. They smiled into each other's eyes, mopped up each other's tears, understanding without needing words.

'Of course you can start again. You can do owt, you. Always have been able to. Isn't that what I love most about you, the way you get up, dust yourself off and bounce right back.'

'Not this time. All my bounce has gone. He's finished me, for sure, sweetheart. Benny's surrendering the lease of the warehouse this very minute, but we'll still be liable for the restoration of it, whether the insurance company pay up or not. It's over, Lucy.'

Keeping an arm about Polly's shoulders, which seemed much too frail and thin, Lucy watched the barge in the cut before her, the mate blowing on his hands this cold frosty morning, having had to put out his fire in the bow as regulations demanded while it slid under the warehouse for loading. How careful everyone had to be to avoid disaster, she thought, just as her lovely mam had always been with the oily waste. Why would it suddenly burst into flame?

'Has anyone discovered what started the fire?' she asked, but Polly shook her head. A tear splashed on to her arm and Lucy wiped it away with one finger. 'What about our Benny? I suppose he was no help.'

Now that a reconciliation had taken place, Minnie edged nearer, to lean nonchalantly on her brush. She was a bit hard of hearing and didn't want to miss anything.

'He's been marvellous so he has,' Polly was saying. 'I don't know what I would've done without him.'

To Lucy's sharp ears, Polly sounded defeated, as if every ounce of her mother's once formidable energy had indeed evaporated and she had no resources left, which in truth she didn't wonder at. Her own opinion of her brother was far less charitable. Hadn't Polly always spoiled him? 'If it hadn't been for Benny, Mam, you'd never have got involved with Hubert Clarke in the first place.'

'Aw, don't blame him. He's worked like a Trojan, so he has. Didn't he only want the best for his little family? Where's the crime in that?' What Lucy said was true in a way. She would never have needed to borrow money from the bank to buy stock, nor been at the mercy of Hubert Clarke's unscrupulous business practices if Benny hadn't begged her to go in with him. And she'd have been spared a great deal of worry. 'What's done is done and can't be changed so why fret over it?'

Lucy pointed out that Benny had always shown a tendency to be careless. 'Look at the way he lost Big Flo,' she reminded Polly who, surprisingly, laughed as she hugged Lucy close.

'Nobody could control that old woman. What a character. Had a mind of her own and a will power second to none, so she did.'

'But...' Lucy caught the expression in Polly's eye and stopped, pursing her lips tightly together as she struggled not to argue that all of this must be Benny's fault. And all because of his foolish dreams and the fantasy tales he used to spin to Belinda, not forgetting his stubborn determination to work for no one but himself. Instead, unwilling to upset this happy rapport she'd at last established with her mother, she grudgingly admitted, 'I suppose he has worked hard, recently anyway, as well as looking after little Matt.'

'Hey up, t'lad's here now,' Minnie said and Benny came running up Castle Street as if he had a fire on his tail.

'It's the bailiffs,' he shouted. 'They're stripping the house clean.'

Polly was on her feet in a second, rigid with fear. 'Charlie,' she cried, her voice little more than a whisper. Benny grasped her arms, smoothing, calming.

'It's all right, don't fret. He's next door with our Matt.' Then he cast an anguished glance from Lucy to Minnie and back again. 'But they're taking everything, every stick of furniture we own. They say they'll have to sell the house if we're to avoid bankruptcy. It's the only way to pay off the bank loan and what's still owed to Hubert.'

Polly didn't wait for any further explanations, she was off, heading in the direction of Pansy Street to save the remnants of her pride. But it was too late. By the time she arrived the last item of furniture was being loaded on to the back of a lorry which drew away, giving a cheeky blast on its horn. Polly might shake her fist at it but that didn't alter the facts. The house was stripped bare, furniture and ornaments gone, carpets ripped up. Each and every room stood empty, just as if it had been scrubbed clean.

'Sorry, love,' said the bailiff. 'I'll have to ask you to leave too.'

'You can't do this!' Benny yelled, beside himself with fury. Baby Matt, being gently jostled in the arms of Doris-next-door who stood by silently weeping, stretched out his arms to his dad and set up a howl of anguish.

'By heck,' Minnie said, too shocked to find a more appropriate riposte as the Pride family filed out again and stood on the street, watching in stunned silence as the man locked the door, pock-eted the key and walked off with a sympathetic nod, shoulders hunched. All that was left was an untidy heap of clothes, a large carpet bag, a few books, papers and other personal possessions all scattered about the pavement. One or two sympathetic neighbours were gathering them up and putting them into brown paper carrier bags.

'So here we are then,' said Polly at last. 'Right back where we started. With not a scrap to our name.'

Chapter Twenty-Seven

Charlie was the only one who could offer comfort. He sat next to his wife on the horse-hair sofa alternately patting Polly's hand, stroking her shoulder or her hair, and sometimes drying the tears as they fell. 'It'll turn out all right, Poll,' he kept saying, without being able to offer any reason why it should.

They were sitting in Minnie's front parlour amongst the aspidistra, the whatnots and the overbearing Victorian furniture, heavy curtains blocking out the sun and the sound of the measured clonk of the grandfather clock loud in their ears. To Polly it seemed to be marking out the final moments of her youth. From now on she would be an old woman with no future left. No warehouse to go to each day, no money to her name, not even a home to call her own. Twenty years ago, less, she would have rolled up her sleeves and started again without a second thought. With youth and energy, most of all a belief in herself, she'd always felt she could achieve anything.

But where was all that now, vanished in the pall of smoke that still hung over the remnants of Pride Carpets.

'We're finished,' she said again, as if by repeating this fact she might drum the awful reality into her head.

Lucy glared across at Benny, who was sitting with his head in his hands in the far corner of the room. 'See what you've brought us to.'

'No,' Polly said, shaking her head. 'Don't blame our Benny. Hasn't he only done what he thought best for us, and for that little treasure.' She smiled softly at her grandson who was sitting on Minnie's rug chewing on a crust. Recognising his nanna's smile

307

he grinned back at her, showing two white teeth, and offered her a bite of his bread. Polly pretended to take one and the baby chuckled, hiding the crust behind his back.

'What are you accusing me of anyroad?' Benny wanted to know. 'Of wanting to make my way in the world, of needing to earn a decent living to bring up my son? Of being a man? You could go so far as to say if only I'd never met Belinda – because that's what set this all off – but I for one don't wish that, not for a minute.'

'Aw no, bless her sweet nature, me neither,' Polly said, putting a hand to her mouth to stop fresh tears. Minnie handed her a handkerchief which Polly took without a word, or even realising who had given it to her.

Lucy, ashamed suddenly of where her accusations had led, hung her head, 'I'm sorry, Benny. I never meant it that way. Belinda was my very best friend. We all loved her. I wish she was here now, alive and well.' Lucy took the handkerchief from Polly and blew her nose upon it as her own tears spilled over. 'Instead the poor love died in that dreadful way because a no-hoper like Percy Sympkin, your odious landlord wouldn't give you time to pay the rent arrears.'

Polly was nodding sadly. 'Aye, for all our Benny had finally been accepted by Belinda's family and had hopes of a brighter future. A tragic irony, eh?'

It was as if a light had been switched on in Lucy's head. As if everything had suddenly become crystal clear. This was no fault of Benny's. None at all. This whole thing had been planned from the start. The loss of Belinda, Hubert's own daughter, had been little more than an irritation to him, an inconvenience rather than a tragic loss, serving only to fuel his jealousy and greed still further.

'Mam,' Lucy said, her voice dropping to a low pitch with a hint of wonder in it at this new realisation. 'You're right. This is none of our Benny's making.'

'I'm glad you see sense at last,' Benny said, still sounding aggrieved.

'None of it is. Hubert Clarke engineered all of it from the minute he discovered Mam had a profitable little business. Once he knew she owned Pride Carpets, he started to put the squeeze on so that he could get his hands on it. What he didn't bargain for, was for Belinda to stand by you. He knew she was used to an easy life and solid middle class comforts. He expected her to come running home the minute money got tight, then he could put an end to your marriage and Mam's business in one fell swoop. After she died, he continued with his nasty little plan, out of revenge, but he'd have done it anyway.'

Shocked glances were exchanged all round.

'By heck, you're right,' Benny said. 'He wouldn't give me the time of day in the beginning, then suddenly, for no reason, his attitude changed.'

Lucy was nodding. 'That must've been when he realised he could do himself a good turn by fattening his own profits while he bled us dry.'

Benny's mouth had gone ash dry. 'And Belinda? Are you're saying it was Hubert Clarke who had us evicted?'

Polly let out a small gasp while Charlie said, 'Surely not.'

'Yes, I am. Belinda loved you too much to go running home, Benny. She'd been bullied by her father all her life and now she meant to stand by you; to protect the man she loved from the one who'd denied her love all her life. Sadly, she was the one who suffered most from his diabolical plan. I can't prove it but I reckon if you put the squeeze on Percy Sympkin, he'll squeal loud and clear that the eviction was not his own idea.'

'Christ! Then Hubert Clarke was responsible for his own daughter's death.'

'Yes. I believe so.'

For several long moments there was no sound in the room but that of the clock ticking in loud solemn tones. Then from deep within its mechanism came a low growl that lifted to a steady whirling tone and finally erupted into a strident bong as it counted out the hour in ten doleful notes. As the last echo died away, it seemed to stir the occupants of the shadowy room back to life, though it was Lucy again who expressed all their feelings.

'I reckon it's time we fought back on Belinda's behalf, don't you? Time for the last battle.'

Polly looked at her usually homely daughter, eyebrows raised in mild surprise. 'Is this my quiet, romantic little Lucy talking, who usually has no other thought in her head than what's on at the pictures, or what colour lipstick she should wear?'

Lucy flushed, with embarrassment as much as annoyance since there was some truth in the accusation. 'One minute you complain I'm too rebellious, the next I'm too quiet and romantic. Whichever, I'm not stupid.'

The teasing smile faded. 'So you're serious about this?'

'I am indeed.'

Benny was on his feet, red-brown hair tousled from the constant raking of his fingers through it, round face a mask of pain. 'Our Luce is right. It's long past time we started to be a bit less *nice*, or fair. Time we were a bit sharper on the uptake. And time we all stuck together instead of falling out between ourselves.'

'The lad speaks sense,' Minnie chipped in, unable to keep quiet any longer for all it was family business. 'If you ask me, him what did this needs to be taught a lesson, hoist by his own petard as it were. And I reckon I know how.' All eyes were upon her, mesmerised. 'Everyone has some sort of weakness, an Achilles heel or a secret they'd much rather keep hidden. Even Councillor Hubert Clarke.'

Polly was staring at Minnie in surprise, coming slowly to life at this sign of new support. 'That's true.'

'There must be summat he doesn't want folk to know.' 'Indeed there must.'

'Well then,' Minnie said. 'All we need do is find out what it is.'

–

Percy Sympkin not only squealed but wept with regret by the time Benny had done with him. Benny picked him up by his coat collar and hung him on a hook in his own front hall by which time he was only too ready to confess that it was Councillor Hubert Clarke who'd forced him to evict the young couple. He added the further information that it had also been Benny's father-in-law who'd made sure that he never did get his allocation licence. Young Ron had gathered the petition signed against him from all those owing Hubert money. 'They did it to buy themselves time, and put the mockers on you, lad.'

By the time Benny had heard the end of this sorry tale, he was purple with rage and flexing so many formidable muscles that Percy was more than anxious to turn the tables on his former aggressor who now seemed chicken feed in comparison to Benny's military brawn.

Benny unhooked him, stood him up straight and gently dusted down his rumpled suit. 'Get me something on him, Percy lad. I don't care what it is, I mean to make him pay. There must be some secret Councillor Clarke doesn't want bruited about.'

It took Percy no time at all to come back to Benny with the results of his enquiries. There was a swirl of snow in the air, cold enough to freeze the waters of the canal when they met late one night, in a place where a discussion could generally take place without fear of interruption. The old stones of the bridges had probably heard more secrets than these two were about to spill.

'This information comes free and gratis,' Percy hastily assured Benny. 'Glad to help, lad. Your Belinda were a right little treasure. Lovely lass.'

'Get on with it, you smarmy toad,' Benny growled, and so eager was Percy to help, he barely drew breath for twenty long minutes. Councillor Hubert Clarke was apparently up to his greedy neck in black marketeering.

'He's involved in so much funny business, stuff he doesn't want the authorities to know about, I'm hard pressed to know where to begin.' Percy took a breath and launched into his tale.

It seemed Hubert bought goods strictly for cash with nothing in writing and sold on at one hundred per cent markup, sometimes twice that amount. 'Other stuff he hardly pays anything for at all. Them chairs he sold to Polly were a case in point. He got them for almost nowt as bankrupt stock and charged her the earth for them. He also has a nifty habit of invoicing a shop for stuff that never gets delivered, or so one of his van drivers told me.'

'Then it wasn't a case of careless paperwork. We really were defrauded of stock we'd paid for,' Benny growled, his rage deepening.

'Sometimes he buys stock in what he calls a ring, where he bids for them at auction but only against dealers who've agreed to drop out, so nobody pays too much for an item. They sort it all out between themselves beforehand, who's having what. Sometimes it's new bankrupt stock, sometimes second-hand. He doesn't trouble too much what he buys so long as it's cheap and he can sell it on to some poor fool who pays through the nose for it.'

'Someone like us.'

'Aye,' Percy agreed. 'And the poor souls who pay Ron week after week, knowing they'll never settle their debt.'

There was a great deal more and by the time Percy was finished, Benny was spitting mad with fury at having been so used. How could he have been such a gullible fool? His former landlord tucked a grubby muffler about his neck and rubbed his hands together to aid circulation. 'I saw another friend of yours the other day. Michael Hopkins.'

'He's no friend of mine,' Benny growled, for he didn't in the least approve of Lucy walking out on her husband, even if sometimes he did feel a tug of conscience that he'd never mentioned that rather odd conversation he'd had with Tom. He'd put it from his mind, deciding the man was a bit sick in the head, and probably couldn't properly remember what he'd been doing these last years, or where he'd been. War did that to a bloke. Anyroad, Lucy had no right to be gallivanting with her fancy man, not while she was still married to her husband. All the same he was curious to hear about Michael Hopkins, and listened to what Percy had to say.

As the two men went their separate ways with a nod and a hand shake, Benny was satisfied that it'd been a most useful half hour. He'd discovered more about his father-in-law than he'd ever have imagined possible. He'd also learned that Joanna was not half so loyal as Hubert imagined. She had indeed spent much of the war keeping the soldiers and sailors happy, but not simply by knitting balaclavas. He took this nugget of information directly to Polly and together with Lucy, Minnie and Charlie, held what might be termed a Council of War.

—

It was agreed that Lucy's task would be to discover more about the nefarious goings-on of Joanna Clarke. 'If she has a few grudges of her own against Hubert, she might be glad to help. Particularly when she learns what really happened to Belinda,' Lucy agreed.

Benny readily volunteered to keep an eye on son Ron, smiling at Polly's caution to 'go easy on him'.

'Don't worry. There are other possibilities I need to follow up first,' he told her, which he wasn't yet ready to divulge.

As well as investigating ways of getting the business going again, they were all given their separate jobs. Charlie, with a lessened degree of pain thanks to the new pills he was on, opted to hold the fort at Minnie's house, keep an eye on the children when necessary and provide meals for them all. This was where they were all now living. Where else could they go? Polly said she was lucky to have such a good friend as Minnie who was prepared to take her family in when she hadn't a penny to pay for their keep.

'It wasn't as if we were ever particularly close, you and me,' she said, trying to find the right words to thank Minnie for her generosity. 'But don't you always manage to be there when one of us needs you? I do appreciate that, to be sure.'

'I thought of leaving you out on t'street and giving you a brick to lay thee head on, but then I thought, happen not. Waste of a good Accrington brick,' chortled the old woman, her cackling laughter making her false teeth click.

For all Minnie's generosity everyone knew it was going to be hard. With no business and therefore no income coming in they would all need to find new jobs which, for Polly and Charlie in particular, wouldn't be easy. Being poor was bad enough when you were young; in middle age, Polly said, it didn't bear thinking about.

'What you need do is to scupper Hubert, then maybe you'll manage to salvage summat from the mire,' Minnie kept reminding them.

It was to be Polly and Minnie who would set in motion the method by which they would achieve this seemingly impossible task, and hopefully win back some of the money he'd so artfully stolen from them. They weren't sure of all the details and implications yet but the intention was to find a way to let him know that at some location, still to be agreed, there were goods for sale at a bargain price, strictly cash, no questions asked.

Minnie volunteered to act as decoy, since she was very nearly sure that he didn't know her well enough to recognise her. Even if he did, she argued, he'd no reason to suppose she was friendly with the family from Pride Carpets but she doubted he'd ever paid much attention to an old woman who lived in a big old terraced house at the end of Pansy Street. 'He might recognise our Michael, if he saw us together, but he's not going to, is he?'

Lucy swallowed the lump which came instantly into her throat at mention of his name, turning her face away so no one would see the flicker of pain that crossed it. She'd had no word from Michael since he left. With each passing week her pregnancy was progressing and he didn't even know about it, let alone the fact that she had, at last, left her husband. Clasping her hands tightly together she determined to hold fast to her strength and keep hoping that one day, perhaps tomorrow, he would come back to her.

In the meantime, perhaps her own marital problems would at least make it easier to prise some information out of Joanna Clarke. Lucy could certainly sympathise with the woman's need for a lover, for all she didn't care much for her choice. Tim Fenton was young enough to be her son, should in fact have been her son-in-law if Hubert had had his way. Lucy wondered if her husband had any idea about the reality of their friendship and rather doubted he did, since arrogant men such as Councillor Clarke, rarely imagined their wives to be capable of asserting themselves let alone having an affair. And not for a moment would he believe that he had subjected her to a miserable existence.

–

Joanna looked far from miserable when she opened the door to Lucy. She was smiling and dressed in a pretty pink housecoat that had a ruffled collar and hem. She looked like the perfect model of a housewife straight from the pages of *Woman Own,* except she probably wasn't eagerly waiting for her husband to come home. Lucy couldn't help glancing up the stairs behind her, as if half expecting to see lover-boy appear at the top of it.

'Mrs Clarke, I'm Lucy Shackleton, Benny's sister. I wonder if I could have a word.'

Joanna coolly responded that this wasn't possible and would have closed the door in her face had not Lucy managed to get in one more short sentence. 'I think I know why Belinda died.' The door stopped closing upon the instant.

She was shown into the conservatory which apparently was the warmest room in the house, kept heated all year round to nurture Hubert's carnations, his pride and joy. The lush greenery and sweet scents of the flowers was almost overpowering.

Joanna brought Lucy a sherry and then excused herself for a moment. She was back within ten minutes or so, dressed in a simple but clearly expensive scarlet wool dress which showed off her elegant figure to perfection. Her face was a carefully presented picture of cream foundation, powder, and a bright red lipstick. As she drifted by, Lucy caught the scent of Californian Poppy, which was almost too cloying in the sickly sweet room. She arranged herself delicately in a wicker chair and reached for her sherry. 'What is this you have to say about my daughter? I hope you aren't here to make trouble or reopen old wounds, Mrs Shackleton. My family has suffered enough.'

'So has mine.' Lucy kept strictly to the facts which she delivered as bluntly and smartly as she could. Then she sat back and waited with some trepidation for the woman's reaction.

Joanna merely blinked and sipped her sherry. 'I know all of this. Tim discovered it all for me.'

Lucy's mouth dropped open but she quickly closed it again, remembering to mind her manners as Polly had instructed her. 'You *know* that your husband was responsible for Belinda's death, and yet you said nothing?'

'*Indirectly* responsible. He didn't personally kick her out on the streets. It was a mix-up, a mistake.'

'Oh, I see. It was meant to be my brother, was it? It would've been all right for Benny to be chucked out. You obviously had no qualms about making him homeless. But didn't either of you ever stop and think for one minute that Belinda might insist on staying on with him, the husband she loved, no matter what.'

Joanna began to look agitated, clasping and unclasping her hands, darting anxious glances anywhere rather than meet Lucy's probing gaze. 'I do assure you that I knew nothing of this at the time. Nothing at all. It was only after... after Belinda had died that I learned the truth. I wouldn't have wanted anything serious to happen to Benny, truly I wouldn't. *I just wanted Belinda to come home!*'

It was very much a cry from the heart yet Lucy felt nothing but contempt for the woman, and immense pity for her friend. Poor Belinda, no wonder she'd been eager to run straight into her brother's arms when he obviously worshipped the ground she walked on, no matter if he was a dreamer. She'd probably have done anything to escape her dreadful parents. Their utter selfishness left Lucy gasping, not to mention appreciate her own Mam and Charlie a lot more.

'But she didn't come home, did she? Would never have done so.'

Joanna shook her head, a sad little gesture which should have been heartrending yet somehow left her beautiful face unmarked. 'No. Belinda always had a strong will but then she gets that from Hubert. Whatever he sets his heart on, he doesn't stop till he gets it.'

'We've discovered that to our cost,' Lucy drily remarked. Then as if to escape the claustrophobia of the situation she got up and began to prowl about the conservatory, fingering leaves, smelling sickly sweet flowers which somehow reminded her of graveyards. She sat down again. 'Did you never think to curb this determination of your husband's to destroy others for his own benefit? Did you never try to put your daughter's happiness first?'

It was Joanna now who got up to stand with her arms wrapped tightly about herself and gaze out through misted glass on to a dull grey winter's day, almost as if she were viewing a world that was strange to her. She looked like an exotic flower held fast in a tropical paradise. 'There's something you should understand about me, Mrs Shackleton. I loved my daughter. If I was inadequate as a mother, she accepted that. We were never, how shall I put it, a particularly demonstrative family. She led her life and I led mine. We agreed to differ for much of the time. Occasionally I would attempt to...' here she paused and drew in a deep breath, '...yes, I shall say it. I attempted to civilise her, and curb her foolish rebellions.'

Lucy almost laughed out loud as she went to stand beside Joanna. 'That's rich, that is. You thought *Belinda* needed civilising? Not yourself, nor Hubert, just Belinda?'

'She tended to go to extremes, just to annoy us. Like her joining the *army* for goodness sake. All on a reckless whim of rebellion to score a point over Hubert. I couldn't let her ruin her life yet again out of stubbornness.'

'You don't think she might have genuinely wanted to join the army? Or that she really loved our Benny?'

Joanna looked confused, as if this thought had never truly struck her before. 'Sounds rather monstrous put so bluntly but no, I never did consider that for a moment. I did everything I could to persuade her out of marrying him.'

'Even though you were sleeping with the man your husband wanted for her?'

She winced slightly, but went on, 'He was no more than a mild amusement. I would've given him up for Belinda.'

'How very generous of you.' Lucy had heard enough. If she stayed another minute listening to this selfish woman, she might spew up at her feet. She half turned to go but Joanna caught her arm.

'Never underestimate my husband, not for a moment. I may be weak and foolish, but he's an utterly ruthless man when it comes to getting his own way, particularly in business matters. He trusts no one, save for his accountant Colin Wilnshaw who makes sure he doesn't pay a penny more than he should in tax. Hubert's made a fortune because he's a man of considerable acumen and courage, always ahead of the market. You have to admire him for that. It isn't the only reason I stay with him, but I've threatened to leave him many times whenever he too blatantly parades his women friends.'

'Women friends?'

'Someone called Myra is the most recent, from Slate Wharf would you believe? She may be history now, of course. Dear Hubert has learned to be more discreet over the years and we rub along rather well, in fact.'

Lucy didn't wonder at it. Joanna's explanations of how she enjoyed the comforts that her husband provided, had unfortunately revealed nothing Lucy didn't already know. 'We've developed a way of life which suits us well,' she finished, smiling brightly, almost as if the loss of a daughter were an unfortunate consequence of a business matter that had gone wrong. Lucy felt physically sick.

'As for Tim Fenton. I'm afraid the poor boy became increasingly dependent upon me, particularly when Belinda refused to marry him. Then when she died... Well, I shall let him down lightly.' The smile became less fixed, the beautiful mouth curling delightfully up at the corners, rather like a woman with a secret, and Lucy wondered if there was another candidate already waiting in the wings. Joanna Clarke gave no indication of a wife scorned, or one eagerly awaiting an opportunity to put the dagger in.

Lucy grabbed for the door handle, suddenly anxious to quit the suffocating heat of this rarefied existence. 'I won't waste any more of your time. There's clearly nothing I can tell you that you don't already know.' Yet despite, or perhaps because of her failure to learn anything herself from Joanna, Lucy paused at the door, the words almost bursting out of her head. 'But I'll have you know that you can't play with folk's lives the way your husband does without creating havoc. Apart from ruining my mam's business and leaving her homeless and jobless with a sick husband to care for, there's no doubt in any of our minds that if Hubert hadn't interfered, Belinda would be alive today. Think on that.

'Benny would have got his allocation licence from the Board of Trade, tried and probably failed with his joinering and then gone in with Mam, as he'd always wanted to do deep down. The only problems they ever had were those caused by your husband which, in my view, is disgusting. You'd think a father would want his daughter to be happy, even if it did cut across his own plans for her. Belinda should be alive now, enjoying her son and a good marriage, well and happy.'

Joanna's beautiful face had turned ashen, her lips thin and trembling. 'That's absolute nonsense. Hubert wasn't responsible for Belinda having a difficult birth. She might still have died, even if she'd had the baby inside the flat.'

Lucy almost sneered. 'Rather than in the freezing snow in a back street where she bled to death, you mean? You hang on to that thought, love. It might be the only comfort you have in a lonely old age.' Lucy escaped into the cold street with tears rolling down her cheeks, and drew in a thankful gasp of coal-tainted air which at least had the benefit of being honest muck.

Chapter Twenty-Eight

It was agreed that a casual meeting in the Queen's on Gartside Street was the best way to arouse Hubert's interest, since it wasn't a pub where Minnie was known, and the beer was good, not watered down in any way. Even so some doubt was expressed on whether Minnie could carry it off, until they saw her dressed for the part.

She looked entirely different, which of course was the whole idea. Having delved into her old employer's trunks and boxes kept in the loft, Minnie had decked herself out in a grey sealskin coat that didn't smell too strongly of moth balls and a pair of well polished court shoes made of finest Italian leather. A shiny black straw hat with a figured veil and a coiled velvet rose sat atop her victory rolls and she sported matching gloves and a large black leather handbag. Instead of her usual thick lisle stockings, she wore a pair of purest pale silk which made her skinny legs look like sticks of coltsfoot rock. The finishing touch was a fox stole which she clipped about her shoulders, the mouth of the stuffed animal opening to bite on its own tail.

'By heck. You look a right bobby-dazzler,' Benny chortled, impressed by the startling change in her.

'Aye, till I open me mouth,' Minnie ruefully admitted. 'Eeh I'll go to th'end of our yard, I'll have a job on, carrying this off.'

'Just soften those broad vowels a bit,' Polly suggested with a grin. 'There's no harm in being a Lancashire lass, just sound a richer one, that's all.'

'I'll try to hemulate the grand tones of my lady employer,' she said. 'How happy hi am to make your hacquaintance.' Overdoing it to such an extent that they all fell about laughing. But the laughter quickly subsided for this was serious, if not dangerous business. Minnie had every intention of taking Hubert for every penny she could.

They went carefully over the plan in fine detail, leaving nothing to chance and finally decided that some trust would need to be established between them. Funded by Minnie from her savings, Polly bought a consignment of three dozen pairs of leather gloves, fleecy lined and in tan, black and mustard pig skin. They cost seven shillings a pair to sell at eleven shillings and sixpence, but Minnie suggested they ask five bob, so as to prove their worth as suppliers. They'd make a loss, to be sure, but this part of the operation was viewed as an investment for future deals.

A brief note was sent to Hubert to the effect that if he came to The Queens tomorrow night at eight he might hear of a bit of business to his advantage. In point of fact he was there ten minutes early and Minnie was the one to keep him waiting. Stricken with nerves she proceeded into the snug and deposited a box containing a few samples of the gloves on the table in front of him. She was sure that he would notice her hands trembling as she untied the string to let him examine the contents. Minnie didn't even dare glance up to meet the glowering expression of suspicion she knew would be on his face. Nevertheless she could almost hear his brain ticking over likely profits when she told him the price she wanted for them, and what he could ask from his own customers. No doubt he would add a shilling a pair at least, to her suggestion.

To her vast surprise the deal was struck in less time than it took to shake a dog's tail as she later told her admiring band of fellow conspirators. Bolstered by success, Minnie was airily promising him she'd keep an eye open for other bargains for him in the future. She might well have a very special consignment coming up soon. In the meantime would he be interested in a dozen or so felt hats? He would. A deal was struck and she promised to include them with the gloves. (Once she'd run round to Lewis's and bought them, of course.)

'He's sending a van round tomorrow evening sharp at seven. You did manage to rent a bit of a warehouse, eh Pol?' Polly had, if only for the day, again with money loaned by Minnie. If the plan didn't work, she would be forever in her friend's debt.

Ron arrived on the dot to take possession of the goods and, as agreed, Minnie was there to greet him, still resplendent in her sealskin coat and shiny black straw. As soon as he handed over the cash, she quickly proceeded to count it before handing over the parcels, 'So's he don't take me for a fool,' as she later explained. Satisfied, she gave the nod for him to start loading the van with the boxes of hats and leather gloves. Within minutes he was slamming shut the doors and on his way. Minnie locked up, taking care to change back into her own clothes before scurrying back home to Pansy Street.

Questions were thrown at her thick and fast the minute she walked in the door of number 179. 'Did he fall for it? Was all the money there? Did Ron suspect anything?' Dim as he was he might just have recognised her but no, Minnie assured them that everything had gone smoothly.

'Right,' said Polly. 'Stage Two.'

–

Over the next few weeks, they bought and sold several more small consignments of goods to Hubert and he proclaimed himself well pleased. 'No wonder,' Minnie said. 'Robbing meself, I am.' Not once did he ask any questions about where Minnie lived, or how she'd come to hear of him. Very quietly, and without fuss, she built up an excellent working relationship with him, while expecting at any moment for Hubert to guess who she really was and not the Violet Davenport she purported to be. This was a name so far removed from Minnie's reality it made her quake to think of it, let alone use it.

They then decided to do nothing for a week or two, watching with interest as Hubert once or twice looked in at the pub and seemed disappointed to find Minnie not there.

'Right,' said Polly. 'It's time.'

Discreet enquiries by Charlie among contacts he had in Liverpool led to them finding a supplier of cheap jewellery, which they thought far enough from Castlefield to ensure complete secrecy. Polly then bought the finest man's watch she could find, one which had a Swiss movement and a good leather strap, together with a matching ladies model. She also purchased a beautiful double row of pearls, very reminiscent of the Queen's wedding gift to Princess Elizabeth. The pearls cost a good deal of money and everyone admired them with something like awe. 'If the greedy tyke's eyes don't light up when he spots these, we're sunk,' she admitted.

No one thought this likely. Hubert was ever on the look out for a new opportunity and Polly was sure he wouldn't be averse to moving a bit upmarket. There were plenty of women with money burning holes in their pockets, now the war was well and truly behind them, and with promises of affluence in the years ahead. The difficulty would come if he started asking how Minnie came by this shipment of jewellery in the first place. A story had to be concocted and memorised by the old woman till she was word perfect.

'I already have him eating out of my hand, and will soon snap his hand right off,' she promised.

'Well just make sure you keep your teeth in while you do it,' Lucy warned, with a grin.

—

Tom was fast running out of patience. He'd waited day after day for an opportunity to get Lucy on her own, but the only time he ever spotted her was out with Benny or her mam. They'd all suddenly become bosom pals, much to his disgust. She hadn't even been collecting the childer from school, lazy tyke, leaving it to Charlie to hobble up the street leaning on his stick, poor blighter.

One of these days, when he got tired of waiting, he might take a stroll up to the school himself, see if he could persuade the teacher to let him take the kids out early, before Charlie arrived. After all, they were his childer. That'd fetch her running back home quick enough, if he had the kids. Tom smiled to himself. He'd more power than she realised. He just hadn't chosen to exercise it yet. He was too interested in watching the activity that was going on, trying to work out what they were up to.

When he'd decided to come back to dear old Blighty, he'd thought he'd be on easy street. He expected to fall back into a job, have a wife eager to do his bidding and children to play at his feet and make him a happy man. Instead there were no decent jobs to be had, save for working for peanuts for his mother-in-law which didn't appeal one bit. That was finished now, of course, but it was doubtful whether it would ever have got any better despite her big talk and ambitions. Serve her right to be brought down in the world. He'd suffered, so why shouldn't she have a taste of that too? Polly'd had it easy long enough.

He was sitting in the Queen's on Gartside Street, since his credit was all used up at The Dog and Duck, enjoying a pint on the slate and wondering if he dare ask for another or whether he would be obliged to use cash. He did have a little money in his pocket but was reluctant to part with it. He was still pondering this vital matter when Hubert Clarke walked in. It wasn't often you saw him in here, so Tom watched with interest as the councillor bought himself a double whisky and found a quiet corner away from the darts players and the domino brigade. A matter of moments later a second person came in, one who excited some interest for all a respectful silence fell, for surely here was money all togged out in sealskin and shiny straw. The woman looked oddly familiar though he couldn't quite place her so Tom splashed out on another pint and, keeping well back in his own corner, continued to pay close attention. His interest sharpened when she calmly walked over, bold as you please and seated herself opposite Hubert.

The two appeared to be in deep conversation for several moments, the woman sipping occasionally at a sweet sherry Hubert had procured for her. Then she seemed to shake her head, clip a dreadful fox fur stole in place about her shoulders and, chin set in stubborn determination, walked from the pub. Tom was instantly torn. Should he follow her to see where she went and what she was up to? Or stay here and watch Hubert Clarke? It was all most tantalising.

The decision was made for him when Hubert himself got up and without a glance at those about him, briskly followed the woman. Just before the door swung to, Tom caught a glimpse of the pair of them standing talking on the pavement before turning and walking away together out of sight.

He downed his beer, slammed down the glass, snatched up his cap and followed. Something was going on and he meant to find out what it was.

–

Minnie led the way along the street with trepidation in her heart, still fearful of discovery. He'd been seriously interested in the watches, she could tell, particularly when she'd told him she had a hundred of each to offer, exactly the same. And she'd seen how his eyes had lit up at sight of the pearls. A sticky moment came when he balked at the price and had interrogated her on the source of her supply. She'd turned huffy, saying she had to respect confidences as she was sure he understood. If he wasn't interested he needn't bother, there were plenty of others who were. Then she'd walked out, wondering if she'd blown the whole enterprise. Now he was urging her not to be too hasty, and to give him another chance. Minnie could only suppose that because of those earlier successes, he was willing to trust her and deal again.

So here they were concluding this piece of sensitive business standing outside some solicitor's house on the corner of Gartside Street. Seemed appropriate somehow.

'It's cash on the nail you understand,' Minnie emphasised, looking him square in the eye so he knew she wasn't one to mess with. She also explained how she'd prefer it if the goods were collected later in the evening. 'Perhaps around nine tomorrow night?' It'd been Benny's idea to arrange a late collection. By that time there would be fewer people about and it would be dark and more difficult to see what was in the boxes if Ron decided to open one. Even so, it would be risky. This time Hubert would be getting nothing but rubbish for his brass. Minnie felt the strain was beginning to tell on her and wouldn't she be glad when she could peel off her stockings and soak her sore feet in a bowl of salts. These fancy shoes were killing her.

'It shall be arranged,' Hubert agreed, and smiled his most charming smile which almost made her shudder, though she managed to respond in kind.

'Tomorrow at nine then? Your son will fetch the van to our warehouse, as before?'

Hubert agreed that he would. Minnie nodded. They shook hands on the deal and she departed, a sprightly spring to her step which gave the lie both to her sixty-four years and her aching feet.

–

It was a crisp cold night down by the canal, a strong smell of tar in the air and the sound of a ship's hooter echoing somewhere in the distance. Beneath the railway arches a match flared, briefly illuminating the man's face as he lit a cigarette. He made no attempt to move from his hiding place, which offered an unhindered view of the road leading to where he'd seen the woman go. Knowing it to be a cul-de-sac, he was quite certain that he wouldn't miss anyone calling to see her, nor her own return trip home. He cupped the cigarette in his hand, to hide its telltale glow and settled down for a long wait.

At the end of the cul-de-sac, by the rented warehouse, Minnie waited, heart in her mouth, ears attuned for the sound of a van's engine. Somewhere deep in the shadows she knew Benny lay hidden, just in case there was trouble. He wouldn't show himself unless absolutely necessary but just knowing he was there gave her confidence. She still wore the sealskin coat but had opted for a more workaday hat in the shape of a black felt and dispensed with the fox fur stole as not quite appropriate for the occasion. What she dreaded most was for Hubert himself to turn up. Ron would no doubt take whatever she offered without question but Hubert… She'd taken some precautions against that unwelcome scenario, but would it be enough?

Minnie sat plaiting her fingers, peering out from time to time into the darkness, lit only by a single light bulb over the warehouse door. Somewhere out in the ink-black night, she heard a sound which made her nerves jitter before realising it was merely the scrape of a barge against the wall as it slipped out into the canal.

'Have you heard owt yet?' she hissed into the darkness, worried that her poor hearing might have let her down, and was loudly shushed. Biting her lip Minnie waited, and waited. Nine o'clock came and went and still there was no sign. By quarter past she was wishing she'd brought those pills the doctor had given her for her blood pressure. By half past she was feeling sick and ready to give up. He wasn't coming. He'd cottoned on to their little scheme. 'Eeh, this is a rum do,' she moaned, half to herself. She was, in her own words, all of a-flutter by the time she discerned the reassuring sound of a van reversing up the narrow alley to the warehouse door. It's black shape emerged slowly out of the night mist, halted and then the driver's door was pushed open and a figure emerged, boots scraping on the slippery setts.

'Evening, Violet. Thought I'd do this trip meself.' The familiarity jolted even as her heart sank with misgiving. It was Hubert himself, just as she'd feared. 'Come inside,' she bravely offered and her voice sounded surprisingly calm, even cheerful. 'Take a nip to warm yourself while I get my men to load up.' This was her main defence strategy so as Minnie preceded him into the cavernous warehouse, she sent up a silent prayer that he would follow.

'I won't say no.'

What it was they talked of in the confines of that hired office, she was never afterwards to recall but it took two whiskies and a good deal of banter before there was a tap on the door and she was able to tell him that the van was ready.

'It's been a pleasure doing business with you,' he told her, evidently feeling benevolent as his stomach warmed to the spirits.

Minnie could hardly wait to get him out of the door but gave no sign of this as she smiled benignly up at him, nodding pleasantly. 'You have the cash?'

'Indeed.' He handed her a large parcel which she ripped open and, heart pounding, flicked the notes casually with her thumb.

'Aren't you going to count it?' She knew she should but that would take time and the notes all looked satisfyingly present and correct. Besides, instinct told her that if she showed no trust in him, he would respond in kind and insist on her opening up those boxes of pearls and watches Benny himself had just loaded on to the van. Instead she shoved the packet into the mysterious depths of her leather handbag.

'I'm sure you and I have no reason not to trust each other, Hubert,' she said, refilling his glass. 'Since we're aiming to do more business in the future.'

'I'll drink to that, and more good profits.'

Minnie was relieved to see him down this third tot in one, though how he would see to drive after so much lubrication she really couldn't imagine. Not that she cared if he ended up in the canal. The money was in her bag and tucked firmly under her arm. Still he lingered, gazing upon her with a frown that could only be described as curious.

'How did you get into this business?' he enquired. 'Woman of your class, I mean.'

Thankful she hadn't consumed as much alcohol as himself, which meant her brain could still register, Minnie told her well-rehearsed and heartrending tale of losing a husband who'd gone down with his ship and her entire family, including two sons, when a bomb flattened her house. 'So I must make my own way in the world, as most of us have to these days, Hubert,' she said, offering a rueful smile.

He shook his head sadly, made the usual remarks about the pointlessness of war, which sounded odd coming from one who'd made a small fortune from it. 'You're still an attractive woman, Violet. Let's drink to a new future for you, and a new love in your life.' Yet again she felt compelled to refill his glass though her heart was beating so loudly she was sure he must hear it. When this had gone the way of the first three and still he made no move but stood, swaying slightly, a vague smile upon his bewhiskered face, it was Minnie who pulled open the door, with just a hint of desperation in the gesture. 'I'll see you out,' she encouraged, but Hubert politely and punctiliously insisted he could find his own way.

'It's bitter out there. You don't want to catch your death, Violet.'

She continued smiling as he tipped his hat to her and took his leave. Then Minnie's shaking legs finally gave way and she sat, rather abruptly, upon a handy orange box.

Benny was at her side within seconds and together they counted the money, relieved to find it was correct to the last shilling. Minnie prudently changed out of her 'disguise' and locked the door of the warehouse. A figure drew back into the shadows as she emerged from the end of the cul-de-sac, drawing her shawl over her head, with Benny a half step behind her. After no more than a brief glance about them, the pair walked away at speed beneath the bridge and since they were engrossed in their own excited hushed whispers, neither noticed the soft sounds of footsteps fall into place behind them.

–

Polly was relieved when they both arrived back safe and sound if slightly out of breath. The incriminating items of clothing were now stowed away back in the loft, wrapped in newspaper and stuffed to the bottom of the chest from whence they had come, never again to see the light of day if Minnie had any say in the matter.

'That's the last anyone will see of Violet Davenport,' she finished with no small sense of relief.

It had been a good night's work, they all agreed, and the bundle of notes felt satisfyingly thick in Polly's hands. 'Nowhere near enough to buy back everything we've lost but it will at least help to get the business going again, once I've paid back what I owe you, Minnie. I still have the name, Pride Carpets, since I managed not to go bankrupt, and the cleaning contracts from the big hotels. They'll bring their orders back to us just as soon as I get the machines up and running, I'm sure.' She heard Benny's groan and smilingly told him that no, she didn't intend just to stick to carpet cleaning but it was a start, was it not?

Benny, buoyed up by the success of the night's scheming pulled a cheeky face, saying he'd make sure that's all it was. But, as agreed, the very next morning he set out to visit every single hotel and boarding house in Manchester and district. It took him several days and when he was done, he returned with the promise of several orders for lengths of new carpet as well as repeat cleaning contracts.

He slapped the orders down on Minnie's kitchen table. 'You'd best keep that warehouse on, Mam. We're going to be busy.'

They all expressed their surprise and due appreciation of Benny's efforts but Polly had some reservations. 'If we start throwing money about, taking on premises, buying or hiring machines too soon, won't Hubert smell a rat? Won't he guess that it was us who stung him?'

'Does it matter?' Lucy wanted to know.

'It does, aye,' Minnie put in, feeling suddenly hot under the collar at what Hubert might do if he ever found out who'd set him up. 'He's not a man to cross isn't Hubert Clarke. Let's hang fire a bit, eh? Then happen you'd consider a new partner for Pride Carpets, Polly, when you do get going again.'

Polly frowned. 'New partner? Who would you have in mind?'

'Me. You don't have to pay me back. Think of it as an invest-ment. As a matter of fact I could put in a bit more, match what you won off Hubert, pound for pound. I was left quite comfortable by my lady employer and it's built up over the years.'

Polly was smiling long before she'd finished. 'Welcome aboard,' she said and would have hugged the old woman had Minnie not waved her off, claiming she didn't hold with such soft nonsense and offered Polly a pear drop instead.

–

The silence from Councillor Hubert Clarke was disturbing. Benny prowled high and low but no word reached him on the streets of Hubert having been stung for a lot of money for watches and jewellery that had turned out to be not half as good as he'd expected. He hadn't even found Ron. 'We've hit him in his pocket, where it hurts most and he's that mad he's keeping the shame of it to himself. He must be livid that he didn't think to check every box before purchasing. But then he never let us check stock in advance either, did he?'

Polly said, 'He rarely waited for us to even order it. Wouldn't he just deliver without a by-you-leave, and then refuse to take it back.'

'Yet we've only wounded him,' Benny moaned. 'He'll recover, drat him.'

This thought sobered them all, then Lucy remembered some-thing. 'He doesn't like paying tax. Joanna Clarke told me so.'

'Nobody likes paying taxes, m'cushla.'

'No, but we pay up all the same, Mam. How do we know Hubert does? He pays cash for goods, with no invoices. So how can anyone prove what he's bought where or from whom, certainly not the tax people and Hubert isn't going to tell them, is he? Joanna said he had an accountant, a Colin Wilnshaw, and it was his task to make sure that Hubert paid as little tax as possible. He also has a woman friend, Myra somebody or other who lives near...' Her mind went blank. 'Oh, lord, I can't remember.'

'Try. Think hard.' They were all keenly interested now, sitting on the edges of their seats. If Hubert was evading taxes, then they might have a stronger weapon over him than they'd ever dreamed possible.

'*Slate Wharf?*'

Chapter Twenty-Nine

It took no time at all to persuade young Ron that it was long past time for him to seek his fortune elsewhere. Benny marvelled at his own self-restraint as he placed the rail ticket in Ron's grimy paw and personally escorted him to Liverpool Road Station. The ticket was to London, one way, and in a fit of generosity Benny gave him a fiver to help him on his way.

He even extracted from him a telling amount of information on what he was responsible for, and what he wasn't.

It was amazing really how grateful the little weasel was as Benny stood on the platform and watched him climb aboard. Anyone would think he'd expected much worse from his sister's widowed husband. He even managed a little wave as the train shunted out of the station. Benny went straight to the gents to wash his hands the minute the train had vanished in a cloud of blue smoke.

His next call was upon Myra who seemed only too willing to allow him into her home, simply because she liked the look of him: big brawny sort of chap, young, good-looking and with masculinity oozing from every pore was the way she'd describe him. Benny couldn't help but smile at her teasing. No wonder Hubert had found her fascinating. She was still attractive and alluring for all she was well over the hill in Benny's opinion. She coyly informed him that he was exactly the sort of feller she wouldn't mind seeing a bit more of. And despite their forty year age difference, Benny could see she wasn't joking.

The cramped parlour into which he was shown with its shaded pink lamps, cherubic statuettes and *chaise longue* draped in some sort of animal fur made him feel slightly nauseous. Benny accepted the drink she offered him but left it untouched on a marble-topped table.

He wondered how to set about the task, whether to be upfront and honest or side-track the issue by asking her about friends in high places, hoping to find out something that way. In the event she forestalled him by seeming to guess what it was he required.

'You're Belinda's chap, aren't you?' she asked, bright blue eyes moist with sympathy. 'She was a lovely lass. Not appreciated by that family of hers and although we never met, I liked and admired her.'

Benny felt a lump come into his throat and it took several moments before he could respond. He still ached for her. There wasn't a moment in his day when he didn't miss her. Sometimes the pain was so bad he thought he'd go mad. At other times, he was acutely aware of her presence, as if she standing right beside him, and it comforted him.

'I loved her very much,' he told Myra. 'I'd've done anything to save her.'

'I dare say you would, lad. I told Hubert no good would come of trying to evict the pair of you but would he listen?' She snorted her disgust then sipped at a violent green liqueur. 'Always thought he knew best did our Hubert. I've seen him only once or twice since she… since you lost your lovely lass, but it weren't the same. I couldn't feel for a man who was so hard on his daughter. I've two children of my own, so I know what I'm talking about. There's nothing more precious.' She stood up and swept an armful of photographs from the mantelpiece to show to Benny. He dutifully admired her son, her two daughters and her several grandchildren, a family in whom she clearly showed substantial pride.

'You're not still with him then.'

'Heck, no. Heartless old sod. I hope he gets what he deserves.' It was all plain sailing after that. She gave him facts and figures, dates, companies he'd deliberately made insolvent, even the combination of his safe where he kept his ill-gotten gains that the tax man knew nothing of, hidden in his study at Potato Wharf. Myra knew all of this because Hubert was apparently loquacious in his cups. And plainly indiscreet.

'Some pillow talk that must have been,' Benny laughed as he later related this tale to the others.

Minnie's eyes gleamed while Lucy simply remarked, 'We've got him.'

As ever, Polly was more practical. 'Fetch pen and paper, Minnie. We've a letter to write. We'll address it "To whom it may concern" and begin "With reference to the business affairs of Councillor Hubert Clarke..."'

–

Tom arrived at the school early, as he'd promised himself that he would. The children's teacher was uncertain at first about letting them go but when Tom pointed out that they both had a dental appointment, she relented. Attention to good teeth hygiene had always been one of Miss Bell's hobby horses and, really, the school dental service left a great deal to be desired. She applauded Mr Shackleton for his care, but then hadn't he suffered himself in the war so was it any wonder if he wished to spare his children the agony of the school dentist?

Sean was so excited when he saw his dad that he didn't notice his sister's more reticent attitude. 'Have you come to take us back to Aunty Minnie's?' she asked in her quiet little voice, so like Lucy's own.

'No, your mam's asked me to fetch you home wi' me. She's already there, making your tea.'

'Sausages?' Sean wanted to know, bouncing up and down. 'Are we having sausages?' Sarah Jane still felt unsure and began to back away, saying she'd left her lunch box in her desk. In her young mind she felt a sudden urge for someone in authority, even Miss Bell, her teacher whom she didn't usually care for much at all, to know that she wasn't really going to a dentist, or even to

Minnie Hopkins's house but back home with her dad. It seemed somehow important that she told someone.

'Don't be daft,' Tom said, taking a firm hold of her arm. 'You won't need it.'

'I will. To put me lunch in ready for tomorrow.'

'We can find you another box,' Tom insisted and maintaining his grip on both children, he marched them out of the school yard and through a maze of streets in the direction of Liverpool Road.

–

Hubert moved restlessly about his beloved conservatory, pinching out carnations in an effort to calm himself. He couldn't recall ever feeling more angry in his entire life. The heat of his ire blurred his vision and left him gasping for breath. Reaching into the pocket of his waistcoat he took out one of his pills, the tightness in his chest having been growing for some days. From time to time he rubbed his arms which were also aching, no doubt from having carried all those dratted boxes out of the van. He wished now that he'd made Ron do the job, then he'd have someone other than himself to blame. But the boy seemed to have vanished off the face of the earth. Hubert hoped he was out collecting money. They'd need every penny after what he'd lost the other night.

He knew he'd been had, and he knew who by. The problem was that he couldn't prove it.

When he'd opened the boxes of watches the following morning, rather late admittedly, due to a thick head, he'd stared in disbelief at the rusting, misshapen bits of metal for which he'd paid well over the odds in the mistaken belief he was buying top-notch merchandise. As for the pearls. Wear them in a rain shower and he suspected they'd instantly lose their sheen and turn back into the cheap paste they undoubtedly were. They might actually dissolve.

No doubt about it. He'd been done good and proper. Polly Pride and her contemptible family had taken their revenge.

The moment he'd realised, he'd stormed back into the house, red in the face and raging about injustice, shouting for Ron and how he'd see the whole lot of them at the bottom of the canal sooner than let them get away with it. Joanna had been so alarmed by the noise he was making, she'd come running from the kitchen, insisting he tell her what was wrong, and Hubert had blurted out the whole sorry tale.

But had she shown him the proper sympathy he deserved? Had she heck-as-like. She'd put back her head and laughed. It had been the most unladylike sound to come out of her mouth in a long while, not to mention the most disrespectful.

Now, several days later, with still no sign of his stupid son, she stood with her arms folded and informed him she was taking a leaf out of Polly's book, and Benny's, by starting again. 'You remember Benny? He was married to our daughter once. Lovely boy, had we but realised it. Bit of a rough diamond but he'll go far, I'm sure. I can tell that he's already making good progress, despite the unexpected setbacks he suffered at the start.' Her blue eyes, so like Belinda's, were sparkling, as if entranced by her own wit.

'What in damnation are you talking about, woman?' Hubert asked, then demanded to know where his breakfast was, as he'd telephone calls to make, business matters to arrange, and a counterattack to plan. His wife was in a mood over something or other, though what exactly it was he couldn't imagine, and cared even less. She brought him a pot of coffee and a round of toast.

'Are you going out?' he airily enquired, noticing her attire of a smart green coat and hat which he didn't recall having seen before. Not that what his wife did with her time was of any great interest to him. 'What about my eggs and bacon?'

'Sorry darling, but you'll have to get your own breakfast from now on. I'm off. I'll send someone round for my luggage later. Oh, I almost forgot, this morning's post.' And she handed him a large brown envelope which he scarcely glanced at as she floated a kiss an inch above his brow.

'Luggage? What luggage? Off where?'

As she swept out through the door he could've sworn she said she was running off with Colin Wilnshaw, but that couldn't be right, could it? Colin was his accountant and absolutely essential to the security of Hubert's affairs.

It was then that the telephone rang. Hubert snatched it up and listened in silence to the voice at the other end for some minutes before slamming down the receiver and at once starting to dial. 'Get me Wilnshaw,' he barked at the unfortunate secretary who answered.

'I'm afraid he isn't in, sir,' she replied, in a quavering voice which, to his horror, sounded near to tears, having instantly recognised Councillor Clarke's unmistakable tones. 'He appears to have gone.'

'*Gone*? Gone *where*? What are you prattling on about, woman?'

'He's left his wife and family, left the firm, taken everything and g–gone. Vanished. There's not a thing of value left in the safe.' Now she did burst into noisy blubbering tears but Hubert was no longer listening. He was tearing open the brown envelope which bore an official stamp, and roaring with rage at its contents before charging out of the house.

–

The man turned up his coat collar so that it almost met the brim of his trilby hat. Keeping as inconspicuous as possible beside the lamp post, he smiled to himself as he watched the Wolsley car roar into the yard and skid to a halt. He'd already seen the two officials go inside and guessed it meant they didn't bring glad tidings of great joy for the occupant of this particular warehouse on Potato Wharf.

The family had done well. Their plan, whatever it might have been, seemed to be working. Hubert Clarke, he suspected, was about to get his just desserts, and not before time. He'd never seen him in such a rage as when he'd stumbled out of the car, slamming the door far harder than usual and storming into his warehouse.

As the man turned to leave, still smiling and longing to know the full details which his observations, no matter how painstaking, had failed to fully ascertain, he saw another figure emerge from a nearby alley. Tom Shackleton. The last piece of the jigsaw. He'd know him anywhere. And with him were Sarah Jane and Sean. More worryingly, both the children looked bewildered and Sean as if he'd been crying. As Tom hustled them towards the canal basin and across the foot bridge, the man slipped quietly out after them.

–

It was while Lucy was sitting in Minnie's front parlour, wondering why Charlie hadn't appeared with the children, that the door knocker rattled. This couldn't be them. They'd charge straight in. Who could it be? Not Lily Gantry with more bad news, she hoped. She really wasn't up to that old troublemaker, not today with all this business over Hubert going on.

Polly had sent the letter days ago, since when she and Benny had lurked beneath the railway arches, keeping a watch on Potato Wharf in case the inspectors came. Lucy felt sick with nerves. Hubert Clarke, as Minnie so frequently reminded them, wasn't an easy man to cross. But as she went down the lobby, Lucy glimpsed a uniform through the glass of the vestibule door. She opened it to find not one, but two very official soldiers in full dress uniform. They looked exceedingly smart with their brass buttons, chevrons glowing white, and red caps on their heads.

On seeing her they both saluted, then one stepped forward and handed her a paper. It identified them as Military Police. Lucy had already guessed as much.

'Would you know the whereabouts of one Private Tom Shackleton? We understand he used to live in this street, ma'am, and, according to our information, has unexpectedly returned home. We very much wish to question him. Looks as though he's been AWOL.'

'AWOL?'

'Absent without leave, ma'am. He's a deserter.' The man's voice was unemotional, official.

Somehow Lucy managed to step back from the door. 'There must be some mistake. I think you'd best come in.'

As they followed her into the small front parlour Lucy found she was shaking. She would like to have sat down but it didn't seem quite the thing to do, so she stood facing them, feeling confused and helpless, while the two MPs proceeded to explain how they'd been given information that Tom had been hiding in Spain for some years.

'Spain? Don't you mean Italy? He was in Germany for a long time, as a prisoner of war,' she corrected, though not with any real conviction in her voice.

'Sorry to contradict, ma'am, but according to our source, he left Italy long before the war ended.' They went on to question her, asking for details of where Tom might be hiding now.

Before she had time to gather her wits the door burst open and Charlie came hobbling along the passage. Lucy could guess by his expression what had happened, even before he got a word out. He was beside himself with worry and by the time he'd told his tale about the missing children there wasn't a breath of colour in Lucy's ashen face. 'I must go to him. Get them back.' She was half way to the door when one of the MPs stopped her.

'If he's got his back to the wall, he could prove dangerous.'

'They're my kids. And Tom is my husband.'

'And our prisoner. I wouldn't be too sure about that. According to our information, he married a young woman out there, a Spanish senorita.'

Lucy felt as if her whole face had grown stiff with shock, 'Married? How can he have married? He already is married, to me?' She felt bewildered, unable to take in what was happening.

The MPs dropped their official stance and for the first time looked shamefaced, apologising for bringing her such bad news. 'We have to take him in for questioning, love. Sorry.'

Lucy drew in a deep, steadying breath, realising they were only trying to do their job. 'He won't hurt the children, or me, if I go to him. Maybe I can persuade him to give himself up. Let me try. It'll surely make it better for you, and him too.'

The MPs conferred but finally agreed to let her try on the grounds that it would indeed go better for him at the Court Martial if he surrendered of his own free will.

'Thank you.'

'But we'll be outside. Watching,' they said. 'Give us a shout and we'll be there in a jiffy.'

—

Lucy saw Sean first. He was sitting on a chair by the fire sucking his thumb. She could see no sign of Tom. When the little boy spotted her through the back window he had the sense not to jump from his seat, simply removed the thumb and grinned at her, then nudged Sarah Jane with his foot. Lucy saw that her daughter was curled up on the rug and her heart leapt to her throat. Had she been hurt? Why was she lying down like that? But Sarah Jane sat up and stretched, rubbing her eyes, making it clear she'd only been asleep. Lucy put her finger to her lips to urge them both to keep quiet as she let herself in through the back door. Within seconds her children were in her arms and she was asking if they were all right.

'Didn't I tell you Mam would be home soon?' Sean said, not understanding.

Sarah Jane seemed more aware of what was really happening. She half glanced over her shoulder, then grasping her mother's arm thrust her towards the back door. 'Let's go to Aunty Minnie's. Quick, before…'

'Before what, Sarah Jane? You weren't thinking of going anywhere without me, were you?' The voice from the door stopped them all in their tracks. Lucy spun about to face Tom and gasped when she saw him. In his hand was a gun, the German Luger she'd once caught a glimpse of in his drawer and dismissed as a product of her vivid imagination. Now here she was, looking down the barrel of it. Time seemed to slow, to stretch endlessly as a sense of utter disbelief swamped her. This surely couldn't be happening.

'Tom? What are you doing?' Her voice sounded calmer than she felt. 'Why don't you put that thing down. You wouldn't want to hurt Sean or Sarah Jane, now would you?'

'I'm aiming it at you, Lucy, not the children. Can't you tell?'

She moved her lips, stiff with fear, into what must be a parody of a smile. 'Yes, of course I do. I'm aware that I've hurt you, Tom.'

'You have indeed hurt me. You're the guilty party. Not these innocent children. Isn't that right?' When she didn't immediately answer, he repeated the question, only louder. '*Isn't that right?*' It made them all jump and Sean to realise that all was not well, and start to cry.

'Hush, sweetheart. It's all right. Yes, if you say so, Tom. But let me send the children out, so we can talk this thing th—' She got no further as he suddenly yelled at her to be quiet.

'Don't tell me what to do! I'm in charge here. I'm the one with the blasted weapon. Can't you see it?' He was shaking the gun now, waving it about in front of her face. Sean stared at it wide-eyed with horror.

'Don't you hurt my mam,' the little boy bravely shouted, and Lucy hushed him again, anxious he didn't irritate Tom into some reckless act. This was the last thing she'd expected. Yet Lucy realised that she should have been alert to the possibility. She'd underestimated Tom for too long. She should have protected her children better.

'Let Sean go. He's just a baby. Let him go. Sarah Jane too.'

'And have them fetch help? Do you think I'm stupid? Once you have the children back, you'll run off with that fancy man of yours. I know what you're up to, Lucy. I've seen all the toing and froing. I've been watching you all for some time. And I've seen him hanging about by the wharf.'

'Who? Michael?' Hope leapt in her but he only laughed.

'That got you going, eh?' It quickly died again as Lucy tried desperately to make her brain work, to think, to plan, to decide what she ought to do. Should she tell him about the MPs waiting outside for her signal? If she shouted could they break in before he fired the gun? Or should she keep on talking and smiling and hoping for the best? While she was still striving to make up her mind, Tom stretched out his hand and flicking a finger said, 'Come here, son. Come and stand by me.' Before she could make a move to stop him, Sean had done as he was told, apparently mesmerised by the chill command in his father's voice. Tom grasped the boy and held him close to his side, oblivious to his noisy crying. Dear lord, why didn't someone help her? Could they hear his cries outside?

Tom was beckoning to Sarah Jane, ordering her to come to him too, before he lost his temper good and proper.

Swallowing her fear Lucy grasped hold of Sarah Jane and pushed her behind her own back. 'No, you're not having her.' Lifting her chin she braved the furious anger that twisted Tom's face into something utterly unrecognisable. 'Listen to me, Tom. I'm not going anywhere.'

'Oh, but you will. Everyone leaves me. Francesca left me for her old lover, just as you're doing.'

Lucy froze. So that was her name. This didn't seem the moment to accuse him of bigamy. 'It's not true, Tom. I haven't seen Michael in, oh, I don't know, ages. Not since before the fire in fact.'

'I don't believe you,' he snapped. 'You *lie, lie, lie* all the time, just to serve your own evil purpose.'

This seemed rich, coming from the smoothest liar of all, but Lucy had the good sense not to say so. 'Don't shout, Tom, please. You're frightening the children. Anyroad, it'll do no good,' she gently urged him, using her most cajoling tones. She let go of Sarah Jane's hand. Pushed her further away. Took a step closer to Tom. 'It's all over. Give me the gun before you hurt our lovely kids. You know you'd be heartbroken if you did anything to harm them.'

'It's *you* I mean to harm.'

'No, I don't think so, Tom. You've had a bad war, I accept that. Now it's all over. They've come for you. The MPs, I mean. It'll be much easier if you give yourself up. Don't make it any worse for yourself.' She held her breath, wondering if she'd done the right thing to warn him as he stared at her in silence. Lucy could have sworn there were tears as well as panic in his eyes, and a curl of hope rose in her breast, swiftly quenched by his next words.

'The fighting at Salerno was a mess,' he told her, his voice scathing, filled with a brash arrogance as if entirely unconcerned by the fact that the truth of his inauspicious war career had at last been revealed. 'A combination of mud and military bungling. I wasn't hanging around just to get shot or die of disease. I escaped through Greece, across North Africa and have been living all nice and cosy in Spain ever since. Then Francesca left me, stupid bitch. Went back to Diego. Not that I really cared, you understand. I was getting bored with her in any case.' He spoke with his famous bravado. 'I decided to come home to you, Lucy, that you were worth the risk of returning.'

'You mean you couldn't think of anywhere else to go,' Lucy responded, the first hint of bitterness in her tone. Tom was quick to respond.

'No, it's true. I did miss you. But I only intended hanging around long enough to persuade you to come somewhere fresh, to a new life. America or Australia. Except you were hooked up with this Hopkins chap.'

'I'm sorry,' Lucy said, though she wasn't at all.

'Now I suppose bloody Benny's grassed on me.'

'Benny? What does he know about any of this?'

'Only that he guessed I'd deserted. But he promised to keep his bleedin' mouth shut.'

Lucy decided to pursue this matter later with her brother, and again held out her hand. 'Please, Tom. It's over now. Give me the gun.' It was almost there, almost within her grasp when there was a loud crack. Then every door seemed to burst open at once and the room was suddenly filled with people, Benny and Michael coming from one direction at the back and the MPs from the front. It was several moments of utter pandemonium before she realised that the gun had been fired.

–

A pair of handcuffs were being slipped on to her unprotesting husband's wrists. Words were spoken, informing him of his rights and where he would be taken. Tom was shouting at Benny. 'I'll get you for this, for shooting your bleedin' mouth off.'

'You're wrong,' the MP calmly informed him. 'It wasn't your brother-in-law. It was someone else. They told us you'd set fire to a warehouse, thereby adding arson to the charges. We'll be investigating the matter fully, of course.' The two MPs were obviously enjoying themselves.

Tom paled and, switching his attack, said, 'Bloody Hubert Clarke. After all I've done for him. I'll kill him.'

'I don't think so, Private. You'll be tucked away somewhere very safe for quite a long while.'

It was only when Tom was safely shackled that an ashen-faced Benny asked if anyone was going to spare a thought for him. The bullet had nicked his shoulder. One of the MPs gave it little more than a cursory glance but assured him he'd live. When Benny groaned in pain, the military policeman laughed and began to strap it up with a scarf, packing it with a tea towel Lucy brought, and promised to drop him off at the local hospital on their way back to base.

'So if it wasn't Benny, who was it?' Tom yelled, glaring at Lucy.

'Actually I was the one who shopped you,' Michael said and smiled with satisfaction as Tom made a lurch towards him, quickly stifled by the two MPs. 'Benny and I met up some weeks ago and he told me about your lies. Then when he confirmed that Ron was innocent of arson, we guessed you were responsible for that too. I thought it about time you settled the debt you owe to society, and to Lucy. As soon as I was sure Hubert Clarke was in the bag, I brought in the military.'

Lucy was glaring at her brother. 'You *knew* Tom lied?'

'Don't be angry Lucy. He did talk about Spain once but I felt I shouldn't get involved, because of you and Michael. But then after the fire I saw things a bit different. I'm really sorry, truly I am. You were right all along. Tom Shackleton is bad news and I shouldn't have made any promises to him. That's why I had to come dashing to your rescue, Luce, like the bleedin' cavalry.'

Lucy's eyes filled with a rush of tears. 'You great daft lump. I could batter your brains in, if you had any.' And putting her arms about Benny's broad shoulders she hugged him, causing him to yowl in protest as she accidentally pressed against his injured shoulder.

'I went all through the war without being wounded and here I am having pot-shots taken at me in Civvy Street. Don't that take the biscuit?'

–

After the MPs had gone, marching Tom before them, with Benny trailing behind in their wake, Lucy found that she had to sit down for her legs had given way. She'd wasted all those years waiting for Tom to come home, all that loyalty and sympathy, all that agonising and believing herself still beholden to him. And when he'd unexpectedly returned, against all the odds, she'd been endlessly patient, not wishing to deprive him of his children, striving to do her duty as his wife. She'd thought she was the guilty one for loving another man, had believed what he'd told her despite her reservations.

'When all the time he was a deserter. Not only that, but a bigamist as well, marrying some other woman while still married to me. What a fool I've been.' Lucy put her head in her hands and began to cry. 'Oh, Michael, you were right, I should have left him ages ago. I love you so much, and Tom has told me nothing but lies from the start.' She at once launched into a flurry of apologies and explanations.

Michael interrupted her. 'Say that again.'

'Hubert has...'

'No, the other bit, about your loving me?'

Lucy looked up and smiled at him, a smile so radiant it lit up her entire face. 'I love you. I love you. *I love you!* There, is that enough?' She could hear the children giggling, Sean with his hand clapped over his mouth in a picture of glee, and Sarah Jane grinning from ear to ear.

'No, it isn't,' Michael said. 'I want you to say it every day for the rest of our lives together.'

She beamed at him, then kissed him softly on each cheek and after that full on the lips. 'We are going to be together then-for the rest of our lives?'

'I reckon so, just as soon as that military court has finished with Tom Shackleton, we'll take him to another for that divorce. Right?'

'It'll be a pleasure. Then I'll say it every day to you, and this little one too, shall I?'

'Little one?'

He gave a puzzled frown as Lucy smilingly laid a hand upon the curve of her belly. 'Our child.'

'Oh, my love!' Michael's arms came about her and Sarah Jane was wriggling between them, Sean jumping and scrambling into Michael's arms, determined not to be left out of the loving.

'We'll have to take the new baby to see the fireworks at Belle Vue,' Sean yelled.

Sarah Jane was shouting too in her excitement. 'You promised us, Michael. You did, remember?'

'I remember. Well, as I always keep my promises, it's a date.' Then they were all laughing and hugging, Michael with his arms full of love, for they were a family at last. Nothing and no one would ever separate them again.